Frances Fyfield is a criminal lawyer, practising in London, the setting for many of her books. She also lives by the sea which, aside from her love of London is her passion. *Deep Sleep* won the CWA Silver Dagger Award in 1991 and *A Clear Conscience* was nominated for the CWA Gold Dagger Award and won the Grand Prix de Literature Policière in 1998. She has also written three novels as Frances Hegarty and her books are widely translated. Her most recent novel, *Looking Down*, is available in Little, Brown hardback.

A HELEN WEST CASEBOOK

FRANCES FYFIELD

TRIAL BY FIRE
WITHOUT CONSENT

*TWO NOVELS IN
ONE VOLUME*

A *Time Warner* Paperback

Published in Great Britain in 2004 by Time Warner Paperbacks

A Helen West Casebook Copyright © Frances Fyfield 2004
Trial by Fire Copyright © Frances Fyfield 1990
Without Consent Copyright © Frances Fyfield 1996

The moral right of the author has been asserted.

A CIP catalogue record for this book
is available from the British Library.

ISBN 0 7515 3630 X

Typeset in Plantin by M Rules
Printed and bound in Great Britain
by Clays Ltd, St Ives plc

Time Warner Paperbacks
An imprint of
Time Warner Book Group UK
Brettenham House
Lancaster Place
London WC2E 7EN

www.twbg.co.uk

TRIAL
BY FIRE

CHAPTER ONE

There were foxes as wild and shy as wolves in northeast
London, haunting the dead railway lines by night in search
of sustenance, running into gardens when the need was
great, abandoning the petticoats of the city to forage in
bins. In the crowded outskirts where city clawed at country in a flurry of picnics between mismatched towns, the
presence of summer and constant supply of discarded
food lessened necessity and made it negligible. High
summer for this fox, sufficiently fed on old hamburgers to
cope with present hunger, but nothing in her stomach as
compelling as this fruity stench, this rich smell of carrion.
She quivered from the sharp, vicious snout of her to the
down-pointed tail, eyes bright with curiosity, hair stiff with
anticipation, a predator salivating in the darkness.

Fox scratched at the loose earth, dry and unresisting
around the human hand. She examined and sniffed. A
mottled set of fingers, earth-stained but still delicate white
and shiny in the waning dark. Her firm teeth gripped the

3

fingers, bit and gnawed the splintering bone within, then paused, shy and wary. In sudden urgency, she closed her jaws over the knuckles of the hand, dug paws into the ground for purchase, and pulled. Better a prize to carry home, not to eat but to bury, less greed in her now than pragmatism. The hand was weighted by a heavier body, resisted beyond the elbow as the earth resettled around the form with a sigh. Fox grasped the forearm, encountered larger bone, pulled again to the tune of a slight cracking sound. Growling softly, she persisted as the light grew, shaking her head from side to side, unable to shift the obstacle. Pausing in the struggle to survey the problem, she tested the air, heard in the distance a car on the road, the infinitesimal dawn sounds of human life gathering force far away, yet too close for comfort.

She turned her head from the carrion and spilt soil in sudden disinterest, scratched, twisted, and danced in the new warmth spotting her coat between the trees, a ritual dance in the rising light, graceful and carefree in celebration. Then she cleaned the earth from her jaws and slipped away into the undergrowth for home. Sunlight, warmth, freedom and safety were preferable even to food.

The grave she left untidy, as if a sleeper had turned the blanket in the middle of a dream. Beneath the surface, the larvae continued their slow and steady movement, out of sight, busy, busy, busy.

One hand remained visible above the ground, finger splintered and chewed, knuckle browner and stickier than before, softened by teeth and the abrasive tongue. It was the shroud of flies that indicated a presence, buzzing in a furious crowd and attracting the dog running through the woods when the sun retreated. The arm protruded crookedly, the wrist at right angles like a signpost. The owner of the dog, once a poacher, regarded the sight with laconic curiosity only slightly tinged with shock; he sat and debated with his slow soul what to do next, holding his animal firmly by the collar as it twisted to escape, enraged by the smell of fox, frightened by the presence of death. As the man rose and plodded towards a telephone, he was relieved he had not seen the remnants of a face, relieved the fox had not done worse. Such a pale, slender arm, the colour of a well-hung, badly plucked bird. Once a woman's.

At eight forty-five in the evening the village of Branston was already somnolent. After seven-thirty, the trains from Liverpool Street via twenty-one stations east, a long and rattling ride in carriages with dirty windows, became less frequent, and even the alternative route, Central Line to Epping, equally elderly rolling stock and even noisier, had diminished its reluctant service. The commuters had faced their last hazard of the day: none remained in city wine bars on an evening like this. 'We live in the country,' they said. 'Wonderful, have to get home. Ever heard of Branston? No? You haven't lived. Marvellous spot, hasn't really hit the market yet, house prices not bad, why, we only paid . . . You must be mad, living in Surrey. Go east, man, go east, the only place to be.' So they laboured uphill from the station carrying tributes to spouses and children, wine in carrier bags held by men, while the women carried decorative materials and ornaments in endless pursuit of style for the solid-built houses, some old, some hideously new, which formed the fabric of Branston. Flanked by woods on one side, flat fields on the other, approached by three roads hidden by hedges, Branston nestled quietly. There was a main street, comfortably ugly and mellow. The Coach and Groom, Bario's plush pink and grey restaurant – 'Terrific place, better than anything we've found in London, I mean, there's everything here' – and a few miles beyond all that, the wider consumer vistas of Chelmsford with Marks and Spencer, Habitat, and all the disguises the human soul could require, places where Branston refugees escaped on Saturdays to avoid contact with Mother Earth. Branston consisted of workers, a village of respectable and ambitious house-owning commuters, pushing themselves ahead by sheer effort, taking advantage of still old-fashioned schools for their new-fashioned kids, watched with amazement by the few High Street natives for their habit of leaving their homes empty for all of twelve hours a day.

Branston did not possess a history. It mirrored the taste of its current age and was resurrected from oblivion by the need for housing an Olympic stone's throw from London. Previously its three streets had almost died, deserted by young and old alike, the young from boredom and lack of opportunity, the old from pneumonia induced by dampness and the right time to go. Now the remnants found themselves revisited, adopted, and conquered by the descendants of their more ambitious children. In addition to those with no instinct to go south or west, there were those seeking the nearest patch of greenish field to the East End convenient for market trade, a touch of fraud, or a place to own a house acceptable to a mother still locked in the fumes of Bethnal Green with her pub and all the blacks. Branston had never been much of a community, simply a place. Now its inhabitants tried to make it into a village. The village format was slightly unconvincing, with the High Street boasting one confused supermarket, one small branch of Woolworth's, a shop selling kits for home-made wine and beer, and alongside the restaurant a kind of café called La Taverna, a pizzeria, and a burger bar, also selling kebabs for those who preferred foreign. The rest of the ten shops included one featuring swanky tracksuits for the unconverted East End wives, one more prosaic and expensive sportswear, an upmarket greengrocer, a jeweller, a delicatessen, and two newsagents, the only ones that were there in the first place, source of all gossip. Aside from these establishments, which maintained half-day closing and lunch hours, the rest strove to cater for the custom living in the newly developed housing estates. Parallel to the shops was a small green, usually hidden by buses panting at two stops before turning around to return to bigger things. People gathered on this green trying to make village gossip, hampered by their underlying London reluctance to know one another.

She could see the point. Occasionally she enjoyed the prettiness and the space, succumbing to the instinct to enjoy all aspects of life whenever possible. But much of the time Helen West, émigré from the dirtier streets of Islington and grimy offices of very central London, found herself hating Branston with a quiet passion that surprised her.

Not at every moment, and not during this one.

Whistling, with her hands in the suds covering last night's washing-up and looking out through the diamond-shaped windows of the modern house in Invaders Court, Helen told herself she had no excuse for hating any place – places were not important enough for the expenditure of that kind of emotion. She slammed a dish on the draining board and did not stop it slithering back into the water. What the hell, better things to do, sun still shining. Bubbles of soap attached to the front of the loose jacket that swung from her slim figure with comfortable ease. Helen was at home in a suit, wore one like a glove, far better adjusted to the professional role it symptomized than she was to the kitchen sink, which she approached with all the caution of an enemy unwilling to do battle. She was small and dark, dressed in the black and white required for a courtroom, enlivened as always with one splash of colour, like a magpie with crimson in the tail. There was a dishwashing machine, which she dared not use in Bailey's absence, so terrifying were its instructions, and she missed his presence slightly the more for that. It was the slightest missing, a constant and distinct preference for the pleasure of his company, abnormal in her to resent time spent alone, and it stemmed from her impatience with the ever unfamiliar sharp edges of this streamlined house. Squinting through the window, she could see Isobel Eastwood toiling past the house on the way to her own, laden with carriers. Oh, goody, I wonder what she's bought today. Where on earth do they put everything she carries into that house? Ducking below the windowsill, Helen avoided the necessity of a wave, which was the closest she and Mrs Eastwood ever came to communication. Helen and Bailey had become gleeful gossips, discreet but avid in their curiosity about other people's lives. They were both unused to visible neighbours and found them the fascinating source for hours of comfortable speculation, their own amazement and observation never diminished. Now he had been called to a dead body, he had said on the phone, no self-importance in the announcement, just a statement of fact; he would be away until late, possibly all night, but at least they could spice the usual enjoyable daily accounts with something more substantial to discuss. In the knowledge of that, and the sudden lack of necessity to clear the kitchen now rather than later, Helen abandoned the attempt, gave herself a generous measure of gin, and purred with contentment in the first sip. Bet they're all pouring drinks, she thought, looking beyond the window at her vista of new brick.

It was an equally sound bet that none of them would invite her to share. The inhabitants of Invaders Court, Branston, were empire builders rather than sharers, and besides, their vague knowledge of the unmarried status and respective professions of Geoffrey Bailey and Helen West did not encourage them to warmth. 'What do you do, Mrs Bailey? I suppose we call you Mrs Bailey?'

'No,' Helen had said cheerfully, 'you call me Helen West. I live with Geoffrey, but we are not married. And I'm a solicitor. No, I don't do conveyancing; I'm a prosecutor. No, we don't have any children, and no, this is not our house, we've borrowed it.'

'Oh. And what does Mr Bailey do?' they persisted, beaming in benign, slightly wavering curiosity.

'He's a detective chief superintendent. In the police.'

She could never keep a note of defensive pride out of her voice when describing Bailey, not for his rank, just because he was Bailey and she could never cease to honour him, in public at least, but she had watched the faces fall.

Mental head count of delinquent children, out-of-date road tax, and unpaid parking fines, end of conversation. 'Well, my husband works in the city.'

Helen's understanding of this reserve was complete. She knew it to be as natural as breathing, not indicative of malice or stupidity, simply a withdrawal capable of reversion if their other interests had been more communal. As the woman of the piece, like all the other women, it was her role to make the social effort, but chatter died on her like the end of sudden rain. She did not despise domestic bliss, but, having ploughed the furrow of thoroughly professional life for a dozen years, remained puzzled why anyone with choice settled to anything else. There was so little to discuss: she and Geoffrey had no children, no company car and, although the details of their identical houses would be enough to fill conversational hours, she did not, as they did, love or treasure her home. It was rented for twelve months, half of them gone. She would never have bought it in a million years and would never have filled it with these fat, hard, uncomfortable, but ludicrously expensive things chosen by her young and absent landlords who were pursuing the upward path of their success on foreign territory. Helen did not feel like a successful woman, didn't expect she ever would, wondered what it was like. Her own environment, lost for this experimental year, reflected only what she liked, rich colours, plentiful pictures, and an element of disorder. In

Helen's mansion, it would take at least a year to mend a broken object; here, anything flawed would have hit the reject heap and been replaced within hours. The pale harmonies of the walls, grey carpets, cream sofa, jarred on her, also the lack of anything middle-aged, let alone old.

She sat on the offending sofa and thought that if it had been taken out of context, it would have been quite nice. The same sort of thin description would apply to Branston itself. A village that was not quite a village, one of a series of villages, this one in particular was caught in a time warp of house prices because of the triangle of motorways and trunk roads that had somehow isolated it with a few miles of protected woodland. But it was still not a real village, because the heart went out of it every day when three-quarters of its occupants remembered it was only an outpost and pushed themselves into taxis and trains. Well, thought Helen, cheerful at the alternative prospect, at least I don't do that. I get in my clapped-out car, drive it to the office as rarely as possible, then to magistrates' courts in Cheshunt and Epping where I prosecute the daily list of thieves, burglars, and even, occasionally, poachers, all at snail's speed to suit the magistrates, saying everything twice. It was in that respect that the contrast was most marked – the pace of it, the deliberation behind decision, the endless repetition of facts. What would have been allowed half an hour in front of a tetchy stipendiary magistrate in Bow Street or Tower Bridge took half a day here, with somewhat dissimilar results. Here they were swifter in sending the offenders to prison, heavier on fines, and inclined to hang them for careless driving, but she had to confess that law and order prevailed after a fashion, not unjust, not innovative either. Less bark, slower bite, more civilized.

Nor did she mind the subtle demotion that her move from central London had involved. Helen was not designed to succeed on the crude hierarchical ladder of the Crown Prosecution Service, or in any branch of the uncivil service, had never progressed far in grade, owing to an embarrassing frankness in interviews and a deliberate ignorance of whom she should please and flatter. Securing further promotion was a Machiavellian exercise demanding paroxysms of sycophancy for which she had no stomach. Bailey's similar indifference had propelled him through the ranks of the police like a secret missile, but Helen's had kept her still and, in the old office, rewarded in a way she had preferred. She had skills beyond those of her superiors. They recognized and exploited her skills by a division of work that took advantage of them, leaving Helen with a host of difficult and dangerous cases. Here in the outback, her sheer competence, the experience of murder, mayhem, drugs, and fraud, unnerved her employers more than slightly and they tried to bar her from the mainstream as far as possible. It was Cheshunt, Epping, and the juvenile court for Miss West. Keep her out of the office; she knows too much. Helen smiled and defeated them further by genuinely not minding. There was a purpose to this beyond career, after all: she had only wanted to stay alive and to see if she and Geoffrey Bailey could make a success of living together. Nothing was more important, nothing more absorbing than that. If some of her remained unused material, it would have to wait.

'Oh, damn.' For the second time in an hour she had gone to the wrong cupboard. Freudian slip, the product of undiscussed home-sickness, making her behave as if she was in her own home. Which she wished she was, even with all the attendant arguments – your place or mine? – that had bedevilled the last year. What an unlikely pair of lovers they were, policeman and lawyer, too scared, the pair of them, too suspicious, and far too independent to begin to decide which house should be home, miserable apart, tricky together. She had thought of abandoning it, could not contemplate that; thought of marriage, could not contemplate that, either. A marriage of true minds, all right, but pulling in opposite directions. Then Bailey was moved to this parish; this very house fell vacant for rent. They would try it for a year, borrowed premises, borrowed time, no commitments. Helen as housewife, the idea made her choke, but there was a nice novelty to it. So far so good in this isolation, though it would have been better if he liked it less. Bailey, after all, hailed from the East End; he might have the same aspirations for a better life. Helen hailed from nowhere and believed in very little.

'We may as well go home,' said Superintendent Bailey. 'If we search in the dark we may ruin the chances. The doc will be here shortly after five a.m. So shall I.'

'I've left Smith and Peters here to peg out the area. All that.'

'And shoot foxes,' Bailey added, smiling.

'With what, sir? It's the ghosts worry them.' The inspector grinned, comfortable with Bailey as few were, grateful for the pragmatism that was going to allow some

13

of them to sleep instead of messing around all night, talking about it until daylight revealed anything they would miss if they moved now.

'Seal off the footpath and the carpark, will you?'

'Will do, sir. Bowles will do that. Funny thing is, it was only opened again yesterday. Been resurfaced, out of action for weeks. They've all been taking their cars elsewhere.'

'Good. More chance we'll find traces of whoever put that body in there.'

'Poor cow.'

'Yes,' said Bailey, looking at the protruding hand sealed with polythene. 'I wonder who she is.'

The inspector grinned. 'Was, sir.'

Bailey sighed. 'Definitely past tense. Was. Come on, let's get some sleep before we have to look at the rest of her, presuming it is a woman. See you at five. Tell them to walk carefully. He may have left some souvenirs on the footpath.'

Eleven p.m. now and too many boots for comfort on that footpath already. Tell them not to deviate into the woods either, for God's sake, crashing about and standing on anything that might have been left by the performer of these rude and hurried burial rites. Looking at the shallow grave, flattened earth, and bent branches around it, Bailey supposed there would be traces. No careful undertaker this; no wonder the fox had found her. Tomorrow would be soon enough for discovery, when all the willing troops were deployed to their worst after brief sleep. All except Peters, Smith, and Bowles, who would not even have their turn to sleep in the morning. Bailey tried to forget them all on the way home, tried, on his way to Helen, to forget that offending, blotched stump of a hand pointing its accusation above earth.

In the carpark, half a mile from the grave, Police Constable Bowles tapped on the window of the single van parked beneath the trees, stood back politely. Inside, beyond the condensation on the glass, he could see movement, a breast rapidly covered, an arm in guilty movement, a face pressed to the rear window, eyes wide at the sight of the buttons on his uniform. More movement, until a youth scrabbled out of the front, buttoning his shirt, furious in the face of Bowles's half-smile.

'Wha's the matter, for fuck's sake? No law agin it, is there? First I knew.'

'Just hope she's sixteen, son. But you've got to move. Got to clear this carpark, see. Sorry about it.'

'Why? Why the fuck . . . why should I?' His fists were clenched, aggression on display like a fighting ram.

'Less of that. This your car, son? Or your dad's? Or your gaffer's? Been for a drink, have we?'

'All right, all right, all right.' Querulous fear rose in the voice. A girl's head, young but not childlike, appeared at the window. Bowles relented.

'Found a body in the woods, miss. Dead. Got to clear the area, seal it off. Hop it.'

The girl shrieked, short and shrill, an eerie little sound, then curled back in the passenger seat, pulling the boy in beside her. The engine spluttered, van spitting away full of the boy's fury, leaving profound silence. Extending the yellow tape across the entrance to the road, Bowles missed

15

the company and wondered how they had failed to see the police car parked in the far corner. Shame on you, boy, you could have done better than that.

The purr of Bailey's diesel engine at the door was a welcome sound. By the time he had collected his case, gazed at the sky, gathered his wits, wondered if Helen was still awake, and opened the door, she had padded into the kitchen, found the Scotch, run the bath, and filled the kettle. This was not the first body he had found in their six months' sojourn in this not so peaceful place, nor was it the first late evening to give Helen the opportunity to practise domestic solicitude, which Bailey neither demanded nor expected, but which secretly delighted him to the marrow of his strong and slender bones.

Bailey welcomed these attentions like a child. It felt like having the wife he had seen described in fiction, a true comforter never encountered in his life until now, and not even a wife in name. Bailey regretted that, and respected it. It was Helen's decision, not his. Sleep, even after thirteen hours of duty, was less important than news and the long embrace of dear familiarity. One day they would discuss his reservations about the place, this frightful house she seemed to like, but not now. There is nothing, he thought, more delightful than a woman who is happy to see you.

There is nothing, Helen thought, more becoming than the wrinkles on Bailey's face.

'Very macabre,' he told her, sitting up in bed with Scotch and coffee, Helen curled beside him, as welcoming as the night had been chill, both of them indulging in a frequent

16

if decadent nighttime ritual. 'Macabre with the usual comic overtones. It always makes me laugh when the divisional surgeon turns out. You know, he who precedes the pathologist and gives us licence to continue.'

Helen knew.

'Dr Flick, busy little man, looks at his hand, this suggestion of body, far from fresh. "I think she's dead at the moment," he says. "I'll do a certificate." Very pompous and Irish. I don't know why we needed a doctor to tell us that. "I'll pronounce it lifeless, I think," says Flick, just as he would if faced with a pile of bones. Pretty clever diagnosis, I thought. Has a swig of this out of his back pocket' – Bailey raised his own glass to illustrate – 'then scuttles away as fast as his legs will carry him.'

'Back to the living. Or the pub. Can't blame him.'

'No,' said Bailey, turning to her. 'I don't blame him. The living have more to say. I'd rather be with you than keeping vigil in a wood.'

She smiled at him, forgetting her preoccupations, seeing him anew as she did almost every day. 'Well, if that's the case, I'm glad you've no other choices.'

'Who said I haven't?'

'I did.'

Later in the warmth, his arms surrounding her. Geoffrey murmured sleepily into Helen's ear, 'You didn't have to run a bath for me, you know. I don't have to touch the bodies. Not these days.'

She stirred. He could feel her frowning. 'But you do. They touch you, and you touch them. You always do.'

'Yes,' he said, remembering the spasm of anger as his

17

own fingers had touched that pathetic and pleading muti-
lation of a hand, felt the ice-cold mottled forearm in the
dark. He had wished her goodbye, disliking the prospect of
tomorrow's disinterment, wishing they could simply leave
her alone.

'You always do,' Helen repeated.

'You're right,' he sighed. 'I always do.'

CHAPTER TWO

Detective Constable Amanda Scott arrived early by fifteen minutes, always in advance of the boss, careful in this and all things to preserve the good opinion she had tried so hard to deserve. She stepped out of her neat car, unaware of its highly polished gleam, but pleasantly conscious of the shine on her leather pumps and the curve of her waxed and tanned calves as she stood away from the door with her precise movements. She checked her hair in the side mirror, reproving herself for her own vanity while locking the car with automatic care. Miss Scott was dressed as she was always dressed in sensible but feminine clothes. White long-sleeved blouse with buttons, pleated cotton skirt in navy blue, matching the handbag and shoes, offset by tiny pearl earrings. Nothing flashy about Miss Scott – not a Mrs or a Ms – clad in good chain store clothes with an eye to economy and perfect presentation rather than the luxury of flair. She had liked the less nerve-racking days of uniform duty, still reflected in her conservative clothes, but she liked this better and knew herself to be modestly, only sometimes raucously, admired.

She sniffed the air. Woodland smells mingled with fresh Tarmacadam in the carpark, completed when? A day or so before, she would have guessed. No common access to the woods from here for over a fortnight. She gazed around her, saw the footpath into the trees, and mentally propelled herself above it all, forming in her mind a plan of the area. Maybe they would need an aerial photograph, but with a facility all her own, she imagined she could see herself and the scene of this demise from the air. A triangle, body in the middle. I stand, she told herself as she would have told a class, one mile from Branston on the Epping road, on the edge of Bluebell Wood. Here is a carpark, a picnic spot provided by the council, and here is a footpath that leads into the woods but peters out after half a mile; only proper walkers go farther, to their own disappointment because there isn't that much of it, really. Only another half-mile, then a valley, uphill to a small field and a bit more woodland surrounding that awful hotel. You could walk straight across to the hotel if you could ever get through that jungle of a garden. About a mile from here to there, with woods extending a mile on either side of where I point, two more picnic spots on the other side. Not a particularly beautiful or pleasant place outside the footpath and even with the dearth of green trees on this border of London and country, strangely unpopular. Might have been less so if the establishment on the other side, which insisted on calling itself a hotel rather than the unfriendly pub it was, actually welcomed guests. Amanda's single visit had coincided with that of a cockroach. She had never returned and could not

20

remember what they called the place now – the name changed with each renewal of the licence and the whim of the owners. The Crown, that was it, and no one, surely no one, would brave entry into the woods and fields through their garden. Compared to that wilderness, the woods were as easy as a street.

Detective Constable Scott paced three steps left and three right, small, clipped steps. Should she stay and greet the troops or walk down the path to the muslin-sheeted grave? She hated being still: she would walk; no, she would wait for the boss and walk behind him. Bailey would talk and think at the same time, dividing the wood into sections for searching, throwing ideas and instructions over his shoulder, and Amanda would remember them all, watch, and learn. She was only there to learn, would never miss a single scrap of knowledge or let past her sharp blue eyes the slightest opportunity for making a quiet contribution. She would be as she always was, his calm, efficient shadow, earning trust. It never occurred to her to wonder if she actually liked Bailey, or any of her colleagues. Amanda's concentration was streamlined. Her own feelings were irrelevant, suspended as Bailey arrived and greeted Dr Vanguard as an old friend. Both their cars were parked crooked, and she wondered why, on such respectable salaries, they drove such shabby vehicles.

The team assembled like the cast of a play, Bailey leading and Vanguard following, as daylight grew sharper, the signal for a hot day. More speed, said Vanguard. The sooner we get her out the better. Police Constables Bowles and Peters rose stiffly from camp chairs as the rest arrived in single file, not deviating from the footpath, as Bailey had

21

told them. Photographers, exhibits officer next with bags, labels, gloves, tweezers, strolling behind the ambulancemen, who were the only ones talking.

'As I said, Fred, it ain't really my turn to do this shift.'

'Never mind,' said Fred. Ordinary grumbles in the mist.

The searchers, combers of undergrowth, pickers of detritus, carriers of bags, would follow, foot soldiers behind cavalry.

Vanguard never seemed to mind the dirt. He who had waded into stinking Thames mud to recover half-submerged limbs, who had pulled a leg away from a hip joint in a cesspit, found this dry earth relatively innocuous. He knelt by the grave and began uncovering the form beneath the soil with all the care of an archaeologist, sweeping away handfuls of leaves with systematic energy until the shape emerged. The photographer recorded each stage of the process. The others watched from either side as the figure came into focus, lying straight with legs uncrossed, face turned flat against the earth as if refusing to watch what was being done. She was recognizably female in limbs if not yet in detail, and as Vanguard's hand dusted the face, Amanda could not suppress the rising nausea, glanced at Bailey, and maintained calm against her shiver of disgust. The face was discoloured green and black, alive with bright white maggots twisting in the cavities of empty eye sockets, active in the distended nostrils, full of hideous and indignant movement in the eyes and lipless mouth where their destruction had exposed teeth bared in an obscene grin.

Bailey wondered why they had attacked the face first, what dreadful lack of mercy; render to earth what must be rendered, but first distort, make unrecognizable what was once so human, may have been beautiful. No greater damage than the face; apart from the half-chewed hand without fingertips, the limbs were intact, stained like green marble, but whole. No doubt the larvae would have found the other orifices, liquid, vulnerable private parts.

Amanda turned her head away as pathologist and assistants lifted the body on to the plastic sheet laid ready to receive it. She was ashamed for the woman's nakedness, knew disgust and contempt for one found in such condition, almost an acute dislike for the dead, resented her own squeamishness and the constant struggle to suppress it. Thank God Vanguard would not be taking his vaginal and anal swabs here: they would be spared that sight until the thing was finally devoid of all humanity on the post-mortem table. In the haze of her own disgust, holding her breath to avoid the stench, feeling her skin itch as if the larvae had attached themselves, Amanda shook her senses, forced herself to look harder. She was not there to feel pain, noted the gash on the forehead, the gaping throat. Well. They would soon know better. The exhibits officer collected larvae from the face, put them in a bag without a word, treating them with gentleness. Amanda wondered what manner of man it was who analysed them.

'How long, Doc? Can you say?'

Vanguard was continuing a cursory inspection, calling up the ambulance boys for the tiresome walk back to transport, grumbling under his breath. 'How long? What, for a report? Oh, I see, how long dead? Difficult to say. At least a week, probably more. Depends if she was left uncovered first, speeds up the decomposition a bit. Do we know who she is?'

23

'No, not yet. No one local reported missing, except children.'

Vanguard grunted, scratched, and Amanda wondered how his wife ever let him inside the doors. 'Well, look for a woman, fortyish, dark-haired, bit big in the bum, but otherwise shapely, probably pretty.' He cackled, Bailey grimaced. He liked the man, had time for him, but occasionally the humour was hard to take. 'And a knife, I would think. Also something blunt. About three p.m. OK? Got another one first.'

Bailey felt the hangover of familiarity. Another session with formaldehyde smells and all the ceremony of an abattoir. His own aversion to the necessary witnessing of the pathologist's knife owed less to squeamishness than to a sense of indignity. Sad enough to be buried, slaughtered first before time, terminally abused, without being disinterred and cut apart, so distant from the dignity of laying out and decent burial that was the ordinary hope of ordinary men. No saving grace for the murder victim, none at all, no stateliness in death or anything that followed and from the disgrace of secret killing there would follow more. In Bailey's mind there grew the dull and familiar anger against the dealer of such treacherous cards, the perpetrator of such brutality, which carried this in its wake. Pitiful nakedness. Not a stitch on her or with her. Not even woman's comfort, the everpresent handbag.

He turned, issued his orders. Start here, fanning out in sections, eyes to the ground. Cigarette ends, notable footprints, broken branches suggesting haste; a week is long enough to hide half the traces if there are any traces, and what a scrubby, mean, depressed bit of woodland this is.

Not real forest or real country, not the oil-drummed, rubbish-filled adventure playground bombsites of his youth, either. He felt dislike of Branston and all its environs rise like a tide, sink in the need for action. Two dozen men, more if needed, comb the ground for a square mile. Amanda, organize a press release, meet me at the hotel, no, I don't need a lift, I prefer to walk, and I wish you were not so obsequious, or that I liked anything about this place.

Bailey had walked every inch of this ground, alone sometimes or with Helen, pacing the territory of his new home like a cat, fully aware that without butter on his paws, he would have aimed for home. For the wider territory of his professional manor he had made it his business to drive every road and take into his brain each landmark, street, pub, station, and anything else immovable. He knew the bus routes and the trouble spots as well as the areas of innocence. The manor extended far beyond Branston, slipped into the sprawl of northeast London where he was stationed in a building of monumental ugliness. The three other bodies whose removal he had witnessed in the last two months had been found, respectively, in a flat, behind some dustbins, and in the front seat of a car. Minicab driver with smashed skull, urban waste, sticky with blood, but found before the predators and the flies got to him. Not like this. This was beyond town limits and the zone of improved chances. The same was not supposed to happen here. For Helen, himself, and all who dwelt here.

An afterthought, catching the man's eye. 'Stay on and help, Bowles, will you?'

'Sir.' The grin widened on Bowles's face. Overtime and, besides that, work he liked, reminiscent of weeding and pruning, pedantic garden chores, which he also liked. Bowles was fifty, with eyes like magnets attracting him to anything out of place. A man of infinite patience which his children did not understand, so that he was forced to pretend occasional irritation foreign to a cultivator of plants and detector of metal objects on Essex riverbanks. Bowles enjoyed sifting lawn seed and grains of sand, also searching ground with his mole of a nose and brown long-sighted eyes, squatting and picking, sorting and choosing. A cursory search behind the carpark area had revealed cartons and Coke tins, hamburger wrappers, plastic bags, and several used contraceptives. Bowles was always amazed by the human habit of congregation even to deposit rubbish. The flocking habit was foreign to him, although his mating instinct was sound enough to let him recognize anything that might have been thrown from a handbag. Ignoring all distraction, Bowles would waste no time looking for the obvious – what had Vanguard said? Knife, blunt weapon. Dimmer eyes than his could find these if they were there to be found, which Bowles suspected they were not, while his own would look for nothing in particular. He hitched his trousers and straightened his jacket, impervious to growing heat. Ah, yes. A plodder himself, he would recognize signs of haste, for a start, even over a week old, and distinguish between adult spores and the symptoms of tag-playing children. He shivered, accustoming a cold, stiff body to thoughts of activity, thinking slowly, remembering the couple he had dismissed the night before. Picnic spot or no picnic spot, this was somehow not a wood for children.

Bowles and the more conscientious of his companions

knew they were looking for whatever they could find. Not an empirical search, simply a collecting exercise. Later, when they found the culprit – Bowles always said 'when', not 'if' – some of their souvenirs might fill in a corner of the picture. 'You never know' was Bowles's most infamous and irritating cliché; the phrase alone had quite rightly blocked his promotion, indicative of his preference for any activity without apparent purpose. In the event, it was Bowles, of course, who found the cigarettes, the packet and the two stubs, one with lipstick and one without. He put the stubs in a matchbox, like a boy with pet spiders, and carried them safely home.

Unlike Amanda Scott, with her preference for the wine bar in Branston High Street, Bailey had no objection to visiting The Crown Hotel, did not confess to his assistant his liking for the place, even though he imagined her discretion hid nerves of steel. Bailey had found the hotel attracting him from the start, a view shared by Helen to the extent that they had visited the place more frequently than any other local hostelry for reasons neither of them could fathom.

'It isn't the food,' Helen had remarked, happily and thoroughly entertained by wrestling with the crust of a cheese roll, putting it down to search for the cheese, finding a huge but dried lump of it in the centre.

'It isn't the beer, either,' Bailey had added, nursing a murky pint with some suspicion.

'What is it, then?' said Helen.

'Unpredictability, unfashionability, and anonymity,' said Bailey promptly.

'Oh, my, long words for a Sunday. You've been reading

the papers again. Do you mean you can hide here without knowing what will happen?' Teasing him, grinning in contentment, Sunday a holiday.

'No, I mean I like it because so few other people do.' He gestured towards the bar with more spaces than people. 'And because I never know from one visit to the next what it will be like or whether it will still be standing.'

'I quite like it,' Helen said, 'because it has all the sod-the-customer attitude of a London pub. You know, the what-do-you-want-a-drink-for-this-is-only-a-pub-for-God's-sake approach. Clean glass? Fussy, are we? What's wrong with a dirty one? You antisocial or something? I only work here. Why should I care? Et cetera.'

'But they do care,' said Bailey. 'They care desperately, which is why it's so odd.' He had paused and grinned. 'Admit it, Helen. You really like it for the arguments.'

'Oh, I do,' Helen sighed. 'You know I do. I can't resist listening to other people's arguments. Especially loud, public, silly, insulting marital arguments.'

'You're well placed here, then, darling,' said Bailey with his smile. 'Seventh heaven for a nose like yours.'

'Actually,' she had said, 'I'm happy most places with you.'

He remembered the conversation with amusement as he skirted the hotel gardens, finally crossing the field at one side and climbing a fence to reach the front of the building by way of the road in preference to ill-mannered intrusion via the back wilderness of garden. Bailey was always courteous. His politeness was the coldest and warmest feature of his public face, giving him entry to numerous social pockets where courtesy could not be defined, let alone expressed. 'Always polite, Mr Bailey,' one streetwalker

28

informant had stated. 'Always knows when you're in the bath.' Knew also when to accept obvious lies without comment to save face or save pain, and when not to intrude even as a friend, although in their bizarre fashion, Mr and Mrs Featherstone, licensees of The Crown Hotel and owners of same, would have welcomed him as such. Our man of taste, Mr Bailey the copper. Anyone who arrived at their doors, withstood the insults and the rows, the dizzying décor, the recitation of plans for improvement and instant riches, as well as the experimental nourishment, became in their eyes a man of taste. Bailey was aware he had reached this class, equated their definition of his taste in this respect alongside stamina and helpless curiosity, carried as always his own immunities.

Regarding him as a friend, insofar as the Featherstone family had friends, was no guarantee of politeness. As Bailey approached the entrance to the bar, door unlocked as both a sign of proprietorial carelessness by the owners and indifference to local burglars, he sensed beyond the pane the sound of an argument. Ten a.m., the Featherstones fighting, all well with the world. Revised licensing hours' allowing longer opening hours made no difference to the trading manners of the establishment, but then the laws had made no difference before. If the bar had been open in the a.m.s and p.m.s of life, the local uniformed police had used their well-known discretion to ignore the fact, saving the same laws to restrain only those pubs that caused trouble. There were no drugs or underage drinkers in The Crown, while the only fighting on the premises was conducted between the licensees. Even the authorities had neglected the place.

In the huge, potentially elegant bar-room, Mrs Banks, cleaning lady, sat in a corner smoking a cigarette and drinking the half of Guinness she had poured for herself, weary from flicking her damp duster. She let herself in at eight, stopped her indifferent labours when the Featherstone family emerged from their pits. 'Can't stand the noise, dear,' she said to Bailey, shuffling into her coat, draining the glass, which she was not going to wash, pointing in the direction of the kitchen. 'They're in there,' as if any announcement were needed.

'Oh, shut up, Harold, for chrissake. Feed your big face and shut up. Let me get on with this cooking.'

'Cooking! You call that cooking? You couldn't get a job feeding pigs.'

'What about you, then? Call this filthy stuff coffee? I wouldn't give it to the bloody cat.' A crescendo, followed by Harold's voice.

'Fuck off back to the smoke, then, why don't you?' Not screamed, but loud enough, calm enough to penetrate the deafest ears, shortened by Bailey's presence. 'Oh, it's you, Mr Bailey. Didn't mean you. I meant her.'

'Shut up, Harold. Shut up.' Very loud, louder than Harold's casual, vicious invitation. Bernadette Featherstone, shriller in voice but quicker to recover, forced a smile so fleeting a blink would have missed its presence. 'Yes, it's Mr West,' she said. 'Superintendent Geoffrey. PC Plod to us. Fancy seeing you. You don't usually need sustenance so early. Mrs West chucked you out, has she?' Bernadette took a delight in referring to Bailey as West, her own way of striking a blow for female solidarity. 'Can't think why. What do you want? Tea, coffee, gin, whisky? Harold's had one of the latter already. Sweetens him up nicely, you can tell.' Her clipped tones, educated, only the slightest undertones of Irish, betrayed a defeat that was marshalling forces. She had decided to allow Harold the last word, a decision made before Bailey's entrance. The why-don't-you-bugger-off-if-you're-so-bloody-miserable routine usually ended round one and heralded the beginning of round two an hour or so later. She never had the answers to Harold's final questions. Looking at her plump frame, wearied face, scarred hands, uncontrolled once-blonde hair, Bailey could see why she had no answer. Here and now might have been terrible, but here was an addiction, and in any event there was nowhere else to go.

'Business I'm afraid, not pleasure,' said Bailey, and to forestall some howl of protest added quickly, 'we've found a body three-quarters of a mile from here. Bluebell Wood. You're nearest as the crow flies, hence the visit. Simply a chance you might have seen something or know who she is. Which is more than we do.'

'A body? Oh, my God,' said Bernadette, sinking her weight into a chair, suddenly breathless, patting hair and chest as if to see that she was still alive herself, shooting a venomous glance at Harold, accusing him of every foul deed, including this. 'Really dead?'

'Very dead. Since a few days. Beyond artificial respiration.'

Bernadette crossed herself rapidly, last remnant of expensive Catholic education long since forgotten in her language, remembered in her fear of hell. 'Poor soul,' she said. Bailey liked her for being shocked, and for expressing pity before irritation.

31

'But why,' asked Harold, always the calmer but sooner provoked to suspicion, 'why are you asking us? Why should we know anything about it?'

'I don't imagine you do,' Bailey replied with casual patience and the smile that creased his face from forehead to chin. 'But you're the nearest building, and I simply thought if I gave you a rough description it might trigger something. She might have been a customer here. You might have seen a couple in here having an argument, oh, a week or ten days ago. Woman of about forty, dark hair, good figure. I'm only boxing in the dark. Maybe someone depressed.'

'Oh,' said Bernadette, brightening, 'was it suicide, then?'

'No,' said Bailey, 'not unless she buried herself, too.'

There was a little silence, sun streaming through spectacularly dirty windows on to Harold's pale skin. An innocent silence, pregnant with the desire to help, or so Bailey sensed it, not the hesitation of guilty confusion, but not a productive interlude, either. Unless this victim had sprung into the communal mind immediately it would be useless to expect either party to this soured but engrossing union to remember what happened the day before, let alone the week. Unless blows had been struck or walls collapsed.

Harold giggled. 'Only dark-haired lady comes in here is your wife,' he said, adding out of malice, 'sometimes on her own, too.'

'Yes I know,' said Bailey, 'but she'd resent the description of fortyish, you know. She's got a few years to go before that. Almost as many as I have the other side.'

'Couples,' said Bernadette suddenly. 'Couples. We never have women on their own unless they sit quietly and read a paper like Mrs West. Think of couples, Harold, you git. There's one or two of the definitely over-the-side kind, always looking at the door in case they're going to be spotted, sitting in a corner pawing each other. Disgusting – well, sweet, really, in a way. Chance would be a fine thing, wouldn't it, Harold darling? One respectable pair – I mean, not kids – used to come in here, woman about thirty-eight, but not for a while, or at least not regular. Maybe last week, maybe not, I don't know, why should I? Only remember her because I tried to chat once, asked her name, and she wouldn't say. "What's it to you?" she said. "Suit yourself," I said, but I like asking names. Maybe last week, maybe not.'

Bailey could imagine some clandestine mistress recoiling from the suggestion she supply her credentials, especially to a request barked like the cross-examination Bernadette used in lieu of small talk to customers, smiled at the thought. 'Anyone else?' he asked mildly. The Featherstones sat at their long kitchen table amid the crumbs of breakfast, their faces a study of concentration.

Across the wooden floor of the bar came footsteps and a calm but carrying voice. 'Is your mother in?' A muttered response, heavier footsteps thudding upstairs, Amanda Scott pushing open the door with a pleasant hello on her face, fading as she encountered the glower from Bernadette, all at odds with the leer from Harold. 'May I come in?' she said prettily. 'Your son said you were here.'

William, son and heir. Bailey had forgotten him; he had a sad naïveté about children. William, listening at the door, poor daft child, a lifetime of listening at doors. Bailey had a vision of the boy – Harold's pale skin on a vacant face, none of Harold's cunning or vapid good looks, clumsy and lonely. A door slammed in the distance; a thump upstairs as the boy threw himself on to his bed. Found out, careless, bored.

Bernadette spoke rapidly, words addressed to Bailey while keeping her eyes and savage expression fixed on the face of Amanda Scott as if she would like to throw a blanket over that immaculate presence. 'Don't speak to William, will you, Geoffrey? Not today if you don't bloody mind. He's in one of his moods.'

Bailey watched Amanda, sensed her waiting in vain for some sign of authoritative insistence from himself, replied calmly, 'No, of course not, if you would rather I didn't. May have to another time once we know more, perhaps not. When it suits him.'

Bernadette relaxed and recovered. 'Who the hell are you, then, Miss Squeaky-Clean?' she asked Amanda in a deliberate attempt to embarrass. 'His bit on the side?'

Even Bailey could not suppress a hidden grin at the brief spasm of furious indignation on that smooth face. He added quickly, 'Amanda is the privilege of another, Bernadette. Miss Scott is my detective constable. Arrives in time to stop me drinking.'

Amanda was mollified slightly, but, as Bernadette intended her to be, uncomfortable, anxious to get on and out, mystified by the aimless chat that followed, disgruntled by Bailey's lack of desire to allocate tasks. There's been a murder, for God's sake, she said to herself, and you stand chatting in dirty kitchens. Not even insisting on seeing that lunatic thug who was listening at the door. Suspect if ever was, known for inclination to violence. Come on, Superintendent, please, come on. I don't like it here, and they don't like me. There are days when I do not care for you or admire you as much as others do, however handsome you are. There is nothing here, there never is. Come away, please, before I doubt you. Stood silent and smiling instead. Bernadette disliked her quite intensely. The feeling was mutual. Bailey was sorry for the discomfiture of both.

Upstairs, half on, half off his unmade bed, William listened with his ear to the floor and his heels drumming quietly on the wallpaper, his head uncomfortably full of blood and little else. William had chosen this small and unpromising room five years ago on the eve of his twelfth birthday, stuck in it ever since although he had outgrown both bed and furniture, and in this Edwardian barn he had the choice of other rooms far more dignified. There was a theory that most of the seven bedrooms were reserved for guests, but few stayed, only the odd misguided travelling salesman who failed to return, or the even odder couple whose passion could not withstand the discomfort, the breakfast, the inquisition, or William listening at the door. William liked the intrusion of the kitchen smells, ignored the noisy accompaniments, or turned the noises into rhythms inside his head, anticipating the next change of pace or silence. He particularly liked the whirr of the washing machine, which made his room vibrate, and he liked the childish chest of drawers, diminutive wardrobe, all ordered for a boy who was now the size of a man – a man five feet ten inches tall, equipped with huge hands, swollen genitals, the mind of a ten-year-old child, and hearing as sharp as an owl's.

They had gone. William heaved himself back on the bed, all anxiety banished. They had been talking about nothing, and whatever they had said would keep the peace. He knew the words of the conversation, could not always establish the links. Grown-ups were always talking about nothing. What took them so long never to remember anything important he never knew. And he would not be lectured for listening at the door, not today at least. They never noticed, Mum and Dad, never noticed at all, all those people who came and went, fiddled about, drank, got drunk, laughed, shouted, all that stuff. He was dimly aware of the limitations of his mind, conscious of the superiority of his eyes and the refinement of his senses, which found all others foolish, his own absorbing.

Spreadeagled on the worn candlewick bedcover, his bare feet grubby from padding back across the garden at dawn, William regarded his domain, still listening to the polite departing voices. He was the only Featherstone who relished his own being.

The washing machine downstairs began to rumble.

William scratched his groin idly, unzipped his jeans slowly, and began a quicker massage, fingering the thing he had always called his stump, for the second time that morning. Donkey William, they had called him at school, an unkind if accurate reflection on the size of his penis as well as his brain power. Silly William, happy as a baby in a sand pile, eyes closed, hands busy, his face in a grimace of repose, shooting stars.

36

CHAPTER THREE

'It's the lawnmowers that get me most,' said Helen to Christine Summerfield. 'Lawnmowers in summer. Trimmers, hedge cutters, tree clippers, anything electrical. In winter it's hammers and drills. Lawnmowers are worse.'

'Did you have a garden in London?' Faraway London, as if it were another planet. All of twelve miles away. A lifetime.

'Oh, yes. Had? Still have. And a lawn, even. Well, a sort of a lawn. I clipped it with shears after the push-and-shove mower gave up the ghost. Rusted beyond repair, seemed undignified to use it in old age. I hope they – the tenants, I mean – look after it. But I never had a high-pitched machine, not like these things sounding like a swarm of angry flies.'

Christine was immune. She had lived here longer, relished the sounds of rural suburbia. 'Won't take a minute,' she said cheerfully. 'Only a small patch of lawn. Anyway, sitting still is so much my favourite pastime I can stand any accompaniment.'

'This is the point,' said Helen. 'I should formally thank you for your company. You saved my sanity in the High Street.'

'Thank me? It's your house, your coffee, your Saturday morning. Such formality. Does that mean you want me to go?'

'Oh, please don't. Have some more coffee, piece of cake, gin and tonic. Stay and talk. Otherwise Geoffrey gets an earful when he gets home. No, I only mean I'm grateful for a kindred spirit, if that's the right phrase. Eat the cake, anything to keep you.'

'Eat the cake? Encouraging me, you thin hypocrite. You can afford to eat the cake. I can't, but I'll eat it all the same.'

'Inside me,' said Helen, 'is a fat person trying to get out. Six more months of domestic bliss in Branston and this damaged butterfly will have gone back to chrysalis. Fat chrysalis. I can't afford cake, either. Cake and country: why do they go together? Eat your calories, get lethargic, sit back and listen to the butterflies. OK, for once I admit the pleasure of it.'

The two women were a sharp contrast to each other. Christine Summerfield bore a seasonal name for a buttercup nature, resembled an attractive advertisement for dairy food – pleasantly plump and fair, heavy bosom, blue eyes, and expression of shrewd honesty. On first sight her role as professional caretaker of man or animal seemed obvious: she looked like what she was. Helen had guessed nurse first, then social worker. Right the second time. Christine resembled the kindly guardian she was, sympathy implicit in every line of her face, while Helen – so easily ridden with pity, guilt, confusion, and fury, so prone to every surreptitious kindness or mercy her job or her life afforded – did not carry her compassion like a flag in her eyes. She was small and dark, slender but muscular, occasionally fierce. She had a slightly lined face full of hidden humour, huge eyes, and a scar on her forehead. Christine considered her beautiful; Bailey did, too. Helen's previous Boss had called her a stubborn little brute. Vividly attractive on any estimate, but unlike Christine, not a thing to be embraced soon after shaking its hand. She was too quick in wit, too articulate to present as the immediate comforter, the bosom for all sorrows, as Christine patently was, and yet they found Helen, the lamed and the disgraced, the troubled and the children. Can we play in your garden, miss? Can we sit in your car? Of course you can. Tell your mother where you are, and if you eat the plants or puncture the wheels, I'll brain you, understand? Any use for these biscuits, have you? Thought you might. Staccato common sense, endless generosity almost gruff in the giving, parameters firmly set. Old men in pubs, young women in shops talking while she listened and understood, patient with fools. An instinctive grasp of what was important in any tale. Christine the caretaker knew herself drawn in the same way to that calm understanding which was quite devoid of criticism, was charmed and relieved when the confidences that had poured unbidden from her own mouth and into Helen's ears were rewarded by confidences in return. Incomplete confidences, but still something tantamount to shared secrets. 'Dear God,' she had said to Helen, 'social worker and prosecutor, I ask you. By tradition we sit on opposite fences, but we manage to talk for hours.'

39

'Opposite fences?' said Helen. 'Rubbish. We're all on the same side. Two professionals doing a job. Tradition has a lot to answer for.' They had gravitated beyond such considerations, still discussed them.

'I like it here,' said Christine. 'But I can see why you don't. You're playing second fiddle to Bailey – professionally, I mean.'

'I've always played second fiddle. That's what solicitors do, after all. We never make big shots, in public at least.'

'But you don't even deal with big shots, not here.'

'True,' Helen admitted. 'It's a bit lower-powered than I'm used to, but that isn't what I mind, most of the time. Some of the time, but not most of the time. It's a bit of relief, and if the truth were known, the small cases are often as complicated as the big ones. Shame they don't get the same attention.'

'What about your little-shot clients, if that's the right word for them? Do you ever have any doubts about their guilt?'

'I very rarely doubt their being guilty as charged, if that's what you mean, especially here, where truthful witnesses are less at a premium. But I still think them innocent in many respects. Fault and blame are so often irrelevant.'

They were content to sit in silence, Christine waiting, Helen finally restful.

'Damn that lawnmower. I never understand how an age that forces people to live in closer proximity than ever before should give them all the tools to make it impossible. Stereos, lawnmowers, food mixers, such a bloody racket.

London was quiet compared to this. Speaking of proximity, how's Antony? Come on, tell me.'

Helen was well aware that her companion had been waiting to tell for the last hour, only needing a cue, ever since they had met in the High Street, grinning over the heads of the shoppers, she buying for Bailey, Christine for Antony, Helen making heavy weather of chores Christine took lightly. Oh, I can't make up my mind. What the hell shall I buy? There's so much of it. Decisions in shops were far harder than professional ones. Even their love affairs were different.

'Antony? He's at home making lunch.' Christine blushed slightly. 'He likes cooking, actually.'

'Now there's luck for you. Still love, I take it?'

'Yee . . . es. With open eyes. Early days yet, very early, but optimistic. I know what he is, you see, and I don't mind.' She curled up in the garden chair, which Helen found the only comfortable seat in the house, settled to the telling. 'I know he's a dreamer, been a bad lad in the past. Knee deep in poetry, bewailing his lot teaching Shakespeare to reluctant kids. Likes it, really. He has this peculiar ability to teach. I'd forgive him a lot for having that.'

'What's peculiar about it? Any special technique?'

'He makes children want to write,' said Christine. 'I don't know how. He says that's the essence of teaching English. Gets them to write down everything they think and put some form into it. They seem to love it, although the results are hilarious and sometimes disconcerting. Tell it like a story, he says to them, and they do. Then, lo and behold, the little blighters began to like reading, too. Much in demand, our Antony. All for his talent of getting them to record their lives on paper.'

'I like that,' said Helen. 'He goes romping up in my estimation. So that's one thing you love about him. You were just beginning on the reservations.'

'Well, he can't help looking like Byron. It's rather turned his mind, given him this fatal attraction for the opposite sex, which includes me, of course. Says he is redeemed by the love of a fair woman, and provided I can put up with that kind of nonsense as well as the naïveté that seems to have survived school, which I can, he's a lovely, generous, open-hearted man. He'll do nicely for a frustrated thirty-two-year-old social worker once he's over the complications. I only wish he was more truthful. The rest I'm happy to take.'

Helen, who knew these diffident descriptions hid a great yawning gulf of love in the only Branston inhabitant to whom she had drawn close, probed further in gentle cross-examination.

'What do you mean, more truthful? Does he fib?'

'Well, they all do a bit, don't they?' said Christine doubtfully. 'Men, I mean.'

No, they don't, Helen thought. Bailey doesn't. Lies choke him. Unfortunately he prefers silence.

'I only mean he doesn't tell the whole truth. This affair he had – you know, I told you, before me – God, has it only been three months? I can't believe it, seems like for ever. Anyway, this married woman whose daughter he was tutoring, extra English lessons . . . you know, he was giving the daughter this knack and habit of writing things down, although I gather she was pretty clever already. Quite rich, this family; he won't tell me who the woman was, but she was older than he. He had an affair with her, more off than on, for a year. All tailed out. She was keener than he, he says, pursued him like a tank across the desert. He insists it's all off; he's met me, the love of his life, et cetera. Swore he never touched her after me, and I believe him. But he met her last week because she cried on the phone at school, threatened to tell her husband, suicide, the lot. He was a bit distraught. They met at The Crown – I'd been forewarned – and finished it for ever, he says, and again I believe him. He may be a bit of a womanizer, but only one at a time. I just wonder, that's all. Didn't see him for two days, and when I did he looked as if he'd done two rounds with a tiger, still does. Says he fell over a bramble bush while trying to mend a fence in his garden. Antony does not mend fences, not that kind anyway. He may cook, but he doesn't mend fences.'

'I see. No word of how the meeting went with the lady?'

'That's just it. I don't know. He refuses to elaborate. That isn't typical Antony: He relates every wretched shameful thing he's ever done since childhood. His honesty's pathological, exhausting at times. He makes his pupils enjoy mild catharsis on paper, and he enjoys it in words. But not over this, and I don't know why.' She crumbled the last of the cake, dispirited.

'He probably behaved as badly as anyone would when there's no kind way to say the things he was having to say,' said Helen. 'Spoke all the wrong words in the wrong way. Maybe honesty was his downfall, he should have lied a lot, and instead they ended up screaming, he for his skin, she

43

for her dignity. No one would notice in The Crown, after all.'

'I see all that. But scratches? Antony's quite capable of violence, you know. Only when cornered. I know that,' Christine added hastily, 'from the confessional of his early youth, not from anything he's ever done to me. He's wiry, with all the aggression of a bullied boy. That's what worries me. If this rejected matron scratched him, what did he do in return?'

'I hope he didn't scratch back.'

Christine shrugged. 'I hope so, too.'

Helen looked at her friend, alarmed by a sudden premonition, a hateful vision of that corpse in the wood, encounters at The Crown, the disjointed memories of the Featherstones, all recounted as amusingly as possible by Geoffrey the evening before, all merging into the landscape of tragedy. She stripped her face bare of thought, dismantled and dispelled the premonition as it rose like an ugly monument in her mind, smiled, and spoke firmly. 'Nothing you can do now, whatever he did then. Wait and see. But ten days? That's nothing. I tell you, in the realms of male silence, especially if they feel guilty, really nothing. He'll tell you when he's ready, surely.' Sophisticated platitudes for a mature companion, not doubting her tentative analysis of a nasty event, too honest for that, simply suggesting that all sounds of alarm could be postponed, perhaps for ever. Allowing time for a good lunch, a peaceful afternoon, and with luck a peaceful lifetime, but not entirely omitting the doubt. Ointment for a troublesome graze, not suggesting a cure. The balm discharged Christine from the house in a state bordering on optimism, leaving Helen pacing the pastel carpets, full of worry without name. Putting a lid on it was as futile as attempting to suppress a jack-in-the-box with a wicked spring and cruel face, unsuitable for children.

Of course she would tell her Geoffrey, her own Detective Chief Superintendent Bailey, of course she would. Or maybe not. She would tell, feeling foolish for once in the telling, no more than an aside: Darling, do you know what else has been going on in The Crown . . . ? Nothing at all to add to the scenario that gripped him in the current search to find a face for this body, a signature for this murderer, preferably appended to a confession. She would tell him, nevertheless, as she told him everything. Almost everything, she reminded herself; no one tells it all. She might have learned to speak truth automatically and had not yet discovered the day when there would be a serious conflict of loyalties, a question of betrayal. So far there had been no conflict, but without conscious thought of Christine Summerfield or of the Branston way of life, which he seemed to enjoy and she to suspect for its very tranquillity, she feared the imminence of decisions.

One thought led to another. No potato peeling today; Geoffrey out on inquiries, plenty of freedom for thinking. Silly disconnected thoughts involving plenty of nonsense, seen as such. Practical considerations above all, such as what to do with a restless afternoon. I could go to London and get crushed and dirty in Oxford Street. Lovely, if I had the energy. I could stay here and pick daisies, worry a bit, sit in the jungle at The Crown, and pray above all that I never have a lawnmowing husband and that Christine does. No, I shall not wash the car, since the children would

45

like it less, or clean out the garage, because of the starlings'
nest, nor shall I deadhead these tidy roses; let them rot. I'll
go and have a meaningless conversation instead or paint a
picture.

Helen could paint. Charming scenes that tended to
become caricatures with captions as well as faces. When
words failed, she would grab pen and paper in her urgency
to explain. 'Listen, it's like this' – gesturing with one hand
as diagram or illustration emerged from the pen in the
other, on a napkin, a tablecloth, best linen not immune, on
the back of a brief or an envelope. In a lecture hall as a student or waiting in court, she would create a litter of
doodles, noses, eyes, hairlines, and winks, summoning up
for Bailey a presence on paper. 'Listen, will you? He
looked a bit like this, as I told you,' producing a likeness of
sorts with all the salient and funny features first. 'He had a
nose like this,' or an animal face, catlike, doglike, snakelike,
or blank, or a face resembling a car, or three lines that
caught some angle of the features.

'As for you,' she said, 'you look like this on first
acquaintance; you really do,' she told him, drawing three
straight lines in a notebook at the head of a blank page, the
lowest of the lines leading into a vertical line for a definite
nose, a wide, curling questioning line for a mouth, and a
short vertical stab for a cleft in the chin, forming at last a
downward-pointing T to incorporate a strong and stubborn jaw. It suggested everything. A face full of hairline
traces like overcooked porcelain: an infinite capacity for
change within definite limits.

He had fingered this face, found the grooves she had
displayed with her eyes away from them, laughed in dis-

belief and a tiny tinge of embarrassment to see himself depicted with such careless accuracy. 'Better than Identikit,' he said.

'Oh, I hope so,' said Helen. 'I know you better than some witness who might have seen you robbing a bank.'

'And the other people you sketch?'

'Them too, I expect. Surely I have a better recollection than anyone who is not being horrified at the time.'

'And Edward Jaskowski, Stanislaus, your clients, your guilty ones, all those you have sent to some kind of prison – can you draw them?'

'No,' she said firmly, snapping closed her notebook, 'not unless I must. Which is never at all, I think, unless they come and ask me.' Then she would draw more; he would try to copy. They would end as usual, entwined and absorbed in easy laughter.

So far these pictorial observations with pen and ink had provided little apart from relief from the frustration of words, with which she was unduly skilled. The most constructive relief was found on a day like this in a spare room, attempting to construct something with a hope of beauty. Helen painted and sketched on a day like this to rid her mind of everything else. Frowning, she quickly sketched the face of Antony Sumner. Widely spaced eyes, a long, sad nose, high forehead, full mouth and a slightly receding chin. A soft face, miscast and starving Labrador retriever, made strong by affection, a touch of stubbornness around the eyes, a temper. The exercise of bringing into focus that scarcely familiar face encountered only once in the High Street reassured her. Petulant, argumentative, clumsy with emotion, capable of eruption but only

47

suddenly. Quite incapable, she decided, of the sustained rage and stupidity that were prerequisites in a true man of violence. She threw down her pen in the top room of the house, drew instead in her mind's eye the garden of her basement in London, full of overblown flowers, cat in the long grass of the lawn, animals instead of city sounds, some child crouching there awaiting her return. Then she went out to watch life on the reconstructed village green, not even really wishing she belonged, not unhappy, not rude, but not trying, either.

The village green had been the creation of the property developers, a cunning thought, to give the place a focus, John Blundell had said. At the other end of Branston, comfortably far from this village green, standing aloof from the edge of the community and half turned away, the Blundell household did not resemble the miniatures of itself that clustered in Invaders Court where Helen dwelt and which Mr Blundell had helped to build. John Blundell, estate agent and developer, had put Branston on the map, first by selling its reconditioned houses, then by adding to them. Sympathetic additions, he said. His motives had not been bad, since although he had lined his pocket, the zeal to do well for ever and to become an elder of the kirk, if there had been a kirk, was foremost in his mind. This ambition for parish pump prominence had at least ensured well-constructed buildings and a manner in Mr Blundell which could be called honest; but recognition for his crusade was not received at home or abroad, since nothing he had commandeered into bricks and mortar could ever make him significant. He remained small, but became rich, pale, cunning, unhealthy, desperate to be liked, if not loved, and quite unable, for all that, to suppress a streak of meanness. Even while knowing by instinct what people wanted in their houses, he could never fathom the slightest notion of what they thought.

His large house, last of the genuine and best in Branston as befitted its only estate agent, turned away from the road into its own garden at an angle of forty-five degrees, just as John Blundell turned his face, always looking into the middle distance in suspicion of being cheated, vengeful if he was, rarely catching an eye. At the moment he faced his daughter Evelyn, failing to see the contempt in her expression, trying to know better, conscious of profound failure. He was dimly aware that the wheel of his fractious family life, maybe his whole life, was about to come off, that notoriety in the form of pity, rather than the respect he craved, was about to become his lot. And even after turning his head aside from the stern gaze of his daughter, he felt the accusation in it.

'Father, you'll have to tell them. If you don't, I bloody well will.'

'Don't swear, Evelyn, sweetheart,' he said automatically. 'It's unbecoming in a child.'

She clenched her teeth, drew breath sharply, banged her small fist on the table. The voice that emerged from her angelic teenage face was strangely mature. 'You'll have to tell them,' she repeated.

'Them? Who's them?'

'Don't be silly, Father. The police. Them. Whoever you tell when your wife's gone missing.' Her eye fell on the short paragraph in the Saturday morning paper: 'The body of an unclothed female was found in woodland near Branston on Thursday night, identity unknown. Police inquiries are in hand.' She did not draw the item to his attention. 'Mother's been gone nearly a fortnight. You've done nothing about it, absolutely nothing. She could be dead by now.'

'Don't be silly,' he repeated her words. 'Of course she's not. Your mother was unhappy, going through a bad patch. She's gone off for a bit of a break somewhere. She told me she would.' The last lie was transparent.

'You don't care.' Evelyn's voice was suddenly a shrill and childish treble. 'You don't care and you keep on pretending. She didn't tell me, and she didn't leave any food.'

'Darling child, she left a freezer full of it,' he said mildly.

Evelyn was shouting, 'She just went out one evening, and you don't know where she's gone and you won't do anything about it.'

He turned wearily, watery gaze and automatic smile fixed on her for the first time. 'And where do you suggest I begin to look? She went out of this house, wearing a solid gold bracelet and necklace worth a small fortune, probably a bit of money in her handbag, too. She could be anywhere. She went of her own free will. What do you want me to do? Have her dragged back in chains?'

'Report her missing, that's all.'

'It's nobody else's business. I don't want anyone to know.'

'That's it, isn't it? Well, it'll soon be everyone's business. What if she's hurt or lost? What if she's this woman here?' Evelyn stabbed at the page of newsprint, pushing it towards him over the table where they sat. 'Then you'll look an even bigger bloody fool, won't you? They'll think you did it. What if she's fallen under a train? When they find her, they'll think you pushed her because you haven't said anything, like you were trying to hide. Please yourself. Make it worse.'

'You've always had a dramatic imagination, darling child,' he said, trying to grasp the hand that pushed the paper towards him. Evelyn snatched it back. She was not there to give comfort. He was weak, ineffectual, indecisive: she knew all these words because Antony Sumner, her very own teacher, had taught her what they meant. Her father had retreated into silence for over a week, leaving her alone as she had always been left alone when he was not gasping for affection like a dying fish. He did not deserve comfort.

The kitchen was spacious and beautiful, solid wooden units with a dull gleam in the afternoon sun, quarry-tiled floor, dried herbs in a copper bucket, a perfect facsimile of magazine country life, showing signs of neglect, a tribute to huge expense and, finally, desertion. Tears gathered in John Blundell's eyes, rolled down his pale cheeks, blurring his vision of one magnificent room and one strangely beautiful fourteen-year-old daughter. She leapt to her feet, disgusted by the tears, snatched the phone from the bracket on the wall behind him, slammed it down on the pine table in front of his twisting hands.

'Do it,' she said. 'Do something for once. Phone the police, and when they get here, I'll speak to them, too. Do it now. Or you'll wish you'd never been born when they all start asking. Think of the neighbours, Dad. Do it.'

*

Antony Sumner wished he had never been born. No, lying in the generous arms of Christine Summerfield in Christine's pretty little house at nine o'clock on a Saturday evening, he could never wish any such thing. But he wished he could take back the last year, and especially the last fortnight, and give it to her instead. Wished he had never set eyes on Yvonne Blundell, who looked like a gypsy; wished he had never agreed to give English lessons in the evenings to that daughter Evelyn who was the last to need them. Another gypsy. He was flattered, he supposed, to be asked, liked money for old rope, liked being flirted with, same old weakness. Christine darling, please cure me. Release me from a frustrated housewife who reads poetry, aspires to culture in a desert. People should not read poetry on top of a bad life. It's like mixing drinks or eating cheese before sleeping, very bad for the emotional digestion.

Antony Sumner turned and kissed Christine. She was fast asleep, blissful Saturday evening torpor, rubbish flickering on the television screen, bottle of wine and a good meal gone. Peaceful, free in conscience. Yvonne Blundell was not like you, his mind continued fondly. She was looking for an affair before she hit forty, that daughter looking for learning like someone starving looks for food, both of them with wonderful eyes, fit to tear him apart. But the girl could write. He wished he had never bedded Mrs Blundell. It was like curling up with an octopus, then having to detach her one tentacle at a time. Oh, why wasn't someone there to save him? Walking in the woods after meeting her in The Crown, taking the argument into the trees. She always knew the way through that garden.

Antony removed a hand from beneath Christine's shoulder, watched her stir. Oh, God, what have I done? Shouldn't have lost my cool, shouldn't have shown all that disgust when she took off her clothes. Darling, I was thinking of you; the contrast was too awful for words. Antony felt the marks on his face, almost gone but still noticeable, the stigma of shame. Christ, what a cat; more like a tiger, hurling herself at him, but all the same, he should never have struck back, never used conduct unbecoming to any kind of gentleman.

Christine readjusted her position, ascending slowly and reluctantly from sleep, muttered, and smiled at him, one eye open. 'Feel like an old lady,' she said. 'Tell me when it's tomorrow and hand me a stick to get upstairs. Can't manage on my own.' The eye closed; she dozed as he stroked her pale hair, movements involuntary to hide the sudden heaving of heart, which was deafening to his own ears. Stick, she had said. Hand me a stick. The word 'stick' beat against his skull like a gong. Walking stick, his own, an affectation since teenage years and his first reading of Wordsworth striding about the Lake District and Keats stirring autumn leaves. Milton leaning on one in his blindness. He had clasped his walking stick like a talisman through his student days of floppy bow ties, floppier hair, and caped coats; kept it now to accompany the heavy cords, designer hiking boots, and poisonous French cigarettes he carried to school. The stick was his adolescent symbol, the adult prop to individuality, and the staff room joke.

Stick. Walking stick. He looked around the room wildly. Where was it? Thrust into a corner here? In his own untidy

53

house? In his car? Probably in his car. Surely in the back of his car where it lay whenever he forgot it, as he had forgotten it often since Christine, forgotten it entirely over the last twelve days. Antony had a vision of the stick, the carved wooden handle – an elephant's head, quite inappropriately – smooth on the top from years of use, with a rubber ferrule that had perished and needed replacement. Everything he had tried to blank from his mind rose like scum on a pond: he heard the swish of the stick as he walked through trees, remembered gripping it tighter as she had moved toward him, shut his eyes and attempted one more time to see it lying in the back of the Morris earlier that evening, failed. There was no denying the last place he had carried that stick, the last thing he had done with it.

Ten-thirty, dark. Helen bound the files together with white tape, each complete, annotated with notes, consigned to memory in preparation for Monday morning. No matter how much she did in her office, homework always remained for the peaceful hours when she could give scrupulous attention to detail. She never made a conscious demarcation zone between home and work. If you were a lawyer, you were one all the time: nothing stopped when you closed the office door. She looked at the room and the empty eye of the television, content with the evening's work, peaceful without Bailey. Well, my man, I haven't had a hard week, but I think for once I shan't wait up for you. Surely you're allowed home before midnight after last night and the night before? I understand completely: I'd be the same in your shoes, but it doesn't stop me missing you by this time of night.

'All depends,' Bailey had said, whether we get any leads on this thing or not. Might know who she is, or someone might tell us. She wasn't wearing so much as an earring. No fingerprints left, but there's always the teeth. See how we go.'

To be fair, he had telephoned once about seven o'clock. Someone, he said, had reported a missing wife, same age as this poor body in the mortuary. Nothing, really, only a disappearance coinciding with a death. Well, something perhaps. Oh, and a daughter, tugging his arm, saying Mr Bailey, let me tell you something: she was always going to those woods. With a man, she went with my teacher, Mr Bailey; I thought you ought to know. My father doesn't know, Mr Bailey. Please don't say I told you. Poor child. Bailey, coolest man in the world, was always a sucker for girl children, especially those the age his own might have been had she lived beyond three months. For these, he suspended judgement and never got it back. What man? I'll tell you that, too. I'm almost grown up, and I've been so worried. And Superintendent Bailey, knowing the full extent of Helen's Branston acquaintance, recognizing the name of Antony Sumner, had confined himself to telling Helen he was likely to be very late indeed. Don't stay awake for me, darling; we'll try to do something interesting tomorrow. Hearing a gurgle of suggestive laughter in her voice, keeping out of his own the yearning to be home.

Now, at midnight, Helen in bed, shocked by the mean imperative sound of the miniature phone by the side of it, wondering if the owners of this ghastly house used to phone their offices from it at dawn, thinking they probably did – then wide awake when she heard not Bailey's apologetic tones, but the shrill, hysterical voice of Christine Summerfield.

'Helen, you bitch, you knew, you must have known. Why did you let me think it would be all right? How could you let me go home? How could you say nothing? What a fool I feel, never mind the rest. Why did you do that?'

'Do what? Calm down, Chris. I haven't the faintest idea what you're talking about. Whatever's the matter? Chris, don't cry. What's the matter? Come on, pet, tell me. I'm in the dark. Please tell me. I honestly don't know.'

The sobbing on the other end of the line dropped an octave, subsided into furious gulps. Then Christine summoned up fury in words, stopped, started, ended in a voice of drab sadness. 'Oh, maybe you didn't. I don't know. I don't know anything. I don't know why the hell I'm talking to you at all. I only know that your bloody man, your bloody paramour of a bloody copper, your bloody bandit of a fascist pig, has just come here and very politely removed Antony to the comfort of Waltham Police Station for assistance with his inquiries into a murder. That woman Antony met. She's dead. The married mistress I told you about so trustingly because I was worried. The one who gave him the scratches. Now who the fuck told Bailey?'

'I don't know,' said Helen firmly, 'but it wasn't me. I might have told him if I'd had the chance, but I haven't seen him. Calm down.'

The sobbing subsided. 'Oh, God, Helen, you're the last person I should ask, but what should I do? What the fucking hell should I do?'

56

'Get him a lawyer,' said Helen, crisply. 'I'll give you the number of the only one I know who lives in Branston. He's as good as any. Call him and then go to the station, wait for him, and ask him to see Antony; take anything you think he might need. And just be there. Got that?'

'Yes,' said Christine, doubtful and weary. 'Give me the number.' Then, as an afterthought, product of emotion: 'I hate you both.'

Helen ground her teeth, resigned herself to a sleepless night. She had just catapulted one pompous and obstructive solicitor into the middle of Bailey's investigation, an act of dubious assistance to him, something that was bound to slow him down. She had instructed Christine how best to make a nuisance of herself because she believed that the legal rights of all people were sacrosanct, whatever they might have done. She had also acted in the interests of a friendship that had become precious to her and that had been mutilated, probably beyond repair, by this evening's work. Bailey would not have sprung Antony Sumner from the house of a lover in the middle of the evening had he not believed there was something important to ask him. Whatever the outcome of the interrogation, her acquaintance with Christine Summerfield was unlikely to recover. She would also have to see how far Bailey's tolerance in civil liberties extended when it was she who had prescribed them in the full knowledge that Sumner might be too shocked to find out for himself. 'Damn your eyes, Geoffrey Bailey. Damn your eyes. Poor Christine.' She was speaking to herself, surprised to find the anger. It had just begun to occur to her – foolish not to have seen it before – that she and

Geoffrey might not always agree. She found the thought a strange and lonely spectre, found in herself the desire to push him away alongside the desire to embrace him. For once, she wasn't eager for him to come home.

CHAPTER FOUR

Such speed, such graceless speed in the wake of a slow-discovered death. Facing Antony Sumner in the detention room of an ugly police station six miles from home, midnight, himself tired but composed while the man opposite was pregnant with information, twitching with nerves, and pasty grey with anxiety, Bailey knew the familiar sense of defeat that whirred behind his eyes whenever discovery was imminent and early. So there's the truth. How banal, how utterly expected, and how soon. One phone call began it: my wife has been missing since this date; she is dark, forty, not in the habit of straying from home, and has never before stayed away. Amanda Scott, quietly excited, had whispered this could be the one, not another potential victim in sight, all of the others missing either fourteen years old or eighty, always the extremes who run away from home. The postmortem notes sat in the folder on his desk, smelling of the postmortem room, reminding him for no reason at all of the mature but childish voice of that man's daughter, so calm beside Papa's distress, pulling a sleeve like a discreet tart on a corner, but, oh, so beautiful. Mr Bailey, sir – a hint of respect in the 'sir', responsive to the wide smile he always bestowed on girl children – about that body in Bluebell Wood: it won't be, couldn't be my mother, of course it couldn't, but she went there, you see; she was always going there. How did you know? An expressive shrug. Never mind how I know, I just know, OK? Mother had a boyfriend. It worried me. Don't tell my father, but she did. Antony Sumner, my teacher. They both went to Bluebell Wood. Well, they used to, anyway. I thought I would tell you.

Slender but convincing, this information, like the child herself. It was enough to provoke Bailey himself rather than a substitute to knock first at the door of Antony Sumner's house, then at the door of Christine Summerfield. He was apologetic but persistent. 'I'm so sorry for disturbing you.' Then, joking: 'You can sue the commissioner for my behaviour, but may I speak to Mr Sumner? He may, just may, be able to help us. So sorry to intrude on your Saturday evening,' Bailey was ready to back away after two or three questions, abandoning hope of that as soon as his purpose was diffidently explained. Not a murder inquiry at the moment, of course, simply a search for a missing woman, but the man's face was white, old scratch marks to forehead, cheeks lurid, and he was trembling, trying not to weep. It was uncomfortable the way such signs of guilt, accompanied by the look of horror on the face of the innocent friend, afflicted Bailey so, like a sudden flush of fever, making him wish he could have pressed Antony back into the arms of the woman who was, after all, Helen's friend, and told him it had all been a mistake. Instead, he invited him into a car. It's not an arrest, you understand, but will you accompany me? Antony nodding, stroking the woman's head, casting a backward look into that inviting room of hers while Bailey detected on him the incriminating, rancid smell of fear and knew that behind that distinctive scent there were words that would justify the fear.

Detention room, transit room, not quite the same as an interview room, but almost. A room where a witness was detained, usually pending removal to a cell but still with the illusion of liberty, exaggerated by Bailey's habit of leaving the door ajar. From the other end of the corridor he could hear the tidy sounds of Amanda Scott working at her ancient typewriter, tapping out on its reluctant keys a prepared statement for Mr Blundell: 'My wife's dental surgery is at 5, Cross Street, Waltham. I give authority for that surgery to produce to the police any records appertaining to my wife . . .' Amanda would use words such as 'appertaining'; she tended to use the long where the short would do. Proud proof of literacy, Bailey thought with a touch of impatience, while this literary animal across the ugly desk from himself, less disciplined than she, but better acquainted with a dictionary, used short, sharp words and expressed himself with ease.

Antony was vainly attempting to regard his polite interrogator as an ape, could not reconcile this urbane manner with his own view on police brutality, had resigned himself to providing explanations. There was nothing else he could do, whatever the advice otherwise: he was desperate to explain and be, in part at least, forgiven.

Bailey struggled with dislike for Antony Sumner's handsome face, dislike mixed with pity for his misery, a dangerous and subversive combination.

Caution the man: advise him of his legal rights. Fetch Amanda to make notes, and start the tape. Let us continue after all these interruptions, please. We were doing so well before.

'Mrs Blundell? I knew her because her daughter had been at my school. She asked me to give extra English lessons to Evelyn with a view to taking exams early, some such thing. I was skint as usual, so I agreed. Went on for a year. I started having an affair with Mrs Blundell. Why? I don't know why: I was lonely and bored, she was nine years older; it was flattering at first, me with the rich capitalist wifey. We went out for drinks last summer, lay on a blanket sometimes in Bluebell Wood, sometimes at my place. She liked my place, she said, shades of Bohemia. Liked poetry, mad about sex. Anyway, I had to cool it last spring. It was never that much fun, and then I met Christine, finished everything else. But it dragged on, you know, and she frightened me with all her intensity. Yes, we did meet at The Crown; her husband, you see, wouldn't be seen dead in there. Oh, God, what a thing to say, and yes, we were there the other night . . .'

Then there was coughing and spluttering, pause for cigarette before continuing. Bailey noticed sadly the crushed packet of Gauloises taken from the top pocket damp with sweat, remembered Bowles's pathetic offering: two Gauloise stubs and a half-full packet apparently abandoned on one side of the clearing. He leaned across and lit the wavering end of a crooked cigarette for his prisoner, listened with his face straight inside the lines of his skin.

'We walked from The Crown over the field and into the far side of the wood – been that way before, very overgrown. A little clearing, don't quite know where. She was frantic, terrible. She loved me, she said; I was her life. She loved me more than anyone or anything. What about your husband, your daughter? I kept saying, but she only screamed. "There's no one else but you, no one; neither of them care for me." But they do, I kept saying, of course they do. She would tell her husband all about us, then tell Christine all I had never told Christine. She and I would run away. It was madness, all of it. She was full of ideas, places, prospects, showing me money in her handbag, escape routes, all realistic, convincing plans to Yvonne, who'd never had to earn a crust, but not to me. I didn't want to say, "Don't be so bloody stupid; nobody escapes that easy even if I loved you back, which I bloody well don't, never really have. Just a bit of fun that has got out of hand." I couldn't say, "I think you're a silly cow." I gave her a cigarette to calm her. She pulled on it twice, threw it away, didn't like them, really. Started all over again.

'I was sick, turned away a few steps, smoked my own. Christ, I thought, this is terrible, worse than I expected. I wanted to go home. Then she began to cry. I kept my back turned, hoping she'd stop, until I heard a series of movements, frantic movements. I couldn't believe it: she was tearing her clothes off. She always wore quality clothes – dull, smooth, expensive lines – and she was tearing them off as if they were poisonous, screaming between sobs. "You wanted me once; want me again. I'll show you how much you need me, more than that tart of yours." I dropped my cigarette, I remember, when she launched herself at me half naked, bare bosomed, skirt slipping down. She was trying to kiss me. I kept turning my face away, I don't know how many times, holding her off, disgusted. I felt I was fighting an amorous sow, and after a while she began to stop. She was quiet for a minute. Then she spat at me, as if she had suddenly understood. She let go of me, and I turned to face her. She was spitting fury, lashed out and raked her nails down my face, reaching for my eyes, taking me by surprise. It hurt like hell: I could feel blood on my face and I was very angry indeed. Can't quite remember what I did, but I know I hit her then, pulled back my arm, hit her with all my strength and sent her reeling to the ground, watched her lying there, weeping and moaning, exhausted by all that rage and hurt, while I kept feeling the blood on my face. Yes, I might have hit her with the stick; I can't remember. All right, then, with the stick, but only once.'

Antony raised his eyes to the ceiling as if looking for inspiration in the fluorescent light, clearly embarrassed, but determined not to weaken his flow by voicing the apologies in his mind. There are elements of the actor in you, Bailey considered. Even now you half enjoy the telling of the story, you who so enjoy making others record their thoughts, maybe you are only pausing for effect. I can see you wooing this poor matron with all the power of poetry, unable to face her passion when she responded. 'What happened next, Mr Sumner?' A soft reminder. Bailey believed they were either near the end of the story or closer than ever to falsehood.

64

'I just stood there. Then I knelt down beside her, patted her. I told her I was sorry, but she should have listened, should have listened before. We had never been real, she and I, and it had always had to end. Go home, I told her, go home now, but she simply stayed as she was, absolutely inert apart from the crying, determined to be helpless. I was confused, irritated, if you want the truth. I could have – No, no, I didn't mean that.'

'Could have killed her, were you going to say?' said Bailey mildly.

'No, no, I didn't mean that at all.' Antony was angry at so obvious a ploy, Bailey angrier for the interruption. He had known far longer than he could remember how empty a gesture of intent was the threat or even the desire to kill, how different from the doing, how frequently relieved in the mere screaming of it. He had shouted these threats himself as a child to his mother, and he remembered more clearly how, in the depths of love for his wife, he had wished her death years before. Then as now he had been incapable of causing it. He had never actually inflicted blows on any woman. Perhaps the intention was provoked into action by the first step towards it. 'Go on, Mr Sumner. I'm not trying to trap you. Go on.'

Antony lit another cigarette, hands unsteadier than before.

'I didn't know what to do. She was so bloody stupid, so helpless, making it worse for herself. She was often like that, like a spoiled child who would scream and scream until she was sick to make someone listen, then say, "Pick me up. I can't do it; you do it." So I just began to walk away, hesitating at first, looking back. I thought it would make her move but it didn't. I saw her from the footpath, huddled there half bloody naked, couldn't bear to see it, and started to run through the bushes, away from the footpath, then back until I came to the carpark on the far side. I walked all the way back round to The Crown, collected my car. Went home.'

'Leaving your walking stick, by any chance, Mr Sumner?'

He looked up in guilty surprise. 'Yes,' he replied, 'leaving my stick.'

Bailey gestured. Amanda Scott left the room, returned with the cane. 'This stick, Mr Sumner?' Instantly recognizable object even wrapped in polythene and decorated with a large label for passage to a dim laboratory with all other blood-marked objects.

'Yes,' he said slowly, regarding the stick as he would a friend who had been transformed into enemy.

'That's enough for now, I think,' said Bailey. Amanda Scott shuffled her sheets of paper in obvious disapproval.

'Try to sleep, Mr Sumner. I'm afraid you must stay here.' Despite the pleas of your indignant lawyer who has already postponed all this, shouted advice, which you chose to ignore, interrupted to the extent that I barred him. No doubt we shall hear more of that. Never mind. No doubt, either, that dear Amanda was pleased to tell me the lawyer was called by Miss Summerfield at the behest of Miss West, your er, wife, sir. Well, well, they are friends, after all, but surely Helen knows me well enough to understand that I know by heart all that the Police and Criminal Evidence Act requires of me, including the fact that a man must be offered a lawyer as soon as he's offered a caution, and of course I did it. He grinned ruefully. Helen would also know there are some invitations that he, as well as custody officers, tended to make less audibly to a helpful witness than to a defendant. The rules were more malleable for a witness. Yawning and stretching, Bailey realized he needed his bed. It was three a.m., and for once he knew that he and Helen would not talk either this morning or tomorrow: there would be no time once he had turned back here for ten o'clock. Tomorrow, if they had raised that dentist and put a name to the corpse, he would be going for Antony Sumner's jugular, lawyers or no lawyers. He would ask Sumner, however politely, about his knife. About his shoes and his silly walking stick with the elephant head festooned with human hair.

Somewhere in all of that, he and Helen would have to make time. Time was a thief in the night, one he knew well.

By Sunday afternoon, Christine Summerfield was only weeping from time to time, and had noticed through the disfiguring filter of tears how dirty were the windows in her house. She wondered if the panes of glass in Antony's cottage were as grubby as usual, no doubt hiding the large uniforms who were taking apart the contents, finding God knows what apart from her own underwear and several dirty dishes. He had preferred lately to stay under her roof, enjoying all the obvious home comforts he had never secured for himself.

Christine contemplated telephoning Helen West, felt in her bones a spurt of loathing, which she recognized as unfair to both occupants of that household, and did not

67

phone. Instead, she cleaned her windows. When Helen phoned her, the response was predictably swift, not actually rude, but not polite, either.

Helen waited for Bailey to wake, both of them reassured by early morning affection. 'Trust me, darling,' words accompanied by a swift hug before he took his long body out of bed.

'I do,' she had replied, smiling at him. 'I do, most of the time.'

The sun was shining. Bario's pink and grey restaurant disgorged the last of the lunchtime trade into shiny cars parked on the green where mothers talked over prams and fathers pretended to teach cricket to sons, while the less endowed waited in vain for buses. One mile away, the carpark to Bluebell Wood was still closed by a tape, the fragile officialdom of which defied destruction, with PC Bowles thrilling the questioners with a brief account of the reason why. The body in the wood was gossip but subdued gossip, slightly irrelevant to any of them yet. Mr Blundell had not volunteered to others what he had volunteered to the police, or the gossip would have been sharper. Bailey had ensured that this particular husband was not left unaccompanied while he waited to see if he was a widower: a large constable remained in the Blundell kitchen, bored with reading newspapers, while upstairs, drunk and tranquillized, Mr Blundell slept audibly. Bailey should have organized a woman for the child, who was also upstairs. Evelyn Blundell had kept to her bedroom, as far as the constable knew, or she had declared her intention to do so before climbing nimbly from the window on to the out-house roof, down to the ground, and away through a series of gardens and roads to the jungled garden of The Crown. Evelyn knew this secret route from her own house so well she could have managed it in her Sunday best, but today she wore T-shirt and jeans and, oddly enough, with such casual teenage attire, a pair of very bright, sparkling paste earrings.

Even The Crown had attracted custom. Today's lunchtime fare had been vegetarian, Bernadette's new ploy to attract the discriminating Branston customer, Featherstones' best with an Irish flavour. The fact that most of the food remained uneaten in relation to the amount ordered only reflected the Featherstones' deafness to complaints. 'Aren't they all fools?' snorted Bernadette, dumping slabs of her grey bannock bread into a plastic sack. 'Don't know a good thing when they eat it.' For once, she and Harold were in accord, a temporary but regular Sunday afternoon peace, especially in summer, when Harold was mellowed by whisky and custom, content to sit in the kitchen discussing plans, believing in the success of their joint venture until his head began to throb and the worse temper resumed. Evening customers received short shrift in The Crown, but for now, all was sweetness and light.

'Aren't they all fools, then? You're right,' he was reply-ing, pinching Bernadette's behind as she passed him, dropping litter on her way to the bin and ignoring it. 'But we'll show them, Bernie, won't we? I've another idea. Now we've got the place in shape, did you see all the people in here today? They're cottoning on at last. I'll set on the garden. Somewhere else for the buggers to go. Might even go back and do something about that garden bar. The summerhouse, I mean. Few enough places with this much ground around, you know.'

Bernadette nodded vigorously but silently, content to keep the peace. Silence was always preferable on the subject of the summerhouse. Like Harold, she was aware that the most recent revamping of The Crown's bar had eaten up another segment of the inheritance misguidedly left Harold by a doting father, the same inheritance depleted year by year since they acquired the premises with the first chunk of it, abandoning their London jobs in the process, because of William, because of wanting a better life, because of all sorts of things they could not discuss, even now. Again like Harold, she was unaware that the same new décor – floral walls, heavy unmatched chintz curtains, checkerboard carpet, red upholstered seats with varied cushions – was a savage onslaught on the eye, almost psychologically disturbing to anyone who sat in it long enough. Helen and Bailey had counted sixteen different patterns in that room and wondered, with enormous, frankly snobbish amusement, how much expense had gone into the creation of such ghastly disharmony. Along with Harold, Bernadette thought it was beautiful, enough of the gypsy in her to adore dizzying colour but when it came to Harold's other plans, she was less enthusiastic. There had been so many, after all. Upstairs there were two unfinished bedrooms, one half-done bathroom, the same state persisting for years while other projects began and ended and the paint peeled on the banisters. The garage next to the kitchen was full of junk that Harold collected from all over Essex: woodworking table of huge dimensions, rusty machinery, old telephone cable, three-legged chairs, bundle of mildewed towels, fire-damaged sheets, chipped crockery, a trough. Anything going free or almost free Harold, scavenger of the world, would have. It was a curious and useless economy in one so reckless with large sums and domestic provisions. These objects never surfaced again, once acquired and put away. If only he could bear to buy something new and use it. 'You're always wanting something for nothing,' Bernadette had yelled, rarely careful enough to avoid trampling on his dreams, but the mention of the summerhouse kept her quiet on a sunny afternoon that deserved a share of short-lived quietude.

Quite simply, he had gone demented over the summer-house plan; it was even worse than all Harold's other fancies. How long ago was it? Eight years since he had started digging like a child searching for Australia, convinced it was only six feet away. 'This is it, Bernadette. We'll double the trade by putting a bar in the garden. No one else has one of those,' and even then she could see it was cockeyed, the way his plans were in direct proportion to the enthusiasm with which he attacked them. Harold's plans were born drunk like the man himself: they had no place in a sober mind. The idea had been to buy a kind of prefabricated pavilion. 'Makes them think of cricket, don't you see? We'll have them playing bowls.' Even Bernadette could see the impossibility of playing bowls downhill. The pavilion was to be placed over a hole. 'We'll do this prop-erly, Bernie darling: a bar has to have a cellar for the beer and the fine wines. The stuff the new rich in Branston and

71

all over will be flocking for.' So, with a little help, Harold had dug the cellar, faced it in brick, then purchased from a brochure at enormous expense a funny-looking structure twenty feet long and ten feet wide to surround the aperture, and constructed inside it a kind of a bar. That was the trouble with Harold: he could do so much, was so clever with his hands and his brain, contemptuous of those with less, but he had a strange inability to complete any project, always discouraged by the failure of reality to correspond with the picture in his mind. There was the same trouble with the summerhouse bar: it had a squiffy character similar to that of Harold's mind, the mind of a man drinking out of a crooked brandy glass, wondering was it he or was it the glass who could not manage a straight line anywhere. The finished product had a cellar the size of a small room, far grander than the structure upstairs, which looked more like an old-fashioned bus shelter than the thing of elegance first intended. The whole beast was odd. 'Cheap' and 'nasty' were other words that came to mind, but 'odd' always came first.

Harold could not hide his disappointment, nor could the customers who were privy to its progress hide their derision. Bernadette would always remember that she had not concealed hers. The summerhouse was comic, a silly little structure of ugly wood looking like a pimple at the end of the half-acre of wild lawn, a sort of hut with windows listing slightly downhill. 'They'll think they've had a drink already as soon as they look at it,' Bernadette had yelled, and William, poor twelve-year-old William, who thought the summerhouse the nearest thing to paradise, had screamed and screamed in fury and rage. Harold, too, had translated the rage of frustration into action by dealing Bernadette a sharp backhander she had never forgotten, while William shrieked in the worst tantrum ever, kicked his mother, and began a course of conduct that became depressingly consistent and frightening. It was not the first of William's spectacular furies, only the most violent. After all of that, the summerhouse was scarcely mentioned, source of mutual shame and failure that it was. Bernadette hated it, never went near it; Harold, the same, reluctant to examine its obvious decay. He could not resist in the early days storing things there, the way he reacted to any available space in order to justify its existence. The bus shelter bar contained kerosene against power cuts – they had no heaters in which to utilize it, but the stuff had been cheap and Harold remembered rationing – a couple of old beds he could not bring himself to discard, and a broken chair or three, all rotting in there, like the fabric of the thing, sloping under the force of gravity, about to disappear in a cloud of guiltless smoke. Harold had not looked at it for years; only the whisky ever brought it to mind, and even then he remembered William's reaction. Remembered, and then discarded the memory. Too close to home and all the familiar spectres of failure.

William was sitting in the corner of the kitchen hoping that the subject of the summerhouse would drop into silence, relieved and grateful when it did and other topics, brightly introduced by his mother, took the place of a dangerous pause. He had slowly learned the value of silence, knew he had them in thrall with the tantrums they dared not question. He had only to begin kicking his legs against the stool on which he sat with his usual dull but insistent rhythm to reduce them to either sullen fear or resentment; either worked as well, but on this occasion there was no need, and he was grateful. William's mental development remained at the age of that of a cunning ten-year-old, untapped by the local schools who had abandoned him one after the other or the child psychiatrist whom he had abandoned, while his manual dexterity and physical strength overreached his years. The combination was frightening. Bernadette treasured his rare smiles, treated him with distant loyalty and affection, while Harold patted his black head occasionally and otherwise ignored him. Bernadette knew that in William's life the summerhouse had more than the significance of memory, but did not know why. She guarded her wilful ignorance on his behalf, aware that the abandoned structure was a lair to him. She suspected Harold knew, but they did not discuss the subject.

'What will you do this afternoon?' She scolded with questions she knew he would not answer, gentle interrogatives. 'Get out, son. The weather's gorgeous; we'll not keep you.' He surprised her with half a grin, half a grunt, slid off his stool clumsily, made for the open kitchen door. Fine if he was ordered out. He would have preferred to sidle away unobserved, but either way he was gone with a blessing, and no one could call him back.

The garden into which he strolled had been planned with an informality quite unsuitable to such a large and impressive house. A cracked and weed-filled path of slippery stones led down the shady side of it flanked by shrubs for the whole length of the fifty yards that led to the summerhouse. A line of small trees marked the end of the

74

garden, perhaps intended to be magnificent but now a scrubby demarcation zone surrounded by thicket. The lawn was punctuated with more overgrown shrubs in islands, designed to be discreet, but now well developed into quarrelling bushes of enormous size, roots obscured by long grass that would have done credit to a hayfield. Cornflowers and cockles from the last year's barley in the field beyond had seeded among the grass, and a dead tree lay rotting across the path. William clambered over it, too old now for the fascination with termites that had once kept him for hours, and quickened his step until he yanked open the summerhouse door.

Inside, the floor was swept, not recently or well, but swept. Most but not all of the jars of kerosene were covered with cobwebs, as were the windows where a fly buzzed insistently. William picked up one of the dusters from the floor and killed the fly instantly. The last broken pieces of chair were piled in one corner along with sacking and newspaper, and through the aperture behind the bar, a hole in the floor normally closed with half a door mounted on a clumsy hinge, he could see a light. Leading into the cavern below was a household stepladder, also broken but still usable. He began a short but dexterous descent of the ladder, which had only three intact steps.

'William? Is that you?'

'Course it's me. Who else would it be, silly?'

'Don't call me silly.'

He clambered down the steps, face wreathed in the smile the world so rarely saw, stood in the light of the butane lamp, and surveyed their domain. There were mattresses beneath a covering of blankets, a chair, boxes doubling for tables and containers, a locked cupboard, makeshift shelves from wood and bricks, a camping cooker that had been another of Harold's bargains, a blackened pan, and a few tins of food. The floor was covered with an old remnant of carpet, dirty but swept, and on the mattresses sat Evelyn Blundell, paste earrings sparkling in the light, wearing her jeans and nothing else, her white pubescent chest catching the glow of the lamp.

'You're late, William. I told you four o'clock. I've got to go soon. I thought . . .' For once the confident voice faltered. 'I thought you'd gone and told them all.'

The edge of fear in her tone sharpened into reproof, a terrible threat implicit in it, and he hurried, tripping over his feet and his words to reassure her. 'Evie, Evie, I wouldn't do that. Couldn't do that, Evie, I promise, not ever.' The sharpness of her face had carried tears into his eyes. He knelt beside the mattress as she sat up, hair tumbling to her shoulders.

'Promise?' she asked, her voice as sharp as a blade.

'Course I promise.'

'It's our secret place. Hide everything when I've gone. Promise. Cross your heart and hope to die in boiling oil if you don't.'

'I promise.' He was looking at her, his eyes filled with rapture, suffused with complete adoration as he sat beside her, fingered the earrings, laughed in loud relief at the softening of her features. Evie could look so terrifying, especially in this light, her tiny figure as threatening as a whip, eyes blazing with scorn, reducing him to one of those crawling beetles they sometimes saw on the floor, blinkered things, looking desperately for light as William

76

sought relief. Not today. Today he could tell she was relieved to see him, had made him a cup of weak sugary tea, which he loved, even without the milk he was supposed to have provided if the kitchen had not been so wary. 'Couldn't bring any,' he explained, gesturing to the cup she handed him, never taking his eyes off her face.

'S'all right,' she said, her favourite phrase. 'Doesn't matter.'

Silence fell. He drained the lukewarm tea in one gulp, set the mug on a box, shuffled closer to her, smiling his beatific, hopeful smile, tentatively reaching a hand toward her, questioning with his pale and vacant eyes.

'S'all right,' she repeated. 'You can. Only today, mind.'

Then she lay back on the mattress, small nipples pointing toward the dusty ceiling, her eyes closed. William lay beside her awkwardly, stroking her slender torso with one disproportionately large hand that could have spanned her waist. She was so small, so neat, her skin seemingly stretched over bone and the taut and miniature muscles that held the flesh to this graceful skeleton. He placed his mouth around one of the nipples and sucked like a child at breast.

'Ow. That hurts.' But William was panting by now, one hand below the waistband of her jeans, button undone as she had left it undone. She always hoped he might change his mind, but gradually learned that there was as much chance of that as of her baby nephew refusing a feed; she considered both pastimes – that witnessed, this undergone – equally inexplicable and unnecessary, but she was prepared for foolishness all the same. The zipper of her jeans fell away at his touch. He felt lucky today: he had been so

77

good, so very good; he did not know precisely why she should be so pleased with him, but she was. 'Can I?' he whispered. 'Can I really, please?'

'Oh, all right,' she was murmuring, eyes still firmly shut, 'but only if you take it out, you know, before. Only if you take it out.' Then she sat up abruptly, pulled the jeans off her legs while he pulled down his loose canvas trousers. 'Oh, God,' she said in the tone of a bored sophisticate, looking at him with a distaste he did not recognize. 'Hurry up, will you, before it grows any more, but touch me, so it won't hurt.' He touched, a rough and peremptory stroking, with his breath arriving in clumsy gasps while she lay supine, legs splayed, faint traces of Vaseline on her inner thighs, her arms loose by her sides in an attitude of resigned waiting. 'A little bit more,' she commanded, and he obeyed in an agony of impatience, then stopped, rolled on top of her, and thrust himself inside, pumping against her unresisting thinness, remembering her order in his final abandon, whimpering as he released his sticky souvenirs on to her stomach and the blanket. Then he rolled to one side, clutching her hand, and was almost instantly asleep, the smile transfixed on his flushed face.

The butane lamp guttered. Evelyn sighed in the silence broken only by his breathing, drew her arm from beneath him, slid down the wall side of the bed. She picked up his T-shirt, scrubbed at her abdomen with something like a housewife's disgust, and then, as an afterthought, placed it over the small remnants on the blanket. After that, she rolled the unresisting form of William on to his chest. She put on her clothes and turned off the lamp, leaving him in the dim glow of daylight filtering through the cellar

78

entrance, and made for the steps. He would waken in minutes; she was only just becoming familiar with the pattern after these occasions. It was time for her to leave, avoiding all the tiresome affection that followed. He might wake on his own and cry for her and that was all for the best, when she came to think of it; it might make him more grateful for these rare privileges, these conversationless and far from invariable Sunday treats that seemed to matter so much to him for reasons she could not really fathom, given the vague distaste they inspired in her. They had learned thus far together from the pile of pornographic magazines in the corner, from pictures that had frightened poor William to death, but they had not quelled her curiosity nor eased his desperate longing.

'S'all right,' she said to herself, as if reciting a litany while emerging into the blinding light outside the summerhouse.

'S'all right, really. Time to go home now.' She remembered the fat constable in the kitchen, the snores of her father, wondered if she might have cut too fine her own timetable, broke into a run. Looking back from halfway down the length of the field, she was almost sorry to have left him. Then she thought of the ridiculous pictures in those magazines, giggled, paused and stretched in the middle of the windswept barley-field, sprinted home.

CHAPTER FIVE

A pile of pornographic magazines and videos, bagged in black plastic, sat accusingly in the corner of the office Helen shared with two other solicitors whose desks were currently empty. The day before, with a speed and deftness that annoyed her senior colleagues, she had gone through the pornography, drafted summonses, requisitioned statements, and demanded the material that was missing – two hours' work to Helen, a full day to anyone else. Now she immersed herself in another exhibit list, professional antennae twitching, gripped by the emergence of the narrative of the Branston murder, working on three levels, absorbing the story, but still ticking off the irrelevancies, isolating hearsay, sorting the appropriate order of witnesses, giving the thing its courtroom shape, conscious all the time of a mistake. Even while she listed the further inquiries and inevitable missing links, she was remembering that Redwood, the branch crown prosecutor who ruled her life, had been out of the office the day before and that was the single reason why she had been allocated the case at all. Redwood's deputy had sent her the papers only because he was free of the insecurities and strange chauvinistic jealousies that afflicted his boss, and he wanted a competent hand at the tiller. Sooner or later Redwood would intervene; the speed of the intervention would only depend on how soon he could find an excuse. Helen was prepared for something of the kind, had schooled herself not to resent it, and was determined to do her professional best for the case before interruption. In the meantime, what she had read disturbed her.

The resolution of the case was so neat, so complete, so quick. A faultless report from Bailey, the contents of which he had refused to discuss with her at home, like a writer being secretive about a new opus. She could see why. Dismissing from her own mind any knowledge of the protagonists, she was dismayed by the comprehensive evidence, the tidy jigsaw puzzle of it, ready to be assembled in front of a jury with no missing pieces. It was hardly the mandate of a prosecutor to query such a satisfying picture. Not for the Crown to show that Sumner didn't kill the woman, only that he did. The defence must raise the doubt if doubt was to be raised, but in Helen's perfectionist mind, that was never enough when life imprisonment hung in the balance. She believed the Crown must show it has explored every avenue, drawn a blank at the feet of any other possible culprit, examined the motives of many, looked closely at husband, woman rival, even children. God forbid. Here the target had stepped into the net without a murmur and never a sideways glance from the investigators for anyone else. Helen's instinct told her to insist that the police begin all over again: 'Where would you have looked if you had not found him? Look there now. We cannot rely on the defence to do it for us. It is the Crown that must see justice done, facts fully explored. Go on; turn a few more stones.'

Fidget, light a cigarette, debate the next move. Phone Bailey in professional guise, lace the conference with a colleague to make sure it is fully impersonal, get on with it before Redwood uses his undoubted knowledge of the West-Bailey relationship to justify massive interference. Still inured with belief in justice and a passion for the truth, Helen wanted to ask questions. Phone Bailey. It was always a pleasure, that amiable conflict between two highly tuned minds meeting on a similar level of legal experience. She relished it.

As she dialled the number she could have dialled blindfolded, footsteps sounded on the worn carpet outside her door, the familiar, clipped steps of the branch crown prosecutor. Helen replaced the receiver quickly, hating conversations with Bailey to be overheard as much as her chief hated the idea of one of his independent prosecutors cohabiting with a senior police officer. Nor did she wish for Brian Redwood – with his penchant for performance indicators, budgets, time spent per case per day, and that integrity of his which only operated at the least imaginative level – to be party to any decision she might make at this stage. He had a love of rectitude and rules, a chronic dislike of all police officers under the rank of chief inspector, and a profound suspicion of Helen West. In addition to all his other neuroses, he believed that if he pushed and bullied his underlings, they would work harder, having failed to see that no lawyer chose this work who could not lead himself. 'Our Brian,' as he was known without affection, remained an interfering and harrying boss whose meddling was not matched by any semblance of support or guidance. He resented anyone who did not share his tunnel vision.

'Not in court, then?' he barked accusingly.

'As you see,' said Helen. 'Paperwork day.'

'Oh. Wanted to see you anyway. Getting on all right?'

'Fine, thank you.' Maybe he simply wanted to talk and she was the only one to hand on a very quiet Wednesday; she would do as well as any, better than most, but with a sinking heart, she doubted that was all.

'You got a file from your, er, boyfriend. Whatever.' Disapproval was implicit in his tone. 'You aren't the right grade to deal with murders, of course.' Helen forbore to mention that she had already prosecuted more murders under the auspices of previous offices than Brian Redwood had in a far gentler lifetime than her own. There was no point remarking on it. She was in the habit of keeping her head down with Mr Redwood, anything for a quiet life, but while putting her in place with this initial salvo, he was clearly in need of her opinion, however much he hated asking.

'This Branston murder . . . Mrs Blundell . . . Do you talk to your detective chief superintendent about it? Bailey, isn't it? Very good investigating officer.'

'No, we don't talk about it,' Helen lied with convincing sincerity, wishing it was not almost true. 'It's better we don't.'

'Quite right, quite right.' He nodded sagely, swallowing

83

the unlikelihood without difficulty and adding inconsistently, 'But you do know the facts?'

'Roughly, yes.'

'The case is quite straightforward,' Redwood said. 'Open and shut. Fellow wants to end relationship with older married woman, loses his cool, hits her, and then stabs her in argument. Funny place to pick, though, Bluebell Wood. He buries her and goes home, leaving enough traces for an army: walking stick covered with blood and hair, hers, of course; heavy footprints all over the place, made by his very distinctive boots; cigarette ends in the clearing, his brand.'

'Have the police found her clothes, jewellery, handbag?' Helen asked, knowing full well they had.

'In the compost heap in his garden. I ask you, what a fool. The handbag and clothes, all neatly packaged. Jewellery and money from handbag, gone without trace, greedy bastard.'

Helen was silent, allowing the exclamatory flow to continue, wondering on the nature of our Brian's problem. Not the same as hers. He never suffered from second thoughts or surprise.

'No alibi, of course, though the girlfriend did try.'

She remembered. Poor Christine had attempted to say Antony had been at her house before midnight on the night of the murder, gave it up when Bailey gently pointed out to her that he already knew she had not seen Antony for two days after the woman's death, a knowledge he had only cleaned because Helen had told him. In view of the prisoner's limited admissions, such a pretence was no help in any event. Any chance of Helen resurrecting her

84

friendship with Christine had died after that, but that was not within Redwood's knowledge, nor should it be.

'One problem, though,' Redwood ruminated. 'Man won't admit killing her.' His voice was hurt, as if Sumner's refusal to confess guilt was a personal insult. 'Intelligent chap, too. Can't understand it.'

Intelligence had very little to do with it, Helen thought, while trying not to smile. Nor was it incumbent on any defendant to admit guilt in the interest of expediency and saving public money, even if he was guiltier than sin. He had the right to protest his innocence all the way to the grave, causing storms of fury and irritation *en route* if it helped him at all. Man must fight like a cat for freedom, fight dirty if he must, lie if he must. That's what I would do, she thought: I'd make them prove every damn thing. 'How inconsiderate of him,' was what she said out loud, the irony of her words quite lost on her companion.

'Quite,' said Redwood eagerly, forgetting in the loneliness of the office that he was in the invidious position of debating with the member of staff he could least afford to admire. In the dim recesses of his mind he suppressed the uncomfortable knowledge that Helen West could run this office better than he could himself, was the natural deputy he never chose, preferring to keep her talents in obscurity. For today's purposes he also ignored the knowledge that the junior troops already flocked to her for any kind of advice from the state of their marriages to the state of the law, and they would continue to flock to her even if Helen did nothing to encourage them. She was popular for her wicked mimicry in an office full of cigarette smoke, bad language, and plenty of shouting under stress; she was authoritative without effort – all the things he longed to be and was not – while all he could hold against her was a less than immaculate conviction rate. Watching her dealing in court, he could find no fault in her except for her turn of speed and what he called promiscuous sympathy for both victims and defendants, but she was as hard as nails when necessary. Yes, take a plea here, she would say, a bindover here; no, absolutely no bail; honestly, don't be such a fool as to ask if he has nowhere to live; I'd help if I could, but I can't. What do you want, blood? The way she had of letting them go, the toothy schoolboy barristers of the opposition, the shifty defendants, and even the megalomaniacal court clerks, gods in their own arena, all placated and left with their dignity. I don't want to humiliate you, she might have said, but I will if I have to; don't push me to be fair, there's no bloody need. Other advocates faced with weary thieves might have thought from time to time, There but for the grace of God go I; Helen West actually believed it. She moved in pity, only occasionally expressing anger over the sad exposure of charlatans, fools, and youth. Redwood's beliefs were not the same. He did not see himself as the same humanity, saw all of the defendants on the other side of the dock as a race apart.

'I wonder why,' he was musing out loud. 'Why, oh, why won't he admit the killing?'

'Well,' said Helen cautiously, venturing a further grim joke, 'he would radically increase his chances of a life sentence if he did. Or maybe he's telling all he knows and he didn't really kill her at all.'

'What?' He looked up, outraged, saw Helen's eyes fixed on her hands, and dismissed the last remark as one made simply for the sake of argument. 'Of course he killed her. He's charged with murder.' As if that was all it took. Helen struggled with the ridiculous corollary: if you want to kill someone, simply get yourself charged with that person's murder and regard the deed as done. Save yourself the trouble.

'Of course he killed her. Mud still on those boots he never wore afterwards, though he wore them every day before. Stick with silly handle thwacked across the brow, his stick, no one else's stick. A sweater full of brambles in his laundry box, and scratches on his face. And after a God Almighty row like that and her acting like a cat, he says he walked away and left her for someone else to kill? Come off it. Besides, who else had a motive? He, on the other hand, was frightened that Mrs B. would tell that girl-friend of his, whom I must say, he must have been fond of, enough anyway to be terrified of her finding out he'd been screwing the other one all the time.'

Helen could not stand it, loathed all this superior sup-position, as well as hating that demeaning word, which Christine would hate equally. Screwing whom all the time? 'He wasn't,' she said swiftly before caution prevented the words, regretting them as she spoke them, unable to stop. 'At least Christine – "the girlfriend" to you, my friend to me – said he wasn't. He'd told her. She would have known. She told me.'

He looked shocked. Our Brian rose from the desk against which he had leaned, as relaxed as he ever would be in the presence of a subordinate.

'She what?'

'She told me,' Helen repeated, still disobeying the

87

careful impulse and following the instinct to defend. 'She's a friend of mine.'

'You, Miss West,' he said majestically, with a pomposity she found indescribably silly, 'you, in cahoots with a defence witness?'

'No, not exactly. Not in cahoots. In conversation, perhaps. Unfortunately no longer, I'm sad to say. But listen to me, you ought to know: Christine Summerfield did know of Sumner's affair. She knew from the start of knowing him. She knew he was going to meet Mrs Blundell on the night he did, and I can and will give evidence of that knowledge if necessary.'

'Helen – Miss West, I mean . . .'

'Well, what do you mean?'

'You are being naïve,' our Brian said indulgently. 'That is what she told you, but perhaps she told in anticipation of exactly this situation.'

'Oh, yes,' said Helen, temper running like a car engine. 'She's a soothsayer as well as a social worker. Bit of double leprosy going on there, Mr Redwood, I mean Brian. And a jury would see it as rubbish coming from a mouth as disingenuous as hers. I'm sorry, I don't believe Antony Sumner killed Mrs Blundell to spare Christine the knowledge of his affair. I just don't believe it. He may have killed her, but not for that reason.' All of this emerged far more sharply than intended in reaction to Redwood's underlying prejudices and also to the fact she had never, but never yet in three whole weeks, had the chance to argue the same toss with Bailey. Our Brian was here; he would have to do.

'Well.' He was standing now, looking down at her with his best supercilious regard. 'At least you concede the possibility of guilt. I was beginning to wonder. I imagine it's preferable I don't discuss the case with you, Miss West. And a very good idea if you don't discuss it with . . . with your friend the superintendent, either. In the meantime, if you would send your copy of the file back to me, I'll deal with this case myself.'

A few seconds of silence, her hand fluttering around the dismembered papers on the desk. She'd had long training in not reacting, had just betrayed it slightly, would not slip further from the self-discipline of calmer silence. He was ready for an unprofessional outburst, disappointed by the brisk, dismissive nod of her head.

'After all,' he added over his shoulder as a mild parting shot, 'you don't want anything to interfere with a conviction, do you?'

She watched his uncomfortable departure, recovering her smile, slamming down her pen as soon as the door closed, then taking it up again and sketching Redwood's face on the lined pad in front of her. A smooth face, pouched like a guinea pig's with firm round jowls and a precious little mouth. A high, unlined forehead with thin hair, slightly coiffed to one side over creased little eyes. Soon to have tunnel vision, she thought through gritted teeth. Nothing must ever interfere with convictions, his or the court's. Nothing. Not even the truth. At the back of his head she drew a curly tail.

Three whole long weeks since the dentist had confirmed that the radiograph of teeth taken from the Bluebell Wood body belonged to the late Mrs Blundell. Life in the Bailey-West household had resumed some semblance of normality. Geoffrey's office hours were as variable as

Helen's and were rarely spent in an office. She liked the variety, enjoyed the peace of solitude as much as he, provided there was no tension between them to fill the solitary interludes with unanswered questions, nothing to disturb the trust. Which was not the present state. She had tried to tell herself not to express undue curiosity in his current investigation, even when Sumner was charged and Christine Summerfield had abruptly avoided her on a Saturday afternoon in Branston High Street. A tension in the Bailey-West household had arisen from a situation in which Helen could not support Geoffrey's opinion, and this tension was quite sufficient to persuade her not to phone him after all for advice on a multitude of cases and questions of police procedure, as she frequently did. Helen was finding difficult the return to greater self-reliance and the gradual denial of the constant turning to Bailey in any moral dilemma that featured one of his tribe. He had always done the same to her: What should I do, Helen? What do you think? The most precious of things shared was this impeccable trust in the judgement of the other, a complete respect neither held towards any other person. Helen mourned the passing of this mutuality, prayed to her own version of God that its absence was temporary. On the calm surface of their lives, there was no more than a breeze, but in the new atmosphere of secrecy engendered by the murder, she felt as if the fingers and toes of her existence were growing numb, losing sensitivity in an early frost.

Bailey, when she first encountered him, had been a silent man, bursting the banks of his own reserve so slowly at first that she had not realized how much he had been giving and at what cost. Bailey's heart had opened to enfold her own in a gentle embrace, always ready to release her should she ever protest or demand freedom. A childhood of genteel poverty, a policeman's life in various sewers the full details of which she learned piecemeal and never completely, things of which he was ashamed, fewer where he was proud, never a member of the club that would let him join, never wanting to be. A marriage long past to a woman gone mad, a woman he had treasured and who was still an unknown quantity in Helen's mind. No jealousy, simply ignorance. The trouble was, he still tried to protect his Helen from hurtful information the way he might have shielded that vulnerable spouse; he would always try to do so, and this case, which touched their personal lives so closely, forced a return in him to the old hesitation that had been his hallmark before love for Helen had overtaken him so completely. He had set himself against any kind of silence toward her, but could not persuade his mind to the same course if the truth might wound or even offend her. In his dealings with Sumner, he had acted with the efficiency of the professional: he had charged the man with murder and known that Helen could not approve, could never have done the same. The charge had been like painting by numbers on a picture that was clearly incomplete, since all such pictures were incomplete without fingerprints or signed confessions. The police had more than enough numbers; therefore there was a charge. Helen would have called this process an upside-down drawing, told him not to stop investigating. And so the body in the woods created not a rift but a hiatus, a time when they took stock of each other's reactions, withdrew to save admissions or accusations, felt more than a little lonely, Helen more than a little disappointed in him. No hostilities; each would have gone to the end of the world to avoid a row, but in the fruitful ease of normal communication there was a blockage, a reversion to the native state of two pathologically lonely and self-sufficient souls who had once found themselves so utterly relieved by the discovery of each other.

At home, that home she could not think of as home, she sat and watched. How gently the police had treated Sumner she could only guess. Gentleness of every kind was inherent in Bailey, perceptible even in the lines of that hatched face of his, so severe in repose, so transformed by laughter. Even his harshest and most obstinate interrogations never carried the slightest implication of violence, but he often used the persuasive force of fear. She imagined him with his pale prisoner, well aware of how intimidating Bailey could be with a minimum of words and gestures. Strong medicine for Antony Sumner, prejudiced, illogical, spoiled, selfish teacher and lover, surely unable to withstand such provocative skills. Few others did, usually those cunning enough not to open their mouths at all in a way she would never have managed. But there it was: Antony had resisted, been charged, and her guinea pig-faced employer found the case straightforward despite gaps such as the absence of a murder weapon. Helen did not: she felt that the evidence was brutally incomplete, the conclusions drawn so far woefully inadequate; she was determined to watch and see if her judgement proved correct, but she was a kind of prisoner, unable to discuss the case either at home or at work, since after a few early forays, Bailey discouraged her interest and Redwood forbade it.

Looking at Geoffrey now as he sat in an armchair after supper, reading a book, the way he was most often seen at leisure, she saw the concentration in his eyes. Sitting upright, reading a novel in hardback, while she felt in her veins the old but still new tide of love for him, she decided to speak.

'Geoffrey Bailey, I know that's a book and therefore the most precious thing on earth, but can you put it down for a minute? Talk to me, you brute. This doesn't feel like a talking house at the moment. Let's go to The Crown.'

He smiled at her with the whole of his face as if he had been waiting for his cue, stood, kissed her lightly, made for the door before she had time to draw breath. 'Come on then, woman.'

Such impressive sacrifice, putting down a book, made her gallop out of doors after him into the evening, grabbing his hand as he swung away up the street. Tradition of a sort dictated they walk to The Crown, a habit winter would change but a pleasant mile for now. Bailey pressed her hand inside his own, put it in his pocket with the usual show of embarrassment as they walked up the road. He, who was slower to volunteer affection and all those signs of possession, responded and returned them with interest, conditioned for ever by a childhood and adult life in which they appeared to have been forbidden. Helen felt the warmth of him, and no, she would not mention Antony Sumner, not on the way. Let them simply walk in the sweet-smelling light while it lasted, along the road that had become deserted. Then sit in the motley company of the garish bar and listen to the Featherstones fighting, or something of the kind. Normality, please, something to remind her of the daily release his company provided in assuring her she was not mad after all. Maybe she would tell him about Redwood and the humiliation of being removed from the murder case. Maybe not. He would worry on her behalf, jealous of her professional pride. For the minute it did not matter. She was back in her native state and happy to be alive.

But it was Geoffrey himself, in some faint effort to clear the air, who shifted the conversation to forbidden ground. 'Saw your boss about our local murder,' he said once a bottle of wine was open before them. 'You know, the man without a profile, Red Squirrel.'

'Redwood,' she corrected, laughing and sensing his irritation with the man in question.

'He has his legal credentials framed on the wall in case we humble policemen should doubt them,' Bailey continued.

'Some people do doubt them,' said Helen, 'especially other lawyers. And whatever the diplomas, they don't include any in the art of conversation.'

'Or the appreciation of humour, I noticed,' Bailey added.

A pause for wine, a sigh of satisfaction, speech resumed more hurriedly. 'He told me he considered the investigation complete – a sort of well-done-chaps-but-leave-it-alone-now lecture. Considers it all wrapped up. Advance disclosure of written evidence will be presented tomorrow, only a few scientific statements outstanding. Leave it to us from now on. He's instructing Queen's Counsel and junior, of course, wouldn't condescend to tell us who, mandatory expense for murder, I suppose. Asked me if I thought Sumner would plead to manslaughter. Arrogant man, Redwood. Had you noticed that he looks like a guinea pig?'

'Yes,' said Helen, 'I had noticed.'

'Anyway,' Bailey went on, speeding over his subject as if to subdue it, 'I told him a plea for Sumner was as likely as a good English summer.' He paused and grinned. 'I saw Mr Guinea Pig as a good vegetable gardener; that seemed about the right level.'

'I'm hedging,' said Helen. 'I do want to talk about it and I don't, if you see what I mean. Do you think Sumner would plead guilty but provoked, or diminished responsibility, or whatever? No, I don't really mean that; you've answered me already. What I mean is, did he really do it?'

There was palpable hesitation, a long pipe-lighting and examination of wine label. 'The evidence appears to show that he did.' Carefully said.

'The evidence as far as you've told me?'

'The evidence, as far as it goes.'

'You don't believe it, Geoffrey, do you?' She subdued a rising note in her voice.

He sighed as if he'd been anticipating this conflict for the whole three weeks of its incubation. 'Yes, I do believe it. As far as I need. I believe in evidence. Nothing else works. Speculation, doubt based on loyalty, affection, or hunches, they don't have the same validity. Besides, it doesn't matter what I believe.'

'I've heard you say that before, and it's the only time I catch you lying.'

He turned his brown perplexed face to hers, determined against seriousness, happy to be sitting next to her and suddenly preferring to be talking about nothing.

'Of course it's true, Helen. I record, I investigate, I repeat in court what I have found. I'm not asked for my opinion. I'm a highly trained parrot – homing pigeon, more like, carrier of messages that amount to the nearest thing you ever get to truth – as far as Red Squirrel and the whole panoply of the judiciary are concerned.'

'All right, all right, point taken for the evasion it is. But what do you believe about Sumner? You must believe something. You, not the parrot.'

'I believe what I've seen. What the evidence indicates.'

'You'll drive me mad. What about Mrs Blundell, then? What was she like?'

'Hardly Sumner's type, I'd say. The only thing they had in common was a blood type.' He was attempting to end the conversation, and she was well aware he would succeed. He was becoming remarkably skilled in doing just that.

From behind the bar, the Featherstone insults rang out, transcending the desultory conversation of the customers whose own sentences became subdued out of both deference and curiosity. 'He said a pint, Harold, not a half, you git.'

'Shut up, Bernadette, shut up, put a sock in it, will you?' – all delivered in hisses the one to the other, louder than any stage whisper. Beer drinkers always confused Harold. His face was red, tension in the fist that slammed down the drink into relative silence, frightening the customer with a glare. In the kitchen, there was a sudden resounding crash.

William Featherstone appeared like a bolt from the blue from the kitchen door, ran across the dizzying carpet toward the stairs, darting glances to left and right as he went. Bernadette moved from the bar towards him. He shook his fist and she stepped back, pretending she had not noticed. William paused in mid-flight on sight of Geoffrey and Helen, pirouetted, granted these familiar customers the benefit of an inane grin, and disappeared up the steps three at a time. The noise of him was thunderous.

'Aggressive lad,' said Bailey.

'Poor boy,' said Helen.

Harold Featherstone shrugged comically: Bailey and Helen chuckled simultaneously at the oddity, the chuckle growing into hidden and uncontrollable giggles in the face of Bernadette's withering look. No reason for it to be so funny, but it was.

'That's why I like this place,' said Bailey, watching Harold beginning to dry a glass half full of whisky, Bernadette watching him aghast, preparing words. Helen, suddenly almost content, placed her hand on the back of Bailey's neck and laughed into his shoulder. The smell of Bailey laughing, the touch and taste of him, was like a patent faith restorer. Let them speculate about the Featherstones and the neighbours, then. Let him win for now; she would not disturb the peace with talk of Blundells and Sumners, murders and lawyers. Dangerous ground, a smooth-surfaced cesspit. Varnish it with laughter, while in her mind there grew a dull sense of compromise. It had been the love affair to end all others; it was beginning to slip, the way of all others.

★

In the posh house, love was a much insulted thing. Blundell's dwelling was three-quarters of a mile from The Crown and owned by a modern man who did not think in yards but made measurements in metres for anything but grief and liquid. Liquid was brown and ordered in inches, with or without ice. John Blundell stood in a room as distant in spirit from The Crown as Mrs Blundell could have made it. She had been addicted to *Good Housekeeping* and *Vogue*, her house bearing souvenirs of the former as much as her clothes reflected the latter. The widower was in their bedroom, which was filled with the same ominous silence that suffused this house and filled it with accusations. His daughter was asleep, he supposed: she had retired to bed an hour since with the minimum of goodnights. The house had become speechless, his own breathing noisy. John had opened the wardrobe – fifteen metres of wardrobe – belonging to the late Mrs B. Inside there were yards of clothes whose existence she would have denied in pursuit of more; a small selection, she would have said. She had favoured camel, cream, and black ever since her figure had reverted to youthful proportions in the last eighteen months. Before that, and for the last ten years, she had taken size sixteen and favoured fluffy pinks and reds. Expensive reds, but shrouds nevertheless. The new image had been streamlined and the new face almost sweet company. Nevertheless he had preferred the old – less demanding, less expensive.

John Blundell moved from the wardrobe to the dressing table where jewellery spilled from a box, slightly dusty but otherwise tidy. The accompaniments reflected the clothes. Unburnished gold was typical, earrings that resembled brass globes, but cost infinitely more, belcher chains in large but elegantly dull links, nothing shiny, the most flamboyant thing of all a double row of old pearls with a gleam only slightly less subdued than the rest. Notable for their absence were the solid gold choker, bracelet, and gold hoops, all discreetly heavyweight and worn on the night she had left, the same plain jewellery he had described to the superintendent. Bailey, having acquired Helen's habits, had made the subject draw the objects in mind, fixing them in Blundell's eye for ever. Fixing, too, his fury at their cost. He had bought them to placate her.

She had donned the gear of more established riches, turned herself into an old-style lady of the manor, with none of the traditional parsimony. The habits of dress had not extended to fornication with the gardener, not as far as her spouse knew, in any event. She had found herself another touch of class instead, had she not? She wore her precious dull metals in rebellion against diamonds, tried to improve her mind, she said. And then taken up poetry in motion in the form of some bloody man who read it. And thought John had not noticed.

John Blundell moved back to the wardrobe. Looked at the line of neatly pressed clothes: lean linen for summer, cashmeres for cool evenings, nothing if not organized, colour against colour in fully ironed harmony, not like his own shirts, buggered by the cleaning lady. He took a dress from a hanger, removed the belt, looked at both, then inserted the spike of the belt at the neck of the dress and tore it from collar to hem. Rich cloth ripping made a satisfying sound. With slow deliberation he destroyed two silk blouses in the same fashion, hung everything back in the same wardrobe as neatly as before, along with the other clothes, some already torn, most not, and walked unsteadily to his side of the kingsize mattress. On the reproduction table stood the whisky decanter, which he grasped in one pudgy fist. Now that she was gone – dead, if not buried – at least he could drink in bed. He might as well have done so for the last four years. Sweet fuck all else going on, always moaning on about housekeeping while spending all this. He wept into the pillow: You could have had anything you wanted; I told you I didn't mind. You kept wanting me to talk to you all the time, and then you wouldn't talk at all. You deserved what you got.

CHAPTER SIX

Post was slow. That was why it fell to Amanda Scott at the behest of Redwood, whom she would never have compared with a guinea pig, to deliver a copy of the evidence in the case of *R. v. Sumner* into the offices of Messrs Amor and Harmoner, Branston High Street.

The title of the firm suggested love to all men with harmony thrown in for free, but Mr Amor was dead and if his name had ever influenced the practice with sentiment it was not apparent now. Henry Harmoner was the mainstay, a deceptively slow-mannered man who was grateful to John Blundell for the swift turnover of houses in Branston and thereabouts, which had trebled his conveyancing practice and his clientele. He was not yet grateful for the legal aid clients who followed, leaving these to his brother George who, for reasons best known to himself, appeared to like that distasteful kind of thing. Henry had been less than delighted to discover that George was the inheritor of Antony Sumner, murderer of Mrs Blundell, whom Henry himself had always fancied, especially at size sixteen: fine figure of a woman before she went thin. Been to dinner in his house after all. Husband author of much good fortune while remaining a frightful little shit, mean as hell when standing a round, but not to be displeased. So Henry ranted briefly at George for accepting the client and hoped John Blundell would understand how business was business and all that, the way he usually did without great show of scruple and hopping from one leg to the other. Henry and George Harmoner quarrelling, even as briefly as they did, resembled two bulls locking horns and swaying around with a certain lack of conviction, for the sake of an audience, grunting every now and then. Both spoke in short sentences while beetling their very full eyebrows, the only characteristic of a family not renowned for anything else except a healthy pomposity. This characteristic was passed on to all clients as a kind of reassurance. George was the brighter of the two, which made him very bright indeed although less prosperous for his slightly younger thirty-three years, graced with middle-aged stockiness nevertheless. He resembled his brother in weight, short phrases, and a perfect if painless passion for the way he earned his daily bread and wine. 'Nothing like the law,' he enthused once. 'Nothing like it, Henry, nothing at all.'

'Oh, I don't know about that, George. Other things as good,' said Henry, patting his own rounded stomach. 'Not bad, though, George. Not bad at all. For a living.'

Even at this early hour, George's voice was raised. 'Don't be silly, Henry. Fellow's murdered someone. Got to be defended. Only legal aid, but never mind. Phoned up at midnight, this woman did, in tears. Nothing I could do but

102

pitch up and be a nuisance. Which I was. Couldn't help him then: not allowed. But I've got him now. Stuck with him. Don't mind, really.'

'Bit much, George, bit much.'

'See what you mean, Henry, see what you mean. The victim was John Blundell's better half, and she was, wasn't she? Ha. John won't like it much if I get the fellow off? Well, sorry about that, Henry.'

'Bit much, George, really.'

'I know, Henry, I know. Nothing I can do, see what I mean.'

They yawed at each other in this fashion, feinting half-hearted verbal blows for a while longer, standing in the modern foyer while three junior solicitors slipped in behind and a receptionist with tinted hair blinked into her telephone. Honour was about to be satisfied when PC Amanda Scott stepped through the door carrying a large buff envelope marked 'On Her Majesty's Service' for the attention of G. Harmoner, Esq. Amanda was wearing blue tights with patterns in lace, a frequent sly adornment to an outfit otherwise perfectly plain, and Henry thought she looked jolly nice indeed. He also felt she had somehow lost his argument for him. George came to the same conclusion as his brother regarding her appearance, apart from considering that her legs in those things looked as if spiders were crawling down them, and he smirked, obviously. When Amanda identified him so easily out of the two, George smirked even wider. Personal delivery from personable young women was not frequent in conveyancing: teach Henry a thing or two. Amanda, after being thanked by name for her service, left as courteously as she had arrived.

Henry barked incredulously. 'That's a policewoman?'

'It is, Henry, it is. Lots of them like that now.'

'Good God,' said Henry. 'I give up. Get the bugger to plead, George. He hasn't a chance in hell. First Yvonne Blundell and then a woman like that: they've done for him.'

George knew the sad limitations of brother Henry's criminal wisdom, but after a cursory examination of a relatively small file of evidence, mostly scientific with Sumner's written confession to half the deed, George tended to agree with the verdict given from the depths of Henry's ignorance. Not much scope here for contesting the evidence at preliminary proceedings; at least a *prima facie* case had been proved. Shame. No fuss in front of the local magistrates. George liked fuss in front of the local magistrates and was very good at creating his only chance as a mere solicitor to harangue the witnesses before the whole thing passed into the hands of a barrister and he took the back seat apart from instructing like an ineffective puppeteer, hand-holding some Queen's Counsel who earned twice his own salary. But if this fellow, this poxy fellow of a bloody poetry teacher – his statement as well as his curriculum vitae made you sick – had a thought in his head about pleading guilty to anything, he had another think coming. Not at George Harmoner's hands would he plead to careless driving *en route* to the pub, never mind stabbing to death a wealthy woman afterwards. George sat back and thought, saving the full and sickening details of pathology for long after lunch. Good business, this, even if it was a pity about Mrs B., but she was still a case bound to attract plenty of publicity, her and her big house and all.

'See here, Henry, the property boom is slowing down in this neck of the woods. Made us rich but may not make us richer. It may be time to revise the direction of Amor and Harmoner. Keeping an eye on the ever-moving ball of lucrative but discreet East End crime, shoving a name in front of all those big, dishonest market traders. Only money, nothing nasty; might not be a bad idea.' Again he thought, Pity about Mrs B., but not a time to waste pity, was it? He'd save the kiss of life for the turd who'd killed her. Not bad, the law: not bad at all.

He hummed to himself, undeterred by the pile of files stacked on one side of his desk. Nothing to it, method was all he required and a sense of order, and with those two qualities, everything was curable.

Then, from the lines of a statement in quite another case featuring the theft of a set of carpentry tools including a paring knife, a thought struck George sideways from halfway down the page. Knife. Stab wounds. He dropped what he was reading, picked up Sumner's file, one line stored in his head from the first hurried look at the pathologist's report. What had he said? 'Wounds probably inflicted with single-edge weapon, a knife.' That was what he had read, the very words his photographic memory had transferred to Compartment A along with the contents of the printed exhibit list. Sumner denied either using or possessing the knife. So where was this single-edge knife, eh? Not on the bloody list. Scrabble around a bit, a good eye glossing pages with speed. No knife: not in Sumner's house, in the dustbins, or on the ground; not the sort of thing a poetic chap carried about, if you see what I mean, especially in Branston on the way out for a quiet drink at the

105

pub. Not a bloke to fish, either, as George was; single-edge sharp knife handy there. Fishing line, that sort of thing; cuts it. Has to be very sharp. George was sharp, too.

He sat back and flexed his fingers. He could see the chance for a showy pretend contest in front of the magistrates after all, if only to find out about the knife. Good bloodthirsty stuff, even if unreported in the press; there'd be enough of an audience at the back of court. Make you gasp and stretch your eyes: wounds, causes of wounds, blade of knife, the very sound of it an incantation.

Passing the offices of Amor and Harmoner, sitting on top of the bus, William Featherstone, otherwise in a placid state, ventured a glance at the law firm's windows, scowled, and turned back to face the road before him. While his parents were not aware of one George Harmoner, William was and knew him as more than one local notable who would not have graced their establishment for a funeral. William had met the man in circumstances unfavourable, a fact his mother would have to learn sooner or later, he supposed. George Harmoner had stood above him in the interview room of Chingford Police Station, called by the police as was perfectly proper in the case of a young shoplifter only just across the boundary of seventeen where the calling out of parents was mandatory. William's response to the question, 'Do you want a lawyer?' had been, 'Dunno.' Quickly appreciating his uncertain temper, the police had been careful to call a lawyer who was local to where the boy lived. He gave them the village, not the address. It was also known that Harmoner never refused a case, but on sight of the pale-

106

eyed William plucking at the fraying crotch area of his grubby trousers and gazing out of the window with genuine vagueness, he wished he had. William did not like George, either. The man had shouted at him slowly as if he was deaf. 'Do you understand, William? They are not going to charge you. You told the lady here' – indicating a very young probationary woman police constable in the corner of the room – 'that you took those things.' William would have told the pretty probationer anything she wanted to know, and had. George continued. 'The big police officer' – here he gestured with his hands, making William imagine that the chief inspector he had seen once was shaped like a balloon – 'will give you what is called a caution.' Oh, he's a caution: William remembered his mother saying that and sniggered. He had not absorbed what Harmoner was talking about, other than the strictures: yes, he would tell his parents, and no, he would not shoplift again. He told the balloon inspector he was sorry, because the inspector was a very big man indeed and that seemed a prudent thing to say. William was backward but, within his limitations, not stupid. He did not tell his mother: he expected he might be arrested again if this was the done thing, and he was not sorry at all.

'Come with me, Evie,' he had said earlier.

'No, don't be so bloody silly. Why would I want to do that? And besides, someone might see us. We'll go on the tube another day.'

Pity Evelyn did not care for riding the buses when she had nothing else to do. Coasting down country lanes, a mile or two of fields between mini conurbations, leaving Greater London behind and then joining it again, sitting above the driver and the throbbing engine, William was in seventh heaven. The No. 61 took him from Branston to Chigwell. From there the 134 – pay as you enter, nasty flapping doors that prevented jumping out between stops, another game denied – would take him to Epping via Loughton. Epping had a long High Street full of closed-in stores. He didn't much like that, either; he could not prowl in shops where they were always asking if they could help, the request made in expectation of denial, a mere shooing-away exercise, which he recognized. Worse than market stalls where he could not get a look in. The No. 206, green this time, a dull colour but a nice old bus with a bell, took him all the way to Stortford where there was a perfectly normal modern arcade, the sort he preferred. Shops were open at the front; he did not have to push open doors and announce his presence. Today was Waltham Cross, at the opposite end of the line from Stortford via the 65 from Theydon, but still as full of glittering things. The heavy hand had fallen on his shoulder in Stortford, so it seemed better to leave it alone for a while. All else failing, he could return to Branston High Street or nearby Woodford, which was probably his favourite. There were endless opportunities for changes of mind. He liked that, too.

William's purposes were confused when he approached the shops. Whether he approached from the front or the rear, he never knew quite what he was going to do next. Heart-beating, nail-biting suspense. His grin so wide that anyone catching sight of him wondered if he smiled in recognition of them, then turned away embarrassed, wondering who he was and should they say hello. Back entrances did not carry such traffic although he still smiled

108

automatically. William had been a clumsy mimic as a child, never picking up more than half the idea, but he had mimicked and now mastered in different form his father's scavenging instinct. Bins filled with combustible paper, straw, and polystyrene foam, bits of wire and yards of tissue, and, oh, so often at the bottom of a box, something forgotten, lost in the packaging, or in another, something slightly damaged. At twelve years old, he had played for hours with discarded tapes, holding the endless ribbon of plastic to the light and winding it around his head. At fourteen, he had begun to carve shapes in packing foam, faces and robotlike hands with angular fingers, cut by a Stanley knife too blunt for any use but this. At seventeen he could spend secret hours in the manufacture of wonderful, if tiny, things made from wire and glass fragments, glittery items half resembling rings, bracelets of bottle fragments, but he was far more selective in what he acquired. Bringing home his own bulk along with more under the arm was too conspicuous these days, even for parents such as his own. He purchased or stole in miniature, all of it acquired with a purpose, and never once did he see it as theft, not even when he took an item from a shop counter. He only grabbed from the shop when it was clear to him that taking one item left a dozen of the same, and no one could possibly want so many, surely. Theft was when you took it straight out of someone else's pocket. He had seen that done once, and it had shocked him.

'How are you today?'

'Very well, thank you. How's your cold?' Showing a mouthful of teeth in a smile as wide as a bay, William was known on the buses as a harmless freak. The motion made him talkative: he would chat to bus conductors if they existed, fellow travellers, if not. Yes, yes, they would say, never quite allowing him to engage their attention unless they were over sixty-five. The subjects of William's conversations were food prices, learned from home; poor bus service and lying timetables, learned as he went along; the weather, which was a constant disruption to his soul; public transport; and aches and pains, which he understood. He debated all these topics intelligently with the pensioners travelling on cheap off-peak tickets. On the last subject, William was highly sympathetic, even offered advice. He liked the elderly and the very young. Those in the middle were a sinister blur.

Chingford. Should he alight here and find a quicker bus to base? No, he hated this bus shelter; wait a few more stops, then change; half an hour at least between buses, but a nicer shelter farther down the road on this drizzly, damp day. An old-fashioned shelter with yards of graffiti on the concrete walls, plenty to examine from proper wooden seats similarly decorated. Dear, dear – a phrase learned from the pensioners – Waltham would be crowded. School holidays, teenagers on the streets poking fun, boys moving in gangs, girls with thin legs, flouncy hair, fat lips. Little bottoms and tiny bosoms in all those funny clothes. Just like Evelyn, but nothing like Evelyn. Nothing, no one, no jewel or treasured thing in his whole wide world compared to Evelyn. He closed his eyes for a moment and missed the stop.

William's treasure and father's darling child was trying to listen to her father, stuck in his stuffy office which did not compare with the posher front of the shop – the good plain carpet, carved desk and chairs, banks of plants in bamboo shelving, a mixture of traditional and the new, blueprint for Branston, et cetera. So John Blundell had instructed the eager designer, knocking her down to a cut price for the job, since she clearly hoped for, and he vaguely promised, other jobs to follow in his modest chain of offices and show houses. None did. Having cheated her slightly, Blundell was perfectly happy with the well-textured result. Since no one else but himself occupied the office behind his, it was not important enough for expenditure. A part of John Blundell was very parsimonious indeed. The most expensive for show, the cheapest for private consumption.

'Daddy, don't be so bloody irritating.'

'Don't swear, darling child, please.' Automatically said.

'Well, don't be so slow, then. I do have ears, you know.' She was astride a pile of house particulars perched on a chair on the side of the desk that was normally his. He, like a supplicant, was slightly lower on the stool facing her.

'Get on with it, please, Daddy. I'm not upset. You can see I'm not.' This in a wheedling tone, a placatory voice she had learned to use especially with the opposite sex of all ages, including teachers and relatives. A little-girl voice. He was always seduced by it; he cleared his throat.

'All right, all right, darling child, I was just trying to explain so that you won't be in the dark more than necessary. People will talk, you see; they always do. They'll tell you something I should tell you first.'

She knew that principle already, but found the opposite to be true. If she went into any Branston shop, which she did frequently in the vacuum of school holidays, silence fell. She was aware it could have been the silence of sympathy, a response to her pale face, but she seethed with hostility, wanting to scream, Shut up, shut up being quiet. Shut up knowing things and talking about us. Shut up being so bloody sorry. Just talk, you bloody twits; pretend to talk if you can't really talk. Stop it, stop it, stop it.

Her father saw the tension in her shoulders, paused.

'Go on, then,' she challenged, irritation subdued to the slightest of edges.

'OK, darling child. This is how it is.' He coughed, rendering his own face an unimpressive red to match the viscous red of his eyes. She looked on without sympathy, waiting.

'Your mother. The case about her murder. Henry Harmoner, our solicitor, has just phoned me to say what's going to happen. The bastard.' He muttered the last two words under his breath, remembering too late his strictures to the child about language. 'Anyway, he thinks – God, he thinks a lot, Henry – that the case will come up before the magistrates in Waltham in about two, three weeks, for a hearing of sorts.'

'That's quick. I thought these things took ages and ages.' He looked at her, perplexed. He'd had a dim idea of the same, not so explicit, and wondered as he often did how it was she knew so much. To him, the interval since his wife's murder seemed a lifetime, but he was able to recall that life moved slower for a child.

'Usually much slower than this, I gather. They must have speeded things up.' Perhaps there had been some deference to his feelings in this. He liked to think so, while knowing at the back of his mind it was scarcely likely.

112

Victims of victims always come last, like the poor house-buyer at the end of some chain. That was how Henry explained it.

'What kind of hearing?'

'Don't really know, but not the real trial. A sort of trial before the trial. Won't be in the newspapers, but they mean to call some pathologist chap in to show how Mummy died or something. I'm afraid' – he swallowed, tears appearing at the rims of his eyes – 'she was stabbed before she was buried.' He looked at the pale and precocious face with its calm and disbelieving regard. 'I'm sorry, darling. It isn't very nice. That man, the one who did it' – he could not bring himself to say the name – 'says he didn't. Didn't have the right kind of knife or something silly. It won't be very nice,' he repeated finally.

'Is that man in prison?' she demanded with sudden venom.

'Yes.'

'Will he stay there?'

'Yes.'

She stood and walked around the office so that he would not see the look of grim satisfaction on her face, then went back to the chair, picking up papers and putting them down as she went. ''S'all right, Daddy. 'S'all right,' she muttered through perfect little teeth until she was back in the chair again looking like a miniature consultant. ''S'all right, Daddy, even if it does go in the papers. I'm going to be a doctor, after all.'

'Are you, darling?' First he knew. A moment's surprise distracted him.

'Yes, I am,' she said firmly. 'Also a writer. I have to

113

know about these things so I won't be shocked, Daddy. 'S'all right.'

No, it wasn't all right. He was acutely uncomfortable with her calm authority and ghastly adult composure, felt the same frisson of dislike he had occasionally felt for her, oh, so dissimilar mother. Blundell was not a thoughtful man, merely cunning; he wondered for the first time what they had done, Yvonne and he, to create such a paragon. Should have been more children, he always said, there should have been more. 'Can I have a son, please?' But no, she hadn't liked the idea. Producing Evelyn had been traumatic; leaving the crowded East End in search of more money and clearer air for the child he had then adored had been more traumatic still. He wondered if the women in his life had been in competition and, if so, why? What was it all about with both of them, and were the survivors only pretending to grieve? Why had his darling daughter found her mother's death so easy to accept, mirroring his own lack of anguish? Tears of sheer frustration began to form again. He wanted a drink. His moist eyes slid to the cabinet in the corner, but he was interrupted by her words.

'Can I go, Dad? To this hearing, I mean?'

'To the what? The murder hearing?' His small mouth spluttered the words as his mind took in the meaning of her question. Surprise turned into outrage as his eyes slowly focused on her. 'The hearing?' he repeated, incredulity in each syllable. 'What? With all that—'

'I want to know what happened, and I'm going to write medical books, Daddy.'

'No,' he shouted. 'No you can't bloody go to any

114

hearing, for Christ's sake. How could you – Stop being so bloody . . . so bloody grown up.'

'Don't swear, darling Daddy,' she replied lightly.

But he had burst into a kind of howl, sat on the stool like a lonely dunce, head in his arms, well beyond his own slight control, all of him heaving with anger and sorrow, fat with the desire to scream. Wearily she stepped out again from behind the desk to stand behind his bent back patting it like a fragile and unfamiliar thing, absent half-blows, half-strokes, as if trying to raise a cough. "S'all right, Daddy, really. 'S'all right. Honest. Closing time now, Daddy. Go home to bed. Have a drink. It's good for you.'

Evelyn knew what was good for Daddy. She could have chanted a list of what was good for Daddy, and did it to quell her own fury. William had guessed, as soon as they met at ten p.m., that Evelyn was very cross and very tired. He wondered if this not unfamiliar condition was one he could choose to ignore. 'Such a busy day,' she had said. 'Daddy's in bed now, goes to bed like a dog when it gets dark. What's the matter, William? 'S'all right, William, really it is. Stop opening your mouth.'

How could it have been a busy day if her daddy was in bed already by nine-thirty? William's father never seemed to go to bed sober, which was a nuisance, and he cried sometimes and drank a lot, like Evelyn's dad. Still, he couldn't see how her day could have been as action-packed as his own, the detailed recitation of which, including all the buses and every single one of the shops, had taken half an hour and clearly bored her. She was stiff with crossness and, for once, openly strained.

115

'Look,' he said placatingly, wheedling while postponing the other news, which he knew obscurely to be unpleasant, sensing without fully knowing why, that it would displease Evie more than most, dreading the disclosure. 'Look,' he said again, 'look what I've brought you.' Feeling in his pockets with stubby fingers, putting on the bed between them his small hoard of glittering things, trying to please desperately, giving it all away in one fell swoop. 'These were down my trousers,' he boasted. 'I stitched two pairs of trousers together, see? All these things were right at the bottom, by the hem. They didn't find these . . .' He faltered on the last words, knowing he had blown it, told it all instead of waiting.

They were sitting in the summerhouse den, Evelyn cross-legged on the mattress, lit by the butane lamp, dark hair falling on her shoulders, ears sparkling like the objects on the bed, which she was sweeping to the floor in a luminous arc. One violent movement of her arm and the diamanté bits sprang into the air, hitting ceiling and wall, falling to the earthen floor in a series of uneven sounds. A gesture of contempt to his gesture of giving. Her face was the colour of day, two red spots and a tight slit of a mouth.

'Who's they, William? What do you mean, they? They what? They when? They where?'

He shifted away from her, cowering, starting to shake. 'They,' he said stupidly. 'Them, I mean.'

'Who's them?'

'Policemen them.'

'Oh, shit,' she hissed. 'You got arrested again, you disgusting little berk.'

'Please,' said William. 'Please, Evelyn, I didn't say

116

anything. Just told them I'd found some things outside a shop. Griffith's shop in Woodford, you know, the one you like. A man stopped me, then a woman came, then—'

She leaned towards him and slapped his face very hard. The plain ring on her finger as well as the fingers themselves left an imprint on his face, stigma of a small remarkably strong hand. William shrieked briefly, a grunting little shriek of pain, louder than the sound of the falling objects, followed by a storm of sobbing. He crouched, knees to chin and head in knees, arms pulling self into self, hiding, hurting, and weeping, making his body as small as possible, shrinking away in despair with her strident voice in his ears penetrating his own enormous sobs.

'What did you say to them, William? What did you say?'

'Nothing, nothing, nothing. Only about the things I had and they found, nothing else. They didn't ask; I didn't chatter. Like you said. Like that big fat lawyer man said last time. If I said anything else, you said I wouldn't be able to see you, Evie, and I couldn't bear that. Didn't say nothing, nothing, nothing.'

The last was a rising wail. Evelyn began to recover. 'Promise?' she asked. 'Promise, promise, promise?' The din he made was terrific. They might have been heard for miles: they had tested the den for sound, found it safe, but there was still too much noise.

Her head ached. She began to pat his back, a circular motion with the palm of her striking hand but otherwise similar to the action she had used on her father only a few hours before. ''S'all right, William. 'S'all right, really,' repeated again and again in her best there-there voice, ''S'all right.' She was sick of saying it, speaking words like this and patting people, especially now with that monstrous fear stuck in her chest like an arrow bleeding into her lungs, making her gulp for air in the stuffy warmth of these dirty walls. All too much: she was not a grown-up after all.

She pulled his hands from his face, turned his head towards her own, stared at him intently. 'Promise, William?'

'Oh, Evie, I did promise before. Please believe me, please.' Broken words from a tear-stained, dirt-stained face.

She did believe. She had to believe, and in the reaction of relief that withdrew the arrow, she crouched behind him and hugged him fiercely, mind in an overdrive of impatience. Thinking how soon she could go home, plan, write her diary, sleep, maybe enjoy the luxury of crying herself, wondering if her bike, a possession quite secret from William, was still in the bushes where she had left it. ''S'all right. Will, really. Honestly it is. Which shop was it, William? Tell me exactly which shop. It's important. Don't ask why, it just is. Sorry, sorry, sorry.' She repeated the word like a litany, until the crying stopped.

'I hate them all,' said William finally. 'Hate them, hate them, want to burn them down. I'll show them.'

'Nothing wrong in that,' said Evelyn. 'Tell me which shop.'

Wide awake at three a.m., Helen wished that Branston were somewhere else, a foreign village, the kind she had visited and wanted to visit again, like a Spanish country village, where for all the silence and lack of light at this hour,

118

the darkness seemed alive, a comfort rather than a dismissal. One long street where a dog would bark for a passerby, alerting the next dog in the next house, and the next, suspicious of movement, endlessly protective. Where sleep thus guarded was an end in itself, not a closing-down against the world as it was here, where all inhabitants were battened in hatches, pretending to sleep, their pets and children as silent as themselves behind double glazing, curtains drawn, blinds at full stretch. In contrast to the alien barking dogs and palpable breathing of real villages, Helen remembered next her own flat in Islington, a street where sleep was never universal. From her basement at any time of night she could hear traffic, distant trains, and from the other side of the house, footsteps on the pavement, late revellers, early starters, walkers, joggers, products of the night shift and city enterprises, living in a timeless zone. The bonus of the metropolis: constant humanity barring the sensation of loneliness, while in Branston people closed doors on their separate walls, switched a series of switches, and slept like battery hens.

Shuffling the pillow, putting one arm beneath it for comfort, her body turned sideways, she pictured the rooms of her London flat one by one. Did that ancient cooker still work? Would her plants live? Would the tenants have taken down her pictures? Did they tend the jungle of garden? Did children still climb over the wall from the school beyond, a Montessori for vandals who were too young yet to do harm. Her arm ached from lying across it, a dull discomfort provoked further by sharp recall of one terrifying night in her own home, remembering at the same time for how long after that she had clutched Bailey in the twilight hours to mitigate the nightmares, while now she merely clutched the pillow. The shock of her own withdrawal made her shut her eyes, afraid to wake him.

'Helen?' His murmured and sleepy voice, a slight stirring from him, suddenly intensified with the speaking of her name, himself instinctively aware of her wakefulness, guarding her. 'Helen, love, what is it? You're wide awake . . . Come here, love.' Crossing what had seemed a mile of bed, folding his long arms around her, turning her, pressing her against his prickly chest, kissing her forehead and eyes. 'What is it, darling?' Saying to himself, If you will not come to me, I am still here and I shall not let you go. 'What is it?'

She might have begun to tell him the half of it then in that silent dawn, grateful for his knowledge of her need to be hugged, for his constant reassurance, but as she snuggled into the embrace, ready to speak secrets, he to listen, the phone shrilled. Bailey was on call-out duty, worse than a doctor, a sound in the telephone buzz suggesting shattering relationships and bad news.

He kissed her once, disentangled himself gently, moved out of bed with the lithe speed that always distinguished his passage from sleep to action, answered with a few terse words, including a question: 'Can it wait?' A silence for the explanation. 'I see. It can't wait; fire still burning. I'll be there, fifteen minutes.'

Helen felt the rise of disappointment and loss as sharp as anger, but it was not anger, only sorrow for another opportunity missed, sad in a kind of inevitability. Back to bed with him, only for a second, only for a hug. 'What is it?' she asked in turn.

120

'I'm sorry, darling. One of those fires.'

'Which fires? Oh, I know, you told me. Backs of shops and bus shelters. That one? Why do you have to go?'

'Because I need to see one fresh. I asked Amanda to call if there was another. Will you be all right?'

'Course I'll be all right.' Automatic professional response of a woman who would have said she felt fine in the middle of an amputation. Smiling while her leg was cut off, everything perfectly OK, since that was what the onlooker wanted to hear. 'How many fires have there been?'

'This is the fifth.' Putting on his clothes with efficient ease, not like her, each morning a dozen indecisions.

'What time is it?' This wide awake, he was bound to know. Bailey was one of those who always knew the time.

'Four a.m. Go back to sleep, darling. See you for breakfast, I hope.'

She clung, arms around his neck, for a fierce moment, smiled to show she did not resent such departures. 'See you soon.'

Daylight was always too late.

CHAPTER SEVEN

Manoeuvring his car out of its tidy space and down the hill into Branston High Street, Bailey regretted his own presence in it, regretted their sojourn in such a litter-free zone, and cursed the fire raiser who had caused him to leave his bed. Between a mishmash of thoughts that refused to assume any order of priority in his mind, he also considered dead Yvonne Blundell, Antony Sumner's committal proceedings, and Amanda Scott's efficiency. It was she, of course, who had telephoned, obeying instructions to the letter. Maybe Helen was jealous. He turned the wheel towards Woodford, smiled at the ridiculous notion of himself causing jealousy in the heart of anyone, wished it was so simple. The tension of his household was not related to anything so petty, more to professional disappointment. They were both trained to examine too much, and Helen West thought that he, Geoffrey Bailey, had passed the buck and was refusing to exercise either his mind or his energy to turn upside-down an unsatisfactory case, that he had concentrated on evidence rather than the more oblique prospect of truth. Ah, yes, he knew very well what she thought. That he was acting like a cipher in doing what he was told, trying to avoid those suicidal tendencies that emerged if he thought too much or became involved in other people's lives. Well, that was her theory, not one he had practised in this case or any other, and if she did not believe that, he was not going to tell her. She might know by now it was only his behaviour that was calm, while anything uncertain festered inside him like a wound. He had to confess an irritation with her for being as uncommunicative in her opinions as he was himself.

There was also this second nature of his, which held that an idea, once revealed, was spoiled, like an unexposed film shown the ruinous light of scrutiny. He could not tell her what he was doing with such badly focused images. The doubts and ideas that vexed him needed to develop in peace, immune from description and guarded like secrets. And if the telephone had not rung so imperatively fifteen minutes before, that is what he would have said twice as clumsily as he thought it now. I love you, my Helen, but I could never talk as well as you, and you cannot be party to everything I think without uprooting those thoughts. I know no other way; you must trust me. I could probably live without you if you did not, but the thought fills me with desolation and I cannot change my own slow machinery any more than you could limit your mercurial compassion, your constant vigilance, your strange fund of anger, and all the other things about you I happen to adore.

There they were as he turned down the service road,

neat Amanda Scott in a summer jacket buttoned up against the chill of early dawn, standing with PC Bowles and two others, chatting in the cold, waiting. One badly parked car and a harassed key holder flapping his arms and looking upset, with Amanda placing a soothing hand on his sleeve to calm him, all caught in a stage set by the spotlights of the fire engine, which panted like a tired monster. As Bailey appeared, the tableau of faces broke, looked towards him expectantly. The five firemen began to retreat, ready to depart.

The fire had begun beneath a pile of boxes stacked against the wall for removal next day, all goods unloaded, nothing of value lost, sir, only rubbish burning other rubbish. The boxes had been lined up in rows against the brickwork of the yard, now scarred black by smoke, some of the tougher fabric smoking still, incompletely destroyed by the bright flame, which must have shot twenty feet into the air at least, such a lovely spectacle for the pyromaniac; it would have illuminated his watching face. Bailey did not doubt that the same first spectator was a mile away by now and still gloating. 'Anyone see anyone?'

'No.'

'Did you look?'

'Of course, sir; still looking.' Amanda Scott answered this time, but the fire must have been going ten minutes by the time the panda car spotted it, and the pyromaniac would have legged it long before then. Bailey felt weary and dispirited. They were looking to him for ideas and he had only one.

There was nothing unexpected here at all, simply another outbreak in a local epidemic. He asked questions, examined the obvious seat of the fire with the same sensation of dull familiarity. This was similar to the other four fires. Two were in bus shelters, which seemed extraordinary. Who could be angry with a bus shelter? The other three had been set at the back of shops rather like this. All five were clearly someone's idea of harmless fun – big high flames and no real loss, started with what resembled strips of cotton sheeting soaked in paraffin, judging from the overpowering smell. The same cheap washing liquid container used to transport the paraffin, then abandoned in the flames and half melted. For the moment, Bailey discounted the bus shelter fires, for which he could not guess a motive, turned to the key holder who was still flapping his hands, but looking less worried than mildly expectant. 'Sorry to keep you waiting, sir.' Always polite to a man worried about his stock, shot out of sleep without knowing if he faced carnage or a very small insurance claim, treat him gently. 'Could you tell me, were you working in the shop yesterday? . . . Good. Was there any bother – you know the kind of thing: arguments with customers, anyone shoplifting, for instance? Common enough, isn't it? Yes, you might not be able to remember . . .' And there, from the mouths of babes, sucklings, and shopkeepers, names tumbled. One William Featherstone, arrested here the afternoon before, same boy, same face cautioned for stealing a month before in another shop on the list, scene of the first fire. What was it Helen had called him, not watching him regarding the boy so closely? 'Poor boy,' she had said. That was the difference between them. Where she said 'Poor boy,' he saw a potential criminal. He was not without pity, but that was always his first observation nevertheless.

Yet she, like him, should understand and know when to ration compassion. Can't be nice all the time, or even most of it.

As he kicked gingerly at one cardboard box, issued clipped instructions to send in another photographer later in the morning, he could see how clearly his next move could make life in Branston even less comfortable for Helen. He viewed himself as she might see him, the man who went around arresting the nearest and dearest of her tenuous Branston acquaintance. He wondered if she still slept while he raked the ashes of a silly little fire, wondering if two coincidences were sufficient to justify the pulling in of one William Featherstone. Amanda Scott was standing like Patience on a monument, waiting for a name and orders, which he did not pronounce. At least Helen never gave him this irritating and exaggerated respect. 'Think I'll go home,' said Bailey. 'Nothing for us to do.'

'William Featherstone?' queried Amanda, eyebrows an arc of surprise.

'No, not yet. Nothing yet.'

'I am getting out of here,' Evelyn announced, 'as soon as I can.' It was the waning of the summer, visible in the days following William's arrest for shoplifting, and the first signs of dampness were apparent in the summerhouse den. William was shocked, watched while she continued. 'And if you're very good, you can come with me.' He brightened visibly. 'Only for a day, well, three-quarters of a day. We'll go on the tube, like I said. Not your silly old buses. We'll go to Oxford Circus on the tube.' He opened his mouth to protest, shut it again. He knew the tube, didn't like it. She knew how it frightened him, but with Evelyn with him it might be a different story. 'Only if you're good,' she added meaningfully. William sat closer, encouraged by the mood, put his arm around her shoulders. She did not resist. After all, it was Sunday afternoon, reserved for special Evelyn treats, with no one calling from the house. The news of his impending court appearance had alarmed his parents until Harold shrugged it away, but their vigilance had not increased in proportion to suspicion. William placed his hand on her left breast over the jumper; she let it remain. 'But you've got to be good,' she continued. 'You know, tomorrow at court. All these courts,' she added crossly. 'You tomorrow, me the next day.' He shot upright.

'What do you mean, you the next day?'

'You know, Mummy's case. No, don't talk about it.'

His eyes had widened in terror. 'Dead Mummy? Bad Mummy?'

'Yes, William, dead Mummy. Very bad Mummy. But after that – Thursday, I think – we're going out.'

His span of concentration, acute in some regards, was now as short as his memory, from which he plucked only what he wanted to retain, while his hands, arrested momentarily by the threat of bad news, continued.

Outside, the rain pattering on the wooden roof of the summerhouse was barely audible. Evelyn sighed softly, distancing her mind the way she normally did during Sunday afternoon treats, half her school days, and most dealings with Daddy. Daddy was not asleep and darling child was not doing homework. Daddy was being brave, sorting through all of Mummy's things, wanting no

127

witnesses. She knew what Daddy would find in Mummy's desk: one hundred bills, all of them souvenirs of a bored life; thousands of photographs of Mummy when young, Mummy as teenage bride and infant wife, and among this detritus not a single photograph of darling child. If she had ever pointed a camera in Evelyn's direction, the results had never surfaced. Evelyn knew that with a spurt of rage: darling Mummy who had never loved her at all. Well, what was love anyway? Daddy's hugs, then William's more demanding hands, all to keep the bloody peace. Slowly she took off her jumper and closed her eyes. This was Sunday, after all. First church, now this. Life was full of chores.

For this summer weekend, Helen and Bailey had fled to the sea, cruising the motorway into another county like children escaping the confines of work, armed with books, a picnic basket, shoes for walking, expecting rain and receiving sunshine like a blessing. They had called on friends, drunk a little too much, passed Saturday in a pub with Spartan appointments and splendid comfort, lost themselves in miles of pine-skirted beach. After two days of tranquil, sometimes uproarious contentment, Branston beckoned back a pair of lovers who had at least remembered who they were and why they were together. If there were subjects they failed to disinter from their own silences, it did not matter any more than shadows on the sun. Bailey had delighted in her and she in him. Helen went to work on Monday morning brown and refreshed, body tingling, mind alert. If there was something Machiavellian about her plan for the week, it had not yet begun to trouble her.

In such a mood, Waltham Court, scene of this week's

endeavours, was the best choice. Although smarting a little from the actions of Redwood in making off with her murder case, Helen had refrained from either comment or complaint and simply concentrated more on the work that remained. Waltham's daily list offered a panoply of challenges, a picture of local life littered with dozens of decisions per morning, enough to tax the brain and leave it reeling. Waltham court was a favourite of hers. Approaching the façade of a building resembling a factory decorated with bird dung among stained concrete and flanked by vandalized trees, the local *palais de justice* did not look favoured. Inside, the worn floors were pitted with cigarette burns beneath No Smoking signs. The corridors were too narrow, the court rooms themselves airless and claustrophobic, the whole interior like a stained handkerchief left too long in a pocket, beyond redemption. But the atmosphere within it was full of jokes, the staff as cheerful as crickets, as if to forestall the building's determination to depress, the magistrates armed with a degree of realism, and the administration chaotically efficient. Despite a daily diet of misery and despite its carbuncular appearance, Waltham ticked with positive vibrations like a good hospital. The foyers buzzed; there was consideration for life, smiles among the anxieties. Even William Featherstone, sitting alone, had failed to lose his vacuous expression.

William was hers to prosecute this morning, product of the small world in which they lived, another unasked-for complication. She would have to confess her passing acquaintance to his solicitor. She hoped he would plead guilty, but she was recognizing a more than normal awakening of interest in his case as a teenage policeman,

129

scarcely older than William himself, was showing her the exhibit bag, clear polythene, sealed once and for all with a label, containing William's choices from the worst of local shops.

'Can't open the bag before we go in court, miss,' the policeman said. 'Funny though, innit?'

'Yes,' Helen agreed thoughtfully. Very. Why on earth would William take these things? And later, at the very end of the session, with sulky, scratching, sadly unaccompanied William in the dock, unimpressed by the bulky presence of Harmoner, the worthy magistrates asked the same question.

The chairman of the bench, a local shopkeeper himself, had arranged the objects before him. 'I know he's pleaded guilty, but can your client tell us, Mr Harmony, why he took these, er, particular things?'

If he could, he wouldn't. William shrugged and, from the height of the dock, looked with regret at the display on the clerk's desk. There were four sets of earrings, mock diamond in green and white; three sets of very silvery bangles fit for a flamboyant slave girl; two sets of hair clips with silver and glittery buckles; two bright dip-on bows for shoes; and a necklace of shimmering paste. The collection sparkled in cheap harmony, reflecting the taste of someone addicted to *Dynasty* and young enough to mistake sparkle for sophistication. So: William Featherstone, a kind of human magpie drawn by anything brighter than his eyes, liked these pretty things.

'Got a girlfriend, have you?' barked the magistrate, profoundly suspicious of any other tendency this frivolous selection might imply. Helen looked at the pathetic collection with sadness, the sunshine of her weekend draining away. He had stolen the illicit fodder of dreams, poor child. Oh, yes, he could be cured by more pocket money or punishment or blows, like hell he could. Poor William. Stop dreaming, boy, it's illegal to dream with your hands. Goods and dreams, they have to be bought.

At the mention of the word 'girlfriend', William went into spasm, a stiffening of the body and such violent shaking of the head he looked about to lose it. He sat down – was pushed down, since he did not respond to orders – still indicating his negative while Harmoner preached mitigation.

Helen was relieved to see that William seemed preoccupied beyond listening, since like many of Harmoner's speeches on mitigation, this one sounded like a paean of insults: 'Poor child, not very bright, unfit for employment, unfit for anything. No parents here today, because he did not tell them the date, or if he did, they chose to forget. Lives in a dream world. Not much use to anyone, spends his days exploring on buses, he says. Should be given more pocket money, therefore less temptation to steal. Says he definitely won't do it again and is very sorry.'

More pocket money, simplistic solutions for incurable conditions, a pat on the head for insurmountable problems accumulating over a small lifetime of not quite wilful neglect. Helen liked the eccentric Featherstones – she never criticized parental inadequacy, for lack of qualification – accepted the fact that William, like any thief, had to sit where he was, slumped as he was, beyond redemption by something as clumsy as the establishment, but for a moment she detested the ignorance that had put him there. William would have needed to be born beautiful to gain forgiveness at this point in his life, but his crumpled face was not beautiful. He was fined twenty pounds, repayable at two per week; handouts would certainly have to be increased. Law was law to be upheld; Helen believed in it, but in William's case, had the feeling it made no impact whatever. He was hereby made a thief before he knew what thieving really was.

Court emptied for lunch; William was gone in a flash. Yesterday in a relaxed moment of communication, Bailey had told her about the fires and William's possible involvement; she regretted the knowledge, hoped that questions on the subject could be postponed even while she watched Amanda Scott follow William from the room. She thought, What a close creature, Bailey, looking at everything. I'm sure that boy doesn't start fires; he hasn't the sense, and he has no resentment at all. Unless there's a connection between a liking for glitter and a penchant for flames. Why not? What's happened to you these days, my love? You're turning savage with suspicion, or maybe I never appreciated what it was like to live with a copper, especially a good copper like you. No good being resentful: you've a closer acquaintance with human folly than I. You're a graduate; I'm a student. She had thought it through a hundred times, not blaming Bailey, only the perceptions that made them different and him a stranger all over again.

'Ha! Miss West! Our delightful prosecutor for the day. Nice to see you. Nice of you to put your facts so fairly if I may say so. How you manage so many cases with such elegant economy . . .'

Bit over the top, thought Helen. Harmoner, with his heavy bonhomie, chose this time to embrace her after eight months of rather more suspicious acquaintance. Woodford and Branston were almost country; they were certainly not town, where professional friendships developed perforce at greater speed, where trust or its opposite were bestowed in a glance, since you might never have seen that opponent before. She appreciated Harmoner's ponderous expertise and lack of dirty tricks, but could have postponed closer knowledge indefinitely. On the other hand, he appeared to have decided all of a sudden that she was good enough for membership of his club, which was not a club at all, simply the local fraternity of those thoroughly committed to their lifestyles.

'We're neighbours, I understand,' he continued with weighty familiarity, standing very close. 'My wife and I should see more of you. Marvellous place, Branston, don't you think? Do you ever have a drink at The Coach? You should come to the Rotary Club . . . Sometimes a few of us get together; you know, good for business all round. Must get you involved more,' he boomed. 'Haven't made you feel at home, have we? Must do better. Jolly good. Lunch, eh?'

'Very kind,' said Helen, smiling convincingly. 'But I must go back to the office. You know how it is. But tell me' – seizing the opportunity suddenly with Redwood in mind – 'are you doing the Sumner committal here tomorrow or are you using counsel?'

'I'll do it myself. Why use a barrister?'

She replied diplomatically, 'Why indeed? You'll do far better. I'm not involved, of course, but you won't mind if

I watch?' Best to secure some kind of permission, however worthless.

'My pleasure. Nice of you to ask.' He beamed, taking her interest in his case as a personal compliment. 'And after that, we'll arrange something for you and your husband in Branston.' He would know very well that Bailey was not her husband in the strict sense: Harmoner knew everything, and used the word as a token of forgiveness. 'Look forward to seeing you.'

Not if I see you first. Waving goodbye, watching him watch her make for the oldest car in the park. Nothing personal, dear Mr Harmoner, but the idea of involvement in Branston's social life makes me itch. Rural pursuits means clubs, committee meetings at the church, maybe. God forbid, wine and cheese parties, coffee mornings, and almost certainly dinner parties to show off the wonders of your house. Not likely. She had many acquaintances, few friends, but such as there were provoking passionate loyalty and the desire to entertain in the full knowledge of their tolerance of burned food. The same was true of Bailey: they lacked the herd instinct. She swore to herself. Guilty side up today: first William Featherstone, and then this wild resentment when some half-kindhearted soul tried to bully her into joining his club. Was she a self-protective freak or simply unclubbable, revelling in anonymity, missing her own city? Helen had a sudden and sharp yearning to escape, forgot the weekend's freedoms, wanted out and home to London, planned it quickly and furiously as she drove to the modern old-style house she could not call home. Later this week I'm off, not for good, mind, but off to the smoke for a day out. With or without you, Bailey,

I'm going home. After I've had a look in court at the evidence you've gathered. Then I'll certainly need to escape for a bit.

She did not know why she wanted to watch the committal, but the desire to do so had been strong from the beginning, growing in proportion to Bailey's reticence on the whole subject of the murder and escalating sharply after she had seen the evidence. She could not remember when this current cycle of silence and countersilence had begun to feed her professional curiosity. Perhaps her own action in recommending a solicitor for Sumner had made Bailey distrust her, but she doubted it; he was far too fair for that. Somewhere along the line, his own doubt had touched him with obdurate reserve, had filled her with angry questions, and she was going to watch these preliminary proceedings to see the evidence in focus. Besides, she would one day return to the prosecution of murder and mayhem, and in case that day was far off, she was not going to lose her knowledge or any opportunity to test her judgement in the meantime.

She was better acquainted with the facts than other watchers at the back of another court in the same dreadful building, ghouls drawn by stories of blood, a local murder from a few miles down the road: would you believe we picnicked there once? Helen did not misunderstand the interest as she saw the ravens and the pressmen gather, felt it herself, this indignant, not always pleasant curiosity following violent death. Respectable blood, not a vendetta knife in the ribs or a drunken brawl resulting in death or domestic fury run riot with kitchen tools, all close enough to London to make them ten a penny. This was *crime passionnel*, illicit passion at that. That her own interest was less prurient did not stop Helen from feeling relieved by Bailey's absence from the court. She knew he was allowing Amanda Scott to assume the role of managing officer for the day, had come to consider he was bored with the whole thing and slightly ashamed of it. A purely academic worry was running riot on this score: she had seen before the catastrophic effect on a case of an officer who had simply lost interest. Murder deserved better. Notebook in hand, making herself insignificant in the corner by the door in case Redwood should turn in his opening speech and include them all in his wide-angled view. She was not attempting to hide, but she felt like a trespasser and knew that was exactly how both he and Bailey might regard her presence. Spying on Bailey's handiwork, looking for some clue to his view of the world, seeking a perspective to show Sumner was innocent because she preferred to think that he was. They might have perceived it that way. Helen saw it as keeping her hand in.

Evidence recited out loud – marshalled into order, read like a story illustrated by faces and presented in court – was a different matter from evidence read in a book. To a casual reader it was not the same book; the overtones were familiar, but the style was different: level voices and the occasional inflection of emphasis or surprise, made as undramatic as possible – no emotion, gentlemen, please – by this quiet courtroom and these calm adversaries who brought it alive at the same time with their grave and silly gestures. My learned friend insists. I beg to differ. If my learned friend wishes, he may interrupt, but with all respect to my colleague for the defence, this is the way it is, brother.

You might have the last speech, but I have the first. One defendant in dock, stripped of authority, almost of humanity, guarded on either side against escape. Poor frustrated Sumner. Bet he wished he never set eyes on womankind. Helen still could not see the murderer in him; could see no capacity for deadly violence in those thin shoulders even while she knew that that potential lurked in almost every soul alive. She watched Christine Summerfield sitting two rows ahead of her, wished she was close enough to touch, even offer the comfort she knew would be rejected. All the world's a stage and all the men and women merely players. Act One, curtain up, amateur thespians delivering expressionless lines, preliminary to final conclusion: sentence to death – sorry, life. Curtain down weeks or months hence. That was exactly what it looked like. Idly she drew her small pad towards her, pencilled a rough sketch of Harmoner and next to it, a cartoon of a guinea pig in a suit.

She knew by experience and instinct that the issues would be all about that knife. While she listened, she sketched, ever so economically, figures for the voices she heard. Come on, Dr Vanguard, I have had you described to me and we have met before. Do your stuff and tell us what you found. The doctor sounded shambly and tweedy with a compost-rich voice. Helen drew him as a gardener.

'The body was found in a small clearing among shrubs,' Vanguard said. 'There had been partial clearance of the soil before my arrival, revealing part of the head, shoulder, and right arm. The right hand had been eaten by predators and the head was infested with maggots, which appeared to be at the first stage, first instar. I proceeded to dig the body out of the ground, collecting soil samples in the process. My external examination revealed a well-nourished woman five feet four inches in height. The face was not identifiable because of decomposition. In the area of the neck there were two stab wounds on the left side. The top wound was one and a half inches, a lateral wound and the larger of the two, while the wound beneath was one inch, just above the thoracic inlet. On removal of the hair it was noted that there was discoloration beneath the front hairline with extensive bruising. There was also a laceration of the skin at the same point. There was similar impact bruising on the left shoulder . . .'

And so on. Blows to head and shoulder with a blunt instrument, but the cause of death was the stab wounds to the neck. So far so good: ponderous, mildly said, and dreadful. Then the questions.

Harmoner lumbered to his feet to cross-examine. 'You say, Dr Vanguard, that the stab wounds on the deceased were compatible with having been caused by a single-edge weapon, such as a knife? Indeed. Not the same weapon, if weapon it was, which inflicted the bruises and lacerations to the head?'

'I don't know. He could have used the knife handle as a club, I suppose, but the head injuries were blows, not cuts. There is a very obvious difference, you see.'

'I do see. Look at exhibit one. This walking stick. Could this have caused the bruising?'

'Certainly, yes, any stick, any blunt thing like this wielded with force.'

'Look at photo six.' Shuffling with usher and one glaring picture passed hands, described as showing two gaping wounds to a brown neck.

'How can you say these were done with a knife, specifically, a single-edged knife?' Harmoner asked.

'Ah. I conclude that from the wounds themselves. There is a single-pointed edge at one end of each wound. You can see it particularly clearly on the upper wound. In my experience the wounds have characteristics compatible with the knife used. The skin is lax, due to decomposition, giving them a gaping appearance, but it would have been a close incision, would have looked more like a slit . . . No, I cannot possibly estimate the sharpness of the blade.'

'I am still confused, Dr Vanguard.'

'All right, I'll show you. See, the upper edges of the wound have some irregularities; the lower edges do not. The irregularities are similar. Thus a single-edge blade, not a stiletto, was used for both cuts. The sharp side causes a smooth line; the blunt side makes the other lip irregular, see?' Silence. 'A serviceable kind of knife. Single-edge knives are commonly used. You don't keep daggers, which would cut your fingers. A kitchen knife, if sharp enough, could have made these cuts. More likely a hunting knife, fishing knife, some such thing.' Silence again.

'My client does not have such a knife, Dr Vanguard. Never did.' A loud statement from Harmoner.

'I cannot comment on that,' said the doctor, clearly irritated by a question asked only for effect. 'You know I cannot comment. I did not know the man. I am only a witness to a body.'

Redwood protested about the futile and misleading question, his intervention also only a matter of form. Helen sighed. What a charade. If Antony Sumner's stick

139

had inflicted the head abrasion, a fact that was already clearly established, then no one was going to believe he had stopped there. Even she found the rest of the story inevitable; so would the bench. The judge would commit him for trial and the jury would commit him to another prison. And then and then . . . She looked at her pad, found she had sketched the back of his shoulders, all she could see of him. She had caught in the lines the slump of a man quite defeated, beyond utterance of protest, rumpled despite the fine head of wavy hair. As she looked, she heard the sharp intake of breath from the seat to the left of her own, sensed eyes turned sharply away from her notebook.

She had been engrossed in the evidence, watching as she always did the style of its unfolding, admiring the dance involved. So absorbed she had failed to notice the small form that had curled itself neatly into the seat beside hers on the very edge of the public gallery, a latecomer, sitting still until the image on Helen's page had disturbed her composure. At the same time, Amanda Scott, turning in her seat to stretch her legs, took in the spectacle of the two of them at the back, visibly startled, making Helen prickle with guilty resentment until she realized that the surprise might not have been reserved for her. She turned and looked towards the creature crouched alongside her, conspicuous in her desire to appear otherwise, with her long dark hair curtaining her face, slouched forward, so obviously not raising her head. Visible beneath the hair was one bright earring, paste and mock marquisite, at odds with the clean jeans and dark sweater, worn like a good luck charm. Assisted by Amanda Scott's look of surprise

140

and by her own memory of a face once pointed out to her, Helen recognized Evelyn Blundell.

There was palpable shock in the recognition, a tactile feeling of horror, no more or less than outrage at the thought of a teenager listening to grim particulars of fatal wounds to her mother's neck, glimpsing the colour of blood on the hideous photographs even from here. In one swift shaft of thought, Helen doubted if the deceased, let alone a single one of the living, would have approved. She was filled with a tidal wave of disgust. A child it was, a child, listening to this. She grabbed the girl's arm, leaned toward her, and whispered into the brightly decorated ear, injecting authority into a voice that might otherwise have shaken. 'Come on, sweetheart, out of here. We're off.'

'No.' A disembodied whisper, not revealing a mouth.

'Oh, yes,' said Helen, intensifying her grip on the arm, rising and pushing simultaneously. 'Move.' With Evelyn in mute protest, the two shuffled out through the door like a pair of conspirators. Amanda Scott had risen, sat down again.

'It is Evelyn, isn't it?' Outside, releasing the arm, Helen was confirming what she knew.

'What's it to you if I am? You've no bloody right . . . I'm going back in. I want to hear what he did. All of it, what he did.'

'I don't care what you want. You're staying outside.'

'No, I won't, I won't . . .' The intensity of their voices attracted attention even in a half-full vestibule well used to intense conversations.

'Look,' said Helen evenly, 'you may as well give in. You're staying outside that courtroom whether you like it

141

or not and whether I've got the bloody right to move you or not. I bet your dad doesn't know you're here, does he?' A slow head shake, uncertain, the suggestion of a slight smile at Helen's use of the word 'bloody', a reversion of the face to a sulk. 'Oh, come on,' said Helen, 'I'll buy you coffee. A drink. Anything you want. How about Bario's in Branston? They serve coffee with too much cream and chocolate.' Instinct told her a bribe might work, especially if the bribe was a visit to a place from which teenagers were usually barred. Without waiting for a response, Helen touched the girl on the arm, waiting for her to follow. Evelyn shrugged and obeyed.

If the short drive was far from amiable, at least hostilities ceased. All Helen established was Evelyn's age, and the fact she was at school. She was grateful for the fact that Bario's, despite its recent attempts to augment luncheon trade by serving elegant coffee, was almost deserted at eleven-thirty, sensed that the girl was similarly relieved.

'My dad sometimes comes in here,' Evelyn muttered.

'Did you think you would get in and out of court this morning without him knowing?' Helen asked gently.

'Yes,' said Evelyn through gritted teeth. 'But now you'll tell him, I suppose. Whoever you are.'

'No, I won't, but someone will.'

'Who are you anyway?' The tone was more conversational. Helen looked at this old young face with its fine intelligence and steely eyes, decided against either secrecy or condescension. 'I'm a solicitor,' she replied carefully. 'I know you from living here with Superintendent Bailey. He's investigating your mother's death. You've met him, I think.'

A look of alarm crossed the smooth face and was dusted away with a flick of the head.

'But I don't have anything official to do with the case,' Helen added quickly. 'I just couldn't bear to have you sit and watch it. Here, drink your coffee.'

She was amused to watch how this self-possessed creature responded like a child when faced with a mountain of whipped cream sprinkled with chocolate, spooning it into her mouth with slow and concentrated enjoyment, delicately eking it out to the last, disappointed to find nothing but bitter liquid beneath it, not so sophisticated after all. The process took five almost comfortable minutes. 'You don't have to drink the coffee,' Helen reminded her quietly. 'The cream's the best bit. Want some more?'

'OK,' and the ice was broken.

Evelyn pushed her hair behind her ears, leaned her elbows on the tablecloth, looked at Helen squarely, and half smiled, not quite inviting questions, but at least resigned.

'Why did you want to listen?'

'I thought I ought to know. I don't think that was bad. Besides, my mother's dead. It can't make any difference to her what I know or don't, and I like forensic details. Pathology, anatomy, bones, all that stuff. I want to be a doctor. Or a writer, maybe. I've read about these things.'

'Do you read a lot?'

'Yes, of course. All the time. You have to if you want to learn things. Especially if you know more than your teachers.' Her expression added, You also have to reply to a lot of silly questions like these.

Helen was puzzled. Something was out of kilter, not

merely the garish earrings, which struck an elusive chord of recognition in her mind. There was something else quite apart, a fact from her reading of the Sumner case, some part of his statement clearly recalled, which now seemed unlikely.

'I take it you're very good at school? I expect you are.'

'Yes, very good. They keep wanting me to stay down, but I'm far too clever. Teachers make me sick. My father should have paid for a better school. Better for science, I mean. He wouldn't, though. Mummy said it wasn't worth it. He probably couldn't afford it after all Mummy's clothes.' There was an overtone of profound if well-controlled resentment.

'And Mr Sumner? Why did he come and teach you out of school?'

The regard was suddenly very wary, then far too non-chalant. 'Oh, I asked if he could. My English isn't as good as the rest, you see, and I wanted to take the exam a year early, to get it out of the way.'

For a child so articulate, Helen found this unconvincing, but refrained from saying so. She was getting close to the limit of acceptable questions, but refused to resist the temptation to ask more. 'Did you like Mr Sumner?' she asked, but the child was uncomfortable.

'Like him?' she said loudly, voice full of infantile scorn. 'Like him? No, of course not. He's a teacher, isn't he?'

Evelyn bent her head to the cream of the second coffee, leaving Helen to wonder why a girl of fourteen, presumably with better things to do, should ask for extra tuition in a subject where she was highly unlikely to need it. She recalled in her own misspent teenage years avoiding

144

official study like the plague, and remembered with sudden clarity her crush on a history master in the dim days of school. An hour alone with him would have been like an offer of paradise. Perhaps Evelyn had suffered the same, persuaded her parents into a course that offered contact with the beloved. An idle thought. She turned and looked out of the window. 'You can see the whole world pass by from here,' she remarked cheerfully, sensing she would receive precious little more response from the girl. 'Look at all these familiar faces.' Adding calmly, 'Your father is coming up the street, Evelyn. I should duck unless you want him to see you.'

The child leaned back, pulled Bario's pink curtain in front of her face, smiled at Helen in sudden appreciation. John Blundell passed into his office two doors down.

'All clear,' said Helen, and Evelyn released the curtain. One dislodged earring landed on the cloth. 'Yours,' Helen uttered as she proffered it back, turning again to face the view outside in order to hide the deliberately blank look on her face, forming one more question she knew would be the last. 'You do like jewellery, don't you?'

Evelyn was clipping the orb back on to her ear. 'Not this stuff, not really. I like the better stuff, but I have to wear this in case . . . Well, never mind. I quite like it, really.' Fastening it back with fingers made clumsy by her distaste.

'Yes, I think I know what you mean,' Helen ventured. 'We sometimes have to wear things people give us. Just to please them.' In her mind's eye was the drawing of Mrs Blundell's missing jewellery, purloined from Evelyn's father, jewellery so different from Evelyn's own the pieces she had seen yesterday, glittering on the desk, exhibits in the short case against William Featherstone. Evelyn was regarding her with a look of fathomless suspicion. 'Oh, yes,' Helen continued artlessly, 'you can see the whole population from here.'

Evelyn accepted the distraction, looked outside. 'Nobody's got any time. They never stop painting their bloody houses, buying bigger cars, and having breakdowns. I hate it here,' she said suddenly and vehemently with a force recognizable as something more than childish pique.

'So do I,' said Helen.

There was a full minute's awkward pause.

Evelyn fidgeted, eager to move on. Home, then, to their no doubt empty houses.

Helen paid the bill. 'Where now?' she asked by way of farewell as they stepped into the street.

'Don't know. Lunch, I expect,' Evelyn replied, eyes fixed forward, secretive again, anxious to be gone.

'Not back on the bus to court?'

'No.' A brief smile, two retreating steps, a new anxiety as she turned on her heel and marched away. A definite, hurried walk, hands in hip pockets, lovely lithe figure that would have been the envy of a mature woman in its immature perfection, still childish nevertheless. On impulse, Helen stood in the next shop doorway, watching Evelyn's progress, partly to see if her anxiety would force her to break into a run, partly to make sure she did not board the Waltham-bound bus, which had pulled into the stop a few yards beyond on the green. As Helen watched, William Featherstone jumped from the exit doors of the bus, bounding toward Evelyn, his face, even from Helen's distant view, alight with his best delirious smile, fading as the girl strode past him, a quick cut of her hand forbidding recognition, moving faster and out of sight. He started towards her, took two steps in her direction, pulled himself up short, and stopped with the guilty embarrassment of one who has remembered some broken code of manners, looking around to see if his infringement was noticed. Then he resumed his grin and crossed the road with studied carelessness, hands in pockets, copying the way Evelyn had walked but with none of her authority. Poacher's pockets, thought Helen: and you know that girl as well as she knows you. William Featherstone, what is your business with Evelyn Blundell and her earrings?

Then the next thought: tell Bailey. Back to the instinct to tell Bailey all the odd details of her day. If he would listen, that was. If he did not choose to listen these days to the neater and far more relevant conclusions of his pretty detective constable. If he didn't say, 'Helen, my dear, just because she has lost her mother does not mean I am entitled to cross-examine all members of the family about all the aspects of their lives.'

Helen went home, looking at her feet, faintly ashamed of spying. I must learn, she told herself, to trust nothing but evidence. Learn to do as Branston does: go home and shut the doors. Stop looking in people's windows. They do not like snooping. It is not the way of a community bent on privacy. This village togetherness hides a sad apartness. Go home, Helen West. Go home and close the door.

Chapter Eight

God, what a poxy afternoon, Amanda silently complained, dreadful day from eight-thirty a.m. until now. What the hell had Bailey been doing all day, leaving her with all the legwork and, as it happened, a fair bit of humiliation thrown in? Perhaps he had calculated that last bit with the Featherstones. Amanda Scott pressed the horn on her car, tried to overtake a truck, realized her own dangerous speed, pulled back, and swore. She only swore in private, found it therapeutic but considered it disgraceful in public. The rage was dying, but she remained angry until she pulled into the forecourt of her block of flats in Woodford, where some sort of reconciliation with the world occurred as she parked the car. Come on, patting her hair in the mirror in an automatic gesture, it wasn't all bad: you might have found an opportunity today. But to be virtually chased out-of-doors by mad Harold Featherstone, behaving and appearing like a caveman, was humiliation indeed. On top of that last labour of the afternoon, she had found

Bailey still absent from the office at five, unobtainable anywhere by phone for her to recount how comprehensively she had fulfilled orders and what a good girl she had been. Amanda needed support, needed him to listen to her achievements, and besides which knew very well that it was imperative for an officer as ambitious as she to have her efficiency on record. She would have to telephone him at home, and if she had earlier been of two minds about whether to tell the dear superintendent or nice Mr Redwood about Bailey's girlfriend bringing Evelyn Blundell into court, she certainly wasn't going to keep her mouth shut now.

Good: lipstick still intact. She smiled at herself in the gleaming window of her car as she locked the door, resigned now to her day's work and the prospect of an evening's wallpapering. Amanda spent half of her spare time in the beautification of her small maisonette. But maybe as a result of her afternoon, she might get lucky with a bigger, better flat. Or luckier still with a rich widower. She'd always known she was not designed for some fellow detective constable with a beer belly and long working hours. A lonely widower with a very large income would be good enough for starters. Chance would be a fine thing. The furore of the Featherstones passed from her mind. So did the fact that she had achieved none of her goals in either of the two households she had visited, omissions easily forgotten in the search for self-justification. Exhaustion, irritation, and conspicuous devotion to duty deserved their own reward.

No, it had not, after all, been such a bad day, Amanda reflected over the soapsuds of her three breakfast dishes

– bowl for museli, cup and saucer for decaffeinated coffee – must look after the health. She had been the one in charge of the committal proceedings, subject of thanks from Harmoner, 'for favouring us with your presence, my dear.' Ya, ya, ya, nice to hear, but nothing he could say was going to enhance her promotion prospects. Better to impress Redwood, and even that was scarcely worthwhile. She did not consider it kind of Bailey to let her take the accolades for his immaculate preparation, suspected he had only done so to give himself a free morning after, and he had obviously taken the afternoon as well. Amanda had a suspicious mind. He was up to something. So what? The man wasn't married, after all. She wondered if his girlfriend knew. She had thought what a good-looking man Bailey was, had thought . . . Well never mind what she thought eight months ago. She closed the subject and put away her tea towel. She didn't think it now; ambition had moved on. So the committal was fine, no problem there. One murderer, fey-looking bastard *en route* to the crown court, quite handsome in a way, and everything hunky-dory, with the prosecution smelling of roses and the police, too, for wrapping it up so quickly. Then the rest of the day's impossible orders issued with a smile, while Bailey had the nerve to imagine that she did not realize he found her neither particularly likeable nor attractive. He was bound to prefer that little woman of his, 'a solicitor you might know'. Although Amanda did not regard police officers of any age as suitable for mating purposes – and Bailey was a bit old, let's face it – she was still mildly insulted by his preference for a bit of social status as well as the sort of casual elegance Helen West managed so easily and she herself could never achieve. You and I came from the same stable, Bailey boy. Stop pretending you didn't. She put the dishes back in the cupboard, looked at her neat kitchen with mixed satisfaction and discontent, admiring its shiny surfaces, stirred by the resentment when she thought of the splendour of J. Blundell's mansion. Come now, Amanda, you should be moving forward in life. You've come a long way in twenty-six years, but you should be further forward than this.

From Waltham Court, she had driven to Blundell's house. 'Call on the man,' Bailey had said, gauging to the minute how long the court proceedings would last. 'He goes home for lunch. Tell him what happened at court, be concerned. But most important of all, find some way to search the house. We've done it after a fashion, but not that thoroughly.'

'Couldn't PC Bowles do that?' she had asked, meaning quite plainly, I'm a detective, sir, not a trooper.

'Yes, he could. But Blundell understandably wouldn't like a few plods rummaging all over his house. He won't mind you. I want a thorough search for that jewellery. Explain to him the formality: tell him we have to eliminate the very remote possibility of her having hidden it in the house, dropped it, whatever, even if he did see her wearing it just before she went out.'

'Don't you believe him?'

'Yes, as far as he thinks he saw it.' Amanda felt a frisson of excitement. 'We don't know if she came back before meeting Sumner. Or whether Blundell was drunk or vague. But I want you to have a look in his room, and the daughter's. A good look in the daughter's. Doesn't matter why. It's important. Oh, and ask after the child. Find out what she does with herself. She's been given appointments with a kind of counsellor, but she never shows up. Don't tell him that, but try to find out why. Use your charm.'

Go and wow Mr John Blundell, in other words. Waste an hour of a sunny afternoon poking around his house looking for jewellery Sumner had clearly sold weeks since. Piss off. Then go and see the Featherstones – gently, mind – and ask them what their son does nights and days. What's that got to do with anything? Amanda asked silently. I'm on the murder squad, not the small-fire-and-two-bit-shoplifter squad. Leave those jobs to uniforms. Not out loud, no point in complaining. Close as a clam, Mr Handsome Bailey, good at delegating work, but not ideas. Dislike was becoming reciprocal. She only accepted the afternoon's dumb-fool assignments for the opportunity of a gander at Blundell's house. Dream house; she wanted it. Or if not that, something comparable. She deserved it.

Detective Scott had found the grieving widower in the kitchen at two o'clock eating a sandwich and drinking a beer, been greeted with enthusiasm, explained her mission prettily, and noticed that he looked a trifle lonely. Talking through the morning's progress, she managed to make Sumner's continued imprisonment sound like a triumph rather than the elaborate formality it had been.

'Good, good,' he said absently, 'I'm so pleased,' which seemed a mild response from the bereaved, but Amanda expected that was something to do with grief. She did not know much about grief, never having suffered such a thing in her life. He was certainly responsive enough to make a cup of coffee, offer a drink, which she refused. 'Quite right,' he said, and seemed suddenly disposed to please.

'How's your daughter?' Amanda asked.

'Oh . . . out, always out. She sees her friends, goes to her aunt, back about tea time. Then studies in the evening, darling child. Good girl, very good girl.'

That would do. Amanda was not particularly disposed to ask more about the daughter, felt capable of inventing details to fill in the gaps. Then she had complimented him on his kitchen, her wide smile and white teeth hiding the savage reflection on how her own abode had the same surface area in entirety, including her share of the garden. She put warmth into her remarks and felt him come alive.

'More coffee?'

'Oh, yes, please, if you're sure you can spare the time.' Charm him, Bailey had said. Looking at this kitchen, Amanda would have whored for him. He was smiling like an angel, quite bearable to look at, and patently well heeled.

'Where do you live, Miss Scott?'

'Oh, call me Amanda. I live in Woodford, actually.' Smoothing the skirt and patting the hair while his back was turned. 'Only a little flat,' belittling her pride and joy with a wave of the wrist. 'I bought it from you, as it happens. Your Woodford agency.'

'Really? What a coincidence. When was that?' Animated chat on what was sold when and where in their own six square miles, why it was sold and for how much. They were rolling on common ground. Both were fascinated by space and prices and value for money and floors and ceilings, he globally, she personally but with the same passion. They revelled in the respective merits of pitch or

pine, sloped roofs or flat, whether the entrance was important. Enjoying herself hugely, she only just remembered to
ease in the proposition about searching the house in which
she was receiving such benign hospitality.

He moved the subject aside adroitly like a bill postponed to another day. 'Oh, no, not yet . . . Must say,
excellent commercial mind you have, Amanda. Ever
thought of taking up estate agency? You'd be marvellous.'

'Do you think so? I've always been interested.'
Flattered, she slid down the tangent, only resurrecting the
searching-for-jewellery business ten minutes later.

'What for?' he asked, puzzled.

'For Mr Bailey.' She withdrew herself carefully from
blame for the intrusion. 'He thinks we might have missed
it somewhere. Have to make absolutely sure it isn't here.
You know, tucked in a drawer in your room, your daughter's room, one of the spare rooms. Or in a coat pocket or
something. You know.'

He did know, turned away to refill the kettle and reach
for a bottle of white wine from the fridge. She was bound
to like white wine, not a whisky lady. Just a glass, come on,
Amanda, won't do you any harm. What she would not like,
nor would he, to ruin this budding relationship, was the
sight of the bareness of his daughter's room. Pretty stingy
furniture in there, disgraceful, really, when he came to
think of it, rotten old desk, very small cupboard and child's
bed. Yvonne had always said that was enough for her, and
after a while Evie had stopped asking for anything else. It
shamed him, the poverty of it. Much less would sweet
Amanda like to see, or he to show her, the rows of clothes
hidden by wardrobe doors in his own room. There were

154

things he might have liked to do with Miss Scott in that room, but they did not include a search of coat pockets. There was not a single item of the dear deceased's clothing that was not torn to shreds. He was beginning to wonder how he was going to get the garments out of the house.

'Now listen, Amanda.' Placing a hand on hers, noting the lack of resistance. 'Why don't you tell Mr Bailey you've been through the place with a fine-tooth comb? Because I have, I can assure you, and you'd never find anything I'd missed. Turned over everything, I did. But fussy, your boss, is he?' She nodded vigorously, tut-tutting at his criticism, but smiling compliance.

'That's OK, then. What I was wondering . . . well, never mind. Presumptous of me . . . I shouldn't.'

'Go on,' said Amanda.

'Well, I was wondering . . . It's nothing, really, but I do like to help. I'm sure we could find you a better flat than you have, you know, a good little bargain. In Branston, maybe, I always hear about them, always know when to pick 'em up, if you see what I mean. Interested? Nice girl like you, kind to an old man. Girl like you deserves to get on.'

Amanda's thoughts exactly. The rout of her distraction was complete and she beamed goodwill.

'Not at all, my dear, and do call me John. It's a pleasure to help someone I like, not all these toffee-nosed solicitors, city people, think they're the bee's knees.' A quick stroke of brilliance, stroking the chip on Amanda's shoulder. 'Tell you what. Perhaps when I've marshalled a few ideas we could have dinner and chat about it when you're not on duty. Ever tried Bario's?'

O brave new world: she had never been to Bario's, had dreamed of living among the select trees of Branston instead of in the service area of Woodford.

'I know a chap who does a wonderful line in discount furniture, too,' John continued, and they were off again, all thoughts of searching the house shoved downwind of his after-shave, her perfume, and the riveting discussion of bargains.

Amanda Scott left the Blundell house well pleased, sober on one glass of wine and three coffees, high as a kite otherwise, a tentative date with a rich widower and a plausible account for Bailey bubbling in the back of her mind.

J. Blundell made for the whisky and forgot his office once he closed the door on her, equally pleased.

Then Amanda made for The Crown and a rapid descent to earth.

'Yes? What the hell do you want? Oh, I know you. Old Mr Bailey's sweetheart, isn't it? The unofficial one. Dear God, have you only got one suit?' Bernadette Featherstone smirked in satisfaction, quick eyes recognizing the same navy blue suit at the kitchen door she had seen weeks since, and only briefly then.

'Hello, Mrs Featherstone, sorry to trouble you.' The pleasantry was like an armour. 'Superintendent Bailey asked me to call and ask you—'

'Don't hello me. There's no bloody need. And I'm busy.'

What a contrast of kitchens. Bernadette's kitchen was invisible to the downcast clients clinging to the bar outside and waiting for evening company, abused by Harold or ignored. It was as large as the Blundells', but twice as antiquated, extremely dirty, and currently full of the smell of

156

baking bread and washing. Amanda, who had an eye for domestic detail, wondered how Bernadette could take such obvious trouble to make her sheets that dusty grey. She also wondered if the smell of the bread was going to be the only enticing quality about it. The washing machine in the corner was churning suspicious suds. Both of them were shouting above the noise; Bernadette was used to shouting, but it was awkward for Amanda.

'Oh, for God's sake, sit down. Stop gawking like a tourist at a monument. What do you want, and where's your bloody leader? Lets you out on your own, does he? In my opinion, policemen should be blokes.' Bernadette cackled. Flattery was obviously not today's menu. 'Have you come about William?'

'Well, yes, in a way.'

'What do you mean, "in a way"? Harold!' she yelled to no response. Bernadette picked up a cloth, dried dishes quickly and absently. 'Get on with it, then.'

'Well, Mrs Featherstone—'

'You're a bit worried about William, I expect,' Bernadette interrupted. 'Nicking from shops, little sod. Don't know why he did it. But you needn't worry. Harold's going to give him seven pounds a week, and we'll be keeping him busy. We've solved the problem.'

'It wasn't so much the stealing, Mrs Featherstone.'

'Well, what then, woman? You suspect him of rape or something?' Another snort of laughter while Bernadette lit a cigarette, her instinct well informed enough to realize how much it would irritate while at the same time hiding her own jangled nerves behind the smoke. She had censured William as gently as she knew. He had erupted; she

157

had withdrawn. He was beyond her control, but it was their battle, their very own, not for anyone else. She might have trusted Bailey with the worry of it, but not this peaches-and-cream piece of neatness who could go and boil her head for all Bernadette cared.

Amanda Scott could sense she was being intrusive. Even she could sense Bernadette's controlled rage, and she wondered if the reputed fits of William Featherstone were really an inherited mental deformity from a mother whose secret pastime was foaming at the mouth.

Bernadette was smoking at the mouth, deliberately exhaling a ragged cloud in Amanda's direction. Amanda opted for the businesslike approach. Keep this as short as possible.

'What does William do with his time, Mrs Featherstone?' The snappiness of her tone brought silence, followed by reluctant cooperation.

'Do with his time? I don't know. He's a grown man now. Everyone knows what he does with his time. I told Mr Bailey ages ago. He loves the buses. He goes shopping. London sometimes, Epping, Stratford, Waltham . . . well, you know about Waltham. That's where you booked him. And . . .' She scratched her head and thought. 'Oh, and he sits in his room thinking about things. And I don't know what else. Apart from making things. Jewellery, as it happens.' Nothing else to be proud about.

She pulled open the drawer in the scrubbed kitchen table, a drawer full of assorted rubbish: tap washers, screwdrivers, receipts, fuse wire, wadded-up paper and half-finished candy packets. The kind of drawer Amanda Scott itched to clear.

'Here,' Bernadette said triumphantly. 'See what I mean?' There was a rough bracelet in her hand, upheld for examination with something like pride. 'Fuse wire and glass, baked in the oven,' she said fondly. 'Don't know how he thinks of it, really I don't.'

Neither did Amanda. There was a kind of primitivism in William's artistic efforts. Silver wire or fuse wire twisted, with small pieces of glass embedded in the twists, all melted to an uneven, unusual shine of colours, like crude enamel, the wire imperfectly smoothed by insufficient heat, the glass still uneven although no longer sharp. Rather uncomfortable Amanda thought. It might look strangely at home in some trendy fashion shop for punks where it could double up as an offensive weapon, but not on her own wrist or that of anyone she knew.

'He didn't like this one,' Bernadette remarked. 'Said it was dull. I don't think so.'

To Amanda the thing was distastefully bright; she did not like handling it, took it politely, put it down on the table with obvious distaste. 'What else does he do?'

'What else should he do? This stuff takes him hours.'

'Does he play any sport?'

'No.'

'Any other hobbies?'

'No.'

'Girlfriend?'

A very brief hesitation while Bernadette bent to scratch her foot. 'No.'

'Any friends?'

'No.'

'Does he work at all?'

'Not officially, no.' It was like a litany of negatives from which William emerged as blank as sky. The telling of it filled Bernadette with guilt.

'Well, what does he do in the evenings?' Amanda asked.

Mrs Featherstone rose in fury. 'Sits in the kitchen, sits in the garden, hangs around. Even talks sometimes. Helps me. Sits in his room and wanks, probably. Maybe he dreams of you, Miss fucking Scott. Harold!' she bawled again in the direction of the bar. 'Come here.'

There was a moment's silence, a heavy footfall, and Amanda felt the first trace of alarm. She was not proofed for insult from shabby, crabby Bernadette. She rose to her feet tight-lipped, Bailey's words in her ears: 'Always give up an interview if it seems entirely counterproductive. If they won't tell you, they won't. Wait for another time.' Amanda was content to wait for ever and to get out while the going was merely bad, preferably before the footfalls reached her vulnerable back. She moved, too late and too awkwardly.

'Ah,' said Harold behind her neck. 'It's Mr Bailey's moll. The pretty policeman. How are you, Moll?' And before she could turn, he wrapped his large, thick arms around her waist, wrists locked in embrace, his mouth in her ear. 'How are you, Moll?' he repeated softly, danger-ously, but laughing, his breath whisky-laden, his skin damp and stale. 'Leave off our boy, Moll. Or we'll set him on you.'

She pulled at the wrists in sickening panic, tearing them apart, grabbed her bag, crashed against the table *en route* to the open back door. William's jewellery fell to the floor; she heard it clatter on the broken quarry tiles, and for a

160

reason she did not fathom she bent and recovered the bracelet, slipped it into her bag as she ran for the daylight, slowed herself to a galloping walk, remembering dignity too late. Soon enough to turn and smile back sweetly, more for her own sake than theirs. 'You've been very helpful. Thank you.' Sarcasm in each syllable, hating the last glimpse of two laughing faces. Rubbing her neck where Harold had touched her, feeling diseased. Uncharacteristically close to tears, pushing through bushes, she walked downhill on a slippery path, spitting into the shrubs at the side like an angry cat. Then stood still, momentarily lost in the garden.

The straightest route to the car was the way she had come, through the kitchen, the bar, and the front door, but she could no more re-enter that furnace than she could fly over the moon. She paused, looking and listening. No choices as she drew breath and calmed herself. Walk to the bottom of this dark, disgusting garden, get through to the field somehow, walk back up the side of it to the road and the front of the pub. In common with most of her fellow émigrés to these country zones, Amanda believed in sanitized country life, disliked muddy shoes, brambles, and the slime of ill-controlled nature. The shrubs visible at the end of the path over a fallen tree held little appeal for exploration, but torn tights and a pulled skirt were infinitely preferable to the alternatives. Swearing silently, she persisted down the path, branches spitefully teasing her face, and came on the summerhouse by surprise, and stopped.

Christ. The shed was as mad as the couple in the hotel. No doubt a Featherstone project, with that drunken look, half done and then abandoned, like the kitchen. She was not interested or even disposed to look – the whole family could roast in hell, the sooner the better – but in passing silently she peeped into one of the windows, frightened but drawn. Through the damp grime on the glass, she could see a dim light, hear sounds of hammering subdued by earth as if coming from a great distance. From a hole in the floor, momentarily blocking the light, a head and bare shoulders, pale in the glow, rose away from her. Perhaps a Featherstone, perhaps an intruder, perhaps big William tunnelling out of the ground like a giant slug. Amanda could imagine white-skinned William, vacuous image of his father, an undressed grinning version of the lout she had met in court, but naked and rampant, lumbering towards her, a vision that was entirely in her mind, since only his back was visible; while she watched he remained terrifyingly still. She ran from the window, pushed through the shrubs, climbed a fence into the barleyfield, and thrashed her way uphill to the safety of her car. She drove well beyond view of The Crown before stopping, dusting down her muddy skirt, cleaning her shoes with tissue and grass, no longer trembling, feeling utterly foolish and simply angry.

Remembering now, looking at the mud on her skirt, Amanda decided on a weak gin and tonic, normally reserved for guests, to make it look as if she tried. The problem with the mortgage race was that it left over so little money for self-indulgence of this or any kind. She drank in tiny sips with relish, forgetting the humiliation as she crunched the ice. She had to get on, whatever it cost, and never mind the drawbacks. A job was a job and this was a good job, a passport. Featherstones or not. She had come a long way from the back streets of North London, and she was not going back. And as for her visit to The Crown, she would tell Bailey all she had learned about William, but not quite how the learning had happened.

'You did well, girl. Really you did. Saw her off nicely. I was listening at you, you know, before I added my three penn'orth.'

Bernadette was lighting the fortieth cigarette of the day. 'Thought you might be,' she said. 'Harold, what are we going to do?'

She put her head in her arms briefly. He moved to her side of the kitchen table, hugged her quickly. Harold was sober and trade was dead at ten o'clock. Amanda Scott's afternoon visit had raised a brief laugh, but dispelled the taste for whisky.

'What are we going to do, Harold?' she repeated.

He slumped into the chair beside her, hating emotional scenes of the noncombative kind as much as he hated responsibility, suspecting most of the fighting was the result of his evasion of his duty.

'Do about what? The pub?'

'Oh, Harold, face up for once. Never mind the bloody pub. I mean William. Our son, William. I don't even know where he is.' She had a fair idea he might have been somewhere at the other end of the garden, and she was relying on the end of summer to bring him back, but even in this extremity she was not going to say. She knew Harold's limitations as well as his temper, felt she had betrayed William enough already for one day – she had even lost the bracelet

163

she treasured, given her as reject gift from the pile of his creations, but still a gift.

'Well, what *can* we do?' asked Harold, mildly belligerent. 'Why should we anyway? All right, he pinched some trinkets. I've paid the fine, given him more pocket money, and that's that. He's not done anything serious.'

'Hasn't he?' asked Bernadette. 'Hasn't he, now? I wonder.'

'Like what do you wonder?' Irritation, a self-defensive and guilty anger, as well as a plea for forgiveness rose in his throat.

'Oh, I don't know, Harold. He's so empty. I keep thinking of that body in the woods, that's what I keep thinking. I don't like it, Harold. Don't know what to do.'

'There's a man in prison for the body in the woods,' Harold almost shouted. 'Stop thinking, Bernie. You're not good at it, honest you're not. And what the hell can we do anyway? If you stroke him he bites. If you pat him he scratches. Interfere now and we'll only provoke him. He's fine, Bernie, just fine. Look at him, always smiling.'

She was too tired for conflict. It was the story of her life, this incessant fatigue kept at bay by quarrelling. Better do as Harold did, simply avoid it and hope for the best.

'If he gets worse, pet, we'll take him away.'

She turned to him with mild and hopeful enquiry. 'Where, Harold? Back to London where no one would know us? Suit me fine. I'm sick of it here. It's like living with a whole load of cuckoos feathering their nest. Just like we do. If we hadn't worked so hard, and I might add for so little, we might have had a better son.'

He sighed dramatically. 'We'd be lost in London, Bernie. Wouldn't own a thing.'

'That's exactly why I'd like it, Harold. So would William.'

Harold hesitated, hating both the forward and backward trends of the conversation. 'You don't really think he's done anything more than thieving, do you, Bernie?'

'I don't know,' she said. 'I just don't know.'

Better not to know, John Blundell had decided. If he did not look in her room, which was always carefully locked – 'I must have my privacy, Daddy' – he would not know if she was there or not, could kid himself she was, hunched over some encyclopaedia or whatever it was she did. Last time he had peeked in there, when Evelyn had permitted access to the cleaning lady, he'd seen a plastic skeleton, the only adornment visible in that Spartan room, before she'd caught him looking and frozen him off with her stare. She even supervised the cleaning. He had never really wanted to know anything intimate about her, and her eccentricities made more sense in the light of her recently confessed ambitions for a medical career. Thank God Amanda Scott had been fobbed off from searching. The sight of a small plastic skeleton in the room of a female teenager struck Blundell as a worse obscenity than a naked man. As for what was in the drawers of her locked plywood desk, he had a shrewd suspicion. There was something else of value as well as a lot of paper. She loved jewellery, and he had noticed how she hid the things she loved. Up here, she was forever writing and hiding. One day he would improve on his glimpses. Not now, later.

But he cared if someone else knew. If darling child wanted to be secretive about her own bits of rubbish, and if he wanted to tear up his wife's clothes, they would do so. Family was family. They had come here to preserve family, whatever kind of shambles this one had been for years. With the careful calculation of two whiskies down, he waited until ten o'clock, dialled the number left by Amanda Scott. He knew enough about the inside of people's houses to hazard a guess at her life-style, saw her with cold cream, cocoa, and nightie, rather liked the thought. Two birds to be shot with a single stone: avoid prying eyes on the one hand and cast a lure for a new woman on the other. Not a bad prospect, Amanda. Might at least know the value of money and be grateful. Yvonne, the bitch, only liked the best.

In the Bailey-West household, peace of a kind reigned. A single phone call from Amanda Scott, bursting with the desire to report something or other, but guarded and satisfied when Bailey had said he would hear it in full tomorrow. No information given or received.

One of their neighbours was sitting on the sofa, complaining to Helen about her children. He was amazed at the picture they made, these two disparate women, even more amused when he contrasted Helen's obdurate unclubbishness with her complete inability to close the door on a visitor. No, she would not attend a meeting, be seen dead on a committee, sign a petition, but she would listen, pour a drink, and extend a welcome, unable to resist. At home in far-off London, her phone had never stopped ringing. Bailey had been irritated by it then, but found he missed it here. Listening to the neighbour, the well-meaning but harassed mother of two, despairing over the decisions made by local school authorities, he wondered at the implications of these empire-building residents of Branston, questioned whether fresh air and keeping up with the Joneses was really an improvement over life in London.

'He does so much worse than anyone else in his class,' the neighbour was saying. She was not tearful yet, simply indignant.

Stop pushing him, then, Bailey added silently to the conversation, wishing she would go. The boy is healthy. No one else is sick. What's the problem? Push, push, push, an endless spiral of improvement. Better houses, better cars and schools, all lined with the same amount of discontent. People nagging away: it's so good now; it can't possibly be good enough. We've come quite a long way, Helen; it might be time to turn back.

Bailey regarded the visiting woman with mild eyes she found slightly unnerving. He reflected that this brave-new-worlder was trapped economically in marriage, like a state-aided couple in a slum, neither with another place to go and no money to split up. The only difference was that one couple was more affluent and lived in a different cage where the padding didn't really help. There were plenty of murders in these situations, plenty of scope for them in cosy Branston. The upwardly mobile, striving for heaven, by some accident curtailing their choices rather than expanding them, leaving themselves no time to think. No time to see how the children thought, either. Would they prefer the posh schools or the concrete playground?

167

Electronic toys or cardboard boxes? He didn't know. There was no time to judge your partner. Maybe Helen had time: she did not need him in the same way he needed her.

Since his contribution to this living-room chat was not required beyond an occasional murmur, Bailey was free to think of his own day. It had been pleasant in its way, a release from supervision, reports, delegation, and listening. Superintendent Bailey trying his hand at being junior detective and legworker – that took him back a year or ten. Getting on and off buses, amazed at how arbitrary they were, how patient their passengers all around the parish, buses that stopped at two burned-out shelters and took him to Waltham and Woodford armed with a copy of William Featherstone's photo, taken on his second arrest. 'Seen this boy, have you?' he had asked, showing the unflattering image in black and white. Odd how these new Polaroids were no improvement on the old in giving every subject the appearance of a villain. 'Yes, I seen him, guv. Often, as it happens, but he usually smiles, poor kid. Been seeing him for years, but he's grown a bit.'

Bailey had been surprised to find in William's travelling acquaintances something approaching genuine affection, at worst a mild tolerance. Perhaps in calling him 'poor boy' Helen had seen something he had missed.

He turned in response to a nudge from her. 'Pardon?'

'Mrs Levinson was asking if we like it here,' said Helen.

'Oh, we like it fine,' said Bailey. 'Lovely place.' Noting with surprise how Helen had passed that awkward question to him. Perhaps the space was not so important to her after all. He noted that, recorded it with amusement and something like hope. Perhaps – an impossible thought in the face of the evidence – she loathed the place as much as he did. And akin to this, a sadder conclusion: yet another day had gone by without real conversation; the weekends of life were lost so entirely by midweek.

Helen thought, I should tell him about the committal proceedings. Then she listened to his polite praise of Branston and held her tongue.

Chapter Nine

Shops. Oxford Street filth drifting on pavements that needed rain. Judging from the sky, they were shortly to be blessed with it. Of course, no one went to Oxford Street to look at the sky. All of them looked ahead or sideways, never upward, occasionally down to see what was entangling their feet, keeping handbag in front and pockets clear. Helen was streetwise, used to standing for hours in Marlborough or Bow Street court prosecuting queues of pick-pockets, dippers in every colour with quicker fingers than Fagin's children, smiling benignly as they passed on the escalator with a wallet already gone to the one behind, netting thousands a day. She was careful in the shops, too, once versed in the Can-I-help-you? conman: urbane and immaculate on the floor of a department store otherwise devoid of helpers, assiduous in assisting with choice of scarf, jacket, tie, before offering to take those traveller's cheques, dollars, yen, Visa card, whatever you were needing change of. Take a seat, ma'am, I'll be back shortly, and you will sit here for ever if you're waiting for me. Famous characters when not in prison. Policemen patrolling this fairground of shops for the parvenues of the cheap to the merely priceless called it simply 'the Street'. The Street was dirty, shabby, crowded, and jostling, downmarket, upmarket, middle market. No one spoke English or walked in a straight line. Rudeness was customary. Pretend stolen goods as well as real were sold on pavements along with tacky souvenirs, overpriced fruit and dangerous toys. Shop assistants either crowded around customers like flies or studiously ignored them. Litter bins overflowed, and the three underground stations were frankly sinister. Bargains and impolite robbery were equally available. There was nothing essential to life or decent to eat within a mile, and there were bomb scares.

Helen loved it.

Nothing better for a shopping addict. She loved shops, full stop. Here her essentially serious nature took off into harmony with the frivolous world. Helen could not shop with any precision, a facet of her that irritated Bailey to the extent he could never accompany her on any expedition unless she set out to buy one item in an emporium that sold nothing else – paint in a paint shop, for instance, nails in a shop that sold only nails. This suited Helen, who preferred to shop alone or accompanied by another female of kindred spirit who understood that when shopping you looked at everything: duvets and food in Marks and Spencer even when you went there to buy a skirt; washing machines, carpets and coats in John Lewis, even if you had gone for a plug. And if you had embarked on a vague search for clothes, there would never be an end to it, not even a beginning.

171

Bailey could not understand how she could return from such a foray armed with nothing but exhilaration, replete with things seen, people met, and everything else, but without a parcel in sight – although that was rare. Something always got hold of the purse, but it mattered not if the product of four hours' wandering was no more than two pairs of tights and a pineapple, one lipstick and a newfangled potato peeler, two light bulbs and a free sample of perfume. Today she intended to do better: this was a prearranged frolic with itching credit card. Helen was looking for the boost of a new autumn coat, replacements for down-at-heel shoes, and a new pair of trousers to make her look at home in ultracasual Branston. Having decided on that, she would not be disappointed to return with a tube of toothpaste. The looking was the thing: that was the way it was with shopping, the way she liked it.

Helen sat on the train, thought of the day ahead, armed with the inevitable book, forgetting to read in an almost empty carriage, so empty she felt the sense of secret holiday. Really, she and Bailey were equally bad. What harm would there have been in mentioning that she had seen part of his case and had met Evelyn Blundell in the process? But she had said nothing, and had allowed last evening's garrulous neighbour to exhaust them. They had gone to bed when she left, Bailey for an early start, she for a piece of truancy like this. What the hell. She was dreaming, gazing out of the window into a lowering sky, nothing ahead but dirty London and crowded shops. She wriggled a little with the sheer pleasure of it, ate an apple for late breakfast, watched world. Thirty-five minutes by train on a good day from Branston into Oxford Circus, more usually exceeding an hour: never travel without a book for distraction or enough thoughts to fill the time. The Central Line rolling stock, running on Central Line rails, operated as a bone-shaker fit to disgrace any subcontinent, requiring restraints between stations, gathering speed with a threat to throw any unbraced passenger from her seat into the arms of the one opposite. Rush hours with strap hangers lurching around like drunkards only became more comfortable when passengers were packed like sardines, each avoiding the eye of the other as they stood in intimate stability, swaying in unison within the purgatory of the train, bottoms and stomachs joined like serried Siamese twins. Emptier carriages made others unwary: neglected parcels on a dozy afternoon would leap from their bonds between Debden and Theydon as the tube rattled and shook with the effort of speed, braked in fury for a deserted stop. Out of office hours the train was depopulated by the further reaches of outer London, as if places like Branston had ceased to exist. Once people moved away as far as this, unless commuting with the herd, they were supposed to remain where they lived. Otherwise, the floor-shaking, arm-bracing Central Line, as stable and sweet as a wagon train, became their punishment.

But in those languid hours, there was the mixture of views that drew Helen into the vortex of beloved London every time she caught the surroundings blurred by the consistently dirty windows of the carriage. Surprising fields around Branston, signs of harvest; then, seen near the rails, looking like an outpost, prefabricated 1950s buildings resembling Nissen huts, postwar construction still standing in lurid pastel colours. Debden melting into

173

the background. Theydon Bois next, known locally as Theydon Boys, somewhat more settled than Debden, but scarcely visible. A tunnel of green approaching Snaresbrook, the presence of trees a sign of prosperity, homes with lawns, mock Tudor, mock Spanish, and older Edwardian houses with outbuilt conservatories, hidden to all but Central Line passengers. She had once sat in a train stopped by signal failure between stations, a frequent hazard of the Central Line, at this very spot, and watched mesmerized as a naked man washed while singing in front of a window, reaching to a shelf out of sight in all his glory, unconscious of the silent audience. Helen had nudged the woman next to her in case she missed it. 'Look at that,' she'd said, unable to resist sharing it, both of them sniggering like children. She thought of it every time she passed the place.

Greater prosperity still as the train chuffed away from Snaresbrook, downhill from the territory of lesser showbiz, and East End crooks seeking new life in security-alarmed houses, into the duller safety of South Woodford's narrower avenues. Earnest small blocks of flats to augment neat tree-lined streets, the territory of hopeful artisans, bank clerks, teachers, and the more modestly prosperous of the age. A tasteless place, safe and dull but green enough to pass. Then a quicker descent to reality: street after street of stocky row houses coming into Leyton, mean back yards bearing signs of loving devotion, covered in washing, a place of crowded roads. On the right, a vast graveyard that looked as if it might have held every corpse found in London over a hundred years. Plunging away from Leyton, another graveyard, this one for cars, bodies

174

of metal in clumps piled up like weeds, rusty and shiny lorries, mangled cars, shells awaiting redemption, looking
jaunty perched one on top of the other, cheerful scrap
heap, metal stripped of all the aspirations and images once
invested in the living machine. Mine belongs here, thought
Helen; I might like it better without wheels.

Then Stratford and a quickening of heart among even
meaner houses, the train plunging underground as the city
began. The rest of the journey a crowded blur, onset of the
true metropolis, train rattling slower, stopping to open its
doors for engorging crowds at Mile End, taking in the city-
bound people laden with bags and haversacks, holdalls and
cases, bound on business, for shops, trains, aeroplanes.
Liverpool Street, a pause for breath with more of the same
in skin of every perspiring colour. Tick, tick, tick, doors
closing, opening again as if indecisive, ever unwilling to
take travellers from the east, unwilling to go on, sighing
and moving with a jolt. Crashing into the gloom of St
Paul's to collect a gaggle of brochured tourists speaking in
tongues, panting into Holborn via Chancery Lane for
lawyers' clerks, Tottenham Court Road for all the world
plus wife, and then Oxford Circus, ever late for waiting
crowds with shopping bags, four deep on the platform,
doubting the train would ever arrive. The uninitiated
pushed in and out, forever terrified of being carried on or
left behind with doors closing on the skulls of half their
families: 'Come on, Jack, we'll miss it. You'll be lost for
ever. Get on, get on, quickly, quickly.' Helen stirred with
the languor of a native, ambled off the train as the others
boarded, unhurried, unfazed by multitudes, refreshed with
the blessed familiarity, the sheer anonymity of it all. From

175

the heaving mass of foreign confusion in the foyer, circulating in search of the right exit, she stepped leisurely into the roar of the circus and thus began the business of the day.

There was, of course, no method at all to the business of Helen's shopping; it did not matter how or where she started, stopped, or progressed. The nearest likely shop was the beginning, the last one the end. In the course of a very slow perambulation around dozens of departments she would stop for coffee in three or four different back streets, cappuccino or black as the mood dictated, teeth-defying bread or stale pastry for energy, cigarette for sheer joy, and back into the fray. Food was irrelevant but part of the haphazard pleasure. Over a space of hours she would try on an assortment of garments, most of them unsuitable; would be happily tired of taking off clothes and putting them on, wishing she had worn something better suited to the purpose like a track suit without buttons and more comfortable shoes; would look at herself in mirrors and detest what she saw, the existing skirt, even the clean underwear beneath it, dead and grey against the backdrop of all the newness. She would shake with suppressed laughter in communal changing rooms at the vision of herself looking like a dartboard in a dress of vivid yellow check; would give and receive opinions, joke, help to fasten hooks and eyes. She would rehang neatly on hangers everything she had taken off because she knew what it was like to be a shop assistant and she would try to be pleasant, however rude or pushy they were, making them laugh in the process. She would pull a dozen faces; considered herself obscenely fat on the beam, too muscular in the arms, too skinny in the shank; be hideously depressed by her own silhouette, obscurely and maliciously cheered by the vision of another infinitely worse, if she could find one. She would be shocked at the prices, discuss them with others in whispered tones, swear at buttons, zips, and the endless obscurity of the ladies' loo that seemed necessary at any given time; would drink her coffee like an addict while recognizing on her wrists the perfume sampled at counters under eagle eyes, by now a cacophony of scents. I smell like a tart's parlour, she told herself finally, while all original ideas of what she had wanted to buy drifted by the board. An excellent afternoon.

She had spent one thousand pounds in her mind and acquired no more than a bar of soap, admired fabric for curtains she would never buy, sat on a three-piece suite she could not own, wondered how the world could be as rich as it seemed and who bought these things, and debated the purchase of a microwave. She dreamed of eating a baked potato and promised herself chocolate on the way home. Not now, later. Stuck in the bowels of Selfridges, looking at do-it-yourself items for reasons she could not and did not want to fathom, since both subject and the practice of it were anathema to her, she even forgot the time. Helen could always forget the time without Bailey to remind her. He never forgot, but with Bailey all this would never have happened. Moving upstairs, thinking vaguely she should go home now and wasn't it time the store closed and forced her on to the street, she also remembered she had first set out in search of a coat, and for the first time in several hours, she went to look at coats.

'Can madam be helped?'

'Well, yes, if you'd tell me where you keep my size. Nothing else, really. Please don't trouble because I probably shan't buy, if you see what I mean. One of those days when indecision is rampant and I'm feeling fat.'

'Ah, yes, I know what you mean: nothing suits a fat day, madam, nothing at all, but please look.'

The shop was becoming empty when she tried on the coat, the first one on the rack, a brilliant non-conservative blue, soft as cashmere, a coat with swing enough for Helen's stride, room enough for Helen's business suits, sleeves and hem corresponding to Helen's size and with style that took away her breath and left her delighted. In other words, a coat in which to live and die after too many changing rooms had reduced her self-image to that of squat scruff with scowling countenance, face slightly drained of colour. But in this coat she was transformed. Six inches taller, suddenly elegant and authoritative. She examined the label and groaned out loud.

'That's our designer range,' said the assistant, beaming approval.

'It would be,' said Helen.

There then followed a procedure as mandatory as it was pointless, quite inevitable all the same. It involved Helen progressing through the racks of coats in the hope of finding similar inspiration in a cheaper equivalent, furiously calculating as she shrugged them off on the hows and whys of affording the first, rounding up three alternatives like sheep in a pen, and looking at them all.

'The first,' said the assistant.

'But the price,' wailed Helen.

'It's the best,' said the assistant. 'I wouldn't lie to you,

madam, honest I wouldn't. It does things for you, madam.
And we close in five minutes, madam. Nearly seven
o'clock, it is. Long day.'

'Oh, Christ,' said Helen, 'late night shopping. I'm two
hours behind.'

'And the coat, madam?' She grinned conspiratorially.

'Yes, the coat, I'll have it. I have to have it, you knew all
the time I would.'

Taking home the jewel-coloured coat, skipping into
Bond Street station, she felt guiltily reborn, and bugger the
bills. Bailey would like it, Bailey never resented extrava-
gance; always mean with himself, he positively encouraged
her to spend lavishly and besides had a rare masculine eye
for style. What else was there to tell him that was fit for the
retelling? The desire to relate her adventures to Bailey was
stronger than ever, which was saying a lot. He enjoyed
shopping as long as the experience was secondhand. Ah,
yes, she would describe the woman asking the seller to
wrap her silk shirt as small as possible so she could get it
into the house without her husband noticing. Assistant
nodding without blinking, understanding perfectly, a
common request, folding the silk into a myriad creases and
the size of an envelope. At least Helen did not have a
spouse like that, and such reflections, plus the comforting
bulk of the coat, were enough to arm her for the rigours of
the Central Line.

This red line out of London was ever erratic, as if sulking from time to time. Nothing unusual to find the thing
promising to go to Branston, but fussing to a halt at Mile
End and refusing to go farther: This is your Central
Line information service. All change, please. This train

179

terminates here. The few passengers were resigned. Seven-twenty in the evening, downtown London suffering a lull while the population arrived home from work, not ready yet to re-embark disguised in different attitudes, towards the night's entertainments. The platform at Mile End was a secretive, vulnerable place, double-edged, unguarded underground pavement for two sets of trains travelling east as well as west, a long and gloomy island punctuated by large flat pillars and copious freestanding signs giving directions. People leaned on the signs or lurked behind them seeking anonymity, making the station appear empty as Helen walked from one end to the other in search of a seat and the same anonymity. She sat down on a bench hidden by a pillar, clutching the coat bag and the overstuffed handbag, from which she extracted the book, reconciled to the world because of the coat, ready to endure the next forty minutes with the help of the printed page, when she heard whispering as diffuse as underwater humming.

'Oh, I'll be late, I'll be so late. They'll be cross. I told you I didn't like the tube: it never works.'

'Oh, shut up, William, shut up. I'll be late, too. It doesn't matter. Nobody's going to hit us, are they? Be sensible, will you? No one will know if we're late. We're often late. You watch out for the train, will you? You might make it come faster.'

Helen slid to the edge of her seat, craned her neck so as to look behind the pillar, caught a glimpse of William Featherstone at the extreme edge of the platform and only a few feet away, standing with hands in pockets, gazing down the tunnel as if willing a train to emerge. He was completely absorbed, tense with anxiety, looking first at the tunnel, then at the tracks.

'Oh, look, Evie, look: mice, real mice.' A whisper of excitement.

From behind the wall, where Evelyn squatted against the support, Helen heard a muttered expression of boredom. Her first response was amusement: two children at play, well, well, well. So they *had* known one another with the familiarity she had imagined; how coincidental to confirm their secret so far from home. The next reflection contained the thought that theirs was private mischief in which she should not intrude. The tube was as good a place for hiding as any; let them be. Helen might have moved away if their next moves had been as innocuous.

William knelt at the extreme edge of the platform, riveted by the mice who lived below the rails: a phenomenon that had often riveted her own eyes. While he watched, making odd little cooing noises to the mice, his voice echoing slightly in the tunnel entrance, Evelyn stood upright on her plimsolled feet, ran towards him, stopped short of him, turned and paced back to her spot. She did this twice, as if counting the yards between them, the second time retreating farther so that her distance from him was slightly greater. Then ran a third time, as silent and light as a bird, the extra yard allowing extra speed, retreated again, as if satisfied.

William was quite oblivious, still whispering to the mice. 'Come here, fella. It's not nice down there. I'll take you home. What happens when a train comes? Please climb up here, please.'

Evelyn was coiled like a spring in a sort of squatting

181

race start, equally unaware of observation; both were utterly concentrated.

Helen watched, mesmerized, felt on her face the slight breeze that heralded the approach of an engine yet unseen and heard, knew it to be ominous, tightened her grip on her package, watched. She is going to push him; that is what she is going to do, push him over the edge just before the train bursts out of the tunnel. I know that is exactly what she is intending to do. She chose this deserted end of the platform, this distant platform, measured the distance. She planned it all. I know.

From the tunnel came the rumble of movement, the distant shriek and hiss of brakes, then growing sound. A slight vibration pushed the air forward, blowing strongly in Helen's face as she rose. William heard it, began to stand upright; Evelyn caught his intention in a glance, and was ready to run. Helen ran too, behind William, blocking the path between them, braced herself for the impact, felt Evelyn's tough little body slam into her from behind. She stumbled against William as the train crashed into the light, dropped the coat bag. The coat half spilled in a flash of blue. William shouted in anger. In an action quite as automatic as her running forward, Helen bent to stuff the coat back into the bag as the train strained to a halt, seeing at the same time from the corner of her eye one pair of jean-clad ankles hurrying away beyond the pillar. She rose, as the carriage doors slid open, to face the puzzled regard of the boy.

'What you doing? What you think you doing?' Furious, confused, looking around in sudden panic. 'And where's . . . where's . . . ?' The train tick-ticking, breathing impatience. People appeared from nowhere, stepping aboard, others, fewer, alighting. 'Where's . . . Where's . . . ?'

'She's gone, William. Get on the train, quickly. You're late.' Her voice emerged with brisk authority.

William's look of animal confusion vanished, replaced by a vacant gaze, the clearing features of a boy who has remembered well-rehearsed lines after a moment of panic. 'Who's gone?' he said loudly, jumping on to the train with unnecessary energy. 'Who do you mean? Must be mad . . .'

But as Helen followed, sat next to him, she watched him stretch and peer through the closing doors, scanning the platform as the train moved past, desperately seeking clues, a sight, a glimmer of the paste earrings or the plim-solled feet. Helen's limbs were trembling; so, she noticed, were his. They sat in silence, drowned by the noise of the train until it thundered through the tunnel into empty, floodlit Stratford. Outside Stratford, alongside the grave-yard for cars, motion ceased entirely. The lights in the carriage flickered.

September summer: humid, storm-filled, feeling like winter darkness, an inky daylight black, scarcely relieved in the heavy-breathing train. Even less light in this last of all compartments and no people, either; William and Helen sitting as silent companions, frozen with unease.

He turned and looked at her with cunning curiosity. 'No one's gone,' he said with conviction. And then, 'I know you. You come in the bar. I know you. And you talk in court. You're one of them.' He nodded vigorously; she nodded in turn. Sitting on a train, the two of them, lately prosecutor and defendant. Helen was glad that the resentment of the defendant was less often directed at the prosecutor than towards the policeman who felt the collar, and William was clearly feeling no resentment at all. Feeling nothing, apparently, apart from anxiousness to convince her in words of one syllable that he had been accompanied by no one. No one had gone: he had asked his questions of air.

'There are mice on the tracks, did you know?' he asked, beaming goodwill.

'Yes, there are,' said Helen. 'William, how long have you known Evelyn? I know her, too.'

'Evelyn? Evie . . . Don't know Evelyn. What you mean? No one's gone.'

'Evie, Evelyn. Evelyn Blundell, the girl with the earrings. Your friend.'

'My friend . . . Yes, my friend. No, she isn't. Which Evie? Don't know her at all. Stop it, that's silly. Stop it.' He muttered in agitation, squirmed, and looked towards the door for escape. The train was obdurately still, locked in a semi-silent signal-failure zone between one civilization and the next, a kind of no-man's-land, while someone was probably calling someone else out of a pub. She patted William's arm to soothe the quivering; she was not a parent after all, not here to cross-examine. To her surprise, he seized her hand, held it, examined it. 'Nice,' he said, 'very nice.' She felt the first queasy tremor of fear as he parted her fingers and scrutinized them, then saw he confined his attention to a sapphire ring, Helen's only piece of sparkle, Bailey's only gesture of ownership. 'Nice,' said William, twisting to look at her with the familiar vacuous grin, still holding the hand, stroking it now, sighing slightly. She smiled back; that action of face seemed prudent while

184

she wished the train would move, which it did, slowly, clack, clack, a peaceful crawl, resigned to reluctant effort. William swayed with the carriage, abandoning himself to movement, suddenly relaxed by the motion, reminded of the buses and the soothing sound of his mother's washing machine humming beneath his room. The train exhaled and stopped.

'I like girls,' he said, apropos of nothing, and placed a hand on her thigh, hot through her skirt. Helen withdrew slightly, rummaged in her bag, discovered chocolate, and offered him some. 'Oh, goody,' he said. At least he was capable of distraction – not completely. William was feeling affectionate, inquisitive with it. He pressed his shoulder against hers, warm through her blouse, hotter to touch than his somewhat grimy hands. He had removed himself from Evie and everything else, attached himself to present company. He liked her.

'Do people . . .' he asked, face contorted with the intellectual effort of formulating a question. 'Do all people . . . people as old as you still do it?'

'Do what, William?' She was slightly fazed by the question, parrying for time without doubting the meaning of his enquiry.

'Do sex, I mean. I know some people older than you do it. I thought they got tired of it. They don't ever have pictures of them doing it. It must be horrible when you're so old.'

'Some people,' Helen replied drily, amused by the question despite herself and despite the hot hand on her thigh, which she gently removed, 'even older than me do it all the time. But only if they want to. Which means it can't be

185

horrible or they wouldn't do it, would they?' The train, having started, slowed again. She felt an overpowering sense of the ridiculous.

'Even when they're more than forty?'

Which is, after all, very old indeed, Helen reflected with even more amusement. I'll soon be over the hill if forty's the limit. And Bailey's already only a few years on the other side. Bailey would enjoy this conversation, seems to enjoy that which William is discussing, come to that. Hope he doesn't think it's horrible. Shows no sign of it, or waning powers either. Must tell him this boy would imagine he is simply doing his duty.

'Oh, yes, even when they're over forty. Or fifty or sixty.'

'Ugh,' said William.

'Why do you ask?' she enquired in calm conversational tones, offering more chocolate.

'To see if I'm right.'

'About what?'

'Oh, everything.' He waved a limp hand, fell into silence. Perhaps they could talk about something different, but William's mind, master of the non sequitur, remained on its own peculiar tangent.

'Mrs Blundell liked it,' he remarked, picking up Helen's even tone. 'She liked it a lot, but we thought she was silly.'

Helen's reactions were suddenly sharper, her body stiller, her voice on the same even keel. 'Oh, did she now? Well, I told you, a lot of people do like it. I suppose you saw Mrs Blundell in the woods?' A good enough guess, judging from the nodding.

William was forgetting his lines. 'Yes. Both of us saw her. With Evie's teacher on a rug he brought. Very, very silly.' He giggled. 'She looked horrible. All bare. Evie was very cross. I told her my mummy would never do that, never.' She was silent, waiting for him to continue.

'I 'spect Evie was cross because they were our woods,' he added. 'She said if her mummy and that teacher went to the woods, they might come up and find the summer-house. Sometimes they passed it. I watched them. They were all silly, like people get after drinking in our place. They came through our garden and out over the field. Evie was furious. "What's she coming here for?" she said. "If she finds us, she'll kill us. You first, me after. No, Dad'll kill me, slowly." Never seen her as cross as that, but she does get very cross. Sometimes. "She'll kill us," she said . . .' There his voice faltered in a dim realization of too much spoken.

'Well,' said Helen, keeping her own voice as untroubled as her throat allowed, 'she didn't find you, so that's all right, isn't it?'

'Yes. I suppose so,' said William slightly mollified, still driven to speak. 'But we found her, though.'

'You? When?' Too late to prevent the give-away sharp-ness of tone. 'When was that, William?' But he was retreating fast, shrinking, remembering stricture and warnings, horrified by his forgetfulness of learned-by-heart promises.

'On the ground. You know, dead. Evie fetched me. No, she didn't; I was there. I'm not supposed to say that. Oh, stop it, stop it, stop it.'

He was squirming in agony, his movements accelerating with the sudden speed of the train, possessed by a pain beyond enduring, electrocuted by the gravity of his own words. Then he turned on her in a fury, punched her shoulder with clumsy violence. Placed both heavy paws on her breasts, pressing and kneading with a force that made her wince in pain. Paralysed by some dim memory of physical attack she suppressed the desire to scream and struggle, forced herself into an unnatural stillness. Even when he changed his tactics and grabbed both her arms, making odd, biting motions in the direction of her throat, his fingers clawing into her flesh, bruising delicate flesh with savage strength. A fantail of raw prints rose under her skin, and she felt a lacerating pain.

'It's all right, William. Calm down, now. It's all right, don't worry. It doesn't matter what you've said. I wasn't listening at all. It's all right.'

The words worked like a slow but magic formula as the train drew into Debden. He withdrew his hands; she resisted the almost overpowering temptation to rub where he had touched. William looked at the sliding doors opening to the dark world outside as if contemplating flight, then decided against it. She contemplated it, too, felt his hand stray to her arm, stayed as she was.

'Hold my hand, William. It's all right.'

'OK, then.'

They pulled away towards Theydon, the prospect of home becoming reality, swaying together in the new enthusiasm of the machinery, pitched and tossed and lurched into the next station. She was beginning to see what the motion did for him, felt faint and sore with the effort of keeping still, decided recklessly to risk one more question.

'Where's the summerhouse den, William?'

He gazed at her blankly. 'In the summerhouse, of course. Daddy was going to make it into a bar. Only the summerhouse,' he repeated, as if it was obvious. The noise of engine and track was a duet of such force that they had to raise their voices. He looked at her with sly affection, pushing his face towards her. 'You're nice,' he said. 'Nicer than Evelyn's mum.' The same hand had moved back to her thigh, squeezing above the knee, fingers spreading in exploration. She removed it again. Ten minutes at most before Branston: she wanted to make him forget all he had said as well as the movement of the train, cast about her thoughts in desperate search for words. Finally, out of the blue, a question emerged.

'What did you buy today, William?'

He sat upright. 'Nothing, I didn't buy anything for me. Not allowed today. You did, though,' he added, pointing at the fallen-to-floor coat bag.

'Yes, I did. I bought a coat.'

'Oh, I love shops, I really do. Will you show me? Please?'

In the bucking carriage, he released her and she released the coat from tissue paper, showed it to an admiring audience of one. William stroked the cloth, grinned at it, tickled the collar like a cat's ears, murmured compliments while she gabbled a little description, words only words, of how she had come to buy it. He folded the coat back into the bag, insisting, 'No, this way: you're doing it wrong. Got to be careful, see? Nice thing, very nice.' Just in time for the single light of Branston and a mutual falling off the train, he carrying the coat, which he immediately handed back, albeit with reluctance. Beyond the

189

unmanned station, William examined his unused ticket, puzzled. Life on the buses was different. 'Here,' he said, 'you can have this,' proffering it to her – his version, she understood, of a gift.

'Why thank you, William. See you soon.' Then in a rush of sudden pity for his look of misery, as well as a desire to walk home unaccompanied, she added, 'You can tell them you came back with me, if you like. Say I asked you, if they go on about your being late.'

William's straight face widened into the vacant grin; they smiled in conspiracy. 'Goody,' he said, smiling and waving, embarrassed at parting. 'Bye, then.'

'Bye.'

She staggered uphill with deliberation. Her thigh tingled from his touch; on her upper arms the purple marks were forming that would show tomorrow over the bones of another possible statistic. 'Woman raped and attacked between Debden and Theydon.' The stuff of the local paper, the thought of it inducing a mild and comic hysteria. Not a woman with a coat, though. Ridiculous thinking: coats were meant to lend warmth, not protection; perhaps the mere existence of this one had lent her confidence. She was surprised to find herself giggling. One way to downplay this whole episode to Bailey: Darling, I bought this very expensive coat and avoided being attacked on the train because I didn't want to damage it. Or, having this new, very expensive coat enabled me to cope. Take your choice. Or, darling, I want to talk to you about William Featherstone and someone who seemed for a moment to want to kill him. He and Evelyn Blundell – they're conspirators. They found her mother, and William is violent enough to have killed her. He's been schooled into silence, but he's like a dummy without a ventriloquist until the action slips. What are you going to do about it? And while we're at it, what are you going to do about us, Bailey, you rat? Can we leave this improving place, please, where people do these things to their children? I'm sorry to disappoint you, but my spiritual home is Oxford Street and North London with all the Cypriots, and drunken Irish, the blaggers and the dirt. I'm frightened here as I never was there, more frightened now than I was on the train, which is extremely frightened, as it happens. I'm also ashamed. I have fingerprints all over me; please let me in.

Her own fingers had lost their sixth sense for finding the keys. To avoid William, she had walked from the station, forgetting the simple fact of her car in the carpark. She was cold, it was dark, she was wet from the drizzle she had failed to notice on the train, and she was still preparing a smile. She dared not look at the time, expected it was well after nine. Dear God, the civility of London was a long way off. Life here was far too complicated.

Bailey wrenched open the door of 15 Invaders Court, feeling and looking savage, his face blank with fury. The smile fell: Bailey's rage, whatever the degree or cause of that rare anger, was difficult to handle.

'Hello,' she said stupidly, and pushed damp hair out of one eye. He saw the scar on her forehead, implicit with dreadful memory. She remembered, quite irrelevantly, that the coat on her arm might be soaked.

'For Christ's sake, Helen,' he shouted, dragging her in through the door, 'I could shake you . . . Where have you been?' And he was shaking her, gripping both arms in his own strong hands, as strong as William's, fingers extended in a grasp more exasperated than affectionate. He was angry and anxious and distant: she was in disgrace. Perhaps his concern for her was uppermost in his mind, but it made no difference on the sensitive spots. She hated him for this exhibition; it simply hurt, body and soul, it hurt. Helen yelped briefly in her own anger and profound disappointment, and in the flurry of the pain she shook her arms free. And briefly, sharply, and painlessly drew back one hand and slapped him.

CHAPTER TEN

The day of Helen's ordeal had begun well for her but not for Bailey.

'Get you, Amanda Scott! Who's the new lover boy, then? Look at that, flowers all over. Champagne next, is it? Boss gave them to you, did he?'

'Leave it out, Jack,' said with ostensible boredom and secret pleasure. 'Can you see Bailey giving anyone flowers?'

Police Constable Bowles paused to consider. Difficult, that, hanging on the door of the detectives' room, empty save for her. PC Bowles was one of Amanda's fans; most occupants of the room were not, preferring to work elsewhere when she was in. Prissy, clever, tidy little bitch. Iron knockers.

'Superintendent Bailey giving flowers? Yes, I can see him doing that, as a matter of fact. But not those flowers and not to you.'

'Push off, Jack. I'm busy.'

He blew a daring kiss in the air, ambled down the corridor whistling, leaving Amanda in contemplation of the bouquet, which he had delivered from the front desk, telling everyone its destination *en route*. Which was nice, to put it on record; so nice she was not about to diminish the pleasure by taking off the polythene and allowing anyone to imagine she had bought the flowers herself. Keep this up, J. Blundell, and we'll get along fine, really we shall. You're doing very well, what with phone call yesterday to celebrate the colour of my eyes and dinner tomorrow night. Don't know if I should. Bailey won't like it, but he'll have to lump it. If he knows, that is, which he won't if I don't tell him. Never mind, never mind, I know how to fix him.

Grabbing handbag, smoothing hair, making for his office with verbal report of yesterday's sojourns with Featherstones et al. already tidy in her mind. Not entirely fictionalized, simply glossed by judicious omission. She always presented the best profile to her information.

Good morning, sir; good morning, Amanda, how did you get on? Could ask the same thing, sir, but I don't, of course, even leaving aside the rude connotations of the phrase. Your days can be secret, mine bloody aren't. Instead of saying that, offering a rueful smile.

'Not much success, sir, in any direction. Apart from the committal, of course; you know about that. But I found out a bit on William Featherstone, our arsonist, sir.'

So did I, Bailey thought. Rather too much, really; can't afford to feel for a fire raiser. I know all about where he goes and what he chooses to buy and steal. He watched with surprise as Amanda produced a clumsy bracelet from a tidy handbag.

'In his spare time he hides in a shed in the garden, and he makes these things in the kitchen,' she said gravely, as if revealing the crown jewels.

The bracelet lay on his desk like a gaudy and lumpish pebble: Bailey wanted to laugh. 'Do they know you have this?' he asked quietly.

She flushed, furious to be caught at a disadvantage so soon. She should have begun at the beginning and gone on to the end of her afternoon, giving her report the authority of chronology. 'Well, no they don't. I sort of picked it up.'

'I think I'll return it at some stage,' said Bailey evenly. 'Someone's treasure, isn't it? Well, well, clever William,' putting the thing in his pocket, continuing. 'No jewellery in the Blundell house, by any chance? Was he helpful?'

'Yes,' she replied with sincerity this time, 'yes, he was. Very. We went through the place with a fine-tooth comb,' repeated like a parrot and, to forestall any further questions on that line, entered a rider that did not follow the question at all. 'Sir, there's something I must tell you.'

'Sit down, Amanda, please.'

So she told him with relish, keeping the spite out of her voice and her whole stance as she had learned to do as a child, wrapping it into a parcel of concern. 'I was puzzled, sir, very puzzled at the committal proceedings . . . I don't think you can have known about it . . .'

'Go on.'

'Well, sir, your wife, sir – sorry, girlfriend, Miss West, I mean, of the Crown Prosecution Service,' to prove she understood exactly Helen's dual importance. 'She brought

195

Evelyn Blundell into the committal proceedings. They sat at the back and listened to the pathologist.'

'They what . . . Helen?' A remarkably satisfying jump.

'Yes, sir. I'm afraid so. Not from the beginning. I was just checking the public gallery halfway through when I saw them. Your . . . Miss West saw me; she grabbed Evelyn and they left together. I thought I'd better tell you.'

'Thank you,' he said drily. 'No doubt there was some purpose in it. She works for Mr Redwood; I'm sure he approved.'

'He didn't know, sir. Not until I told him.'

You would, wouldn't you? Well done, Amanda, and what are you hiding with this taking-the-wind-out-of-my-sails kind of exercise? Shrugging it away, pretending to do so. 'You're sure there's no jewellery in Blundell's house?'

'Only what she left, sir.'

The revelations about Helen had the ring of truth, were in any event verifiable and therefore not the subject for lies, while the helpfulness of surly and difficult John Blundell had the tincture of dishonesty, but for the moment, Bailey was too dispirited to persist.

'And were the Featherstones co-operative?'

'No, sir, not very.'

Good, serves you right, but I'll remember the bit about the garden shed. If our William starts fires, he also stores paraffin. That will do, Amanda, you have played your upper hand with great effect; you deserve an Oscar.

Helen, why did you do it? How dare you interfere with such crass, such unbelievable insensitivity? He could not believe it, had to believe it: Amanda would never lie with such vulnerability. He had been aware for a little while now

196

that she was in the habit of lying, but never where she could be caught. He wondered how much her impressive record owed to lying and to her delightful habit of always ducking the sort of awkward situation where careers were blighted. The question of Helen dogged him more hour by hour, often minute by minute; an explosion of incredulity, not yet anger; an indignation of disappointment, still capable of being placated by reasonable explanation, but hardening into firm belief of the worst without scope for forgiveness each time he rang either her office or home to find her defiantly absent. Who did she think she was? Frustrated detective, trying to fiddle with the jigsaw pieces to find a reaction? Mad scientist playing with poison on a younger life? He had gone home early to expiate the anger, bring forward the explanation, forced the same anger to new heights in the long hours of waiting. The anger was overlain with appalling anxiety as he listened to the rain, pacing the modern room he privately hated, smoking cigarettes he felt inclined to grind into the carpet, too sick to eat or drink, apart from two furious whiskies consumed without effect. By now anxiety had the winning streak, a tyrannical fear, premonition of Helen's loved body broken by bus or train, victim of something or someone; some tentacle of this case reaching her in punishment for her wilful involvement. He could recall as vividly as the shape of his own hand feeling the same anxiety the last time she had been hurt and he had seen her as battered and bruised as he now imagined her, obscenely injured.

Half past eight o'clock: no phone call. No word from this woman of his who was punctilious in such courtesies. And then she knocked at the door. He pulled it open, expecting some bearer of bad news, finding her instead smiling, carrying a bag. Been shopping. Like a father finding a lost child, his first reaction was the sheer fury of relief. He wanted to shake or hit or shout at her, to establish the reality and let her know she had cost him about ten years of his life. Of course she had neither wanted nor needed that. And even when he had yelled at her, shortly after the slap, he shouted, 'What were you doing bringing a child into court to listen to her mother's death being rehashed? How could you do it?' He witnessed her disbelief that he could ever imagine she had done such a thing, heard the reply that she had removed the girl, certainly, yes, but never conducted her there. He knew it was true, it still did not shift the anger. Anger remained with him like a leaden weight throughout the rest of her words. The slap and the guilt rendered him impotent to change his feelings; even when he saw how white and drawn she was, and he pretended to listen, the anger, like indigestible food, refused to shift.

'Listen to me, Geoffrey: I'm too tired to talk long. I'm sorry I slapped you, sorrier that you should think so badly of me, but listen: I took Evelyn out of court; she had sneaked in without anyone seeing. We had a chat afterwards. I saw William Featherstone recognize her; then I saw them together today. They're buddies, probably something more. He adores her, but I got the distinct impression that she was trying to push him under a train.' Bailey did not interrupt this recitation to ask for details, and in the light of the living room it did indeed seem incredible enough to defy elaboration. 'Anyway, she ran off, and he pretended she'd never been there, some

198

prearranged story in which he was well drilled, but then he let it out. He seemed to like me.' She laughed shakily. 'He also told me that both of them saw Mrs Blundell dead after having seen her perform live. He was very distressed in the telling, acted up a bit. He's not with it, Geoffrey, this William, and he's got the hormones of a raging bull, brains seated in his underpants, and a weird gentleness with it. Don't you think it's probable he could have done something to Mrs B? He'd do anything to protect Evie, I don't know from what, or keep her. Perhaps he's bedding her.'

It sounded to his ears like so much nonsense. 'She's only fourteen, Helen, for God's sake.'

'So what? They begin at twelve elsewhere; you know that as well as I. But not in Branston, where they're civilized by nice houses, is that it? Suppose he thought Mrs Blundell was on to him, they watched her, maybe she watched them. Suppose—'

'For Christ's sake, stop supposing, Helen. Will you let that bloody imagination of yours rest? Go to bed. You've been sitting in a clapped-out train listening to the ramblings of a crazy boy, and you've constructed a whole scenario out of air. Who knows what he's read in the papers or imagined for himself?' Then in a gentler tone, 'You're whacked, Helen. Go to bed; I'll bring you a drink.'

She looked at him, defeated. 'All right,' she said. 'I'll stop thinking too. Like any policeman.'

And then, in the bathroom, Bailey saw Helen washing, half crying, grey and tired, fingerprint bruises on her upper arm, similar to the marks he had seen on countless prisoners arrested in struggles: the autograph of heavy, sometimes careless, needlessly painful hands. Bailey was appalled. 'What's this, Helen? What the hell is this?'

'Nothing,' said Helen. 'Absolutely nothing. I told you William Featherstone was violent. You weren't listening.'

'Oh Christ,' he said taking her limp figure into his arms. 'Oh, Christ almighty, Helen, I'm sorry, darling, I'm so dreadfully sorry. Tell me—'

'That's quite all right, Superintendent.' She spoke brightly, her voice brittle with pride, eyes sparkling with quiescent tears. 'Perfectly all right. No problem at all. I'm going to sleep now. You can do what you like.'

Christine Summerfield got up to tend her garden, intending it as therapy organized for a day off, but found it already tended, the same therapy last empty weekend having rendered it cleaner than a new pin. She got in her car and drove doggedly to Antony Sumner's deserted cottage, to which she held the only key at his request and despite the wailings of his parents, relatives, and colleagues, who suggested selling it, burning it, or ignoring it as if he were already dead. Christine Summerfield had cleaned it; that was therapy, too. The place had never been so clean or she herself so bare of hope. She was sickened by her inadvertent discoveries, made while she was in search of the inevitable bills, which were not suspended during his imprisonment, and she was dismayed by her own resilience. She moved towards the cottage like an automaton, trying to think of him and resurrect her early belief that this was all a mistake and one day he would live there again, even live there with her; it was larger than her place. But that early optimism had faded despite her

200

persistent nurturing of it, turned brown and desiccated like the leaves in the garden, helpless in the temperature of her own cold realism. She had little faith in a system of justice that spewed so many of her clients into her lap, but was fair enough to realize the same system, clumsy but relatively incorrupt, got it right at least half of the time and was as necessary as breath. She knew very well how casualties were created by life itself, not by authorities, and was also aware that Antony, her lover, had been treated as fairly as most. It was nothing as simple as the system that begat her own tremor of doubt; it was Antony.

While tidying his study in search of the gas bill – this indescribable mess of a man was so hooked on the printed page that he could never dispose of a single sheet of paper – she had found the beginnings of a novella, snapshots of his childhood, which made her weep, pictures of previous girlfriends, which made her peculiarly, possessively irritated, and a little bundle of fairly recent love letters from an unknown pupil, sadly signed in childish, educated script with the anonymous words, 'Yours Ever,' which made her furious. She knew they were recent because of references to local events, such as 'I saw you at the carnival last week, by the rose float; you looked very handsome'. She knew, too, he would never have responded to this moony devotion, but he should have established through the handwriting who had written them, returned the first letter with an admonition and surely not accepted more. Encouraging students to make a habit of writing was one thing; keeping the results was another. Whether he hoarded from carelessness mattered not. Whatever would he do for flattery, such a precious gift to him, poor man, the same weakness leading him to dead Mrs Blundell and all of this betrayal? Before the discovery of the letters, Christine had always respected Antony's integrity despite his mistakes, liked his enthusiasms despite his excesses, cherished his affections with all their past lack of discrimination, but on sight of those letters, the whole image of him began to slip, the respect fading by a dangerous degree, tinged by treacherous memories of his passion with its underlying violence. Were all men thus, madness lurking in their veins, following their organs to disaster because of a kind word, blindly obedient to subliminal commands? She suspected they were, was very tired of the breed, angry with him for what he was.

An element of disgust began before the committal proceedings. Evidence had unfolded while more doubts formed like a mushroom cloud. Christine sat beneath it humbled to camp follower and only supporter, fighting back reluctant belief in what she heard, while there gathered behind her eyes a huge resentment. Not for what he had done to Mrs Blundell – she could not in all honesty bring herself to care about that, although she wished she could – but for what he had done to her. For better or worse, from poorer to poorer, she knew, whatever the outcome, she could not forgive him. She had seen him in a new light while trying to shade it, viewed what she should never have seen, found him lacking, and wondered how she could ever again love him, and she was full of remorse for having come to doubt him. Even when she had never loved anyone half as much before, her mind had already moved to planning life without him, just as she was constantly advising her clients: Think of yourself, dear, you must, you know, no one else will. The last rat leaves the sinking ship; I don't know how love goes, but when it's gone, it's gone. Not without a self-hatred so acute it left her breathless.

So this was duty, obdurate, labour-intensive duty to prove to herself she still cared; she owed him that much, at least. Thou shalt not be guilty, dearest Antony, before trial, but after that, my pet, I shall have to leave you. I cannot sacrifice my life to you, only part of it. Tears hot on a flushed face, attacking this messy garden of his. Oh, why did he never do anything about it and why did he shatter my peace of mind? Look at this mess. He never looked after it, lived here three years and never raised spade or trowel. How could he? What a waste.

The previous owners had made an effort, left him with a format. It was a tiny garden: small patio from the kitchen, twenty feet of lawn bisected by path, shrubs standing like soldiers against each fence, a miniature shed, and a patented compost thing looking like a large and ungainly dustbin. She raked the overgrown lawn and the scrubby beds free of leaves. She had carried her rake here for the purpose. Why had he never bought one of his own? Sweeping up leaves awkwardly, putting them in the compost bin with disgust. That was where he had put the dead woman's clothes and handbag – sorry, someone else had put her clothes and handbag there. That was what Christine was supposed to believe and couldn't any longer. Strangely, that piece of evidence had failed to register with her at all until she had heard it read out loud, hadn't thought of it until it slapped her in the face. Now she did, and she was suddenly arrested by its incongruity with everything she knew of him. That he would strike the woman, yes. Take her money and jewellery, no. Put the remnants here, no: he simply wasn't materialistic enough.

The gate at the side of the cottage clicked. Full of sinister thoughts, she turned in alarm, faced Bailey, dear Superintendent Bailey, the bastard, standing in his workday suit, beginning to speak. She stood up like a lioness in a cage, snapped in a voice that was all teeth, 'What do you want?'

'Nothing specific. Passing, and saw your car.'

She was angry, turned back abruptly, and began attacking the leaves, which floated from control, presenting her behind conspicuously, determined to ignore him. He simply fell in, grasping piles of damp leaves with skill and efficiency, shoving them into the compost bin, pressing them down, going back for more, quietly ignoring the effect on his suit and hands. They worked in silence for fifteen minutes, clearing the leaves with speed, she found herself oddly mollified, disliking his presence less and less. She even felt the beginnings of a faint amusement, glad of the company. 'All right,' she said finally, flinging down the rake. 'You win. Now, what was it you really wanted?'

She sat on the single dirty patio chair. He sat on the wall next to it.

'I was wondering,' he said mildly, as if the conversation was the most natural in the world and this was the middle of it. 'Looking at this garden, I was wondering how Antony ever knew where the compost bin was. Or that he had one at all. Surprising. Not a keen gardener, I take it.'

'No,' she agreed curtly, suddenly reminded of the incongruity that had struck her before he arrived. 'He

204

usually forgot he had a garden. Didn't really recognize its existence.'

'I see.'

He did see, she thought; he saw what others had failed to see. He was all nerves and nerve, a complicated man, looking for something. In one fleeting instance she could imagine what Helen had found in him.

'Did you like him?' she asked gruffly. 'Antony, I mean.'

'I didn't – don't know him well enough to say. I do try to distance myself from suspects, murder suspects particularly, because I hate, loathe, and detest violence. I find it difficult to take the rest seriously, but violence sickens me.'

'That means you don't like him.'

'It means I don't dislike him too much. I can't afford to.' His eyes strayed to the compost bin. 'But I don't see him as a thief. I wonder if I could look at his desk, even though we've looked at it before. I don't want to remove anything. Simply look.'

'For the investigation or for your conscience?'

He laughed. 'Helen's my conscience.'

'You've got a bloody cheek asking, but yes, you can. I doubt he would have allowed it, but I shall.'

Sun shone directly on her face, exposing the lines of worry and grief, making her look older and harsher than her years. The suggestion in his words of the case being incomplete did not bring a glimmer of hope as it might have done even days since; it created no bloom of excitement in her very pale cheeks.

'How's Helen?' Faintly polite and dim memory of manners, but a blank face.

His brow furrowed into lines. 'While quite understanding why you avoid her, she misses you greatly. She finds it very difficult to live with a policeman, I think.'

'Oh.'

It provided a strange relief, hearing about the difficulties of other couples; it was oddly comforting. Christine wished Helen no ill, could not contemplate that, but all the same she would not have rejoiced in her happiness. This phase of her life would pass, she hoped, but at the moment the transparent contentment of others made her feel faintly sick.

'May I look, then? Do you want to come with me?'

'No, I'll trust you. Can't quite understand what you're doing, though.'

'Listen,' he said, standing above her like a slender and gentle giant. 'I may not like Antony, but I don't want him convicted of something he may not have done. Helen's always thought I didn't look far enough, doesn't realize that I never stop looking in my own way. If I find anything helpful to his defence, I'll tell them. I always do.'

'Oh save your energy. He did it all right.'

'Do you really think so?'

'Yes, I do. Look, what's the point? Don't pussyfoot around here piling on the agony. Oh, shit. What I really mean is that whether he did it or not, whatever the verdict whenever it happens, it'll all come too late for me. I can't even apologize for sounding so selfish, but that's what I think. I can't even think of him. It's too late for us.'

'Perhaps not,' said Bailey, well used to the aftermath, the grateful media-blessed reunions of the acquitted and their families with whom they would never again live in

206

peace. He was using tones of brisk optimism, a voice she recognized: nurse addressing the patient. 'Supposing he was acquitted. He'd get back his job, hasn't lost it yet; he'd come home. Life would go on as before.'

'No,' said Christine. 'Don't give me that shit. No, life wouldn't go on and couldn't. You know that very well. And you don't have to answer.' She spoke quietly, turning her face away from the sun as if ashamed of its resignation. 'Now bugger off and look at his desk. I've put the correspondence in piles. There are some letters from a schoolgirl that are particularly entertaining. They were of no interest to the others who looked. See yourself out.'

Bailey knew better than to repeat his platitudes, knew when and where he simply could not help, departed indoors for his unofficial exploration, his patient retracing of all the tracks he had delegated to Amanda Scott. Leaving Christine trying to erase from her eyes the relief of tears, looking at the garden denuded of all the early autumn leaves, feeling older than winter and already bereaved. She was right; she knew she was right. What was it she had said to him? 'Whatever the verdict.' The great big irrelevant verdict. Mrs Blundell had won after all.

Helen had yanked herself into daylight, redeemed into humanity by Bailey's kind but speechless provision of coffee, the rest of her stiff and immune from touching. Get in car, go to office, court this p.m., home early given a single chance to duck, more sleep if possible. Anger and pain were dissoluble in sleep, especially an insufficient, dream-filled sleep like hers. Her normal good nature reasserted itself and gave her enough cheerful self-control to reach her desk without hitting anyone *en route*. 'See Mr Redwood' – a note falling on to the blotter, which was covered with telephone numbers and shopping lists, slipping out of an in-tray the size of a house end. If yesterday had been the proper cue for an easy day today, someone somewhere had forgotten the lines.

Red Squirrel was suspiciously bright and know-all. 'Ah, Helen. Tried to get you yesterday, but you were off.'

'You're dead right I was, in all senses. But I did buy a coat,' she added irrelevantly. The coat continued to comfort. He looked puzzled.

'Little matter, Helen, of the Sumner proceedings. Why were you there? You were supposed to be in the office.'

'Ah, yes. Well, I wasn't; I was at the proceedings. I did the office work first, of course. Why was I there? Curiosity. It's also good for me to see an expert like you at work.' He would miss the irony and take the compliment; she knew he would. 'I asked Harmoner if he would object if I watched; he didn't, so I did.'

The pace of this left him slightly disconcerted. He cleared his narrow throat.

'Detective Sergeant Scott says she thinks she saw you with Evelyn Blundell at the back. She thought you arrived and left together.' Questions and accusations hung in the air. 'I rather had the impression she must have been mistaken about the arrival. Others saw the departure.'

'Evelyn came in after me. I hauled her out. I knew her by sight and thought she had no business there. That's all.' Helen was sick of this explanation and could have done serious bodily harm to Amanda Scott. She was relieved and grateful to see Redwood nod his acceptance of her explanation.

'I rather assumed something of the kind. You're rather too headstrong, Helen, but not lacking in wisdom.'

'You believe me, then?'

He looked surprised. 'Of course I do.' The fairness was reluctant, accompanied by another clearing of the throat. 'Whatever else I think of you, I've never known you to be other than professional. You might be rash sometimes, but you do have judgement. Of course I believe you.'

Which is more, Helen thought sadly, than dearest Bailey bothered to do. He didn't give me the benefit of the doubt, didn't make a single check before doubting my judgement, did he? But then, how could he? Whatever the verdict, patience and understanding had played no part in it. She listened politely to the guinea pig delivering a lecture.

'Miss West, you should not have been in court, should not have abused office time. Keep your nose out of other people's cases, do you hear?' This was not entirely sincere, since he was beginning to wish he had never interfered and had left her to it. The Sumner case weighed on him and he wanted help, but he could not concede out loud that she was the best person to give it, so he lectured her instead.

Helen, on the other hand, felt entirely disinclined to confess her extramural activities which had resulted in knowledge of the dual entanglements of Featherstone and Blundell. Nor did she wish to reveal her own frightening suspicions. Let Redwood speak directly or not at all. He had his case and his corpse and was going to run with it. Funny, seen like that: she could imagine him lugging a corpse across a courtroom floor. Her mind had slipped long before the end of the lecture and only shifted gear when the hectoring tone, mercifully mild, moved back into the conversational and she noticed the subtle way he had of soliciting opinions. She decided he had left it too late.

'Anyway, the committal went well,' he said. 'Very efficiently run. Sergeant Scott must be a great asset. I can see why Bailey was able to leave her to it.'

'Yes,' Helen said vaguely, not tuned in to praise for such a little telltale, still perturbed by the way Bailey appeared to have listened to her. 'Well, I'm glad everything's fine. Miss Scott's obviously the flavour of the month.'

Redwood disliked her quiescence, her equanimity in face of speeches from the throne, and the absence of anything suggesting co-operation or even acceptance of what had been his own version of an apology. He wanted to shake her, undermine that unnerving composure.

'Yes,' he said, rising to finish the interview. 'A highly successful case so far, but keep away from it. It's not yours.' He moved by instinct into a heavy teasing vein. 'Bailey owes a lot to Amanda Scott. Attractive girl. I should look to your laurels, there, Helen.' Playfully delivered words, like a punch in the arm, a kind of revenge.

'If you mean by my laurels my own superintendent,' Helen replied, returning the smile with saccharine, 'she can wear him around her head for all I care.'

'Oh. Right, then.'

And that was all she needed in order to ignore the rest of what he had said. For the remainder of the day she only recalled the last bit. She needed, she decided, a full frontal lobotomy, a new job, and a long holiday. And all she had was a new coat, while he, dear he, had brand-new Amanda Scott. Well, so be it. He was welcome to her. Jealousy was beneath Helen. Her instincts told her simply to give up.

Evelyn was profoundly suspicious of her father's cheerfulness. Only that morning he had suffered an attack of meanness, going on about housekeeping and other mundane activities, chuntering through a lecture on the cost of living, but now the desk in the back of his office was littered with brochures, each featuring on its cover people smiling in bikinis and swimming trunks of indecent size, bikinis to the fore, each couple in Evelyn's eyes as identical as the grains of sand on which they sat. 'I was thinking,' said her father, 'of going on holiday.' Evelyn, fairly slow today, had gathered that much. He was looking at her with questioning anxiety. 'Somewhere exotic. There's no trade here at the moment . . . well, not much. I want to leave all this unpleasantness behind. I need sun, sea, sand, all that. You've wanted to travel since you were ten, you always said you did. You'd like a holiday, wouldn't you, Evelyn?'

In another age, when she had still asked for things, before she gave up asking, when there was less to do, yes. 'When?' she asked with visible alarm.

'Oh, as soon as possible. Travel agent can get us a discount. In a day or two? Next week, maybe?'

'No,' she said loudly.

He looked at her dumbfounded. There he was in a sudden effluxion of energy, and yes, a touch of guilt, planning treats for a daughter and a suntan for himself to take away some of the years he would need to subtract before

211

grappling with one Amanda Scott, and darling child said *non* with all the defiance of a General de Gaulle. 'Why?' he asked stupidly.

'School starts next week.'

'But you've spent all summer gummed up with books, haven't you? Never let up for a single evening, ever since Mummy . . . left. Missing a week's school won't matter, surely?'

'Yes, it will.'

'Oh, Evelyn, please.'

Oh shit and blast and bloody hell. Tears again, lurking in his eyes. More therapy indicated. The sooner he went back to ignoring her the better. Look at him with his beseeching eyes, like an ancient puppy with none of the appeal. 'Later, Dad, later. Take someone else. I'll be all right on my own.'

'No, you won't, of course you won't. I've had that Mr Bailey in here only this morning asking about you. All about homework, washing up, and did you have a bicycle, for heaven's sake. Everyone seems to think I bloody neglect you and I'm not having them thinking that. What would you do if I left you here?'

Meaning what would they think, all of them out there. Mind my own business, that's what I'd do, if you and everyone else would only mind yours. Words at the back of her throat ready to be shouted in sheer exasperation and gut-wrenching panic: Why don't you leave me alone? Can't you see I've got far too much to cope with already? It's a bit late to look after me now, Dad.

'Later, Dad, like I said,' stammered in a voice of wheedling humility. 'I couldn't cope. Not just yet. I'm not

212

quite ready.' A better note to strike with him unable to see her little fists clenched behind the desk.

'Sure, darling child, but I don't see why.' The eyes filled with tears again. God, he had an inexhaustible supply that his customers never saw. He came around the desk again with his automatic gestures, automatic voice, patting her back.

''S'all right, Dad. 'S'all right, really it is. Let's just stay still awhile, shall we? After that man's been tried, Daddy, then we'll go, shall we?'

He thought of the hideous expenditure he was offering and might be avoiding, considered the business he might miss if he went away, thought of the evening ahead with delicious Amanda Scott, found himself suddenly less tearful, and patted Evelyn's behind in turn. She leapt away like a scalded cat, calmed immediately, and sat down away from him, smiling her placatory smile.

'OK, darling child. Anything you say.'

Evelyn could have wept during her afternoon of industry, ploughing through the list of shopping he had given her and she had not dared refuse. Father was watching her: it seemed everyone was watching her: she felt it when she walked down Branston High Street like a grown-up with a grocery bag, sick of it, very sick. She was even watched when she was out of bounds with William. She'd been seen on a tube platform, and he'd gone home alone, saying God knows what. If they found out about William, and what darling child did with William, that would be the end of holiday plans, school, and just about everything else that made life tolerable, like being ignored, for instance.

William had to be protected and that was all there was about it. Going on holiday and leaving that vulnerable lump was quite unthinkable. He had to be protected from himself was what, and both of them had better stay protected from the outside world.

'Buy more groceries, will you, darling child? Especially washing-up liquid?' As if she was the skivvy her mother had wanted her to be. 'I don't know what you do with it,' he'd said. 'Do you drink it or something?'

'I like the dishes clean,' Evelyn had said primly. Yes, she would love the holiday, even with him – she could lose him somewhere; he would soon be bored with her – but it was impossible. She bought the washing-up liquid, cheapest brand, like he said, looked at it quizzically. Quite impossible to leave now. Not without William sorted out first.

CHAPTER ELEVEN

The flames were still murmuring towards the beginnings
of stars when Bailey arrived at this fire. The fury of them
had diminished, but the display and the noise were still
significant. Most of the noise was the row of human
endeavour, but as he walked towards the scene, there was
a cracking of glass above the shop yard, then warning
shouts as broken windowpanes clattered into the tiny yard
below, musical and sinister, loud above the spitting of
flame. The fire had long since engulfed its own beginnings. Bailey knew on first sight exactly what fuel had been
used, watched the hungry heat that had stroked the windows into explosion. A low pyramid of boxes was tumbled
by water. The firemen always used too much water, causing more damage than the fire. It was dramatic but
pathetic, the whole sight, but it was under control. He
noticed Amanda Scott's presence and her slightly festive
clothes. Beneath her cloth coat, he could see the shiny
material of an unusually flamboyant blouse catching the

reflections of the dying flames, which also threw into focus the hard planes of her face. Her eyes shone like crystal: she was stiff with resentment at the interruption of her evening. Without a word she handed him the souvenirs she had found so efficiently, knowing he disliked her for it. For one bizarre moment, Bailey imagined her incandescent with malice.

'Coming out through the front, sir,' said another voice, irritatingly cheerful.

'Thank you.' He ducked down the smoke-filled alley beside the shop, followed the light to the road beyond.

'No problem here, sir, no one dead. They're in shock and all that, shock and smoke. One of them is cut. They live in the flat upstairs, sir. No, they're not the owners. They're an elderly couple who were watching TV, saw the flames at the back, and panicked. Couldn't get out, smashed the front door of the shop.'

Cut and crying, controlled tenants who lived above an upmarket gift shop in peaceful disharmony. Now they were consigned to a night in hospital and a lifetime fear of flames. The ambulance rolled away. One panting key holder was conferring with the fire brigade on the boarding up of his shattered plate-glass window, moaning about ruined stock already accumulated for Christmas, what a mess, what a bloody mess, a man disliking his life in the semidarkness and the acrid stench of the smoke. Bailey was momentarily oblivious of the fate of the survivors. His mind was busy with its own stock in trade; he was puzzled, alarmed, quietly angry. Deep in the pocket of his raincoat – Burberry, generously bought by Helen, stained by the smoke and by his having stooped to examine the dusty ground beyond the shop's back yard – his long fingers closed around the discordant collection of things given to him with such lack of ceremony by Amanda. Strange things to the uninitiated eye, so obviously placed, almost trampled in the rush as if the depositor of the incrimination, with a greater faith than Bailey in official vigilance, had wanted them found and relied on the eagle eye of a policeman to do so. Souvenirs. To Bailey's mind, in the sight of anyone with even primary knowledge of the boy, souvenirs with the hallmark of William Featherstone, almost bearing his autograph. A pile of bus tickets, a piece of chipped enamel half fashioned into a brooch, William's jewellery and William's favourite pastime scattered on the ground like his flag.

Early yet. An early dark, as if this arsonist had seized the first opportunity evening offered for the kind of display that would be spoiled by daylight. Even the timing served to illustrate how easy it would have been for him to arrive and depart prosaically by the bus that stopped outside the shop, timing his operation perhaps in accordance with the fictional timetables that only became fact in the early part of the evening, buses disappearing into total silence with the onset of night. Nine forty-five now. The work of minutes to stack boxes as he had done before; apply paraffin, as he had done before; discard the tickets and the shiny thing by the gate, as he had never done before. Flung apart from the other souvenirs was an empty washing-up liquid container, cheapest brand. Bailey thought fleetingly of the Featherstones' brimming sinks, the ever-expensive tastes, the mismanagement of provisions, buying the best and misusing it. It was too impractical a household for economy, not parsimonious enough. A richer, more successful household would feature such cheeseparing.

He thought of William with savagery. You have gone too far, boy, and you wanted to be discovered. This time you endangered lives; you could have killed that elderly couple with your flames. No, I have gone too far with my strange reluctance to arrest you sooner. This is my fault, you little bastard. Those deaths would have been on my conscience; now it is only these lives. Tramping back to the front of the shop, he regarded the damp but tasteful stock, saw in the key holder's hands the smooth edges of dull and tasteful jewellery, smooth handbags dusted down, and wondered with one slight tremor of shock why William had chosen such a place, so different from the tacky glitter he preferred. Looking at the damp tissue paper billowing in the road, the broken display stands crashed into by the old couple in their panic to escape, he had a sudden vision of the leaves strewn about in Antony Sumner's garden, the letters scattered on his desk with the same manic untidiness. There had been such control in the lighting of this fire and the others, such a sense of order; he could not equate this with an untidy mind. Again he thought of Antony Sumner's garden with the dead Mrs Blundell's clothing folded with such precision and placed in his otherwise disused compost bin. Her jewellery and her handbag, both purchased in exactly this kind of expensive emporium. Image crowded upon image. Untidy minds, unhinged minds, like William's. Bailey hunched in the street, trying to fathom how minds worked, confused by all the images in his own. Perhaps in William's swimming grey cells there existed this sense of order, imposed on his actions to save himself from the constant mess of his environment, but suddenly Bailey doubted it, doubted everything, sensed at work an alien mind devoid of William's clumsiness. He remembered the boy's lumbering, his strange popularity with the elderly on the buses, what Helen had described as his weird gentleness. Despite his violence, Bailey could not see him doing this, despite the evidence.

For once Amanda Scott would have to forgo the chance to make an arrest and be allowed to go home to her interrupted evening. For once, he would not phone Helen. He ordered a cursory search for William in the vicinity but not at home, please, I'll see to that. Then he went back to his office and the murder file – all the material, snippets, nonsense, rumours, documents marked 'unused' and labelled 'irrelevant' – and started again.

All right, said Helen to the kitchen ceiling. All right, all right, all right. He hasn't come home: he's doing to me what I did to him. Surely not: I've often wished the man would do something petty like this, allow me the excuse, once in a while, for a tantrum, but he doesn't, he won't; he's far too reasonable. So where the hell is he? Working, as usual? Spending his time productively? Or is he telling me something? Is he reconsidering his position in this bloody-minded household? Look at this squarely: none of it computes. His work rarely involves being away from a phone for hours on end; he had only to snap his fingers and someone would make the phone call for him; Amanda Scott would even snap his fingers for him if his knuckles were tired. Oh, be quiet. As with Bailey the night before, concern and anger intertwined in a mixture of growing unreason. She looked at the clean kitchen and envisaged the contents of the fridge: special foods, peace offerings, a good bottle of wine, rehearsed words now chilling with the rest. Bailey, we have such capacity for happiness. We must talk, or if you won't talk, at least tell me a story. I've made all these efforts with all this food . . . Was that what she was reduced to – Branston housewife in newish home seducing spouse with tidbits? Helen snorted, nine months' experience of domestic bliss, even with the long spells of contentment, curdling into a shout of resentment. I hate to cook, I hate to play second fiddle; I did not join this partnership to be a drudge, to sit around waiting for the man as if he kept me. She paused, struck by the imminence of yet more furious resentment, sat on the modern sofa. Wait a minute. There is a corollary to this: you are hooked on the man; he is a superior policeman; his partner must have self-sufficiency and endurance, and if you stay, this will be the story of your life. It cannot be otherwise, would not be otherwise were he doctor or parliamentarian; you would still be left waiting, and you would not like it, not like at all the fact that he has, in the scheme of things, greater value to the world than you. But I have even less importance here than I had in London. Branston diminishes me and no, I do not want artificial aids to fill the gap of uncertainty joining a club or taking evening classes. I cannot stay in a position where I am scolded like a child, I cannot live with a man who won't talk. And at the moment I need to talk; it's the only way I can find perspective on anything, so I'll go out and find some company, dammit, out. Where? Out. Somewhere.

Suspending judgement on her own reaction to the possible sight of William Featherstone, Helen flung on a coat, not the new coat, left Bailey a note mentioning her whereabouts and walked to The Crown. Let Bailey find the note and meet her there. Better a meeting on neutral ground: if he walked into that anonymous living room now, she might stain the walls with shouting. Not that The Crown's discordant atmosphere was likely to provide balm, but it was 'out', and the walk to reach it was preferable to static impatience, which was fast creating in her a kind of destructive electricity.

''Lo, Helen. How you been? Not seen yourself in ages. Too smart for you, are we?'

Bernadette Featherstone's greeting was offered from the depths of indifference, or so it sounded, surfacing against her better judgement; Helen found it cheering all the same. There was a party often in the bar, rowdy, post-races, post-wedding somewhere else, the revellers having found the only pub on a deserted road now had Bernadette to serve them with sullen efficiency.

'Where's Harold?' Helen asked, missing his presence leering over the counter.

Bernadette kept her eyes lowered, a posture that Helen did not know well enough to recognize as the symptom of a lie. 'Gone out with William. To the pictures.'

'Oh.' Helen found that surprising, given her knowledge of the Featherstones' habits, unprecedented even, but why not? It was pleasing news. She accepted it as truth, no real reason to doubt it.

Bernadette passed her a glass of wine without glance or comment. She was not about to confess that dear Harold

221

was snoring like a drunkard, dead to the world upstairs, the combined effect of a bender and a row with William, whose whereabouts were currently, not unusually unknown. For once, Bernadette was conscious of her lack of control in her own family, bitter and ashamed of it. She was worried enough for her mind to be crossed with the idea of asking for help, but the thought died in passage.

If Helen had hoped for some biting conversation, perhaps a piece of invective, she was disappointed, but relieved all the same to retreat to a corner with a newspaper and book, only half of her waiting for Bailey; if she'd stayed at home, she would have waited with deathly, furious concentration.

'Himself coming down tonight, is he?' Bernadette shouted from the bar in the second tribute to manners.

'Maybe, maybe not. He'll please himself. I don't know.'

'Bloody men,' yelled Bernadette, startling the customers, granting Helen a transitory sensation of solidarity.

She read, drank a second glass of wine, watched through the door daylight fading with reluctance, the sky clawing at the remnants of summer, conscious in herself of the trickling away of patience and concentration. She had resisted the impulse to swig a couple of large gins, but in the bloodstream of her thinking, the dry red wine provoked slow ideas, speculation, and the return of the restlessness that had driven her out of her home and into the harsh plush of the pub's seat. With all this itching, she had deflected her mind from her own condition into thinking of William Featherstone. She remembered his reference to the summerhouse den, his retreat, a place that somehow offered him a curious safety and comfort. Helen felt a childish wish for the same sort of hiding place. She wondered if Bernadette knew of it, imagined she must; surely she did. There must be some place to which you consigned a child such as William with your blessing for his absence. Helen's desire to see this refuge became suddenly overpowering; this impulse was not entirely the effect of the liquid, more the last resort of a weirder kind of stress. But the drink always had this kind of effect on her, making her wilfully stupid when she should have been cautious, active when passivity was appropriate, talkative when silence was better advised. She wanted to see the den so much she did not have a choice; it was like that coat, there was no choice at all. There was this den, something to be discovered before darkness was complete, something to do. Professional solicitor plays amateur detective. How rude, how intrusive, how silly. She reflected she was merely curious after the most vulgar of fashions; she had no right to explore or trespass and would not have done so without the wine or the constant irritation of Bailey's absence. She got up and went to the bar.

'You trying to tank up or something?' said Bernadette briskly, avoiding her eye.

'Listen,' said Helen, 'you've got a summerhouse bar or something like that, in the garden, haven't you? Can I look at it?'

Bernadette blanched, grinned, and frowned in quick succession, looking in one moment the image of her uncertain son, mirroring his vulnerability. She forgot the obvious remark – 'What's it to you?' – and all the aggression that usually followed any question she regarded as impertinent. Her shoulders sagged and her face crumpled

223

instead. There was bravado in her voice, but not in the way she stood, like a rag doll.

'Yes, there is. A bloody great shed. Want to buy it? It's William's, you know.' This she said in a great rush of confidence. 'At least I think it is.'

'I know. He told me.' Tactless, thought Helen as she said it, very tactless.

Bernadette's face showed a whiplash of hurt. 'Did he, now? Well, I won't ask when and how, bugger never talks to me. Look all you want. Why should I bloody care? He never tells me anything, that boy, my bloody son. And if he's out there, send him in.'

'You said he was at the pictures.'

'So I did, so he is, of course, with his dad. Sorry I spoke. At the flicks.' Moving away in dismissal. 'Go on if you're going. Look out for the tree on the path. Sod you.'

It was this invitation that committed her; that and her own tactlessness dispatched her on a mission. Explore and report back, discover this den, since you already know more than Bernadette. Report back with reassurance if you dare, damn you, some hurt to be justified. Crossing the dark path leading downhill from the kitchen, Helen was defensive rather than fearful, bold rather than afraid, ridiculously active in any pursuit rather than sitting still.

After clambering over the fallen tree, still visible in the semi-darkness, she saw the shed looming before her and almost laughed out loud. It was a ridiculous lopsided structure, a Featherstone masterpiece. Oh, what a fine abandoned dream, lovable on sight, redolent of her own childhood, a place she would have adopted, woven ghosts for, dreamed of, kept a secret from sisters and brothers,

224

loved. Still aware of the unkindness of her mission, the rudeness in her curiosity, she determined not to linger despite her delight in this eccentricity. She would take one quick look around the back, a few more glances of furtive admiration. Then she'd go back inside, make peace with Bernadette, walk home, and face whatever music happened to be playing when she arrived. She was making for the window when the door of the shed creaked open like a prop in a horror film, and there, squinting into her own startled face, were the equally startled features of one William Featherstone.

'Who's that?'

She could not open her mouth.

'Oh. It's you.' He stood with his arms by his sides like a gorilla, face in a frown of confusion, unable to decide between anger, irritation, and relief in the knowledge that the eyes which met his own were neither unfamiliar nor unsympathetic. He flushed with disappointment, searching his mind for some sort of precedent or rule that would cover this situation. Evie had never mentioned or rehearsed him for this: he did not know what to do, but found in the end that anger was impossible. There was something here he liked; he could not remember what. He rubbed his hands across his eyes, felt exposed, while some strange code of manners afflicted him. Lumbering alongside the remnants of social graces forced into him as a child and all but forgotten now, there lingered his pride in the den itself, his own creation, something he had always yearned to show while knowing he could not. And Evie was not here to forbid it. At this time of night she would not come here, and if she did, she would be angry, he knew it. Yesterday she had abandoned him to this woman; today she might have done the same, no telling.

Helen smiled, the expression intended to cover a feeling of fear still half formed. William found himself smiling in return. 'You'd better come in,' he said, and tugged her arm in clumsy invitation.

She was suddenly diffident, genuinely shy herself. 'Should I?' she asked. 'Are you sure? You don't have to show me . . .'

'Course I'm sure. Come.' Some equally strange code of manners made it impossible for her to refuse.

He went back inside the shed. Helen followed, seeing herself in one brief glimpse in the window as the kind of character she had always hated in films, the one who walked off into the dark danger by herself with the whole audience shouting, 'Don't do that, you silly bitch. Can't you see it's the last thing you should do?' After negotiating the lethal steps and entering what appeared to be a kind of shallow grave, she found herself in a haven so bizarre she almost giggled with relief.

William lit the lamp before she descended the broken stepladder, something he could always do in the dark. Then he stood by like an anxious estate agent showing a house, waiting for her reaction, hoping for approval. With his arms extended, he could almost touch both walls, his head nearly touching the ceiling. The den in Helen's eyes was cluttered but reasonably clean, equipped with all the necessities of life, like a fallout shelter prepared for a siege: a few tins of food, two piled-up mattresses, a cupboard on which was pinned, quite incongruously, a bunch of tinsel pinched from the gaudy supply of The Crown, William's latest homemaking attempt, glittering foolishly in the dark. Helen had a fleeting picture of submarine life, men living in restricted airspace that smelled like this, of bodies and dust and perspiration, a threatened prison bedecked with pathetic tributes to ordinary humanity in an ordinary world.

William regarded her hopefully, his face a question mark, his mind working out why he liked her. Oh, yes, she had not told on him about being in London. Was that it? Something of the kind registered, and, oh, yes, she had a coat she had shown him, pretty. She was old, of course, teacher-old, one of them, but nice. He had longed for adult approval, longed to show this place to someone other than Evie, who visited with intermittent grace and who was frequently critical, rarely admiring. His longing was a version of domestic pride. 'I made all this,' said William, the excitement of the achievement clear in his voice, 'and no one else comes here, except—'

'Except Evelyn,' said Helen neutrally. 'Of course she does. William, it's wonderful, really it is. Where did you find all these things? Oh, look at that, you've even got cutlery. You could live here for ever and no one would know.'

The thrill of approbation seemed endless: he shook with it, mumbling in shy embarrassment, remembering again his strange and erratic code of manners. 'Sit, sit. You want tea? Only I got no milk. Plenty sugar but no milk.'

'Black tea, plenty sugar, will do fine.'

He was busy, flustered beyond efficiency, managing nevertheless to heat water on the other arm of the gas camping stove that held the light. He put tea bags in mugs surprisingly clean, and finally, after providing a running commentary on each of his own movements, brought forth tea of a kind. It tasted as it looked, lukewarm, flavoured in her mind with the smell of butane and the heat of the camping stove, the taste at odds with the last of the red wine. The place had ambience, she decided, suppressing hysteria by concentrating on the tastes in her mouth. The scents of the room were both domestic and animal. Her wandering imagination, which had lit first on the image of a submarine, dwelt next on the notion of a fox in its lair: William must not be made to feel at bay. With the image of a fox prancing through her mind, her hands curled around the mug and she remembered Mrs Blundell's fingers, thought of her predators, human and animal. She looked at the hulk of William sitting beside her on the makeshift bed, talking as if there were no tomorrow, benign, amiable, dangerous.

'I keep my tools in here,' he was saying, eager to display anything and everything there was.

'Do you, now? And did you make the cupboard?'

'Yes, of course.'

'Why do you need so many tools?'

'For making things, of course.' He threw her a look of condescension reserved by males for silly females.

'What things? Can I see them?'

A sigh of exaggerated, completely hypocritical impatience, 'Oh, all right, then, I s'pose you can . . . You won't tell?'

'Why on earth would I tell?'

'Don't know, but you might. They'd laugh.'

'I promise I won't tell. And I shan't laugh, either.'

'OK.' It had been enough to stroke William's burning

228

impatience to show off his handiwork. He opened the crooked homemade compartments of the cupboard, showing his collection of polystyrene figures, recognizably human but odd. 'I don't do these any more,' William remarked in passing. Then he revealed things carved in wood; then rings, bangles, and strings of strange glass beads spilled into Helen's hands. 'I like these things best,' he said simply in explanation for their existence. The shelf below this treasure chest held a hand drill, hammer, pliers, mallet, and the dull gleam of a blade.

Helen dragged her gaze to the glitter he held out for her inspection, and even while murmuring in genuine amazement, 'Oh, William, what's that?' or 'How on earth did you make this?' let her eyes go back to the knife on that shelf, an old horn handle and the pristine blade of a single-edge working knife, settled as comfortably as a carving knife in a kitchen. She admired William's possessions, silently remembering courtroom descriptions of wounds to the throat made by a single-edge knife that was never found. Oh, don't be silly, the world is full of knives. And throats cut within a half-mile of this shed?

William's sharper instincts caught her second glance at the weapon. He reached into the cupboard with the swiftness of a snake and pushed the thing to the back, looked at her in doubtful trust, withdrew it again. 'I saw you looking,' he remarked. 'You may as well see. Nice, isn't it?'

'Lovely,' said Helen. 'Only I don't like knives much. They frighten me.'

'They don't frighten me,' said William. 'I know what to do with them.'

'What do you do with them?'

229

'Oh, carve things most of the time. And kill people.'
This was a boastful shout.

'I don't see why anyone would want to do that,' said
Helen.

'I did,' said William, puffing out his chest.

'Oh, put the knife away, William. I like the jewels better.
Show me some more.' He did as he was asked, anxious
again to please, his memory as short as the moment.

Against her will she was impressed and frightened.
'Perhaps you could make things for a living, William. I
mean, you could learn how to do all sorts of work . . . oh,
I don't know, carpentry, making pretty things like these.
You'd be earning your own money. Wouldn't that be nice?
Would you like that?'

'Oh, I would, I would.' He looked so vulnerable, like a bull
terrier puppy, all pale snout and clumsy power, musclebound
brain, confused reactions of confused strength.

'Perhaps you could talk to your dad about that.'

'Perhaps,' he said gruffly. 'But I don't talk to Dad much.'

'Why not?'

'Evie said not to. She says when I talk I always talk too
much, and if I talk too much she won't come here any
more, not even on Sundays. Besides, I don't like talking to
Dad. I'm no good at it.'

'You need more practice. Then you'd make more sense.
You get better at everything if you practise.'

He was not insulted. 'Practice? You mean like I got
better at making things by doing it all the time? That's
funny. Talking to Dad's not like that.' He laughed, a yelp-
ing, snorting sound, unnaturally loud, and she laughed
with him.

'No,' she said, 'talking isn't quite like that. But the idea's the same.' Dear God, Bailey, where are you?

But the laughter had stopped, William fallen into a dreadful stillness as sudden and complete as a paralysis. He grabbed her arm, fingers digging into her wrist, face paler than a ghost.

'What is it, William? What is it?'

'Shhh.'

From above their heads there was a whisper of movement, then a silence unnervingly complete. Into the silence crept the sounds of the gathering night, the faint and distant noise of wind in the trees, the tiny whisper of an aeroplane overhead, nothing suggesting an intruder. William loosened his grip on Helen's arm, the puzzled look still stuck to his features, mouth open, eyes wide and clownish, softening into repose. ''S'all right,' he said in a whisper. 'Mices, I think. Keep quiet, though.'

She sat silent and obedient, relaxing slowly, recognizing in him antennae that she did not have and a wariness she could not share. Then, as William opened his slack mouth to speak, there was a flurry of steps, a grunt of effort, the expulsion of breath in one great gasp.

Over their heads the trapdoor slammed into place, knocking aside the ladder and filling the cellar with choking dust and debris. Both of them gasped, retreating to the farthest corner of the room, she upsetting and extinguishing the lamp in the process, he turning off the hiss of the gas in one swoop, actions felt rather than seen in a darkness that seemed total. Then silence fell again for one pregnant and endless minute, full of the sound of breathing. In that long interval her eyes adjusted, sharpened by overpowering claustrophobia, until she could see the cracks between the wooden slats of the trapdoor and the shape of the trapdoor itself. She stuffed her fist into her mouth to prevent herself from screaming, choked on her fingers, and grabbed for William's arm, anything to touch. As she groped for him, he hugged her with one paw and wrapped the other around her neck. He placed his hand over her mouth, gently, but brooking no argument.

Silence followed the thunder upstairs. Then a sensuous scraping as if an animal or a human had lain across the trapdoor. There was a long, contrived sigh, an adjustment of clothes, then the sound of humming.

'Evie,' William screamed. 'Evie!'

A muffled sob, then heels drumming on the trapdoor, stopping as the voice began, petulant, seductive, and slow. 'You told, William Featherstone, you told. Crybaby, tell-tale. You told.' The voice was hardly recognizable as Evie's, a droning monotonous adult whine.

'I didn't, I didn't.' A responding shriek from William. 'I didn't, no I didn't.'

'Did, did, did.'

Helen struggled briefly against William's grip. His bitter-tasting palm remained clamped over her lips, forcing her to be silent.

'What did I tell? Who? When?' Another shout, irritation mingling with fear in his voice. 'What'm I supposed to have told?' This he repeated on a rising note of hysteria. Fumbling in the dark, Helen shuffled closer to the trap-door, one arm feeling for William's shoulder, leading him in a single step, smelling the stale, earthbound smell of him, sensed the beginning of his tears.

The figure moved on the slats of the trapdoor, face pressed to the wood, voice more composed, louder, but still an insistent drone, monotonous, childish. 'You told, William, didn't you?'

'No, Evie, I didn't. Open the door, stupid.'

'Don't call me stupid.'

A silence of great length, William controlling his breathing, Helen standing absolutely still. Then, peculiarly, Evie sobbing, lying on the dirty door above and whimpering, whether in rage or in grief it was impossible to determine.

'I can't let you out, William. They'll be looking for you, all of them, I thought you'd be safe, but you aren't. I know you've told about us, and you'll tell the rest. So soft you are, William. You can stay here now, in the dark. Then you'll know better.'

'No, Evie, please.'

''S'all right William, I'll be back.'

There was scuffling, shuffling, thudding, a dragging of something heavy across the floor, sounds of more effort from Evelyn. William screamed again. 'Come back! Don't go, Evie. I'll tell them whatever you want. I'll tell them I did everything if you like, everything.'

'Did everything what, William?' Evelyn's voice was sharp and normal now, but fatigued and impatient.

He hesitated before answering in quieter tones, sinking to a mutter. 'Don't know. Everything.'

There was a tut-tutting of annoyance while Evie digested this and Helen stiffened. 'No,' said the upstairs voice, leaden with despair. 'That isn't what you were supposed to say at all, is it? You can stay here now until you remember what you should tell them if you're daft enough

233

ever to say anything. That way people will leave me alone. So if you want to say anything, you can tell them you saw Mummy's boyfriend kill her, which is just what happened, isn't it? But you're useless. You've got to stay here now.'

The object she had pushed and pulled across the floor was shoved once more, falling on to one side against the slats. Liquid began to trickle through the wood in a steady stream, striking their upturned faces, hitting hair and clothes until William dragged Helen back out of reach, his hand still clamped on her mouth. Evelyn's quick footsteps died away; the door of the summerhouse banged into silence. William released his hand, slumped on the mattresses, began to sniff, while Helen felt the strongest urge yet to scream into the darkness, a reaction suppressed only by the more pressing need to cough and choke. He recovered, banged her back, unaffected by the smell that filled the place.

'Silly,' he muttered, an adult attempt at bravery, taking strength in the act of patting her, 'very silly, it'll be all right, you wait. Not to worry, missus, I can get out of here easy. When I can see,' he added, shuffling around on the floor, then standing and feeling in his pockets.

'What do you want, William? What are you looking for?'

'Matches,' he answered. 'Ah, found them.' Somewhere beyond his head, the liquid was still dripping, hitting the stone slab on the floor where the ladder had rested. Helen grabbed at his arm. ''S'all right,' he said again. 'I can get out of here easy, once I've found the lamp.'

'William, do not light a match, *don't*, whatever you do.'

'Why?'

234

'Because,' she said, speaking slowly and carefully, enunciating each syllable, 'because Evelyn just poured this stuff all over us. You must not light a match, William; we are covered with paraffin.'

She could hear the rattle of the matchbox as he dropped it to the floor. 'Oh,' he said. 'I see.'

CHAPTER TWELVE

Bailey disliked the exterior of this pretentious house and took particular exception to the gravel outside the front door, placed there for the sole purpose of making a sound of satisfying richness. *Nouvelle richesse*, in Blundell's case, no worse than any other kind, simply more offensive. The snobbery of it appealed to Bailey's own subdued inversion of snobbery, which had prompted him to allow Amanda Scott to deal with this man and his neighbours instead of doing the job himself. Bailey knew he had no right to his prejudices. Some people chose houses that advertised their wealth, but they bled and suffered the same as those who had failed to make such conspicuous improvement in their lives. Still, the gravel irritated his soul. So had Blundell on their first meeting, when he had been diffident, sedulous, and crawling to please in a man-to-man kind of way, even when reporting the absence of a wife. 'Sorry to bother you, old man,' he had said. For God's sake.

Whatever resentment Bailey felt then would be

reciprocated now. No man enjoyed visits from the police at eleven-thirty at night unless he was in pain or truly desperate for company. Only the form Blundell's resentment would take remained to be seen. PC Bowles, large and uniformed in the car outside the gate, could lend an air of officialdom if necessary, but Bailey hoped not. He knew the purpose of his visit to be tenuous, knew his pocket should contain a search warrant, and had already rehearsed the alternative approach, an example of the kind of benign trickery he had often used: 'If you won't let me in to look at your house, sir, I'm sure you won't mind waiting with this officer here while I go and wake up a magistrate to supply me with the piece of paper that will force you to comply. Up to you, sir.'

'And why do you want to search my house, Mr Bailey?'

'Well, I don't rightly know. There are questions lingering here.'

'Get out, Mr Bailey.'

He tried the garage first. Open and empty, nothing to steal apart from a bicycle – old, battered, hidden by a tarpaulin. Clearly labelled in Bailey's mind were two preoccupations: letters, and the gleam of gold. Letters taken from Antony Sumner's desk, the ones Amanda had failed to secure so sure was she of their irrelevance. Perhaps other, similar letters she had failed to discover here. And maybe the jewellery worn by the dead woman, the bracelet, earrings, and necklace that Blundell had described so uncannily well, as if he had seen them very recently. Bailey could not rid himself of the conviction that they were still in this house. Certainly the man was mean enough to keep them and claim his insurance, but Bailey

237

doubted if that was all he'd been up to. He was clever enough, or maybe simply rich enough, to deflect dear Miss Scott. 'And every time she shouted "fire," the people answered, "Little liar".' Bailey recited the old rhyme to himself, stopping to survey the front door, trying to decide upon the most appropriate pleasantries for the occupants. Sometimes he managed the most sophisticated approach of all, making himself think and feel like an ordinary visitor, imagining himself with an invitation and sure of a welcome. People allowed extraordinary privileges to their guests, showed them the sanctum of their own lives, displayed everything from the beams to the contents of the bathroom cabinet without turning a hair. If Bailey could think of Blundell as his host, he might influence events. Then again, he might not. He could not imagine John Blundell offering him a drink, and the thought reminded him not only of the taste of whisky but of how difficult he would find it to refuse. A whisky would be nectar.

But within feet of the front door, he knew the house was empty, giving off from itself the scent of vacancy. He had spent enough of his life approaching doors and windows unbidden, in the dark, in daylight, in the eyes of storms, and instinct told him immediately when human life was absent. He had learned in the bitter experience of failure how to avoid the pitfalls, and how and where a man could hide indefinitely, learned to sense emptiness and its opposite. He had sat in a room for two hours on guard, uncomfortable, but unaware of the one silent Indian hidden behind a wardrobe two feet from his own back and still carrying a knife. Now he knew when to turn, when to look, when to ignore logic and obey his instincts. There was nothing live in this house; he was sure of it. But for all that, the place was lit up like a Christmas tree. Blundell, it seemed, was losing his grip: door unlocked, lights on, not a soul to be seen, like the *Marie Celeste*. When Blundell left, he had believed his castle to be still occupied.

Bailey shouted into the empty hall and was relieved by the answering silence. Acutely aware, if only for a second, of the dubious legality of his presence, he began to walk from room to room. Kitchen empty and tidy, heart of a heartless house, two glasses on the table. Living rooms and handsome stairs muffled by carpet and soft beneath the feet. Calling 'Anyone at home?' he trod heavily up the stairs, moved along the hall and into the largest room, being deliberately noisy, both as a warning to others and as a sop to his conscience.

He was indifferent to the fact that this exercise could blight his career, a consideration that had persuaded him to leave Bowles behind to avoid tarring him with the same brush of disgrace for so flagrant a breach of the rules. Bailey forgot the professional madness of his illicit search as soon as he stepped into what was obviously Blundell's room. Handsome mirrored wardrobes lined one whole wall. Wealth consumed by vanity, thought Bailey, opening the first door. Good God. A row of shredded garments hanging from padded hangers like streamers, resembling tired flags ripped by a malicious wind long after the celebration. Another door revealed more of the same, rags replaced neatly as if the creases of them still mattered, zips gaping like wounds, sleeves in shreds. He was stunned, closed the doors with something like reverence, furious with Amanda Scott, his mind jangling with possibilities, entertaining the thought of Blundell as murderer. Then he put the thoughts back into order, stored the vision of this graveyard of clothing for future reference, went back to the first purpose of his trespassing, left the room, and went to the next.

An unpromising door, bolted from the inside, light from the interior colouring the dark floor in a brilliant band. He had quickly identified the remainder of the upstairs rooms; this door was the only one left for the daughter of the house. Evelyn, darling child, whose writing on a shopping list seen in John Blundell's office bore such a striking resemblance to that on juvenile love letters to a teacher currently in prison. He did not know what was in his own mind other than writing, the gleam of gold, and a familiar feeling under his skin.

Bailey put his shoulder to the door, felt the breeze from the open window beyond as the softest splintering of wood shrugged off a cheap bolt, clumsily constructed as a barrier against a world that had never wanted entry in the first place. More a symbol, this bolt, effective only because it was completely respected. On the other side of the door, a room so Spartan it almost defied occupation: small bed, tacky wardrobe, cheap wooden desk bought for a child, spitefully at odds with the luxury of the rest of the house. A plastic skeleton hanging from a cupboard and a hoard of books, tidily placed. Thin curtains moved in the breeze, flagging the presence of Evelyn Blundell's own back door. A small transistor radio was playing quietly but insistently. He sat in the childish chair by the desk and began to open the drawers. Somewhere out there, walking the streets in the quasi-countryside of this artificial part of the world, looking at the better life, was darling child, a malevolent, determined, and beautiful presence, perhaps protecting a murderer. Somewhere in this anonymous room was the rest of her, arrogantly undisturbed.

Evelyn sat at the edge of Bluebell Wood, half frozen. She had embarked on her evening enterprises dressed for action, but her cotton T-shirt was inadequate against the cool night. The wood behind her was black. She had no fear of darkness but was chilled by her impatience and the cold. From this end of the wood, she could just see the outline of The Crown in the distance, partially obscured by trees, nothing else visible: her eyes fixed to a point between trees and horizon. Do it, William, just do it. Put your hand in your pocket, feel your silly plonker, leave it alone, and get out the matches. I couldn't, but you can. Go on, you just don't understand fires; you never did, not even after the first one I made you try. You were too thick; you couldn't even see it was fun. You only like doing that thing. You don't really like anything else except all that foul jewellery you make and, even worse, what you steal, and putting your plonker in me, and I'm so bloody tired of that, really I am. I'm sorry, though. All that fiddling about wasn't enough to keep you quiet; it makes me mad. I can't stand all that squidgy stuff. You'll talk to that woman you went with yesterday, went back on the bloody train with her, too frightened to go on the tube by yourself. It's no good, William, no good. You'll be like putty. All those questions, it's no good, William; you've got to go. Out like a light. Oh, I'm sorry, I shouldn't have said that, shouldn't think it, even without anyone hearing. She giggled at her own bad taste. I'm sorry, William.

Her shivering was becoming uncontrollable. She remembered the bicycle rides, huge physical efforts, the sensation of palpitating heat as she had watched the first of the flames outside the shop, then more pumping of pedals and heartbeat and emotion as she had entered the summerhouse, flexed first her hearing, and then her muscles to drag the paraffin across the floor, having closed that door. She had not intended to use the paraffin at first. A spur-of-the-moment stroke of brilliance, the same ultimate solution she had played with yesterday, not really intending to use it until she had seen his cringing and knew despite his denials that he was slipping. She'd heard the lie in the shrillness of his voice and had realized in the same moment that the general discrediting of William by having him labelled a loopy arsonist as well as a thief was not going to save either of them; all it meant was that no one would believe a fire raiser. He had to be put away where no one could talk to him at all. Now, in the absence of any flames hitting the sky, the sight for which she had grown hungry, she doubted her own wisdom, wondered if she had underestimated him. Surely not, she decided. She contemplated going back, but no, let him face his family stinking of paraffin if he got out – family and policemen, if they had found her clues. What difference would it make? They would never listen to him now.

The field below her inclined gently toward The Crown, the stubble of it shining like dull gold. Slinking down one side, barely visible, was the fox, a mere suspicion of movement, a flash on the eye like a ghost in motion. Its presence was a blow of surprise, a dark premonition of disaster, filling her mouth with vomit as she watched to see how close the thing would pass before detecting her presence. She loathed the sinuous progress of it, Mama's fox coming back, the one that had bitten off her hand, or so she had heard in some eavesdropped aside. No animal, no living thing, should have the teeth or temerity for that. Mother had been hers, the revenge all her own. Evelyn jumped to her feet, shouted wildly. 'Go away, go away,' waved her arms, watched the fox freeze, flatten, turn, and double back into the undergrowth at the foot of The Crown's jungle of a garden. She was shaking with relief; she kicked her feet and wagged her hands, jogged on the spot, circled the tree against which she had sat, settled down again to rest, flexed her fingers, looked at her watch. Midnight.

When she got home, she would write it all down, the way she wrote so many things, as Antony had taught her. It's all in your head, Evelyn: writing is only learning how to get it out, make sense of it. She remembered the alien familiarity of her room, the papers in it. They were safe, of course, the mildest of risks, because Papa could be bribed with the gold in the end, and no one had ever wanted entry to her sanctuary. No one ever had. Her only risk was what she had written; her only legacy from the teacher. Her eyes began to close.

She would wait one more hour. Then she would go and see.

Still no sign of fire.

William was sinking into sullen inactivity, shuffling and speechless.

'Cheer up. Nothing's ever as bad as it looks.' Helen's

voice rang false in her own ears, repeating a cliché she hated.

He grunted with short laughter. 'Nothing looks like anything in the dark. We can't see anything in the dark.'

'OK. Sorry I spoke.'

'Not your fault.'

'Couldn't we try again, pet? You lift me up, I push the door?'

'No, I can't. I don't even want to. I'm tired.'

So was she. Their several attempts to shift the trapdoor with a certain clumsy co-ordination but without the benefit of the shattered ladder, had resulted in nothing. The first shove had shifted the paraffin container, dousing them further, while the second had damaged their ankles and knees. They were filthy and stinking. Helen's hope for eventual rescue via Bernadette, whose punishment for her interference would surely not be as extreme as abandonment, had sunk to a dull glow of optimism. Her greatest fear was the return of Evelyn, but her fear was William's greatest wish and she tried to distract him from it. Even in the course of their efforts, in the flow of her own chatter, the odd joke which had succeeded in making him laugh, William's stone mill of a mind had been grinding out conclusions. She had begged him to think; now she wished he could stop.

'She isn't coming back,' he said.

'Well, she's obviously cross about something.'

'I don't mean now. Ever.'

'Oh, I expect she will. People don't stay cross for long.'

'She tried to kill us. No, me.'

'Oh, no, William. This is just her idea of a joke.'

'She knows I don't understand about fires. She tried to teach me, but I couldn't learn.'

Helen paused, unwilling to stretch him further but desperately seeking clues as to how to deal with the dreadful possibility of Evelyn's return.

'Why is she so cross, William? Is it about you and her being special friends, you know what I mean, going to bed together? Is she afraid her father might find out, or what? There's more than that isn't there?'

'We weren't always special friends. She wouldn't let me . . .' He wavered away into uncertainty. Helen imagined Bailey as interrogator. How quickly he would persuade this boy to tell, shuddered at the thought, listened. 'I suppose she didn't like it very much. She only let me after . . . Oh, never mind.'

'After what?'

'After her mummy was dead. I cried. We buried her, Evie's mummy. She hated her mummy, but not as much as she hated the man she says killed her mummy.'

'Oh.' Helen cleared her throat. 'What about her mummy's coat and things? You know, the things women always seem to have, rings and bracelets and handbags. And clothes of course.' She could sense the puzzlement she could not see. William had lost his power to contrive, forgotten his small ability to keep secrets.

'She didn't have any clothes and things,' he said finally. 'She was all bare. Like a big chicken.' He gave a giggle of embarrassment.

'Goodness,' said Helen. 'And how did you dig the hole for her?'

245

'With our hands, mostly, and Evelyn's knife. The ground was very soft.'

'Is that her knife you showed me?'

'Yes. She told me to throw it away. I didn't, though. She never looks in the cupboard. I thought' – he struggled with the idea – 'I thought afterwards, long time afterwards, she might have wanted me to say I killed her mummy. I always said I would say that if she liked, I'd say that again and again if anyone ever said she'd done it – Evie, I mean.'

'You go to prison for things like that, William. For a long time.'

'So what? Doesn't matter for me,' said William stoutly. 'Why should it matter for me? But Evie's clever, going to be a doctor. Only Evie matters, not me. I love Evie better than anything. Only Evie ever cared about me.'

'She didn't—' Helen tried to make her questions as diffident as possible. 'She didn't see someone kill her mummy, did she?'

'I don't know,' said William hopelessly. 'I don't know, and I wouldn't care if she did. I don't know anything any more.' Sobs were rising again like a storm. 'I don't know. Her mummy was horrible. I only wanted to help. And now she wants to kill me.'

'Of course she doesn't. She'll come back.'

'She wants to kill me,' he repeated. 'And I don't know why.'

Helen put her arms around him, prayed for rescue, hugged him, and rocked him to and fro, a part of her wishing in fury a fate worse than death for Evelyn, the other part wondering how long it took for paraffin fumes to evaporate. The skin of her face felt flammable, her arms were weak, and the boy was growing ever more helpless. Wait for daylight. Another thought occurred to her with appalling clarity. 'William, will you give me the matches? I'd feel safer.' He handed them over. Her recognition, in this simple demand, of his despair and his longing to be dead made him cry more.

'There, there, no crying, love. Think about something else. There'll be nice things to do in the morning. Shh, now. Listen, I'll tell you a story.'

'I'm frightened,' said William. 'Hug me. No one's ever going to hug me again.' It was said with utter and final conviction. She hesitated. Hugging William, even in this filthy pit, was a dangerous activity for a boy who could not distinguish between affection and desire. She hugged him all the same. They might neither of them see morning.

'My mother never hugged me,' Bailey read. 'Never did anything like that, ever. Dressed up and all that all the time, but never went in for hugging; it smudged her. Don't like her a lot and reckon she hates me. Jealous as sin. Hates me having friends. Always calls me darling child, like I haven't got a bloody name.' Bailey was examining one of a hundred fragments he had found in the desk in Evelyn's room, a mess of paper crammed into drawers, half-written letters and portions of school essays.

This page was mildly corrected in Antony Sumner's hand: 'Evelyn, no need to swear in essays. It diminishes your considerable talent for description. Please remember to write in full sentences, not a series of fragments. Try this paragraph, "A Description of My Family" again.'

She had tried again on the bottom of the same sheet:

'My mother is always staring into the distance and prefers I do not have a real name or identity. She has never loved me and always tries to prevent me having anything I want. The more I treasure something, the harder she will try to take it away.'

'Much better, but give examples,' Sumner annotated in a bored hand. 'An essay should illustrate the points it makes.'

'Well, she took away my camera, my new desk, my best clothes. She would never let me have friends or anything,' Evelyn had continued on an uncorrected sheet, apparently written for her own benefit, the standard of the English beginning to slip. 'Amazing she lets me have these English lessons. Because I asked Dad first, because it's pretty cheap and because she doesn't think it would be any fun. Didn't know, did she, how I love you. Thought she'd just be keeping me indoors while she's so bloody fat and I'm so thin. Ha ha.'

Beneath these fragments, of which Evelyn had kept dozens of pages corrected in Sumner's handwriting, Bailey found a pile of poignantly incomplete letters on primrose paper: 'My darling Antony, I love you so much it hurts. I want to kiss you all over, I'll do whatever you like. No one else listens to me except you and no one else notices me. Even if I had any friends, I couldn't bring them home, especially not Will. So I'm free to love you to pieces, and I do, I do. Hope you got my Valentine. Now that we have lessons with just us, I shall have you all to myself. She doesn't know. How can I write how much I love you?'

Scattered among the sheets of compulsive writing were random diary jottings, as if Sumner's tuition had brought about an obsessive habit with the pen and a constant urge to record, albeit incompletely. On scraps torn from exercise books lay the evidence of a saga of bitter disappointment. 'August 5: Mummy losing weight like an Ethiopian. Ha ha. Buying new things. I wonder if she wants him. Oh, God, she can't, she's old. Why? Because he's mine, that's why. I watch them going out for drinks. Dad pretends he doesn't notice.'

Next, a torn sheet, crumpled, straightened out again, kept against her better judgement: 'Watched them in the woods. Disgusting, yuck. He sucks her big tits, puts his thing in her, grunting like pigs. Why, why, why? I would have. I'm going to find William. Must stop crying. Can't stop crying. How can you do this to me? I hate her, hate her. Only thing I ever really wanted.'

'October 4: Dad buying things for her, only she never lets him buy anything for me. Gold stuff, lots of it. Suppose she thinks she looks bloody wonderful. Dad trying to buy her back. Silly wanker. Antony talks to me, nice to me, but pathetic, head somewhere else. That gold stuff is mine by right. What about me, Daddy? What about me, then? I am beginning . . .'

'November 10: Where will they go in the cold? Not Bluebell Wood. In his car? Yuck. A whole winter in a car? That won't do. Ha ha. I wonder about telling Dad but what difference would it make? I got William to rap on the car window and scare them.'

'March 15: She's gone funny. He's gone off her; I knew he would. Now he'll come back to me. I want to, I want to, but he's making excuses not to come any more for my lessons. Why not? What have I done? How can he leave me?

Surely he knows I don't mind about bitch face as long as he comes back.'

Then a flat statement on May 10: 'Followed him again. He was with someone else, kissing. Watched them a long time. He doesn't come here any more and doesn't even say hello to me.'

A gap of weeks and then more animation: 'Mummy phones him all the time, but he won't come back. She's done it, hasn't she? Driven him away. She doesn't know I can listen to her on the phone, doesn't even care if I do. Jangling gold and making phone calls. I can't say how much I hate her stinking face. She took him, she took him. Serves her right. Hate him, hate him, hate him.'

'June 5: She gets him to meet her! I'm going, too. With my k . . .'

Bailey paused in his reading, opened the next drawer. More paper, roughly torn sheets with crossings-out, sketched maps, a tube map of London, and a picture of a local craft shop, one of William s favourites, Bailey seemed to remember. There were lists, terse reminders on paper: 'Get washing liquid, v. useful. Hide bike, ask Dad for new one, don't tell.' Interspersed with the lists were strange descriptions, like brief catharses, literary attempts to distil an experience, full of slang in a deliberate and rebellious departure from the favoured style of the essays. A passage dated the day of Sumner's committal: 'You'd like this, Mr Antony fucking Sumner. Ain't this kind of neat? You were in the wood again with the old sow who wants to shag you like a bitch in heat – she never let me have a dog, so I don't know how I know. Says she'll run off with you, doesn't give a fuck for her daughter, husband, etc. Tell me news.

Ha ha. Ants in her pants, ripping off clothes. You hit her with the stick and leave her there with her bum in the air and your stick on the ground. Gives me the idea. So I tiptoe up with my knife and then I tiptoe away again. Get *my* gold later, also clothes. I want to . . . Go on, then, rot. Daddy's the same today. In I come in the evening, go downstairs. "All this time studying, darling child?" he says. "Of course," I say.'

Bailey put down the page and found his hands were trembling. Sifted through the rest finding none of equal length or savagery, some of a similar degree of crudeness: 'At least I now know How to Fuck. William taught me. See what you missed, A.S.? Ha ha.' A few expressions of regret about something: 'Shouldn't ask Will to help, have to do something about Will.' Nothing else but reminders, dates, and scribbles, staccato scrawls like spittle on a page, a mind seized by itself, each day a new plan. On the desk itself, a notice to the occupant: 'Holidays, Dad. See to W. Buy: (1) . . .' The remainder of the white sheet a panic-stricken blank until the tiny scribble at the bottom: 'People watching me now.'

Oh, you are wrong, my dear. People have been entirely consistent in their failure to watch you. You might have known, thought Bailey, they would not change. We should all have watched you sooner, and where the hell are you now? He visualized her approach to the sobbing form of her mother, knife in hand, seeing in one wide-angled glance the evidence left to incriminate another, using the same neatness to litter the ground by one of the fires designed to discredit the hapless idiot who had assisted, perhaps, in the burial. What had one interfering policeman found here? No true confessions, but enough to release one Antony Sumner, that teacher of impossible stupidity, who had nevertheless taught her a powerful use of the written word. Not evidence enough to convict the darling child. And here she would sit in her room, keeping secret her books and her contempt, aware that someone must feed her.

He froze at sounds from outside: car door, footsteps on gravel. With systematic speed, he began to search the remaining drawers in the desk, refusing to acknowledge the distraction. He registered an explosion of argument inside the front door of the house. Raised voices: Amanda Scott, John Blundell, and the patient, apologetic drone of Constable Bowles. At that same moment Bailey's hand closed around the semi-chill of metal. In his fist was the gleam of a gold necklace, heavy, elegant, dull-coloured. He might have known. Of course William Featherstone would never have craved this. And William Featherstone was never watched either.

'If you're so bloody worried, you go. Why should I be woken up? Let the little bastard get on with it.'

'He's not little. That's the problem. And he's not a bastard.'

'Yes he is. You've only to look at him. He's not my flesh and blood, is he, Bernadette?'

'Oh, so that's your excuse for never watching him, is it? Can't stand the thought he might be your responsibility after all this time? Well you can't get away with that, however hard you try and God knows you've tried often enough. Fucking's the only thing we ever got right, and he's the result. Now go and find him, fuck you.'

He recoiled from the explicit crudeness. Bernadette swore, cursed, and abused frequently, but rarely so personally. Harold was half awake, shaken from fully dressed sleep, dragged into his kitchen and his life disbelievingly, bereft of anything but slight shock and the merest semblance of cunning.

'In the summerhouse, is he? And that copper's woman went out there three hours ago? You've taken your time, haven't you, sweetheart? No worry like real worry. She'll have gone home hours ago, interfering bitch. What'd she be doing with a great dolt like William?'

'God alone knows, but she never came back. We'll both go, if you're too frightened.' For once he was not defensive, but did not move.

'Course I'm bloody frightened. Bloody summerhouse. Lights and ghosts, full of them. I've seen 'em. So've you. It's you who's frightened.'

She was pulling on a coat, stubbing out her cigarette, simultaneous movements of fury.

'It's two in the morning. Leave it out, Bernie, for Christ's sake.'

'Two in the morning, he says, as if it can wait. We've a violent son at large and a missing copper's wife. Does it never occur to you, Harold, that two in the morning means that by now someone, somewhere, might come looking for her if she hasn't gone home? Like now, for instance?' Bernadette's eyes were levelled over his head towards the kitchen doors leading to the bar. Slowly Harold turned, imagining the presence of a silent blue-uniformed cavalry. Through ill-focused eyes, he could see nothing but emptiness, a sound suggesting the approach of car engines.

With one automatic movement, he stuffed lighter and cigarettes into his top pocket, grabbed her by the arm, pushed and pulled her through the back kitchen door. Down the slope with stumbling, cursing steps, around the tree with ease, ceasing to hold Bernadette, who plodded behind.

The night was completely still, apart from the slightest breeze, a self-satisfied stillness auguring heat and lassitude under a late harvest moon, the garden awash with half-light, to which the eye could adjust easily. The summerhouse loomed ahead. Harold paused, listening for sound, hearing a muffled banging as he approached the door: *boom*, *boom*, weak inflictions of wood on wood almost below his feet, the sound of ineffectual effort, pausing as he paused, unconscious of him while he was acutely aware, all trace of whisky gone now except for the bile in his throat. Inside the door, voices, thank God, some normality. And at the opposite window, a fleeting, pale image of a face he had seen before, glimpsed quickly and gone, ignored for the moment.

Inside, the shed was half lit by the moon. Harold could see the trapdoor weighted with one full paraffin can, another one lay on its side. He remembered these surplus containers, heavy as hell, but he could not remember their purpose, strode towards them, began to heave them aside, conscious of spilling the last of the liquid from one, disgusted by the smell. Stopped to the sound of a muffled question from under his feet.

'Evie? That you, Evie?'

'No, it bloody isn't, son.'

'Oh, God, it's you.'

Harold was repelled by the leaden disappointment in

William's voice, audible through wood and heavy with rejection, even in extremis. It carried the sudden, strangely unacceptable truth that the loathing he felt for his son was entirely reciprocal, and it angered him. The voice continued with dull, indifferent calm.

'Can you open the trapdoor, Dad? You pull from the left.'

Harold felt splinters enter his skin as he scrabbled for a gap on the left of an ill-fitting door, scarcely remembered now. He pulled, surprised by the ease of it until he saw the pale glow of Bernadette's hands pulling beside his own. Breathless with effort, he peered downward into the pitch, saw two upturned faces.

'Hello,' said one. 'We're very pleased to see you.'

Harold swore, passed his hands across his eyes, squinting. The cigarette lighter fell from his top pocket, plopped on the earth below. He had the vague, irrelevant sense of William stooping to retrieve it. In the distance, his ears caught the sound of a siren, an intrusion in the night, sounding the imminence of invasion. It increased his anger beyond his own believing.

'You're a filthy little bastard, William, that's what you are. Bringing women here, are you? Saves them looking at you. They'd need the dark, you pathetic little shit. You can stay in this stinking pit for ever, as far as I'm concerned, you little sod.'

'Oh, be quiet, Mr Featherstone, will you,' said the other one, only now discernible as Helen West, speaking in a tone of almost pleasant urgency, not free, he noticed, of a slight overtone of disgust. 'Just shut up and help us out, will you?' She touched William's arm in the vain hope of giving him the comfort of conspiracy. 'Someone locked us in here by mistake. And the ladder's broken.'

'Take her, Dad.' Instructions from William, now utterly calm. He seized Helen by the waist and lifted her on to his shoulders. 'Reach, missus, go on.' Miraculously swift, one balletic lift and an agonizing yank of shoulders taking her through the aperture virtually into Harold's arms. She pushed him away, knelt by the opening.

'Now you, William. Come on, the air's fresh up here.' Fresh with newly spilled paraffin seeped from the empty flagon, fresh with sour whisky breath, controlled rage, and the whimperings of Bernadette. Apart from the relief of escape there was little to recommend such freedom for William. It was unloving, threatening, full of retribution.

'Go away,' said William. 'Leave me alone.'

'I'll tan your bloody hide,' roared Harold, his fists clenched.

'Belt up,' said Helen. 'Go and fetch a ladder, will you? And keep your mouth shut. He doesn't deserve that. Your bloody son deserves a whole lot better than that.'

Her furious face was upturned, eyes glittering in skin streaked with dirt, making Harold recoil in shock. He moved to the open shed door, Bernadette retreating with him, obedient.

''S'all right,' William said to Helen. 'Honestly, 's'all right. I can get out now. Just let me stay still a bit. Till he's calmed down.' She nodded agreement.

And then, from beyond the summerhouse came flashes of light and crashings of sound, footsteps thundering from the direction of the pub, crashing through bushes in directionless haste, men searching with raised voices, Helen at the opening: 'Wait here, William. You'll be out soon. And you won't be in trouble, I promise,' leaving the trapdoor in response to one familiar voice, running outside to find it. She had heard Bailey. She was sure she had heard Bailey, saw nothing but torchlight approaching the shed, the sound of male humanity, indistinguishable as anything but a ragged procession, the first breaking into a run, wavering torch beam catching first her own face, then something farther distant.

'There she is, there she is.' Bailey incredibly running into her, touching her shoulder *en route*, not in comfort, simply to deflect her from his path, running beyond her. A scuffle out of sight in the darkness, the meshing of several urgent bodies in an orgy of contact, the tableau of Helen and the Featherstones standing still, oblivious to what was happening outside their view at the boundary with the field. Then, snarling and screaming, one girl child embraced by many hands, spitting like a cat, swayed back towards them in a fierce huddle that squirmed to a halt, still moving. The space outside the summerhouse door was suddenly crowded. Bailey transferred one arm of the cotton-clad figure into the grasp of another large form. Evelyn Blundell slumped between them, and the officers now grasping those thin arms tightened their hold to keep her upright. Three more men hovered breathlessly behind. Bailey's face was a mask of incredulity, the voice short of breath but accusingly calm as the beam of his torch caught first Bernadette's pallor, then Harold's sweating skin, Helen's face last as if noting them for memory. He spoke with a final weariness. 'What the hell are you doing here, Helen? Go home.'

Evelyn looked up, face contorted, towards Helen's familiar face, the Featherstone parents, the dreadful presence of her captors. Helen's own reactions to Bailey's words, those verbal slaps to her own existence, might have been more audible than her own recoil of rejection had the girl not interrupted, flinging back her head, arching herself forward, the lithe body jackknifing itself straight in a moment of enormous strength. An officer twisted one arm up her back with sudden brutality. She did not scream in reaction, simply screamed like a howling animal, long, loud, and pained, words clear in the vicious harmony of her yelling.

'William . . . you bastard! You told, you told, I hate you . . .' A scream going on and on and on, until Bailey slapped her hard. Her head jerked back with the sheer violence of the blow and the scream stopped. Their ears rang with the sound and the message of it, spitting hatred, the echo of it floating and settling on perspiring bodies and stunned minds, until slowly, very slowly, the group began to shuffle and re-form. Into Helen's numbed consciousness there floated the image of William downstairs in his den, listening to this crescendo, thinking slowly on what he had heard. First abuse from a father, then Evelyn yelling condemnation like a valedictory curse. William, searching for the matches that were safe in Helen's pocket, thinking, thinking: Evie came back, she came back, and she hates me. Wanted to kill me did Evie, and I thought she loved me. No other bugger does. The thought in Helen's head became an arrow of alarm, a sense of his loneliness, sharper because of her own in the face of Bailey's vituperative stare.

Alarm became a premonition of fear, turning her back to the door of the shed. She ran the few steps forward, shouting, 'William, William, it's all right.' Bernadette running with her, both guilty for momentary forgetfulness of his presence, victim of them all. As she reached the door, there was an internal explosion like the long-delayed lighting of the gas in an oven. She felt Bailey yank her back with enormous force, sending her sprawling to the ground while Bernadette ran on. Not a summerhouse for a child. A tinderbox.

From the distance, the flames sprang into the air like a beacon. Only the very nearest heard the thin shriek of sublime pain, brief and lost in the crackling of the wood.

END PIECE

The rain was buffeting the windows. Brown leaves from the station's single tree were plastered to the glass by the wind. Dead, they looked, dead and getting deader, pathetic. Bowles did not want to move, obscurely comforted by the sight and sound of autumn desolation outside the warmth of the police station canteen. He was still in a state of half-mourning, half-shock. Come off it, his wife had said, you've seen worse. No, he told her, I haven't, not really; nothing like that. Or heard worse. He had recognized in Bailey a condition similar to his own, liked him better for it, both of them suffering a kind of moving tension, a sort of sleepwalking where all sights, all sounds, were shoved into the background by the memory of a single scream. Shock, the doctor told him, you'll recover, but he knew neither his life nor his perceptions could ever be quite the same. He wished he had been a drinker like the boy's parents and had fallen into the habit of watching his own children with obsessive protectiveness, could not stop hugging them, hated letting them out of his sight, patted them and kissed them, was easily moved to tears. They were irritated by all the anxiety in his attention. PC Bowles dragged his eyes back to his companion. She had not been invited, but he had been too sluggish to object.

'Of course, I always thought it was strange,' said Amanda Scott. 'A bit too neat, you know. But if sir thought so, too, he never said. At least no one's making any formal complaints. Well, they couldn't, could they? Nothing we could do. Not about the boy or anything. How was I to know?'

He could not imagine where she found the energy to chat. It was out of character for her to sit with uniformed plods like himself, failing to perceive the indifference in his eyes or to recognize it for what it was – contempt. His blithe approval of Detective Scott had arisen less from any kind of enchantment than from admiration, and the same guileless glance was currently cold. She was just another tart after all. Out with the rich widower, was she? Quicker to spot pickings than a magpie. Never a word of pity in her ten-minute monologue, not a thing on the death, the boy, the fires, the pity of it. What price a career like his or hers without pity? What point in doing it? Bowles looked at the scum on his tea, crinkling the brown surface as he heard the desperately casual words of a woman with no one else to listen, speaking to him only by default, decided pity was not appropriate here. She didn't deserve it. You might have tried courting Blundell when he was one kind of victim; bet you've abandoned him now. Are you worried about complaints? I hope they hang you. He pushed back his chair and left without a word. She sat where she was, surrounded by an ocean of empty seats. On her lap, she scrunched up the piece of paper informing her with crude politeness of her transfer back to the streets from which she came.

Bailey drove back from the coroner's office full of messages. Yes, the parents may bury the body, after Bailey's own punishment of identifying the remains, the only pain he was allowed to spare the parents. Whatever their failures, neither Featherstone deserved to see the curled and black, utterly obscene remains of a son shrunk into a charred foetus. Helen had offered to go with him to the coroner's; he had refused, wondered if that had been kind. Perhaps he was not the only one who needed to exorcise this crushing burden of guilt. He had never in his eventful life felt so critical a sense of failure, been haunted with such dreams. He had watched inquests and postmortems, seen physical evidence of barbarism and betrayal, been saddened, sickened, and angered, but in this instance alone, he felt himself the betrayer. He sat in the car outside Branston waiting at the same junction for more than one paralysed minute. The car behind hooted; he moved towards the spread of new houses, a contrast to the shabby old East End office of the coroner. 'I like this old place,' the coroner's officer had said. Bailey had agreed. I hate newness for its own sake, he thought. I loathe the deception hidden in new things, all that promise that they will alter the state of the same old humanity by making people happier or even nicer. At least in the comparative poverty of his childhood the neighbours had nothing material to distract them from what their children and those next door were doing. Might have been happier with a little more, no telling, but they would certainly have been less caring and far less observant. Here in the new houses there had been no one looking.

As he drove down Branston High Street, the windows of Invaders Court blinked at him like a series of blind eyes. He had failed to watch like a parent, failed to act and to analyse, earned himself a lifetime's nightmares, but the introspection and the blame would have to find a place alongside all the rest. He could not afford to go to pieces, was too sinewy for that, too practical, but still soft enough to be racked from top to toe with pity and self-recrimination. He thought of Helen, less proofed against sorrow than he, and almost regretted his thick skin. A year of progressive failure for both of them, and if he had not been dissolved by it, he was beyond making decisions concerning their future. Except for one. She must lead him through the rest and he would follow humbly. Only do not lose me, Helen, not now, not in the future. Do not lose me. We were wrong to come here. Branston's new life has stunted our growth, impoverished my vision, eclipsed your career with this horror at the end. That cannot be altered: the boy is dead; you have finished weeping for the parents who would not or could not weep and we need a wider compass, greater anonymity for our lives. We cannot live as others try and fail to do. You must accept me for the deficiency I am – not perfect, neither great nor good, guilty in part for this. I am an embarrassment here, ripe for transfer back to the dirty depths of London, out of the way. Come with me. Before I do any more damage. Poor boy, poor little bastard. I must try to do better with your kind.

He shifted gears, checked his mirror for the impatient one behind, acutely conscious of his hands moving through every movement, his own strength influencing these minor events, progress towards no known goal but the next destination. There was no other way to conduct life. The shadow of William Featherstone which had wrapped itself around him lifted slightly. There was a duty to live; he had made too many mistakes to be overwhelmed now. He noticed the sun was shining wet on the windscreen, raindrops pushed to the edge, glimmering like William's jewels.

'Where now?' asked Redwood. 'Where now? The law's an ass.' He looked at Helen, blaming her for the inadequacies he had in mind, holding her half responsible for his own predicament and the law's powerlessness. 'We've already arraigned Antony Sumner, but we'll offer no evidence, and discontinue the case against him. He wasn't even grateful.'

'Should he be?' Helen said. 'He's been in jail for nearly three months.' One high summer of life gone as well as one crucial love affair reduced to ashes, a reputation ruined for ever. For what should he be grateful? She was silent.

'And the rest,' Redwood continued. 'One juvenile psychopath silent as the grave, apart from insisting that her own confessions on paper, delivered without caution, of course, were simply the stuff of fantasy.'

'The possession of her mother's gold was not fantasy. Enough fact to charge murder.'

'Yes, and we will, but without William Featherstone,

who is too dead to deflect the accusations her inventive mind will shovel in the direction of his memory. We have no more than a forty per cent chance of getting a conviction. Counsel says less than that. Without him we can't even prove he didn't start all those fires. She did, to discredit him if ever he should talk, tell someone about the body, lead everyone to her. But I can't charge her with arson.'

'And her father?'

'Ah. Counsel also says no to a charge of harbouring an offender. Besides, we don't know if he actually did so. He simply knew darling child had the gold, and he chose to ignore the implications. He saw the jewellery in her pocket the day after the murder, he told Bailey, knew she had it. It strikes me that both of them, father and daughter, preferred Mama to be dead. He would have seen the murder as a massive economy drive, but she committed it.'

And then you and I and all of us fell down while the obvious flowed over us. We were outwitted by a child who delivered the unkindest cut of all. Redwood had dissociated blame and himself from Amanda Scott, but like her, he ignored the second tragedy in deference to the prospects of criticism, recrimination, blame, extrication, and getting a conviction. William had robbed him of that chance. I am going mad, Helen thought. Is it only Bailey and I who feel William to be the only loss, the only innocent, killed by the wilful blindness of us all? You could not blame such a clumsy hand as his own. You don't cure by convicting his assassin. Without our intervention he might have lived, under the shade of what dominance and how poor the quality of life does not matter; it is still life lost.

But if her own capacity for guilt was endless, Redwood's was nonexistent. Like the law. She should have known better by now, but because of the guilt, could not criticize either. She had no right.

'We'll try to avoid using you as a witness.'

'Thank you. I don't see how you can avoid it, but no doubt you'll try. You know I'm transferring back to London?'

'Yes.' He had the grace not to pretend regrets, looked at her with respect, even a tinge of affection. 'I'm sorry. When do you go?'

'Tomorrow if I could. More likely a week or two.'

'I should stick to road traffic cases if I were you when you go back,' he said with heavy sympathy. 'Less traumatic.'

'No,' said Helen, surprised into indignation. 'I've learned plenty.' In the saying of it, she recognized her first positive thought in more than three weeks.

Oh, Bailey mine, what do I do with you now? The cloudburst that had blackened the sky and drenched the ground lifted before brilliant sunlight shimmering on the Tarmacadam of the carpark. The force of the rain had cleansed her car of weeks of sticky dust. Clean enough for a funeral. Go home, Featherstones. Go back to the city where you might at least find like kind. They were bound to attend the last rites, surely they must, although Bernadette had lately taken to the same liquid remedies as her husband and John Blundell, all of them in search of oblivion. Why live? Why open your eyes at all? Because then you can see, and like the force of this sudden sunlight on her own tired eyes, it hurt.

266

As she started the car, she thought that of all the omnipresent nightmares which had disturbed her sleep in the days and weeks preceding this, there were none as compelling and selfish as the one featuring Bailey running towards her in pursuit of a criminal, pushing her aside in the process, sublimely indifferent to her presence, so seized was he with the urgency of the moment, acting as if she had never existed.

Do not lose me now, Bailey. We have eyes, both of us, a duty to live and do better, cannot afford our superior overview of the world: look at how blind we are. We should not have come here; this place does not suit us. Living under one roof may not suit us; we are both too secretive. I was so angry with you, so full of blame, keeping my mouth shut until I realized that was unfair. And then I look around and see that, whatever your failings, you are so much finer than the rest. And if I do not completely understand your methods, the workings of your soul, if I am sometimes alienated by your tunnel vision, the hard realism of your policeman's psyche, which sometimes investigates what it needs and nothing more, unable to afford curiosity, I still understand you more completely than anyone else, however incomplete the knowledge, and there is a sort of privilege in that. As you in your way almost accept me, even admire me. Careless of me sometimes, refusing to share, ignorant of me often enough to wound and enrage me, but still knowing me better than any other living soul. I am less of a stranger with you than with anyone else. I do not want to live without that. You are waiting for me to speak. I have marshalled my packing cases, prepared my own home for my return, but I shall not leave you now. What was wrong with the indecisions before? Why did we come here? Why were we subject to the universal belief that life is always capable of that kind of improvement? You have injected too many poisons into my conscience, Superintendent Bailey. You make me feel the business of the law is futile, while I know it is not. But it has to be done by someone well equipped, not someone who is tempted to give up. Do you know something? I do not feel as if I love you at the moment, but I know I do. There are times when I have to say it to feel it.

She pushed open the door to number fifteen Invaders Court, looked at the automated kitchen, imagined with relief her life packed into boxes. On the draining board, glittering like a warning, lay one of William's bracelets. There was a lump of cheese and half a loaf, Bailey's contribution to an evening meal, hopeful rather than skilled. Helen put down her files and her shopping, heard his footsteps upstairs.

She would save the next William. Bailey would be more careful, grow eyes in the back of his head. Listen sometimes. One of these days she would grow into an interfering old bitch.

'Come on, Bailey,' she said out loud. 'We can do better than this.'

WITHOUT
CONSENT

'It is an offence for a man to rape a woman.

A man commits rape if (a) he has unlawful sexual intercourse with a woman who at the time of the intercourse does not consent to it; and (b) at that time he knows that she does not consent to the intercourse, or is reckless as to whether she consents.'

PROLOGUE

Home was where the heart was.

She smelt. Stank. The rank smell of perfume mixed with grass and sweat, city smells and those of harvest, soil beneath her fingernails. Shivering in the heat of the night with the jacket round her shoulders which she wanted to shake off although she needed it for warmth. Needed it, needed it, the lapels damp with saliva, and oh yes, there had been real tears in her eyes as she stumbled home. Look, we don't have to do it this way, she'd said. We could do it nice and ordinary in your car; take me away from all this and I'm all yours, she'd said, and he'd laughed. A lovely laugh, he had, low and sexy and full of promise. Jesus. There was nothing to fear. But she had been so frightened, like now, feeling the air had been punched out of her. She could imagine the fingerprint bruises on her ribs. You're perfect, he'd said; a few bruises won't harm you. Bruises to the sternum where he'd held her down. They'll fade soon, he'd said. I'll make them in the shape of a flower.

She heard footsteps coming down the stairs, imagined, accurately, a young man in carpet slippers coming down to put out the rubbish, closing the door quietly, knowing that what he did was important. Then she began to cry.

Silence. Only a kind of semi-silence in this man's room, high above the street. The slight vibration of anxious traffic but no voices.

It was not enough for him, the ordinary way of doing anything, or so he told himself. Or maybe it was the humiliating fact that it was shameful and undignified to be so obsessed by anything at any time. Sex is not life, simply a part. For some, he supposed sex was a necessary release of tension, instead of this idle curiosity of his in which he could never admit that necessity ever played a part. Bearing in mind what women submitted themselves to all the time, he could not see that he did any harm.

Such women. The shapes and sizes of them filled him with wonder; each body as unique as its own fingerprint, each set of reactions different, each set of needs and stimuli unquantifiable if broadly similar. The thought of so many of them blundering through life without anything amounting to satisfaction filled him with pity. He saw himself as a man who loved women and wished that they could understand and value themselves more, and also take themselves a little less seriously; appreciate a joke, perhaps. God knows, there had been enough jokes played on him to last a lifetime, and he was still smiling. In his view, a feminist was a person who considered it morally indefensible to cause pain to any woman; the object was to cause pleasure; there was no point otherwise. Of course, if the life were already so diminished, so beyond the prospect of pleasure, it might be as well to cause pleasure in the ending of it, but he was not sufficiently practised to consider himself in the role of God. One of these days, he might perfect the most poetic form of death. A sublime accident.

You were born to make women happy, his own mother had told him. Also for the healing arts. Yours is a double vocation, my child. The ice clinked in the glass beside his desk. There were flowers in the vase, variegated carnations, rather sterile in their perfection, he thought. A box of chocolates. He sipped the drink reflectively. Alas, ice and lavender oil were not sufficient for every kind of burn. Nor were drink, pleasure and the exercise of power always sufficient antidote for life's crueller reversals. So many of his ageing women acquaintances could have told him that.

He pondered these and other matters in front of his computer. The blankness of the screen did not alarm him at all; it was hardly the same as facing an empty page with nothing better to do with himself. He could copy onto this space sections of alarming medical and legal text, although the latter, with all its Gothic splendour, always made him regret his choice of career. Medical science was not ennobling. In his experience, doctors were worse liars and rogues than their legal counterparts who tended to be at least more guarded in their promises.

Physician, heal thyself.

The vase holding the flowers was an artful sculpture of female genitalia. The broad base represented the uterus; the ridge at the base, by which he would lift it, the cervix, opening out realistically into a flower-like shape of the

275

labia minora and labia majora. An artist's slightly fanciful impression of the vulva, in other words. A frivolous creation which the girl who cleaned consistently and typically failed to recognize for what it was. He often found it helpful to explain anatomy if one began from the outside in. In actual life, as he knew, the labia closed with the tidiness of a bud, concealed beneath a convenient mound and carried round as normal by women who scarcely knew how any of the reproductive and sexual machinery worked. This polished wood structure was hardly a useful educational tool for hopeful men either, but it was warm to handle and looked, without the flowers, like a decorative candle holder.

He could not explain why he was as he was or did as he did. The random development of his own tastes astounded him as much as the history of his life, but he felt saintly and worthy in comparison to some mindless procreator of the aggressively macho sort. *He* would never foist some unwanted, unsupportable, screaming child into the world; that indeed was a sin, raw and unadorned in its sheer wickedness. He nodded at the screen; the screen agreed.

He smoothed his already smooth pate, tapped it with the middle finger of his right hand. He had his own rationality, that was all; along with the conventional overtones which were enough to show him he was not really mad in his entirely sane fear of retribution. His was the fear of an innocent man who can never really be understood.

What was it they could ever say that he had done wrong? Nothing! And who would give evidence? No one? Nothing was done, my dears, without consent.

He looked at his watch. It was not a distinguished implement but a type made by the million. Dark outside now, but still warm. His lovely little girl would be home. Fearless about the dark. Safe in the hands of a man who would never awaken her.

Almost a soul mate. Not a friend.

Almost a lover.

CHAPTER ONE

Listen, Bailey said.

Once upon a time, there was a girl, going out.

Dressing for the party, she had felt she was worth a million dollars. Somehow that phrase meant more than the sterling equivalent of the day – the last of her life as she had known it – and she might have been worth more. Coming down for a moment from the quarrel with her mother, the third this week, and putting a jacket over what her father called her itsy-bit skirt and the skimpy top, wearing it as if she would never part with it, rather than shed it as soon as she got there, she had a sudden surge of rebellious love for her repressive parents. They weren't so bad, some of the time. For a brief moment, she knew that she was safe as houses, because she had this room to come back to and this number to call, although the only reason she was worth so much to herself was the fact that after three weeks' diet, her waist was where she wanted and her ribs stuck out. Not a milligram of surplus flesh, although, if she ate as much as a bread roll, her stomach came out like a balloon. The answer was not to eat.

'Bye, Mum. Bye, Dad . . .'

'Let's see you,' he called. She stepped into the living room, pretending great haste even though she was early. The jacket was buttoned. She had on a prim little choker round her neck, which would go from throat to handbag before she had reached the end of the road. The make-up would go on in the bus.

'Very nice,' he said, reassuringly, thinking nothing of the kind. Why did this child have to look so fierce and why on earth was she so addicted to black? Why did she go about with that girl who was so much older and prettier? One quick peck on the cheek, given and received in an over-powering atmosphere of multilayered perfume, and she was off before Mother came out of the kitchen. Because Mother was harder to fool.

Later on, when they picked her up after the police had called, she stank of booze. The itsy-bit skirt was torn and stained. The child whimpered, but did not hug; could not bear to touch. Her thighs were scored with scratches; there was detritus under her nails. She was scantily dressed; it was presumed she had been stripped prior to her foetal curl in the gutter where she was found. A few bruises.

No knickers, no jacket. In the presence of her parents, she said she had lost them. That was all she uttered, apart from sobbing. Even after hours with a sympathetic woman in a nice little house with pictures on the wall.

'Well?'

Helen West, Prosecutor, sat on Bailey's sofa, still listening. They did this sometimes, a kind of dress rehearsal for

280

tomorrow's challenges, both occasionally mourning the coincidence of their professions. Senior police officer, experienced crown prosecutor. It was not a relationship she would recommend, but she was stuck with it, like the fly which had fallen into her drink. Bailey had a creased face and a fine way of telling a story. He animated his narrative with verbal cartoons and embellished the whole thing with gestures, but as soon as he said, 'Once upon a time', she knew the story was going to be doctored with his own opinions and recounted in a style he would never use in front of a judge.

'Drugs?' She questioned crisply

'Negligible, from her demeanour. I'd guess not.'

'Booze?'

'Plenty.'

'Semen?'

'Saliva, yes. Here and there; not there. Semen, no. Several abandoned condoms around, but a lovers' trysting place. Bodily fluids also in the gutter. And no, she isn't a virgin. Not quite.'

'That's not enough,' Helen said.

Bailey watched the graceful figure of his betrothed cross the broad expanse of his living room and thought of his ex-wife, for whom his traveller's tales from the police force had always taken second place to what they should do with the bathroom in preparation for the first child. He might as well have been out to stud. Oh, silence, he told himself, don't fall into clichés as if you were obliging someone on the psychiatrist's consulting couch. That woman had her needs, you had yours, which coincided at the time and might still if the child had not died. A child who would be

281

the same age, give or take a year or two, as the girl in the story. He found himself repeating, what a pity, the trite words hiding a multitude of sins. His stomach growled. The last year of his life had seen the development of an ulcer.

'The way you tell it,' Helen said, settling easily into the big fat settee he would never have possessed in his married life, 'gives me all the clues to the verdict. Silly little seventeen-year-old goes out to party, as described to parents, to whom she lies habitually, about dress code, about everything. Goes shimmering in there, dressed in nothing.' He was silent.

'The bloke for whom she's wearing all the glitz does not pitch. So she salves her disappointment by drinking a bit more and then a bit more and ends up in a scrum with a stranger. She doesn't have the faintest idea what a half-naked, flirtatious girl risks.'

'She wanted love.'

'She had love, the silly little bitch. She wanted attention.'

Helen took a sip of coffee. One bottle of wine in an evening was enough. He could continue, since it never seemed to affect him; she would not. There was a level of control in her he both admired and resented. She was a beautiful woman, after her own fashion. The kindest he had ever met, easily the most imaginative, the most elusive, the most measured. He wondered if she had agreed to marry him for the same hormonal reasons which had affected his wife. Helen was in her late thirties, about a decade his junior.

'Her parents are howling for blood. They insist she was

raped,' he said. 'Someone must hang, they say, namely the boy with whom she left. Spotty little oik, who says he tried to kiss her, but she shoved him and ran off. He says she had other fish to fry. Someone she was meeting; someone older.'

'No case,' Helen said. 'Not even if she swore it was him. She could be a victim; she could be a cock-tease. Unless, of course, he caused the scratches. But I'd bet she did them herself.'

'Right. Her own skin beneath her fingernails.'

'And tomorrow, how come *you* have to explain to mum and dad why the evidence is insufficient?'

'I don't. Ryan does. He asked my advice on diplomacy.'

She made a mocking gesture, using two fingers to point a gun at her head, and pulled a sympathetic face.

The lovely Ryan was not always her favourite man. Bailey's bag carrier when first they had met, progressing since then, onward and upward. Capable of being outrageous and treated by Bailey as the son he never had. There was a fidelity between the two of them she accepted, because she had no choice. Personally, she doubted Ryan deserved it but there it was: a mutual devotion without rhyme or reason just like any other kind of love.

'Ah well, early night, then.'

Bailey moved to sit beside her, put his arm round her shoulder and felt her rest against him, willingly. They were easier together since their decision to marry; she joked it had probably caused the ulcer, but it had altered something, although he was not sure how. In a moment, he would clear the last of the glasses and papers from the table. In Helen's flat, litter remained at least until morning, perhaps the same weekday of the following week. One thing they had proved: compatibility need not involve a common domestic attitude.

'Tell me, love, do you always regard this subject with such a bold and jaundiced eye?'

'Do you mean sex cases? Rape? My current, almost exclusive stock-in-trade? Yes. But drunken teenagers don't raise my heartbeat. Oh, I'm sorry for a kid like that; something happened to her, but you can't make a case out of *naïveté* betrayed.'

Would they make love tonight or not? The idea rarely lost its appeal, except when she was tired to her bones. Perhaps she would let it happen, perhaps not. If she did, would that be rape? The idea was laughable. Rape was the exertion of force; Bailey had enough power over her already, although she did her best not to let him know.

He was sound asleep by the time she reached him.

The night light was a pale darkness, glowing through the window. Bailey lived so high above the ground, there was no need for the curtains he despised. From the front windows of her basement flat, Helen could see the feet of people walking past, sometimes peering down, but at the back, there was nothing but the garden. She missed her home, especially the solitude of her garden, and then, when she was in it, she missed the light of Bailey's vast attic. When they were married, they would live in exactly the same way.

His sleep made her perversely sleepless. He would wake if she touched him and his sleep was the unfeigned unconsciousness of the just, the result perhaps of a pragmatism she could not share. He believed in fate, and telling himself that you could only do the best possible with what you were given. No 'if onlys' for Bailey. You did what you did, apologized if necessary, and then you slept. Soundly. Did he really want this marriage, or was it his version of courtesy? In Bailey's eyes, a relationship as long as theirs would have to be honoured somehow. Loving Bailey was one of the best things to happen in her life, but she had a mortal dread of being owned and knew she could still throw it all away. Out of fear.

Failing to sleep opened the floodgates of all those things left undone or badly done. Cases swimming before her eyes. Visions of her previous married life, plus visions of all those odd and brutal couplings she read about on paper and which filled her waking hours with speculation, making her feel like a voyeur.

They should not have been talking about rape before going to bed.

Something had happened to that little girl. She wondered what it might have been.

'All right,' Aemon Connor said, in tones which combined both aggression and resignation. 'That's fine. That's absolutely fine. If you don't want to, that's fine by me. You frigid little cow. Was a time you couldn't have enough of it. Don't worry about it. I can always get someone else.'

Brigid whimpered in the darkness. He was refusing to hear it; he had listened long enough and conversation never cured anything. She complained it hurt; so, if it hurt, why couldn't she use her imagination? He could tell her what hurt, all right, and that was a mammoth state of arousal with nowhere to go. She was his woman, remember; his wife, even; what a joke, when she just wouldn't do it any more.

He lay on his side, him fuming and her still snuffling, opening his mouth to speak. He could not stop talking.

'I could get someone else tomorrow. And then where would you be?'

There was a long silence, until he felt her fingers moving timidly to touch the back of his head.

'Changed your mind, have you?' he muttered. 'Thought you would.' Forcing himself inside was difficult enough, even without listening to the sounds she made or noticing the passive resistance which seemed second nature. The process was brief and noisy. He held her down by the shoulder and in the aftermath of climax fell into a deep and suffocating sleep. Later, having eased herself from under the bulk of his huge drowsy body, she felt for the marks of his hands and wished herself dead.

The bathroom to which she tiptoed was splendid. There was a power shower among the black marble tiles and a bidet with gold-coloured taps which she used religiously, especially at times like these, to wash away all traces of him.

She had no idea how to live outside this house. It was her home and her prison, and living in such a place represented the pinnacle of all achievement. She liked this bathroom best; she had made it her own, and she could hide behind the door after doing her duty as a good Catholic wife. She could also sit and lie here too long in contemplation of avoiding it. Praying to God and occupying the bidet at the same time seemed faintly obscene, but

Brigid imagined God would forgive her that, at least, since he demanded so much of her otherwise, and was supposed to forgive a great deal more than her husband. Dedicating the act of sex as a penance for the holy souls also seemed indecent, but might ensure a blessing in advance. Maybe Aemon was right and she should have been a nun.

You used to love it, he'd said. He said that every time, taunting her. There was a muffled shouting from outside, her name called, 'Brigid, Brigid . . . where are you?' sounding as if he was lost. God help us, he was awake again after insufficient drink to anaesthetize. She touched the lips of her vagina, swollen like cocktail sausages, almost screamed, reached for the lubricant from the cupboard and answered him.

'I'm here, I'm here, in a minute.'

He hated to wake up and find himself alone. It was an insult to his manhood: it gave him nightmares.

Aemon and Brigid, happily married.

In a neat little terraced house, light showed from every window, as if the occupant owned shares in London Electricity, or could not stand the dark. Around three a.m., a solid form could be seen, balanced on a ladder, silhouetted against the window to the left of the door, painting the ceiling of the living room. Anna was in a sweat. The radio played softly only because she was a considerate neighbour. What she really wanted was a house pulsing with vapid, heavy-beat noise, amplified to fill her head. Anything to block thinking and aid the manic activity which had continued since early afternoon.

Ceiling, two coats, a small area, quickly covered; the

whole place a bit of a doll's house. Walls could be finished in an hour, possibly tomorrow. The washing machine hummed in the kitchen; third load today. Curtains hung damply; she would paint round them. The carpet had already been shampooed. She was doing things out of order, but perfect décor, logically created, was not the object of this exercise. The achievement of cleanliness was.

The ladder wobbled; Anna clutched, swore, saved herself from falling, and watched the paint tray fall to the floor, face down. Scraping the white ooze from the ruined pile with desultory energy, she realized that bending over made her dizzy and she could not see straight. All that white, glimmering against the unsteady light of the naked bulb which swung from the ceiling; her eyes were no longer able to comprehend colour. Or the fact that there might be someone outside, looking in.

She might as well paint the carpet, too, and be finished with it; the thought made her smile. All this work had done the trick; she was so tired she could scarcely put one foot in front of the other, and at last the place smelt of nothing but emulsion.

Anna held one hand in front of her face, watched its tremor, and delivered the now-familiar lecture. You can cope, girl, you can cope; it's all the rest who can't. Talking to herself, out loud; that was another thing to be cured, but not yet. The hand trembled; the burn marks on her arms were fading; her legs had the substance of jelly. She could sleep now.

As Anna tried to ignore the spots in front of her eyes while sticking the paint roller in a bucket of water which

suddenly seemed red instead of white, the phone by
Superintendent Bailey's bed bleeped without apology. He
did not need to look at his watch to know that it was
shortly after three; he always knew the time.

'Bailey. What do you want?'

It had been a joke on regular squads that Bailey always
sounded as if he had a woman with him. Probably had too;
the man had been a bachelor a long, long time. Going out
and staying in with a lawyer from the Crown Prosecution
Service was seen as another lascivious eccentricity which
went with his good suits. The wearing of the one on his
back and the other on his arm bordered on some unde-
fined treachery. The men who claimed to know him
longest were placing bets on this marriage. Ten to one, it
would not take place at all, five to three it wouldn't last a
year. They had different kinds of faith in Bailey. The existence of Helen West did not exactly do him any favours.

The voice on the other end of the line appeared to hide
an element of amusement. Sometimes, in the comparative
regularity of his newish role, Bailey forgot that working for
Complaints and Discipline was still, potentially, a twenty-
four-hour shift.

'Islington. Sorry to disturb you, sir, but we've got a
problem. Allegation of rape.'

'Against whom?'

The officer sounded as if he was reciting from a reading
primer for under fives, spelling the sounds as he spoke.

'Detective Sergeant Ryan, sir.'

Bailey paused for a moment's palpable shock.

'I can't investigate allegations against Ryan,' he said. 'I
know him.'

The voice coughed. 'That's the problem, sir. We've tried everyone else on the complaints rota, but everyone knows Ryan.' He paused for effect. 'Everyone.'

Bailey knew what he should do if he were going straight by the book. Get up, look up all other available numbers, tell this sergeant who did not yet have a name to continue his exploration down the list, because yes, he knew Ryan. Far too well. Knew him as a man of flawed intelligence, deliberate blindness, sexual fecklessness, indiscretions of all kinds. A man lacking in imagination, dogged in loyalty, but finally, in the last two years, emerging from a chrysalis, abandoning frustrated youth in favour of some degree of wisdom. Bailey had tutored him, forgiven him, covered up for him, believed in him, right up until that recent point where the belief was justified and Ryan had suddenly taken off and learnt to think, wonder, take responsibility and ask real questions. He had grown, shed his juvenile prejudices like unwanted skin, and learnt the art of patience, the way Bailey had always hoped he would. Looking at Ryan as he was was like looking at the man Bailey himself had once been. What retrograde nonsense was this? Stupid, stupid bastard.

The pause was long enough for the sergeant to cough again. 'Sir?'

'On my way.'

Bailey was precise. In the same way that he knew the time, he knew where to find his clothes. Helen stirred, listening. Bailey knew she couldn't quite fathom his absurd loyalty to Ryan any more than he could himself, and felt a flash of annoyance that the phone call should make him peculiarly, defensively embarrassed, as if she could guess that this was more than his paid duty. He touched her shoulder and left without a word of goodbye. Singing in his head as he went for the car, not Ryan, not Ryan, please. Not just as he was making good. Not Ryan and rape.

With that good-looking boy there would never be the need.

Bailey made himself drive slowly, although the instinct was to race and the sheer emptiness of the streets was an invitation to speed. Emptiness was a relative concept in London. There were always people. In these God-forsaken early hours there were simply fewer, plying the night-time trades, some of them innocent, some not. The factory making dresses for tomorrow's market, the loading of goods, the post-midnight clearing out, the parties which never stopped and the increasing numbers of those sleeping rough. He regretted that his duties no longer really included this twilight zone of all-night pit stops: conspiracy, danger, chat, street light. The night isolated people, made them more truthful. You poor old man, he thought to himself ruefully, they'll make a gardener of you yet. Set you to trimming roses in distant suburban police stations, or polishing the commander's shoes. Instead of this loathsome business of pruning, examining the varied complaints against officers of his own kind.

Oh, surely this was a storm in a nightclub cocktail? He knew in his bones it was not. Ryan, you bloody fool. What now? You always had a weakness for women and they for you. Bailey found he was thinking of the girl with something akin to dislike, already formulating disbelief in what she would say. He shook his head. This would not do.

The back of the station yard was lit with orange light as if to reduce the white paint of the cars to a sickly cream. Bailey went to the back door. Better than going to the front and possibly running the phalanx of waiting relatives, supposing there were any. The interior corridor was a similar warm and oppressive yellow. He was met with the distant courtesy his role demanded. Everyone knew Ryan, a convivial and popular character, while several more knew Bailey, who could not be thus described. No chance, Bailey thought, of an incident like this failing to enter the history books.

The duty inspector was embarrassed, a symptom rarely apparent on ruddy red features such as his, unless he was talking about his daughters with the boastful and nervous pride he reserved for their achievements. The existence of a family made wild men tame, gave them different perspectives; it had done that for Ryan, albeit slowly. However many years he had taken to fall into respectful love with his own wife, he had still done so, although only after he had led her a merry dance, and she him. Boys will be boys, and girls retaliate. The rape story was told, dispassionately, the voice avoiding judgement.

'Decent enough girl. No record, works in a shop. She knows Ryan on account of being a witness in one of his cases. Seems like she went to a disco with a girl who got into some kind of trouble on the way home, and she's giving evidence about what time they got there, what time the girl left, that kind of thing. Anyway, Ryan takes the statement and they get along fine, and he goes back to tidy it up, and they still get along fine. Then, according to her, he meets her for a third time, purely social. He starts to

292

pester her. She lives with a bloke. She and Ryan – Shelley Pelmore she's called, sir – go out for a drink. On the way home, he suggests a walk in the park and he rapes her. Or, at least, he tries. Penetration, but no ejaculation.' The inspector coughed apologetically. Another source of ridicule for Ryan. Didn't even make it, poor bastard; couldn't keep it up.

'Obvious signs of resistance. Sir.'

The police service was an army with a self-appointed officer class, so Bailey understood. Respect had to be earned and in the eyes of this man, he had not earned it yet.

'Now why on earth would he do that?' Bailey wondered out loud, making light of it. The inspector caught his drift, laughed briefly.

'See what you mean, sir. Usually he only has to ask nicely, although everyone says he's quietened down. But then why do politicians go with tarts, even when they've got groupies and their fragrant wives at home, sir? Dicing with death, someone's idea of fun.'

'Do you believe her?' Bailey tried to get the plea out of his voice. The cough was repeated.

'Can't say, sir, can I? I haven't met her, wouldn't know if I did. They were seen together in the pub. He says they met by accident, chatted, that was all, gave her a lift, went separate ways.'

'Who reported it?'

'The boyfriend. Found her on the doorstep. Brought her in. She's in the rape suite up at Holloway. We can't deal with her here for obvious reasons. Ryan's in the detention room.'

'Well, come with me, will you? I can't see him alone.'

Another long hesitation.

'Oh, one more thing, sir. When she came in, she was wearing Ryan's jacket . . .'

He would need a witness to ensure fair play – no hidden intimacies between himself and an old pal – and also because he needed someone to stiffen his own backbone when he saw Ryan. Bailey might as well have been looking at the victim of a car smash, one who was resigned to being told that apart from being blind for life, the legs would have to be removed as well. Ryan's handsome face was puffed; he had not avoided the disgrace of weeping, which had made his eyes red and his skin blotched as if it was bruised. There was a smell of drink, not overpowering but noticeable, and the different, overlying smell of perspiration and soap. He sat on the bench in his shirtsleeves above creased cotton trousers. On their entrance, he placed his hands behind his back, guiltily. Bailey had the distinct impression that he had been biting his nails. He swung round on the other officer, almost falling into him.

'Has he had a shower?'

'Sir, yes. At home, before we collected him.'

Ryan's face had opened into the beginnings of a smile before Bailey spoke. Then it closed into sullen lines and he turned his eyes to a long examination of his hands. Nails bitten to the quick, Bailey noticed. In as long as he had known the man, Ryan had never bitten his nails. Not even in the long reaches of the night, when nerves turned men into anxious boys.

'Has he been examined?'

'Not yet, sir . . .'

'For Christ's sake, that should have been first.'

Bailey swung on Ryan with the anger of a parent trying to prevent himself from slapping a child out of sheer disappointment.

'What have you got to say?' Bailey barked at him.

Ryan shifted. His voice was surprisingly firm.

'Nothing, sir. Nothing at all.'

And he turned his head to the wall.

CHAPTER TWO

'. . . if at a trial for a rape offence, the jury has to consider whether a man believed that a woman was consenting to sexual intercourse, the presence or absence of reasonable grounds for such a belief is a matter to which the jury is to have regard, in conjunction with other relevant matters, in considering whether he so believed . . .'

Rose Darvey measured the distance, sprinted up to the empty cardboard box and kicked it. It sailed upward and hit the casing of the neon light with a satisfying crack, bounced off the wall and landed. Inspired by the length of the corridor and its dull grey paint, she repeated the kick from the other side, watching as the box hit the casing for a second time. That should do.

'Yeah!' Rose shouted, waving her fist. Who said football training was no use to a girl? 'Punch their lights out,' she muttered. Dribbling the box before her, she made for the swing doors. She had to do something – anything, as long as it was overtly physical – before a day in court; frustration was the price of dedication to a career which involved so much enforced immobility. Perhaps she should have gone in for politics. That, at least, allowed a person to shout. In the life of Rose Darvey, Helen West had much to answer for.

Redwood, self-important yet timid Branch Crown Prosecutor, master of this flagship, came out of his office with the speed of a startled guinea pig. Rose beamed at him with the usual unnerving effect. Rose Darvey and Helen West were clones of each other, he thought fearfully, the pair of them separated only by a decade and a half in which Helen had learnt alternative methods of insubordination. Helen could smile just as sweetly as Rose, but relied on guile, abuse of dignity and dumb insolence, while this one, who could have been her daughter, played her games with more palpable falsehood. She shimmered with energy, like a fighter hanging on the ropes, impervious to the strictures of a referee, waiting for the chance to punch a kidney.

'Lovely day,' said Rose.

'Isn't it,' he said faintly, noting the crack in the neon light which everyone hated, wanting to say something about it, but not daring.

'You're in early, sir,' Rose chirped with a terrible display of politeness, her smile reminiscent of a small animal baring its teeth. She could make 'sir' sound like an exquisite insult, no offence intended.

'Yes.' He felt himself beaming in response; fat old cat. Redwood was always in limbo; once he started a conversation, he did not know how to stop, but stood there, hovering. Rose knew that one sure way to make him move was to pick her nose, an action which, understandably, sent him running for cover. At the moment, she had other things in mind.

'Why are we turning down so many rape cases, sir?'

He rocked on his heels, felt for the wall to give him support. The suddenness of the question jolted him into an untypically truthful response.

'Because they don't work.'

'Pardon? Don't work? That ain't no legal phrase I ever heard of.'

'They don't work,' he repeated.

'Don't work for who? The fucking Treasury?'

Redwood fled. The corridor fell into silence.

From the distant end, Helen West hoved into view, coming closer beneath the subterranean lights, three of which Rose had managed to damage. She looked good today, Rose remarked to herself: loose jacket; nice skirt, fitting like a dream; good legs. No wonder that dour old scroat Bailey liked her. She wasn't bad for an old lady.

The cardboard box landed at Helen's feet. Lacking the benefit of football training, she picked it up without a second glance and put it over her head. Rose whistled and prayed for Redwood to come back out of his office. Two demented women would keep him demoralized for a week.

It was cool in here, air-conditioned freezing. Helen continued up the corridor, blind as a bat, and turned left into her room without breaking step. Some day, Rose thought, without wistfulness, all this will never be mine.

She was one third of the way through legal training, and so far she had found the exams a breeze. She could count on her fingers a fistful of achievements, namely, the beginnings of an impressive qualification, a borrowed family and a man she was going to marry in a matter of weeks. The career posed several questions and many more

298

doubts; the marriage did not. Rose scurried down the corridor, looking out for signs of her own vandalism. Now they really would have to replace the fucking lights which drove everyone mad, but then, if the establishment refused to listen to intelligent requests, they had to be otherwise persuaded.

The office of the Crown Prosecution Service, north central, lay at the apex of several insignificant streets and was not itself a landmark. Facing Helen West's small room over a narrow stretch of road, there was another set of offices, with remarkably better equipment and a plethora of underworked employees. Helen had suggested rigging up a pulley over the road so that they could send over photocopying, or receive, in recycled carrier bags secured with clothes pegs, the day's faxes. Over the road, the people were engaged in the long-distance management of a paint production company; their office was light, bright and far from grey. Over here, the office fixtures bore signs of wear, redolent of a surly atmosphere and an environment devoted to the creation of nothing but hierarchies. The pursuit of justice was an unprofitable sideline.

Each occupant of each office was supposed to operate on a 'clear desk policy', translated by Rose to mean, put your mess in a filing cabinet and close the door. Policy directives such as these reached the in-trays on a weekly basis (word processed, single spaced), three-page essays on how to use the new expense claim forms, operate the front door, apply for stationery and photocopying or retrieve a file from the distant limbo of storage, where it could only be accepted for final oblivion if subdivided into

299

bundles no thicker than three inches. Helen had asked if anyone could keep a clear desk when the bureaucracy spat forth such volumes of forms, statements and exhortations which had nothing to do with the practice of law. Redwood said rules were rules.

Helen kept her room in accordance with the keep-the-desk-tidy policy by storing most of the paperwork which she was not actively hiding on the floor. There lay white files, bound with tape, bulging with paper in varying thick-nesses and states of order, festooned with yellow post-its, reminding her of the next thing to be done, and when. She stepped in between the serried rows each morning, read her own messages to herself and hauled forth the ones where some kind of action was imperative. An immaculate system, she thought. The files were slab-like stepping-stones on a grey carpet patterned with coffee stains.

Rose piled one file on top of another and sat astride them. Helen had removed the box, once used for copying paper and invaluable for other purposes, from her head, improving her appearance dramatically. Her hair was not even ruffled and remained tied back neatly in a black scrunchie. Very lawyerly, Rose thought. You could almost believe she was the real thing. Rose adored Helen with a fierce devotion which was not always devoid of criticism.

'Are we really going back to the Crown Court today, Aunty H? Are we really?' she asked in a passable mimicry of Redwood's whine.

'Only if you're good.'

'What does that mean?'

'You should know by now. Don't taunt Redwood so early in the morning. It's bad for his digestion.'

'Is it OK in the afternoon?'

'Yes, especially in the afternoons. Especially during policy meetings.'

Helen was passing down the first line of files, kicking them into symmetry before she pounced, hauled the burden to the clearish desk and struggled with the tape. Rose pointed at it.

'Is this one going to work? I mean, to coin a legal phrase not yet found in the Latin, will it work?'

'Doubt it.'

'Why? That poor cow was raped, good and proper.'

'Nothing proper about it. Date rape. He says she consented; she says she didn't. It all depends on which of them makes the more impressive witness. She wasn't very good at giving evidence in chief yesterday, was she?'

Rose shrugged. 'I believed her, but then I s'pose I'm nearer her age. There's a couple of girls on the jury listening hard, but then there's a couple of mothers who've probably got sons just like him. Testosterone tits.' Rose clasped her hands between her knees, an automatic reaction which was nothing to do with the subject matter of the trial. It was all in the air they breathed: the pollen of rape.

'What beats me,' she continued, 'is why even girls don't believe other girls. It's not as though every female over the age of sixteen knows much about sex. Oh, I mean, she may have done the business, but that's not the same thing as knowing anything about men. You want them to like you. You can't believe they'd actually hurt you. You think they can stop and you think they can read your signals. Girls are romantic. That's why it's so horrible. It can't be

301

half as bad being raped when you're older. You've got less belief to shatter.'

'Oh, I don't know about that,' Helen said drily, checking the papers, looking at her watch. She had clearly stopped listening and Rose was annoyed.

'The problem with you, Aunty, is too much respectability. I think maybe you've got it in for youth, you. The number of rape cases you personally have turned down over the last three months . . . well, speaks for itself. You're positively encouraging testosterone to tread all over timidity. I mean, why did you bother to run this one?'

'Bruises.'

'You turned down the husband and wife one, too. What a pig he was.'

'There wasn't any choice about that. Those kind are virtually impossible to prove unless the couple have separated. One person's word against another.'

'And you turned down the one with the man in the basement flat,' Rose went on, hotly.

'Oh, come on, Rose. You know that gave me sleepless nights. She picked him out on parade, but he was nothing like her description of him and there was no forensic and he had a sort of an alibi . . .'

'And he's done it again. And he'll do it again . . .'

'Probably. Keep your door locked when Mike's not around, won't you?'

The concern in her voice broke Rose's antagonistic mood. She smiled, the grin lighting up her bright eyes, creating dimples in her cheeks and even softening the spikes of her hair.

'Naa,' she said. 'If I get any intruders, they won't be

after my body; they'll be after his, or the wedding presents. Time to go, is it?'

'Yup.'

Rose stood in front of the small mirror to the left of Helen's desk. A policy statement on dress code for court was expected daily. She ran her fingers through her hair.

'Mike wants me to stop being punk and go curly. Only for the wedding. What d'ye think, Aunty Helen?'

Together they considered the most serious problem of the day.

'No,' Helen said finally. 'Unless you buy a wig.'

'Blond? To go with my flowers, d'you think?'

'For sure.'

Rose's infuriation with the random nature of justice was always an item festering on a hidden agenda. Although she could recite it, Rose did not understand the Code for crown prosecutors, which so clearly underlined the difference between truth and pragmatism. The Code said that prosecutors should only initiate those cases where they considered there was a reasonable prospect of securing a conviction. That meant, in Rose's eyes, that they had to consider the likely result before considering the facts. It seemed outrageous to her that these middle-class wankers should base their decisions on second-guessing what the jury, or the defence, would do; taking prejudice, skill and incredulity into account before they were even expressed.

She stood up and began systematically feeding paper through the window, passing through the policy dictates contained in the in-tray with all the delight of an old lady feeding birds.

The taxi fare to court would require a form in triplicate

if it was ever to be reclaimed. Helen was unlikely to bother, happy enough to have the prickly Rose alongside again for the day. As they plunged into the gloom of the court foyer and dumped their baggage for the usual check, Rose pulled at Helen's arm.

'Look, I meant to ask you earlier. One great big favour . . .'

'What, buy you the wig for the wedding?'

'No. I want you to talk to someone.'

'About what?'

'Rape.'

At this time of year, the yellow fields of the north were full of rape. Brilliant yellow flowers, so vibrant they were positively vulgar in an English landscape; luminous by night, brighter than wallflowers, but the scent of the blossoms heavy and foul. As a farmer's son, Detective Sergeant Todd approved of his homeland, approved of rape in that agricultural context. Rape-seed oil, fit for a thousand uses, his father said. He was homesick for the sight of those flat and ugly fields so full of valuable produce. It would be nice to harvest something in the spectacular dryness of this August, and see what you had done.

'What's he trying to do?' Todd asked Bailey.

'Kill himself,' Bailey grunted.

'Clever, when you think of it, although I suppose when you do, it isn't, really. Not for a copper. You go straight home. You have a shower and put your undies in the washing machine. I bet Ryan does that every night he's home late.'

'Ryan's wife might have put the stuff in the machine.

304

She may well swear she did. Just like she said he'd been in all evening, when you lot went to pick him up. Poor woman.'

DS Todd reserved his small supply of sympathy.

'Well, she wouldn't pass her GCSE in telling lies, that's for sure. It was obvious she was saying the first thing that came into her head. Pointing the finger at him even more. As if she'd assumed his guilt.'

'Don't leap to conclusions,' Bailey said mildly.

'Difficult to avoid. I don't see, at this stage, how even the CPS could find a way of turning this down. Even without any forensic. Even if they don't go for rape, make it attempted rape or indecent assault; same difference. She's covered in marks, wearing his jacket, and all he'll say is, no comment.'

Todd was keen as mustard. Imported from another police force, he was one of the few who did not know Ryan, even by reputation. He was not a man for gossip, Bailey concluded, but one whose sharp nose touched the grindstone with dedication every week he was not on yet another training course. Bailey smiled at him to cover the dislike he would not show. He recognized all too well the necessity of having about his person throughout this ghastly mess a nit-picking stickler to whom Ryan was a stranger.

'Was he drunk, I wonder?' Bailey asked.

'Oh, merry. Not so drunk that he didn't remember to take his wallet and warrant card out of his pocket before dunking his shirt into hot soapy water.'

'Hardly evidence.'

Nothing was more debilitating than Bailey's strange

sense of grief. Todd and he sat together in the canteen, relieved at its relative emptiness. From the direction of the counter, over the Formica-topped tables and plastic plants, raucous laughter sounded as two large West Indian ladies poured glutinous soup into the heated container which would render it inedible by lunch-time. Soup was always on the menu, even in August. A few coffee drinkers huddled together, as far distant from Bailey and Todd as they could make it, as if whatever contagion they carried could drift and move above the smell of fried food.

'C'mon on then,' Bailey said reluctantly, uncurling his long legs. 'Got to go and see about a girl.' The chair he pushed back made a loud fart-like noise on the floor. The place fell as silent as a church.

The station by day was an entirely different building to the station by night. This time, they traversed the front counter as an easier route to the suites at the back, passing *en route* the counter queue. It comprised mainly young men shuffling and scratching, signing on for bail; drivers producing documents; ladies with tales of stolen handbags, the air thick with subdued anxiety. While Todd excused himself to find the gents, Bailey took his chance, nodding to the custody sergeant, who pressed the buzzer through into the cells, watching without a word while Bailey practically ran to Ryan's cell and opened the flap.

'You all right?'

There wasn't much else to say. Ryan was sitting still, staring at nothing. He turned a blank face on Bailey, then looked away. Something was said which Bailey almost missed.

'Pardon?'

There was a glimmer of a smile, the voice only slightly louder.

'I said, I never liked that jacket, sir. Never.'

There was little enough Bailey could do for Ryan without showing signs. Keep him clean and tidy for one. Get him out of the cell soonest and try and use some form of telepathy to stop him crying. His gaolers, those solid uniformed men, were bound to see that as an admission of guilt.

There was something terrible about a man weeping. Mrs Mary Ryan had read many a magazine article about the virtues of the new kind of man who wept at the drop of a hat, in case the hat was hurt, and was otherwise honest about his emotions, but it was not a culture with which she was familiar, or one she expected any man of hers to embrace. True, she would have preferred more honesty from her husband, or at least a greater ability to articulate when something was on his mind, instead of which he would put on a mood and hang around like the walking wounded, sulking and barking and waiting for her to guess the cause. Crying, however, was another matter. Tears were her prerogative, and even she did not shed them often. Daughter of a police officer, married to a police officer, with one of her sons dreaming of nothing else but becoming one of the same, she was watching the possible demise of every tradition which kept her family afloat, and there was her husband, her conquering hero, with a face puffy from tears.

Mrs Ryan hugged Mr Ryan and, in its way, the embrace

was heartfelt. She was not a hard woman, merely a practical one, and they had been together a long time. Married far too young, of course; twenty-one apiece and with all the sense of a pair of kids, so that each of them had kicked over the traces a few years later, taken their marriage to the brink once or twice, then, after more than a decade, got a grip. On her way here, driving with automatic care and rehearsing a dozen versions of what to tell the kids, she had made herself remember all she respected about Ryan. He was generous to a fault, he was funny, he did not judge, he was ultimately reliable, and yes, she loved the way he looked; always had. She scorned the assumption that sensible women did not bother so much about a man's looks, when really, the way they looked, if they looked like Ryan even on a bad day, always helped them get away with murder. That handsome mug would go down well with a jury, she told herself, and shook her head in disbelief that she should think such a thing. It would never come to that.

He was not a pretty boy today, though. Seedy was the word which sprang to mind.

'You'll be out this afternoon,' she said briskly.

'Who says?'

'Custody sergeant. Your bloody precious Bailey left a message with him to tell me.' Mrs Ryan, who had always secretly credited Bailey with the development of her husband from imbecile to grown man, now felt and spoke of him as an object of hate, purely for his current power over their lives.

'Bailed for further enquiries. Something like that. What did you tell them?'

'Nothing.' She nodded, approving, but wanting more.

308

'What's the Brief like?'

'OK. I only did what he said.'

'For once.'

Mrs Ryan produced the Thermos of coffee and Mars bar which the sergeant had allowed her to bring in. They seemed such a pathetic offering in the circumstances, she almost put them away, but the chocolate seemed to bring colour to his skin.

'A Mars a day helps you work, rest and play,' he remarked, his voice a touch stronger.

'Did you get any breakfast?' she asked, resorting to the lowest level of wifely consideration, conscious of what she was doing and even more acutely aware of the atmosphere of the place. Echoing footsteps, a muted banging on the wall from somewhere, the conflicting smells of disinfectant and urine.

'Didn't want breakfast.'

She could see why.

'Oh, I bought you a newspaper.'

'Thanks.'

All speech was desultory. She felt as if every word was being overheard and could scarcely raise her voice above a whisper. There was also that sensation peculiar to hospital visits: the fear of saying anything which was not banal and the acute guilty desire to escape. Get out. He seemed to sense it, and for that, she felt a rush of love for him.

'You'd better go, love. No point both of us being stuck in here, is there?' He attempted a laugh. Although she wanted to go, being invited to go still felt like rejection. Perhaps he simply wanted his space back, so he could cry in peace.

'S'pose not.' She rose to her feet gratefully and rang the bell, then sat down to await the response, dying for those footsteps to come down the corridor towards them. She was aware of him watching her.

'What are you thinking?' she demanded; a last attempt to make this encounter fruitful.

Ryan stretched his legs so that they touched the wall opposite. Single cells were not designed for the swinging of cats.

'I'm thinking that I shall never, ever again, bang a bloke up in a cell without thinking long and hard about it first.'

You might not have the chance, she thought. You might never have the chance. You are going to be formally suspended from duty this afternoon, whatever else happens, and our world will come to an end. How could you do this to me?

'I never think of Old Bailey, without thinking of your Bailey,' Rose said as they stuffed the bundles of paper and files into the back of the taxi, this time without attempts to keep them in order. 'They have the same craggy appearance.'

The afternoon sunshine made them blink. Out of the cooler corridors of the court, they felt like moles ascending into daylight. Rose's face shone. She was chattering for the sake of making noise, hiding the fact that she was angry and disappointed.

'Didn't take them long, did it?'

'No, not long. Probably the weather.'

On a day like this, even the most conscientious juror would want to be gone. Back to a flat, a house, a bus ride,

310

away from sordid tales of bodily fluids, out of the gloom and the security checks, into the warm sunlight.

'Half an hour.' Rose tugged at the ends of her hair, found one longer lock, stuck it in her mouth and chewed. 'Half an hour to brand that girl a cheap little liar.'

Helen protested, mildly.

'No. He only had to show that his belief in her consent was reasonable at the time, even if he accepted in retrospect that it was wrong. The clever part was that he was careful to avoid calling her a liar.'

'Won't make any difference to the way she feels.'

'She'll probably recover,' Helen said. She looked cool in the heat. Her right foot steadied a box of paper at her feet.

'What a cold-hearted bitch you are, Aunty West, honestly.'

Helen did not reply. There was clearly a better occasion to mention that the deepest and most terrifying of humiliations, rape included, did not always send a life into an inevitable downward spiral. Rose herself was a fine example of recovery. Rose, who was still so young, but had never been allowed innocence. A father from hell, a history of abuse and promiscuity, from which she had risen, like the phoenix from the ashes, frightened of nothing. Proud of her, Helen also envied that huge capacity for life which had made the transformation possible, and, while trying to ignore Rose's comments on the frozen state of her own soul, wondered if the remarks were true and whether it really was a cop-out to make yourself indifferent to the things you could not change.

'You were saying something earlier on about a favour,' she said. The taxi bowled out into Ludgate Hill. The vast spectre of St Paul's rose before them in majesty, the steps littered with brightly coloured people. They looked normal; they had decent lives, wore their best and most garish clothes, each with his own history. Helen wanted to go inside, feel the cool, mingle with gawping visitors and pretend superiority. Rose was fingering her hair into sharper spikes, a sure sign of determination. Hers was a life which made religion, even religious buildings, anathema. Her father had always carried a Bible, even on his way to abuse little girls. Rose now believed in a different set of gods.

'Yeah. I want you to talk to this friend. Well, I don't know. You might bite her head off and tell her to go and get a life or something.'

'Oh, for Christ's sake stop talking in riddles. What do you want me to do?'

Rose took a deep breath of exasperation, then enunciated her words as carefully as any real lawyer on a pedestal.

'Michael's cousin. She's doing my flowers. I like her a lot, as it happens. Eight years younger than you; nine years older than me. Work that out for yourself. Only, she's been attacked, by a man. She told Mike's mum, but she won't say much and Mike's mum says it's been like watching someone shrivel up, but she won't do anything about it. You met her at my engagement party, remember? You two got on like a house on fire.'

'And you want me to talk to her? Forget it. There's social services, Rape Crisis, Victim Support, all that . . .'

'And none of it would do. Don't ask me why, it won't. You're the right age, you know what it's like to be attacked, you can pull words out of people. Will you do it?'

'No. I haven't got the skill.'

Nor the time and certainly not the inclination. She was trying to recall the woman she had met, remembered a large girl, a midwife by profession. The taxi turned sharply, diving through a dark narrow street, throwing them together. Helen could feel the heat of Rose's skin. Papers littered the floor, ignored. All that paper, representing nothing but loss for everyone concerned.

'Typical,' said Rose, righting herself. 'Bloody typical. I can just hear what's in your head. Me? Never! I just prosecute; I can't do anything else; I don't want to understand. I don't want to find out what it's like, and I don't have time to help anyone, 'cos I'm so busy doing my duty. Like some doctor; I just inject, I just prescribe, I can't prevent. Look, it's because all these counsellors are such bloody experts that she won't go. She doesn't want psychobabble. She wants a nice, dry, sympathetic lawyer. One with my personal seal of approval, which you are about to lose.'

'Why won't she talk to you?'

Rose turned her head away.

'Oh, don't be so silly. I'm too young.'

Rose, you have never been young. Youthful and energetic, yes, but never young, Helen thought, slightly amused and certainly perplexed. Odd that she could withstand the bullying of a judge, the intimidation of Redwood, the vicious dislike of defendants and still have absolutely no armoury to defend an unreasonable request from Rose. She had a sudden flash of what it must be like to be Bailey, locked in his friendship with Ryan, made as malleable by it as a piece of putty.

'When?'

313

She meant, when was the woman attacked? but the single word was taken as acceptance of the demand. Rose was good at that. She had an angular face with a wide generous mouth made for smiling. Redwood was right to remark that Helen looked like an older, calmer version of Rose; she seemed unaware of how much the girl modelled herself on her. If she had her hair transformed into soft curls, Helen was thinking fondly, this little devil might be able to fool even more of the people more of the time.

'Triffic. I'll give you her address. I mean, I did tell her this evening would be fine, but I expect you could rearrange.'

There was no such thing as totally free will, Helen decided. Nor any such thing as predictability when the will was so weak.

Much of the time, she did not like being in charge, especially of human beings. Rose could have been right. It was a dangerous state to have reached if she really did prefer to meet them on paper.

CHAPTER THREE

'The House of Lords have upheld the Court of Appeal in deciding that there is no implied consent to sexual intercourse within marriage, and that it is therefore possible for a man to rape his wife. The argument that "unlawful" meant outside the bond of marriage was mere surplusage ... it was clearly unlawful to have sexual intercourse with any woman without her consent and the use of the word in the subsection added nothing.'

Brigid Connor was taking tea among the friends of the parish, ostensibly to organize preparations for the visit of the Bishop, who would confirm several children in their as yet half-baked faith and inspect the church with a view to allocating funds. This seemed to necessitate a wholesale spring-clean of the church itself, although Brigid privately thought it would be better to leave it as it was, since there was little point painting over the cracks which they wanted the man to see. The episcopal visit was distant enough to take second place to gossip of various kinds; Brigid would be able to add little. She detested parish activity and had no great affection for the other ladies who approached it with the enthusiasm she was capable of assuming, but never feeling, and she disliked the uneasy knowledge that they were all in the same boat.

They formed a sanctimonious posse of the better-off kind of matrons, who did not work, either because they did not know how or because they had no need. They were an unglamorous version of the ladies who lunch, all of them considering it poor taste to be flashy, to show off the baubles or the boobies, while each, to a woman, pretended they were poorer and busier than they were. It was the cars that gave them away rather than the clothes. Each time Brigid met one or the other, she hoped for a kind of break-through into friendship. Or, failing that, some kind of clue as to how it was they seemed to manage their lives so much better than she did; something she could copy, so that she could laugh as they did. But she stood on the fringes, looking in, watching intensely, making them uncomfortable, all the time afraid they might discover how much she envied their self-command.

Did they live in a state of mortal sin? Did they fear hell and any repeat of pregnancy as she did? They were a small element of this particular parish; minimal in comparison to those parishioners at the other end of the scale. This coterie existed to give, the bulk to receive, like a vast nest of baby birds with open mouths, Brigid thought, without condemnation. She had often wished she was one of the needy poor, then she might have greater licence to trouble the priest. One of the other women, only a couple of years Brigid's senior, married young and looking forward to grandmother status by the time she reached a well-preserved forty, was showing the others photos of her daughter's wedding. Brigid had attended the service, without an invitation to the reception. She saw herself, skulking in the corner of one of the photos outside church, with her hat askew, and, looking at her shadowy depiction, felt shame in it.

'Didn't she look a dream? All that lace . . .'

'Her granny's veil, that was, you know. Must be a hundred years old. Beautiful, isn't it?'

There were photos pre-ceremony, photos after, careful to include costly cars and all the best frocks, or so it seemed to Brigid. The one thing which struck her most was the picture of the bride arriving with the veil over her face, ready to float down the aisle in ghostly anonymity, although everyone knew who she was. The veil said it all, Brigid was thinking. You arrived for your wedding shrouded in complete ignorance, thinking you knew about life, the universe and everything, while knowing nothing. Least of all the fact that you were a sacrificial lamb, for whom being in love was not going to help one whit. At least that was the way it had been for her. Might not be the same for a modern girl; but eighteen, this bride, for God's sake. How much could any girl know at eighteen?

The photos were bringing forth a flood of reminiscence, some of it surprisingly frank by their standards.

'I remember my wedding night,' one remarked. 'Lord, what a fiasco. I never thought I'd recover.'

'Was it such a great thing, Mary? Did you have to step over it?'

They all snorted with laughter.

'Course, it's not like that now,' Mary continued. 'Not that it ever really was. I was a virgin, God help me, but as for my sisters . . . Nobody actually produced a shotgun, but Daddy might as well.'

'That was me,' Brigid murmured, suddenly spontaneously bold. She only had to know, within rough parameters, the ages of these women's children to know that the had-to-get-married scenario applied to more than herself. No one was shocked.

'Me too,' said another, after a pause. She was another plump one, who knitted between bites of her cake; the last thing she needed. 'Not that I have regrets, mind: I mightn't have got him any other way,' she said with her mouth full and they all laughed again. 'And surely,' the plump one went on, 'there's few enough years when the sex stuff matters that much. Thank God the old man seems to have forgotten all about it.'

'If only,' Brigid said, further emboldened by the laughter. She spoke too fervently, her voice too loud. Now they were all staring at her, waiting for elaboration. She giggled, feeling herself blush.

'I mean, I wish mine would forget about . . . it. He never does though.'

The pause this time was distinctly awkward. The hostess stood up to refresh the tea.

'Well aren't you the lucky one?' she said, not unkindly. Everyone knew that Brigid, even in the maturity of her late thirties, was one brick short of a load. 'After all those years. It must be a wonderful thing to have a man who still wants you.'

Brigid knew how she must have sounded: boastful instead of bruised. And her Aemon such a handsome man, too. Barrel-shaped, with the kind of ruddy complexion which suggested rustic honesty. A big man with vivid blue eyes and a fine crop of hair, like his brothers. And his daughters, playing with their cousins for the summer. She had failed them all.

She went home via the church, where confetti drifted across the steps and the traffic roared by. God help her; it was only a small thing to bear, wasn't it? Sex, marriage, her own existence.

At the junction of the main road and the avenue which led to her home, she faltered and made an excuse to detour to the shops. It wasted another twenty minutes. The front door to the apartment block was a door of glass, which threw her own reflection back at her with warped accuracy, like a silly mirror at the funfairs of her childhood. She bent in the middle; her forehead was huge, the carrier bag enormous and the necklace round her neck too bright. Nearer the door, as she climbed up the steps, she became a small neat woman with an overlarge bosom and overtinted red-blond hair which was nothing but an artificial imitation of what it had been. She looked capable enough, but with shoulders too narrow for a body to cry upon and a dress with a pattern as busy as the confetti she had seen.

From the windows of the apartment Aemon had built, she could see downhill to the bowl of London. In the near distance were the gasometers of St Pancras. Touches of green between rooftops; railway lines sneaking out from the vast sheds of the station, suggesting freedom. All she had to do was go, but there had been a touch of cold in the morning air, an early-warning sign of a summer on the wane. Brigid did not want to be up here; nor did she want to be down there in those streets, either. Even in those shaded areas of green which showed the coolness of a square or a park.

Too soon for a drink, or was it? Drink, bath, warmth within and without. Ablutions and alcohol to rid herself of the dreadful guilt about taking pills and going to the doctor. Confessing things she should only confess to a priest, without hope of redemption now. No, no drinkies, not yet. She had will-power sometimes; it was the will itself she lacked.

If Helen West was resenting the superior will-power of Rose Darvey, Anna Stirland resented it more. Rose had a talent for subversion which was nicely complemented by her appetite for conflict. Anna could see that someone might rue the day when Rose had been persuaded to train for the law, even though the day when the child would qualify was still a long way off. She could imagine Rose filling the courtroom with her own version of heavy breathing and an office with the same. The effect on her fiancée's family was exhilarating: they were weak with love for her.

Because of Rose, Anna had agreed to meet Helen West. OK, she had liked Helen on one meeting, but she would have preferred another context for the second. Anything to get Rose and Rose's future mother-in-law off her back: she should have kept her mouth shut. Anna was rehearsing the lines to make this less embarrassing, such as, I'm sorry, this is all a big mistake, fuck off. The sheer lack of imagination in her own nervous anger infuriated her all the more, but at the same time, there she was, tidying in

320

expectation of a guest who would notice. Dusting surfaces already clean, looking at the whole doll's house with a critical eye, as if she were selling it. Some chance – she'd sell it if she could – she hoped that the sound of the doorbell was announcing someone responding to the advertisement. People might think the hasty decision to sell was the reason why she had suddenly taken to spending hours after midnight painting the walls. That was the way it went, she chanted to herself in the same singsong rhythm she used to the agent. Once you make it nice, you don't want to leave, do you?

If the woman on the doorstep had said hello, extended some nice warm paw for shaking and announced herself with platitudes or small talk like the estate agent, Anna might have gone into her pre-rehearsed speech, but the visitor stood sideways on to the door, looking away down the street, one hand extended in Anna's direction, offering a bottle of wine, which, once accepted, left Anna no option but to ask Helen in. A clever ploy, she decided later; they had not even looked at one another's faces before they were both trapped.

She noticed again the scar on Helen's forehead. It curled from one eyebrow into the hairline and could easily have been covered by arrangement of her long hair, but she did not seem to mind it. Anna remembered Rose's verdict on this woman, heard Rose's lecturing voice, telling her: she may look buttoned up, you know, Anna, and she may talk a bit precious, but there isn't much she hasn't done. She didn't get that scar in a road accident and she has been known to bite people.

'What a nice kitchen,' Helen said, genuine enthusiasm

taking away the polite banality of the compliment. Anna looked around; it was a more than nice kitchen, full of old pine, carefully chosen pictures, dried herbs and flowers lending it a musky smell. A door stood open, leading on to a small backyard laid out with narrow flower-beds in full bloom. Pink and white geraniums prevailed in tubs; roses climbed the wall. The glass panes in the door gleamed.

'I know what I want in my kitchen,' Helen continued, 'just as I sometimes think I know what I want in my life, but I never quite seem to achieve it. Something goes wrong between concept and execution. I expect it always will. I'd have thought about hanging dried herbs there.' She pointed to the wooden clothes pulley above her head, holding pans and flowers. 'And then I would have continued to think about it. Not done it.'

Anna fussed, uncorked the wine clumsily, poured unsteadily, the sound of it comforting. The glass she handed Helen was unusual, heavy and old; the wine cold and pale. Nothing in the kitchen was new; all of it revealed an owner who specialized in thrift as well as taste.

'I make an effort with my house,' Anna said, choosing words carefully, 'and I love flowers, because I can't do much with my person. I think I do it to compensate to the world. Or myself. I'm not sure.'

'I don't think I quite follow.'

'You should,' Anna stated with a touch of impatience. 'But then you probably live in a different world. Beautiful people do. I'm a rather ugly woman, in case you haven't noticed. It follows that I feel obliged to create something like beauty around me, so that I can justify my own existence.'

She was plain. Not plain enough to warrant the description of ugliness, but still a slab of a woman, apart from the eyes. The kind of woman who had never quite looked like a girl; too full a figure from the age of eleven. The type who would play wallflower and act chaperone for lovelier, livelier sisters or cousins. A face which had assumed responsibility as soon as other children shed it, but not, Helen thought, as plain as all that. Anna spoke of herself ironically, as if she were birthmarked or disabled to the degree that she was an assault on the human eye, instead of being on the wrong side of ordinary.

'I think you should get a new mirror,' Helen said honestly.

Anna rose and placed the wine in the fridge. She had the light-footed step of the heavy woman who had somewhere learnt to dance, a grace and economy of movement which also cast doubts on her own bitter self-deprecation. She did not seem a person who accepted defeat lightly, nor one who had looked at her world without issuing a challenge. If anything, she would be obsessive about making the best of what she had, Helen guessed; not today, perhaps, but on other days. She felt uncomfortingly obtrusive, warning bells telling her to leave because Anna was right to resent the presence of anyone who could not mend her fractured self-esteem, least of all someone who did not want to try. Am I a man's woman or a woman's woman? Helen asked herself, remembering teenage years in which she had eschewed the company of either sex, but especially the female, for the sole unspoken reason that they were the ones most likely to expose her deficiencies. She had been a beautiful reserved child, features which, taken together, had isolated her so much she had envied the big, fat, fearless and competitive girl who led the class and was the doyen of all their opinions. Anna could have been one of the same kind, who took her bulk and her dimples and turned them into virtues, moved on to another popular persona. Becoming one of the boys; something Helen had never been.

'You would suit lace,' Anna said, her face suddenly breaking into a grin which did indeed show dimples, hollowed into the cheeks, bunching the flesh of her face into a picture of good nature. 'You could get away with lace and ribbons. Rose tells me you're getting married.' She could deflect conversation away from herself with suspicious ease, Helen observed; she did it as to the manner born. They could quite easily have sat as they were and discussed the wedding garments.

'I hate lace, ribbons, buckles and bows,' Helen said. 'And Rose tells me you were attacked and can't talk about it. Can't, won't. Rose talks a lot, about other people.'

'So does my aunt. I didn't swear her to secrecy. Obviously not,' Anna said, quick to defend Rose. 'I've been dripping on people, that's all. I shouldn't have. Rose is too young and too happy, it isn't fair.'

She leant back in her chair, which creaked under considerable rather than formidable weight. Shapely weight, as if all her proportions were exaggerated. Not fat, simply too much. Not a lady for wearing Lycra, that was all.

Helen liked her. She had liked her on first sight. For all her reserve, she could fall into instant and profound liking and, all of a sudden, it was imperative to help. She put to one side the thought of Bailey's terse phone call with the news about Ryan; also the daily cases which made it seem that rape was an epidemic, sexual assault an everyday occurrence which she judged by a set of well-established, horribly objective criteria. The questions here were different.

Anna Stirland shrugged and let out a sigh.

'I'm a nurse,' she said. 'A midwife. A competent caring person with professional skills. I've been wiping bums since childhood.' She hesitated. 'In other words, I'm one of nature's sensible people and I'm ashamed of how I've dealt with this so far. And yes, I can talk to you; I have to. Perhaps you could regard it as a piece of dictation. Take it down like a lawyer. That way it might make sense.'

'I shan't fall into a fit of the vapours,' Helen said.

'Because you've heard it all before?' Anna asked mildly. 'You haven't, you know. I bet you haven't.'

At six-thirty in the evening, Detective Sergeant Ryan was formally suspended from duty, denied access to his office and instructed to go home and await the result of enquiries. His own detective chief inspector did this with Todd as witness, Bailey lurking on the sidelines. Ryan looked as if they were sending him out into the world naked, Todd thought with some satisfaction. The DCI thought the same, albeit with greater sympathy. Ryan had been so indefatigably popular, a man's man with a taste for women; the sort they admired. It was Bailey who arranged the car to take Ryan away; no one else had formed Bailey's conclusion that if left unattended, Ryan's departure from the station would demonstrate the shortest route between the back door and the nearest public house. Ryan looked at him wryly, each of them second-guessing the other.

Bailey watched the car disappear, driven by a woman constable. He wondered what, if anything, the two of them would say to one another and reminded himself to ask her later, slightly ashamed of the subterfuge. The pursuit of truth was all, was it not? All legitimate means were allowed. Or perhaps the pursuit of some niggling ambition that Ryan would let slip in private to the driver, some definitive clue to his own innocence. Rape is a crime which calls for vengeance, Todd had said portentously, revealing a churchgoing tendency.

Barring Bailey's progress in the carpark stood a blonde girl, hands on hips, looking at him belligerently. He recognized her as a detective, one of Ryan's sexual offences team. It occurred to him that, so far, the irony of Ryan's current work taken in conjunction with the offence they would likely charge him with, had escaped him. Yesterday, Bailey had been giving Ryan advice on the diplomacy of dealing with incredulous parents; today, he was *en route* to see another set, the ones who belonged to Ryan's own victim. It was all offensively circular.

'Sally Smythe, sir. What are we supposed to do with Ryan's cases?' It was an accusation, spat out with minimal pretence at politeness.

'I don't know. Carry on. He won't be back for some time.'

The blonde looked at him as if he was solely responsible for the doubling of her workload, the demise of her life and the appearance of her first grey hairs. Bailey began to walk towards his car, away from Todd; there was an implicit invitation for her to fall into step beside him.

'Which was his biggest case?'

'They're all big. Indecent assault, buggery, you name it. And he had an ongoing thing . . . Oh, shit.' She was gabbling, on the verge of tears. 'How could he do it, sir? How could he?'

'To you? To me? To the victim?' Bailey asked lightly, touching her arm with the slightest gesture, enough to suggest commiseration, but not camaraderie.

'He was good,' she said fiercely. 'Really good. Getting better. I know none of us liked the appointment at first, but he had this case, eighteen months ago. Broke his heart. After that, he seemed, well, he seemed able to identify with the victims. If we can't, he said, who can?'

'Tomorrow at ten,' Bailey said, watching Todd catching up, 'I'd like to look at all his casework. There might be a clue to his alleged behaviour. It is only alleged, you know.'

She nodded dumbly, peeled away and left him to watch her plodding footsteps with regret. If Ryan's career was blighted, then so, by infection, was hers.

The evening sun raised a pink haze as they drove north, Bailey at the wheel with no need to consult a map. Vague directions would do equally well; he had known these streets since childhood. They were in the no man's land where Islington merges with King's Cross in a series of used-car dealerships, traffic lights and treeless thoroughfares which hide from view the pleasanter, leafier roads of a mixed hinterland. They sat behind a belching bus, watching it shiver with fumes in the heat, Bailey longing for the privilege of a fast vehicle with a siren to move everything from their path. Traffic cried for vengeance, as

327

well as rape. He scorched past the bus and into the side-streets, put on a turn of speed through a series of back-doubles. He flung the car round corners on a small industrial estate, took it up a cobbled alley-way, round the back of a parking lot and back on to the main route again, tyres screaming. When they arrived at number fourteen Roman Court, Todd was pale and Bailey felt calmer, not ashamed for shaking his passenger's composure.

They would not be talking to the victim. She was resting in her own flat, her mother said, and that was not, in any event, the purpose of the visit. Bailey had seen her statement already, it was background he wanted. Something to make the girl more than a silhouette and a name on paper. Something, perhaps, to stop himself disliking her.

The parents were not of the kind accustomed to being deferential to the police. Middle years, old enough to have watched *Dixon of Dock Green* on TV and then read three decades of newspapers detailing the destruction of that avuncular image. Mr Pelmore had twice been stopped for speeding and Mrs Pelmore had once been the victim of an overzealous store detective, so both of them were experts on the law. They saw themselves as minority honest citizens; fully employed, subject to harassment. Shelley, their daughter, was one of three children. Looking around, Bailey imagined he could guess an enthusiasm to leave home, even, as in Shelley's case, to live with a boyfriend less than two miles away.

'She's a good girl,' the mother said, as if anyone had yet suggested otherwise. 'A sweet girl. Quiet.'

A parent would always claim a girl was good. Bailey had

waited years for one to boast that his or her child was gloriously, colourfully bad. The father was silent. Both sat in their living room, defiantly occupying their regular oatmeal fabric covered chairs with uncomfortable wooden arms. Two dining chairs had been produced for the officers to sit facing them, perhaps to emphasize the fact that the interview was on sufferance. Tea was not offered. The room itself personified contemporary gloom: dark-blue carpet, patterned blue curtains, light-blue wallpaper with heavy borders near the ceiling, fittings of orangey-coloured wood. The shelves housed no books, but contained instead carefully arranged china figures of ladies in crinolines, shepherds and shepherdesses, dogs, cats and horses, all prancing together in sterile contemplation of a large loud clock on the opposite wall. Everything was depressingly tidy. Bailey remembered that his own flat had been given a similar description by Helen some time since, but his flat was different. It was eclectic. There was another passing thought, as he let the words flow over and around him, while he arranged his own face in an expression of rapt and kindly concentration. Would he and Helen sit thus, in chairs like this, when they reached the stage of Darby and Joan? The thought made him shudder. He never wanted to be fastidious. Not about emotion; not about anything.

'Yes,' said father at last. 'A very good girl. Always worked, Shell. Never cost us.' Bailey could not help himself, he leant forward with his arms resting on his thin knees. His legs were too long for the narrow room; Todd thought he had a face like a hatchet.

'What exactly do you mean by "good"? Do you mean

329

good in school, good at helping blind people at zebra crossings, kind to animals, or not many boyfriends?' He spoke with all the congeniality of a cobra, but quietly, scratching his head as an afterthought to suggest genuine confusion. Both mum and dad bridled; mother spoke first.

'I mean a good girl, that's what I mean! Not one of those dole spongers! And she lives with this decent bloke. Been going out with him since she was sixteen. Works hard, he does, too. Electrician; works shifts. They got a flat on a mortgage. Getting married.' She spat the last with a note of triumph.

'She liked animals,' father added as a delayed reaction. 'Least, she did when she was a kid.'

Mother darted from her chair and produced a photo album, as if by magic. She placed it on Bailey's lap with a smart thump and retreated to her own seat to sit with folded arms. Todd sensed a conversational hiatus, filled it blithely, looking at the bovine face of dad.

'What kind of animals?'

'Pardon?'

'She didn't really like animals,' mother interrupted, anxious to avoid anything which might suggest a lack of hygiene in any sense. 'Only gerbils and things.'

Bailey was suffering from a desperate desire to laugh, another to scream. He was turning the pages of the album, seeing Shelley as an overdressed baby, held aloft by her mother like a trophy; Shelley at school, earnest in socks; Shelley with her mates and cousins on her thirteenth birthday, a pretty child, refusing to smile for the camera. He felt only relief that these parents had never met the age of the camcorder, the better to depict in movement what was, to

330

his jaundiced view, that fleeting sly expression of their child. Did not like animals. Having reached the point where the photos tailed off, Shelley aged fifteen, he snapped the album shut and placed it back in Mrs P's lap. She had the impression of a large pale ghost coming towards her and retreating, quailed slightly and blinked. By the time she looked again, he was back as he had been, legs crossed this time.

'When was she getting married?' Todd asked, looking like an earnest bank manager, almost cocking his hand behind an ear for the reply.

'What do you mean, *was*? She still is, isn't she? Next month, sometime. She isn't dead, is she?'

Oh, she lied, she lied. All mothers know the date of a daughter's wedding. Did they? Bailey was getting married himself, sometime next month. When the weather was fine, whenever; month decided, date not fixed; a register office do. Left deliberately vague, God help them both. Summer, Helen had said. We'll think about the arrangements two weeks before. It occurred to him, in this frozen room, just why they might both be so diffident. This daughter's mother seemed to regard a wedding as a prize for winning a race.

'He's a lovely lad, her fiancée,' Mrs Pelmore said fondly. 'Lovely. It was him reported it. Then, after the police came, he phoned me. He's good to her. Steady.'

'Did you know about her other involvement with the police?' Todd asked.

'She's never been in trouble with the police,' dad cut in.

'I know,' Todd said easily. 'But there was an occasion, not long ago, when she went out clubbing with a friend, and the friend had an accident on the way home. Shelley helped us with information. We think that's how she met Mr Ryan.'

Mrs Pelmore looked blank.

'How often do you see Shelley?' Bailey asked.

There was a long fidgeting pause. Mother opened her mouth to speak and closed it again. Father hauled himself upright, the bones of his elbows crunching on the uncomfortable chair. Mother put out a warning hand which he ignored.

'She never comes near us,' he said flatly. 'Not if she can help it. He comes, though, her boy. He comes to see us. That's how we know how she is.'

'I know,' said Anna Stirland, 'about rape. Oh, I don't mean in a legal sense, I mean I know about violation. I work with women, you see. It's a kind of violation, having a baby you don't want, by a man you don't love. I don't meet many men, though in my kind of environment there are a lot of them around. Men seem to like me well enough, but they don't, well, look at me. I'm one of the lads, a good sport; they'll put that on my gravestone. To tell the truth, I don't do much looking either; no point in a great lump like me flirting, is there? Only when I look at these baby kids, I know how I'd like my life to go: in the direction of a household with a nice man and a couple of children. Especially children. Well, I'm over thirty and the prospect gets ever more remote. I just don't like men well enough to try. Then I met John. That isn't his real name. I'm not going to tell you his real name.'

'Why not?'

'You'll see. And if this is dictation, you aren't supposed to interrupt.'

'Sorry.'

'He worked in the same place as me. We got on well. I used to watch his hands and think, God, you are the most beautiful creature nature ever invented. He had all the humanity I like in a man; vulnerability, too. Not the sort of drivel you'd put in a statement, is it? I suppose it might have been obvious that I went into spasms whenever I saw him, but the others didn't seem to notice, so I thought he hadn't either. We copers have self-control, you know. Yes, you probably do know. What would have been more obvious was the fact that I sparkled when he was around, became the life and soul of the party, full of wit and energy. Falling in love must be like that. I've always hated the phrase. I thought the best thing would be to be friends first, let love, or whatever you choose to call it, grow like a plant. But desire isn't like that, is it? It's a bloody affliction. It has nothing to do with approval, mutual feeling and appreciation, nothing at all. It's a ghastly virus, immune to medicine.'

She gulped her wine. Helen sat in front of her notepad, trying to make herself as anonymous as a shorthand-taker at a board meeting.

'And we were friends, I thought. He has a special smile he reserved for me; he seemed to seek me out, even when every other female in the place simpered and would have thrown their knickers at him, given half the chance. So I let hope spring eternal. Perhaps one day he'd say, let's have a drink? How about dinner sometime? The one thing I wasn't going to do was make the suggestion: I was too scared of rejection. I sort of prayed it would come from him. It's always better to live in hope than risk the negative, don't you think? Well, it is if you look like me. Such sensitivity, I have.'

Her fingernails were neatly trimmed, Helen noticed. There were flecks of paint on the back of both wrists. Anna stuffed her hands into the long sleeves of the kaftan she wore, as if hiding them.

'But no, he didn't take whatever bait I was offering, not in months, and then he was posted somewhere else. A man with a career path, you see. I was devastated at the thought of not seeing him again. So there I was, acting out of character, saying, why don't you come round to supper before you go? He said he couldn't, but he'd drop round for a drink sometime. I had to be content with that. Had to? I *was* content. Doesn't take much to please me. I worshipped him.'

Helen caught a waft of scent from the garden. It would be pleasant to eat at this table, with the doors open like this and the blaze of flowers outside.

'I waited, of course one waits, but not all the time. He turned up, like they do, when least expected. It was that hot spell, a couple of weeks since; freakishly hot. Midnight or so, too late for a casual call. I looked a mess; it made me flustered. I was in the living room.' She jerked her head in the direction of the first room off the hall which Helen had only noticed briefly. 'I was doing my ironing. Well I tried to smooth myself down, fetched us a drink, but it isn't easy to look both alluring and casual when all you have on is a long T-shirt. I was too flustered to get the ice; he did that.' She gulped.

334

'I put down the drinks: gin and tonic, first things first; I was joking and had my back to him. I wanted to unplug the iron, put the board away, because I didn't want the damn thing littering up the room. I wanted . . . I wanted him to see what a nice room it was. Admire me for it. Pathetic, isn't it?'

'No,' Helen said. 'It isn't.'

'And then he was on me. No preliminaries, no nothing. I thought at first he was hugging me from behind, fooling around, and I didn't want that. I didn't want a quick poke, for God's sake; even I can get one of those if I want nothing more. I wanted sweet words, admiration, some sort of tentative beginning, some curiosity about *me* . . . Oh, I don't know what I wanted, I didn't even want him to see my bare knees.' Her voice fell into silence. Helen wondered if it was permissible to smoke a cigarette and decided not.

'Oh, do smoke if you want. I think I'll have one too. It's amazing the number of nurses who smoke, you know. Doctors, too.'

'Was he a doctor?'

'Did I say that?' Anna said sharply. 'No, I didn't say that. Of course he wasn't a doctor, how could he be? A sort of technician, really.' She took the cigarette with a shaking hand.

'I fell onto the iron. He pushed me down against it; it fell over. I don't know if he meant to do that, but he must have known it hurt, because I screamed. My arm was burnt.' She pulled back her sleeve. There was a triangular imprint of a fading burn mark, still livid.

'The board fell over. I fell with it, I think; on my stomach, against the iron, then I rolled over against it again. I was lying on top of it, screaming; he seemed to be pressing me down. I think it was then I realized he meant to do me harm. I started struggling, but I was kind of paralysed, too; I could only focus on how much the burning hurt. Next thing I knew, he'd hauled the T-shirt over my face. I was on my back, couldn't see anything. I began to cry, I think. I thought he was going to rape me, kill me, I don't know what. I couldn't move. He held my arms down, but there was really no need. Even when he moved and I heard what I thought was the rustling of paper, I didn't move. Then I felt this thing going in between my legs. I think I'd already made a half-conscious decision to stay still. Something stuck up me. Rammed. I might have passed out for a minute.'

The ash on the end of her cigarette smouldered and dropped onto the clean table. Helen brushed it away; it burnt slightly against her palm.

'I don't know why, I thought of a sixty-millilitre syringe.' Anna's voice had gone down to a murmur, as if she was speaking to herself

'You can use them for irrigating a womb . . . and other plumbing operations; they're sort of phallic shaped, cold . . .' Her voice hardened. 'I was simply aware of being fucked and being icy, icy cold. My stomach in contractions; me, fighting with the T-shirt, getting my face free. The fucking stopped. I certainly can't call it anything else but fucking. Certainly not making love. I somehow sat up, got the shirt over my head, and there he was, sitting in the chair laughing. Me, naked, flopping all over the place; him, sitting with his legs crossed, immaculately dressed as usual. He favoured the smart casual. Nice white cotton tops, smart linen-look trousers, handsome belt.'

'Dressed?' Helen murmured, incredulous.

Anna extended both her arms, shaking them free of the purple kaftan sleeves. The colour of it suited her. The burns were almost symmetrical.

'So was I, dressed, I suppose. I was wearing three large burns. And I was so cold. And then what did he do? Swallowed his gin, came over to me, kissed me on the forehead and said, there, poppet, that was what you wanted, wasn't it? Then he left. He was . . . pleased with himself. As if he'd done me a favour. There's more wine in the fridge,' she added. 'Could you get it?'

The fridge was empty apart from the bottle. It looked new and reeked of cleanser.

'Isn't it funny that I can put wine in that thing, but not food?' Anna said chattily. 'It's all his fault.'

Helen kept her expression calm, privately thinking, The woman has flipped. This is not making sense.

'I hadn't even got to my feet by the time the door slammed,' Anna continued. 'And I heard his footsteps going down the road before I moved. Then I looked down between my legs and I thought I was bleeding. A sort of red-coloured trickle was coming out onto the carpet. I stood up and it dripped on the floor. By this time, I was imagining some major haemorrhage. What had he done? Was it a knife? Hadn't I noticed any pain, only cold, because the burns hurt so much and that was all I had room to feel? Bleed to death, go on, I told myself, but I knew it wasn't blood.'

Anna started to laugh. 'It was a popsicle. One of those cheap ice lollies kids like so much, like a long icicle, wrapped in polythene; horrible things, but I kept them in the freezer for neighbours' kids. Should I laugh? He laughed. Get the girl all lathered up, then cool her down . . . it is funny, isn't it?'

'No. It isn't funny.'

'Promise me it isn't funny . . . When I sat on the side of my bed, I was weeping strawberry juice. Tell me, lady lawyer, was that simply a joke, or was that rape?'

Helen cleared her throat, reached for wine and cigarettes simultaneously.

'According to the letter of the law, no, that wasn't rape.'

Anna began laughing, a grim and mirthless chuckle.

'No,' she said, 'I don't suppose it was. That's me, isn't it? Not even worth that.'

CHAPTER FOUR

'Where, on the trial of any offence under this Act, it is necessary to prove sexual intercourse (whether natural or unnatural), it shall not be necessary to prove the completion of the intercourse by the emission of seed, but the intercourse shall be deemed to be complete upon proof of penetration only. According to the old authorities, even the slightest penetration will be sufficient ... It is submitted that this remains the law under the present statutory arrangement.'

Shelley remembered that when she had finally reached home on the fateful night of her meeting with Ryan, she had smelt. Hot-night sweat of rage and fear with overtones of heavy perfume. There was mucus on the jacket, tears in brown mascara rivers on her face, filth embedded in her torn clothes. When Derek had found her, he had not touched her. This had been, he explained, the actions of a careful man who had seen films about the need to preserve evidence in cases such as these.

First, he had put down the rubbish bag he had been carrying and then sprinted for the phone. Highly sensible, a police officer had conceded, but Shelley did not think she would ever forget the fact that he had not hugged her.

Their lives were full of patterns and plans. Derek was like her mum and dad: constantly in a state of vigilance against the awful threat of the unpredictable.

Derek Harrison watched Shelley Pelmore get up and open the curtains he had just pulled closed. She did not open them completely, since she did not wish to contradict him, but enough so that she could see the opposite side of the road and the darkening sky from her window seat of oatmeal coloured fabric from Ikea, identical to that possessed by her mother; such good value. They now had a matching pair of such chairs, replacing the cushions she had possessed. Derek's reason for the replacement was that sitting on cushions meant you had to go such a long way down to the floor and such a long way back up again, and even though she might reckon herself double-jointed, he was not. The same argument prevailed when it had come to acquiring a new bed to replace the double mattress. Derek was the master of do-it-yourself, but he liked to have her around when he did it, requiring an assistant and admirer for his skills. Mostly, it was his money that went on improvements.

I don't resent it, Shell, how can I? he would say as she demurred every time another length of wood appeared. It's our future I'm building.

A future in bricks and mortar, shelving and three-piece suites stretched before her. Matching crockery and washing machines to save them from falling into animal behaviour. Ready-made, machine-washable curtains in pastel shades to make sure they could distinguish themselves from the creatures in the jungle outside. Shelley was twenty-two and worked in a shop in the West End. She got a discount on clothes of which Derek approved; he didn't like her shopping anywhere expensive, so that when she did, she scrunched the garment into a small parcel and hid it away. Brick by brick, Derek built their future; she could feel the walls of it surrounding her. Sometimes, the prison had the comfort of a padded cell; at others she wanted it bulldozed to the ground. Derek was so kind. Everyone approved of him. She had everything she wanted.

'I think I'll go to work tomorrow,' she said.

He looked up in surprise. On the floor between his feet, sitting neatly on a double thickness of newspaper to save the carpet, were the innards of their vacuum cleaner which Derek was mending.

'Oh, no, I wouldn't. It's too soon, lovey, after all you've been through. It's only a couple of days since . . . You need your rest.'

'Two days. I don't need rest. I need something to do. I feel much better, honest, and if I don't go to work, the old bat will think it's time she got someone else . . .'

Shelley could hear the whine in her voice; a rising note of panic singing along tunelessly behind it.

'There are laws against unfair dismissal,' he said primly.

'I know there are, but they don't count for nothing if you get the sack. You can spend weeks fighting it or you can put up and shut up, the manager knows that. Anyway, a couple of days on the sick is all I can get away with before anyone asks questions. And we've got a sale this week.'

Shelley liked work, usually; work was a laugh. The

corollary of not going to work was having to stay at home, in this flat, cleaning it, fussing round it, making custard for apple pie. Derek worked on the vacuum cleaner. Silence reigned, apart from the sound of a screwdriver, tapping the filter free of dust.

'I don't want to tell them, at work, I mean, Derek. I just don't.'

'No, of course you don't. Why should you?'

He dusted his hands, stepped across to her and patted her head indulgently. Then he sat down again and continued tapping the filter. The small sound grated on her nerves. She knew his industry did not imply any criticism of her for fouling up the machine in the first place, but that was what it felt like.

Between them both, the television glowed and people were murmuring at one another. A police officer appeared through a door on the screen and Shelley squirmed at the sight of him. The trembling spread throughout her limbs; she pulled her knees into the chair and clasped her hands around her calves.

'What's going to happen, Derek? What are they going to do to him?'

He looked at the screen, puzzled.

'Sorry, love, I wasn't watching.'

She wanted to shout.

'I don't mean the man on the telly. I mean that copper. Ryan.'

Derek's hands ceased moving and he gave her his full attention. She had had the benefit of his 100 per cent solicitude for forty-eight hours; he never seemed tired of giving, darling Derek.

'Charge him, put him on trial, lock him up and throw away the key, I hope, after what he did. But we don't know, love. Most likely they'll cover it up, just because he's a copper. They stick together, you know.'

'I don't want to give evidence,' she said, her voice tremulous. 'Do you know what he did for a living? He was doing sex cases. That's why I had to go so far, all that way, to that other police station; I couldn't go where anyone knew him. Why didn't they take *him* somewhere else? 'Cos I couldn't be on his territory. I don't want to give evidence. What's the point?'

'You can't let him get away with it, Shell. And you mustn't worry. I'll be with you all the way. Now and for ever.'

Such a good man, the best she would ever find. The girls told her so, warned her not to lose him. Shake him off a little from time to time, sure, but never risk losing such a man in a million who worked hard and didn't mind if she went out alone, didn't even mind if she came home late; loved her enough to give her freedom. Look, Shell, he would say, I don't like clubs and discos, and I got all these late shifts, so you go on and have fun, girl. I like you having a good time. The unspoken context was his own plan to have her knee-deep in babies and living a million miles from town within a couple of years, but perhaps that was an unfair interpretation. He wanted any wild oats sown so he could reap the crop; he would turn one blind eye, admire with the other, as long as he kept her.

She looked at the world outside, listened to the traffic, felt her heart contract with fear.

'I'd better iron some gear for the morning,' she said, uncurling from the chair.

'I'll do it for you,' he said. 'You just sit still now. Want a hot drink, love?'

'Tell me again,' Helen asked Bailey. 'Just so I get it straight in my mind.'

The meal was finished, to mutual satisfaction. Steak for him, fish for her, because fish was something she reserved for the occasions when she did not have to cook it. She was superstitious about fish and always imagined it would leap out of the bag on the way back from the shops, find a drain and try and swim back home. There were lights in the roof of Casale's, suspended from branches, giving the effect of Christmas decorations in a barn. The floor was uneven, the chairs rocky and the proprietor rude to a fault. It was a small price to pay for the food.

'Not that much to tell. I'm told Shelley Pelmore seems nervous, truthful and she's very pretty. I'm never quite sure whether it favours a prosecution case to have an attractive victim, or a plain one. Depends on the argument. If the issue's consent, it's better to have them pretty, because juries will believe she had every right to refuse . . .'

'Well, well . . . I take it you aren't actually saying that a plain woman hasn't any right to say "No"?'

'Helen . . . I'm simply saying that a jury is more likely to assume that a pretty lass can pick and choose. She'll have more men after her. She's likely to have more confidence, reject what she doesn't want, demand more. A pretty girl has more power, that's all. On balance, unless she's provocatively sexy, when her looks go against her, she's more likely to be believed.'

344

It was not a conclusion Helen wanted to accept, but she remained silent.

'Anyway, this pretty woman, girl, is out in a pub, West End, after work, a regular hang-out for the girls. She's met Ryan before, I told you about that. He knows where she lives, because he's been there to take a statement . . .'

'About the other rape case? The non-starter case he was telling you about, where the girl won't say . . .'

'Yes. Ryan happens to be in the West End, meets her this time by accident. They get chatting in the pub. She liked him in the first place, she said; he made her laugh. He says he'll give her a lift home, but they stop in another pub, near her flat, for another drink, ostensibly to talk about her friend. As far as Ryan will say anything at all, he says she wanted to stay in this pub near St Pancras, decided she'd wait for another friend and didn't want to go home yet, so he left her there. That was it. The sum total of his evening's acquaintance with Ms Pelmore: one lift, two drinks, left her to meet someone else. Shelley says they get back in the car to complete the journey to her flat, but halfway there, Ryan stops on the edge of the park and makes . . . suggestions. She laughs at him; he seems to lose his temper, comes round to her side of the door and says, OK, get out and walk. She gets out, not particularly worried, but shocked as hell, because she doesn't expect a copper to come on like that. He drags her into the bushes, telling her she's asked for it; she resists and then stops because she already hurts, and bingo. He mucks her about, tears her knickers, puts on a condom, shoves it in, but can't come, gives her a slap, then leaves her. He drives off; she staggers home.'

345

'Where the ever-loving boyfriend finds her on the step. Wearing Ryan's mucked-up jacket. How does he explain the jacket?'

'He doesn't. He won't. Not even how there came to be another condom in the pocket. Such a responsible man.'

'Traces of her in the car?'

'Bits of straw from a straw bag she had on the back seat. Not conclusive, because she was in the car anyway. Bits of hairy fabric under her nails, from his jacket. Soil. She had scratches . . . bruises.'

'Her friend had scratches. The other one you told me about.'

'Not the same. The only skin under that little girl's fingernails was her own. Shelley had soil from the park. There might have been skin under Ryan's fingernails, but there wasn't, for the simple reason he'd bitten them to the quick before anyone took samples. Now, would you say the man had a case to answer?'

'Yes. I'm glad it won't be coming to me.'

'What a crying, bloody awful shame, and I still don't want to believe it.'

Bailey looked as if he might begin to beat the table, an outburst curtailed by the arrival of coffee and four chocolates which he ate absent-mindedly.

'Shall we talk about something else? Weddings? Births, marriages and deaths?' he said. She had once thought his habit of changing the subject with such speed was evasive, now she knew it was merely habitual, a symptom of a crowded mind, full of separate, easily accessed compartments.

'Marriages first. I thought later this month. Two weeks

346

tomorrow. We always said we'd do it by special licence, midweek. No time for thinking. Put the date in your diary, for God's sake. We can have a party later. To dispel second thoughts.'

'That's just a couple of days before Rose. Fine. Daren't tell her, though.' She hesitated. 'I thought you might want to postpone it until this business with Ryan's over.'

'Nope. If life's negative, I want to do something positive.'

Helen nodded. So they had agreed. Their wedding would be spontaneous, eccentric and private. Suddenly, he grinned, leant across the table and kissed her.

'This is your ever-so-decisive husband, Miss West. Don't change your mind about changing your name, will you? I like it as it is. We can be like all those characters out of Jane Austen. Husband and wife addressing one another as Mrs Smith and Mr Smith. Never Helen and Geoffrey; far too familiar. You'll be Miss West, even first thing in the morning, and I'll be Mr Bailey.'

'Don't expect me to call you sir.' She was laughing now, covering the slight feeling of awkwardness and embarrassment which afflicted her whenever she thought of this forthcoming event, a thought recurring every single day but only long enough to put back in a box marked secret.

'Take ourselves by storm. I'll fix it. Think of it like a medical appointment. This way you haven't got enough time to plan an escape.'

He grinned again, the smile which was imprinted on her imagination. Bailey's smile lit up his lined face and made it look like a map. Age was only intermittently kind to him: he could look cadaverous, but his eyes were brilliant, aware of her ambivalence about marriage; accepting it. He was not bullying her, just following out their mutual conviction that this was the best thing to do. God knows where we'll drift if we don't.

You will be a very distinguished old man, Helen thought, and how well, how very well you know me. I do not think I really deserve you at all.

Ryan loved the City of London with a passion. He could have opted to be a City of London constable instead of an officer serving with the Metropolitan, had it not been for the little matter of family tradition, and the more important detail of his size. Six foot had been the minimum for the City; some of the men looked like giants in their helmets. He was only five ten in stocking feet. In boyhood, he had attempted to stretch his own size by holding on to the wardrobe door with his outstretched arms, his feet hooked under his bed, maintaining the pose until it hurt. In retrospect, he reckoned this exercise had stunted his growth rather than increased it. I should've been stopped, he told himself; I should have been stopped from doing a lot of things. Dozens of defendants had told him the same.

The City was quiet on the brink of dawn, with a pink sky flowering above it. Six o'clock in the morning and the place was beginning to exhale the dark, inhale the prospect of the day. Too soon for all the ants to begin scurrying. St Paul's station disgorged cleaners and dealers into tall and taller buildings. The steps of the cathedral were empty of tourists. Ryan felt as if he was a free man, in charge of his car, without hindrance from traffic, therefore in charge of his own destiny. Life might have been different if his career had been spent in the heart of the financial centre, where crime was white collar and committed on paper and the pubs shut at seven, turning it into an elegant and substantial no man's land, inhabited by security guards and less temptation.

He cruised past the Central Criminal Court, crossed the lights and entered into the square by St Bartholomew's. The contrast delighted him; beautiful buildings: the church, the ancient hospital, and the throng of the meat market which had been in full swing since five. If all else failed, he might become a porter, lugging carcasses into vans, but porters operated a closed shop, even if his size didn't count. Shame; he enjoyed working the early shift. Ryan stopped to buy coffee, sipped the froth, replaced the cap, and put the carton on the passenger seat, carefully. The pink of the sky was fading. He turned the car east.

'What did you do with your jacket?' his wife had asked, persistently. 'How did you lose your jacket?' Then she tried to make a joke of it. 'I don't know, one of your best jackets remaining in custody; you could have given it to the charity shop. I don't understand you, really I don't.'

Ryan could see that she was being courageous and that he, by sticking to his story of simply forgetting the jacket, was making things worse. He had always been so punctilious, if generous, about clothes. If he had said he had given the thing away, he might have stood a better chance of being believed, and if his wife doubted his story, she was making a spirited attempt to hide it, although incredulity leaked through the façade, like honey through a comb.

No jacket this fine morning. Jeans, old trainers, sweatshirt and a two-day growth of stubble. He might have been back in the old days of early-morning stake-outs with Bailey, dressed like the yob they were trying to catch, hoping to find him at home with his pyjamas round his ankles. Ryan tried to remember how many times he had conducted a raid on the wrong house, always careless about reading the warrant when he was all fired up and ready to go; he shivered to remember how Bailey's subsequent ingratiation with outraged citizens had saved his bacon. That and countless other times.

Could details of the defendant's past behaviour be given in evidence? Ryan wondered. Would he be vilified for all his flirtations? The female's sexual history could not be given in evidence, that he knew, but could they put the historical screws on him?

For the moment Bailey's help lay only in all that early training in self-discipline. Much of which had been ignored.

I loved you, you sod.

Ryan reached the public house where he had encountered Shelley Pelmore on the night in question. It stood, locked and barred, with a pile of rubbish sacks outside; only the pubs in Smithfield were open at this hour, another reason for the attraction of the City. He waited outside with the engine idling, an underpowered car, to his mind, but reliable enough for his short-distance-driving wife. His own car, like his jacket, was still in police custody. Ryan remembered with a stifled groan, how new that car was, how much of a novelty to him. If the car had been an old banger, more like the Peugeot, would he have given the girl a lift? Probably not. He had wanted her admiration and respect; he was still a show-off, and she would have despised a runabout like this.

350

He drove on, taking the route he had used from the first pub to the second, remembering something else. That car, his car, had been so new that it had still had paper covering the rubber floor mats in the front. The girl had remarked on it, torn the paper on her side with the heel of her shoe when she got in. For no reason he could fathom, he had found this annoying, and since the annoyance highlighted a fussiness of which he was faintly ashamed (a car was only a car, for fuck's sake), he had crumpled up the paper and thrown it away. That had been on the way home, when he was sick of her silliness. She'd remembered the paper, of course.

Stupid, worthless little cunt. Silly bitch.

The backstreets shaded him from the early sun, which hit the windows of The Wheatsheaf, an incongruous name for a pub hard by a station, in territory best described as an urban wilderness of roads, but still the best of the local soulless drinking barns. By now, Ryan was halfway home again, going against the traffic which was perceptibly heavier. Pedestrians were still abed. He left the vehicle and crossed the road, uncertainly. Which way were they supposed to have gone, he and the girl?

He had pretended not to understand the question during his interview, where all his energies had been spent in saying nothing and avoiding Bailey's eyes and his all-too-familiar voice. Instead he had listened to his lawyer asking for clarification of this and that, making sure they both knew the exact extent of the allegation and its geography. An interview under caution, even where the suspect remains stubbornly silent, must describe the case against him completely. Bailey knew that. Ryan had known that

351

too, even as he had clung to the dim hope that Bailey's comprehensive questions, articulating every detail of the accusation, were designed to help him build a defence. Really he knew otherwise: Bailey was only being as thorough and beyond reproach as Bailey normally was. There had been an ice-cold atmosphere in that interview room.

There was a slight morning mist over the park where, according to the questions, he had stopped the car and dragged her out, put on his condom, tried to do the business after a few choice threats and blows, left her there and driven off. Only a prat, and a very angry prat, would have done that, but he had been angry. What was he supposed to have done with his condom? Ryan brushed away a fly which buzzed round his head, sounding almost friendly. A careful prat, more careful than the average rapist who never used rubbers, would have taken it away, put it somewhere, like on the floor of his car, possibly, then chucked it. He would have put it on the paper on the floor, passenger side, which she had torn with her heel. That would have been why they asked him about the paper, wondering out loud why he had chosen that evening, of all others, to dispense with it on the way home. Because it was torn. If he had decided to break his silence and say what a clever bitch to remember the paper at all, he would have been doubly damned. It was always the details which counted. Hairs and fibres and paper.

Any amount of penetration is sufficient.

There was a crowd of chattering starlings above the trees in the park. He knew this lovely shabby park well. It was somehow preserved while the buildings around it,

352

marooned but still splendid, bore witness to better days. The trees, in full leaf, screened the small area of grass, making it cool; the planting of blooms was meticulous. Pinks and blues in serried rows, neatly interspersed with greenery. Ryan loved gardening, an anomalous but not uncommon addiction for a policeman and the one thing which reconciled him to living in the suburbs. That and his kids.

There was an old lag sitting on a bench. By daylight, this was an old lags' park and Ryan wondered how many of them, old, young, indifferent, knew about the mortuary at the far end with the separate entrance for wagons, next to the coroner's court. You could hear the refrigeration hum, close to. Ryan fished his cigarettes out of his pocket, proffered two and watched a wizened and dirty hand take them from his own fingers and hide them in one of many pockets.

'They can accuse me of anything,' Ryan told him earnestly. 'Anything at all. Only they mustn't ever suggest I'd roll all over the flowers ... Think of that! Would I ever?'

The man nodded. The day had begun. Ryan heard the squeak of a baby carriage and saw a woman coming towards him, making noises at the infant in the pram. He wondered if the child was hers, or if she was simply employed to guard it, and whether he could ever think fondly of any baby which was not his own. The sun through the trees caught the brown of the girl's hair, dishevelled round a pretty, utterly preoccupied face. I may never look at another woman again, Ryan thought, except in a magazine.

353

He felt the time without looking at a watch. Parking restrictions in half an hour. Shelley Pelmore lived three streets east. Ryan tried to envisage the easiest route between that address and this park and then tried to envisage the route a girl might take late at night. One route if she were trying to get home without being seen, another if she was simply trying to be quick. He jogged the first choice in ten minutes, the alternative, back to his car, in eight.

That was enough for this morning. Give it another half-hour and his wife would be awake, ready to resume her persona of stoic, all-forgiving, casual calm, and only ask him one more time about his jacket. She would never once dare to ask, did you fancy that girl? Did you? Afraid of forcing him to admit the truth. Oh yes, I did, I did, I did. I wanted her.

Helen West had taught Rose the importance of the written word. Rose did not realize quite what a flair she had for it. She could write as she spoke, with the same clarion quality, never pausing for a better way to say it, as if she had understood all along that a person who will not listen is also one who will not read, so there was nothing to be achieved by compromise or prettying it up. Rose had had an excellent education in the fundamental rules of self-expression. Granny next door had done that. Dead now, like her mother. Rose had the kind of family history which might have curtailed her capacity for love, instead of increasing it.

Now look here, Mike, you bum, I'm sorry we had

that row yesterday, although I'm not sorry, really. I'm only saying I am because I can't tolerate sulking. I hate those plants, always have; they look so bleeding dismal and I don't care who the fuck grew them, neither of us has time to water the buggers so they're dead, OK? You said our attitude to living things made us incompatible. You do talk a load of shit. Go on then, leave if you want, before it's too late. Getting out of a wedding is far less trouble than a divorce. You don't have to do this bridegroom stuff if you don't want, even if it was your idea. You don't have to do anything you don't want, right?

As long as some things are clear. You've given me more breaks than I ever knew existed and I just want to say thanks for that, and if anyone ever bad-mouths you when I'm around, I'll break their jaw . . .

It took five minutes to write. Rose cut the crap about how she loved him to death and felt she would die without him. If he didn't know now, he never would. She left the note on the kitchen sink, thought about splattering water on it to look like tears. Naa, that was creepy and she knew what ailed him: all that stuff about family planning and pills; they never agreed. And then pre-wedding nerves and everyone getting at him. Hated to be on show, did Mike, unless it was in some sporting event, and he could not regard his nuptial celebrations as that, he took them far too seriously. He'd hang for her and she for him, but he regarded their wedding as a solemn sacrament, while she viewed it as the best party ever.

A man on the crowded underground stood too close;

closer than he needed. Rose twisted round, so that the overlarge buckle of her handbag hit him in the soft of the groin, making him flinch. She smiled at the ring on her hand and then smiled at him with her white teeth clenched in a growl.

A woman loved.

She thought of the man she had told about all of this, in the clinic.

It reminded her of another thing Michael didn't always like: her, talking too much.

CHAPTER FIVE

'It must be proved that the accused had sexual intercourse with the complainant. The prosecution must prove either that the girl physically resisted or, if she did not, that her understanding and knowledge were such that she was not in a position to decide whether to consent or resist. If, however, a woman yields through fear of death or through duress, it is rape.'

He did so prefer the legal text.

No one has ever been afraid of me, he told the screen. There was never any need. I would never make a woman pregnant and that is so often their greatest fear. Besides, they will let me do anything. They all need love.

It is noble in me to give it.

There was a difference, of course, between a woman and a girl, but no difference in their peculiar kind of endurance. Insane stoicism. Didn't they know how to avoid? To take the pleasures of passion without the risks of childbirth and disease? What issue of consent could there ever be if women from recent history submitted to this?

'In the application of leeches, so often necessary in cases of

inflammatory congestion of the cervix uteri,' he read, 'the patient should be placed in the same position as for labour and a conical glass passed up to the uterus; care being taken that no part of the vagina is left around the rim . . . as the bites of the leeches are not painful when the uterus only is wounded, but excessively so if the vagina is . . . Eight or ten being the usual number, the speculum applied closely to the uterus, carrying the leeches along with it, and allowed to remain until the leeches fill . . . generally, twenty minutes.'

He had never seen a leech, except in illustration. They had a greater association with jungles than surgeries in these unenlightened days, but, come to think of it, both places had plenty in common, and a medical man was really only a kind of leech.

'Occasionally it is necessary to detach one . . . readily done by dipping a camel-hair pencil in a solution of common salt and applying it to the head . . . It is a good plan to apply the speculum so that the mouth shall be external to its margin, as in some cases, troublesome symptoms arise from a leech crawling into the cervix uteri and there adhering . . .'

He gave a brief snort of laughter, which echoed loudly in the quiet of the library. There was often something comical in the most pedantic of texts. He turned the laugh into a cough and rubbed his head, in order to look as if the cough troubled him. Then he examined his neatly trimmed nails and wiped his hands down the synthetic fibre of his trousers. Silence prevailed. In the late afternoon, the heat had become stultifying, even in here. He thought of the hungry little leeches and he thought of ice in a long glass, a mild form of anaesthetic to the skin, a deceptive ameliorator of heat. Ice and leeches; they might have done for him as well as anything else. No one should despise

358

primitive medicine in favour of the supposedly more sophisti-cated.

A leech could be useful. Provided it remained detached about its business. Common salt will detach a leech. Air will dispatch, and detach, the woman or the girl.

I want to be loved, he admitted.

I want, even more, to be in control of passion.

They called it the Rape House. It stood two streets distant from the police station, conveniently placed for Sainsbury's and the market. Inside were five small rooms of miniature, late-Victorian terraced building, similar in size to the home nurtured by Anna Stirland, less than a mile distant. The area was roughly boundaried, tapering away into the complicated wilderness of King's Cross on one side, some of the streets gentrified, some defiantly refusing. The Rape House – for use of vulnerable persons only – lacked the polish of its neighbours and the key tended to stick in the lock, making DS Ryan repeat one of his familiar ribald comments, *ad nauseam*. 'Can't get it in,' he would mutter. 'Story of my life.' Ryan's remarks did not always stop on the right side of downright offensive. Personally, Sally Smythe did not think it mattered as long as his actions showed respect and he didn't wisecrack in front of the punters. Sex remained the stuff of rude humour, whatever anyone did for a living, she thought. Police officers were allowed bad taste, same as doctors.

The local authority had given the house to the police, for indefinite use, as an alternative to the rape suite inside the police station, which had been comfortable enough, but only reached via the front desk and a mile of corridor, which was enough to make any nervous victim back out quickly. No paperwork was done in the Rape House; no computer terminal was visible. The décor reminded Bailey of a dentist's waiting-room: three prints on the wall showing landscapes, each aligned with the other in remarkable precision; a chintzy sofa; glass coffee-table and venetian blinds to block out the light. There was a slight smell of disuse in the kitchen, drifting into the surgery, and another room designated for use as a nursery; enough residual stuffiness to indicate that no one lived in the house. Nightmares might find themselves embedded in the clean walls, but no one slept here.

Bailey felt slightly out of date and ashamed of it. He and Ryan's colleague were padding around one another like cats, with her muttering, I'll make you a cup of tea, shall I, treating him with condescension because this was her territory not his, adding in a touch of sarcasm with the sugar. For Lord's sake, the man could read; he'd read the files; why did he want to chat again, and why here? Lucky for him there was no ongoing investigation, no late-night allegation, no current attack which would demand that she sat here with the complainant for one day, two, three, as long as it took to piece together a statement which said it all with minimal need for revision. The Rape House was redundant for a few blessed hours and, even in the heat, felt chilly.

'What was it you wanted to know, sir?'

'How many of these cases get as far as the Crown Prosecution Service?' he asked mildly. The easy questions came first.

'About half. There's no point them seeing the complete

non-starters, is there? A DCI has to mark them off, though. No point sending them the false allegations either.'

'Many of those?'

She fiddled with her hands in her lap, feeling faintly treacherous.

'Yes.'

'Any particular reason why, do you think?'

Sally Smythe warmed to a theme. Perhaps this austere man, whom Ryan had mentioned so often, really wanted to know.

'There's always been a lot, but it's hardly political correctness to say so. Sexual attack and women's rights get a high profile. Probably more complaints now because it's common knowledge we take them seriously, so the rotten complaints increase in proportion. Girls know they risk nothing in coming to us. They get kid-glove treatment, no recriminations, no lectures. Don't get me wrong, I'm not over-cynical, nor was Ryan, but a lot of the time we're a free counselling service. Victims they may be, but not always victims of rape.'

Bailey frowned. Sally did not scent disapproval; she didn't scent anything; his lack of reaction disorientated her.

'Was Ryan tolerant about that?'

'Very. Although he did less of the interviewing than we did. Obviously, some of them don't want a man in the room. There's always two of us. When he was here, there was always a woman officer as well.'

He stirred his tea and smiled at her. The effect on his gaunt face was almost shocking, making her respond with a grin before she knew it had happened.

'Give me a typical outline for a false claim. If there is such a thing as typical.'

She thought quickly and shrugged.

'A woman or a girl says she's been raped, attacked, say, three days earlier. She's thought about it, wants to complain, but she'll give three different versions of how it happened. The description of the attacker will vary too, but she won't know his name, even if she says she's seen him around. We don't try and trip her up; she does it herself, trying to tell us things which can't be proved or disproved, not clever enough to get it right. Sometimes it's sheer fantasy, sometimes a real event from some time past, or a real event distorted, sometimes it's straight off the telly. Troubled ladies. Then there's the semi-false, like, oh, I dunno, someone having it off with a family friend, relative, something; wanting to tell themselves it was rape when what worries them is the fact they consented, or were outmanoeuvred. Then there's those getting revenge on boyfriends. Or hiding an illicit encounter.'

'Do you always know the liars?'

She hesitated, outraged. Liars was a harsh description for the desperate.

'Yes, I think so. After several dozen, yes. I didn't to start with, nor did Ryan. You learn from the ones who tell the truth. There's a difference; it hits you in the eyes.'

She was becoming a touch impatient, slightly self-conscious, felt as if she was giving evidence which could be used against her. She was not fond of the sound of her own voice. Bailey had uncurled himself, begun pacing. You would never hold down my kind of job, sir, she wanted to yell at him: the person asking questions is supposed to ask in a manner which will put the person answering at ease, and then keep them there; it says so in the training manual. Her mind ran on to other things to fill the silence. Pathos and bathos, such as how to get back from the lab the patchwork quilt on which a brave and honest victim had been raped and buggered by two burglars. The quilt had been made out of cut-offs from her children's clothes, pieces of it torn in the process of analysis for stains, but she still wanted it back, if only to prove that the one set of memories it invoked were far more important than the other.

That's what I deal with too, she wanted to tell Bailey: bravery. And that's what Ryan was good at. Finding the truth.

'What I really want to know,' Bailey said carelessly, as if all previous conversation was irrelevant, 'is why Ryan kept this file?' He was flourishing a slim folder, using it to fan himself before he handed it across.

'Which file?' she asked stupidly, blushing as if Bailey had unearthed something incriminatory. There was no such thing, after all, as a totally clean record. If he were to delve around in anyone's career, even if their daily progress was far less documented than that of any police officer, this spy could always find some embarrassing piece of shit. Even furry little rabbits leave turds. It must have been Ryan who said that.

Bailey sat and the room grew smaller. Putting on his glasses failed to make him human. He rose again and pulled open the fussy venetian blinds, letting in light through the small window-panes. The blinds had always stuck before, even when new – Ryan had comments for

363

them, too – but these long fingers of his older mentor commanded obedience out of inanimate things and, suddenly, there was light. Sally was afraid of Bailey, the way, as a child, she had been afraid of the old woman in the story who lived in the forest in a cottage made of cake.

The computer print in the file blurred in front of her eyes. She sat bolt upright, reading the faint lettering, resentful, ready to come up with any old answer. The print was made for daylight. She was half aware that Bailey had left the room; there was a distant flush of the lavatory cistern and the sound of the kettle boiling again. Then he was back. Sounds echoed in an unoccupied house. More tea, as if to prove he could make it better. She hated tea, the drink of comfort and a swollen bladder.

The windows needed cleaning, she noticed; he made her aware of such details. They were smudged rather than filthy, but enough to deserve attention.

'I know what it looks like,' she said. 'He's got the names and addresses and descriptions of several no-hopers. Girls who've been in here. Cases which'll go no further. And their witnesses, few that there are. He's got that disco girl and Shelley Pelmore, the one he's supposed to have raped. And I suppose you're thinking it may be his version of a little black book, aren't you?'

'They have one thing in common,' Bailey said evenly. 'All those names. All those girls, women, I mean; he's quite specific about that, they're all unmarried. Perhaps one or two of them would appreciate a visit from a good-looking sympathetic policeman. Liars maybe, vulnerable maybe, but so far, incapable of completing their accusations and maybe needing a nice broad shoulder, or something of the kind.'

She would have flared at him like a rocket hitting the ceiling in that confined space; she could, after all, see exactly the way it looked. To the naked eye this small compendium of names and addresses was horrifying. We do not rely on photos of victims, she wanted to say, but surely he knew, even in his old-fashioned way, how that would make them feel. We make pictorial histories; we write notes as if computers did not exist. Here was Ryan's inventory of the victims who had never got beyond the DCI's no-action dictate. Not all of them; only some: five, or was it six? Bailey seemed drunk on tea. It was an added insult that he had the kind of long lean frame which need never resort to saccharin in order to keep it in that awkward state of angular thinness. Skeleton on legs, Ms Smythe thought, despising him with a clarity of thought which took in the file, too. Her face was red and chubby. It was her turn to get up and pace the room.

'It wasn't a file for Ryan's personal use. It was *ours*. Ours; the product of 'ours and 'ours; oh, he did like a pun. If you'd read further, you'd see.'

'What would I see?' he asked gently.

She sat, but moved again.

'Oh, I can't expect you to understand his code. Or to see why there was any sense in him recording these particular women, I mean, or the kinds of places they lived in, what jobs they did. Even Shelley Pelmore's friend; you see they all had jobs.'

'Jobs, I presume, they wouldn't want to lose? By doing silly things like shouting rape for the second time, for instance? Unlikely, also to report a smiling police officer at the door with a bottle of vino?'

Sally forced herself to stay calm.

'Look, you were the one who talked about gut reactions, I didn't, and he didn't much. Oh, for Christ's sake, the gut digests, doesn't it? Look. What we've got on this patch is a serial sexual pervert. He's been around for a while. He doesn't have an established way of doing anything, sir, but he rapes without trace, and he may have killed without trace. All the ladies in this file are those who would not, or could not, complete a statement, however long we gave them. They could not, would not, name an assailant. They were blurred in their accounts, they described fantastical things . . . There was never any forensic evidence . . .'

'They were dead ringers for the false allegations you describe. No names, no precision, change of story. Vulnerable ladies. Fantasists maybe; unhappy, maybe. Ideal for a man with his prick out at every traffic light.'

It was at that point she twisted her left hand into the cord of the awkward venetian blinds of the doll's house which was the Rape House; regretting politics, regretting everything apart from the fact that if Ryan was going to be done to death on evidence such as this, she had better put the record straight.

'Look, you sanctimonious, dirty-minded bastard. They weren't even the prettiest. Can't you read?'

'Sometimes,' Bailey said humbly. She continued at the same speed, well beyond listening, her voice stronger and stronger.

'This was Ryan's collection. It has a system, you see. A small collection, you will note, not quite the stuff of a little

366

black book. A few witnesses, maybe working alongside, giving evidence of victims' habits, maybe a link. What we think these girls had in common was one single perpetrator of whom they were ashamed. Some nameless shitface. And Ryan's got the pathologist he's spoken to on the file as well. No one would dare seduce her.'

'I know the pathologist,' Bailey said. 'She's very attractive. And I don't understand,' he added, sounding obtuse, a man without visible gut and all too apparent guile. 'Don't understand.'

She took a deep breath, spoke carefully.

'The ones in this file are the real no-hopers; nowhere to go, no names, no forensic, nothing to toy with.' She was so close she could have spat in his eye, which was exactly what she wanted to do. 'But they were the ones we believed. We believed them. You hear me? They had no case and we believed them.'

The cord from the venetian blinds came away in her hand and she sat down abruptly.

'The problem is, sir, no one believes *us*.'

'Perhaps I should go and see them. Check the black-book theory.'

She laughed.

'You do that, sir. Not a long list, is it? Especially since two of them are dead.'

There was a moment, later on, when he sat in a pub, nursing a half pint and mulling over what Sally Smythe had told him, that Bailey missed Ryan so intensely it was painful. And pathetic, he told himself, to find no pleasure in a drink unless that silly fool was sitting next to him.

Ryan had a rare cunning for finding an excuse to get into a pub. He could fabricate an informer who must be seen, or a rumour that the drinks were free, but Bailey had never thought that such petty deceptions made Ryan a liar. He was fond of conspiracy theories, though; capable of inventing drama when life was too dull to be endured, and plenty capable of getting Sally Smythe to go along with some fantastic theory if he believed in it himself, even if his commitment to the idea had some ulterior motive.

What theory and how fantastic? Bailey spelt it out to himself, as explained by Ms Smythe, a woman under Ryan's influence, of course. Oh, what a joy it would be to have the luxury of listening to someone and believing what they said without a second thought.

Ryan's theory hinged on his belief that there was, out there, a rapist with a difference. Quite a different animal to the rabid man who leapt out of bushes to satisfy a sudden surge of lust on any female, of whatever age, who happened to be passing. Different, also, to the ex-lover, raping out of revenge, or the sly next-door neighbour or date rapist who mixed rape with seduction and pretence. These were merely distant cousins to Ryan's rapist. One way and another they wanted sex. This one wanted gratification of a peculiar kind.

Bailey looked around the bar. No candidates here. Ordinary men with ordinary desires and shirtsleeves.

At best, at his most normal, this creature was a performing trickster, a manipulator, who learnt as he went along. A man who wanted to tease and control, who made up the rules *en route*, sometimes clumsy with it, because the delight, of course, was crude. The achievement was to leave a victim so ashamed that, even if they began the formalities of a complaint, they would never complete the process.

It was an awful pint in a pub for those on the dole, with the Catholic church about next door. Downhill were the train termini and a view of London, swathed in a mist of heat.

A foul kind of magician, then, this mythical attacker, with blunt factual Ryan on his tail. Possibly a man with allies. Or a figment of Ryan's overfevered imagination, created to add purpose to the sometimes mundane and ever-seedy business of the Rape House. A fiction to allow him to preserve the names of the fantasists; keep a dossier of vulnerable women who might, after all, like indoor love with a married man, no strings attached.

The door of the pub burst open. A young woman with a dog, regretting the row of her entrance, went outside and did it again, only quieter, as if the second entrance would make her invisible. Something to sell, or buy, perhaps; nothing to celebrate.

Bailey could not see subtle plotting as part of Ryan's stock-in-trade, not for the sake of sex alone, unless he saw himself as some romantic counsellor, helper of the afflicted. That was more like it for a heavily romantic man who still believed that people could be helped despite their own resistance. He lied sometimes; an honest liar. Try that for a character reference, as if any character reference was going to help a policeman charged with rape, or save him from the extra brutality reserved in prison for his kind.

The thought made Bailey sick. His stomach growled.

If Ryan were put on trial, on the decision of some

separate faceless bunch of lawyers whose decisions Bailey felt he could quite safely predict, the defendant could be acquitted. Easier, for such a good-looking man with so much to lose, charged with such an offence; the jury might not have it: they were soft on police officers. Ryan could come out of there, the exonerated darling of the tabloid press, but Bailey despised that kind of result. He was either innocent or guilty, not to be consigned to that half-life of disbelief in between.

Look at the black book, then, find an excuse.

The bottom line was wanting him free.

'Well? What did she say?'

'Who?'

'Anna, of course. Who did you think I meant?'

'Rose, if I was going to tell you, do you think I'd do it here?'

'Oh, see what you mean.'

The Central Line of the underground was tolerable for once, although not a suitable venue to discuss anything personal, even for someone as uninhibited as Rose. They sat together; Rose fished into her purse for a list.

'All we've got to buy, Aunty H, is a complete transformation of me for less than a hundred pounds. Inclusive of shoes, bikini and a full frontal lobotomy. Got to put the old me through the mangle of the Dickins & Jones sale and collect a fully-fledged wifeling at the other end. Got that?'

'I thought you said you wanted a dress.'

'Oh, that too. I don't think I've had a dress since I was twelve.'

Rose would be married in an outfit yet to be found. She

had drawn the line at a frock of virginal white, not on account of any hint of hypocrisy it might imply about her lifetime's experience, but because she thought white was tame. The closest she had got was a sort of ivory shirt, tried on beneath Helen's critical eye and giving rise to smothered laughter in a changing-room. Rose had resembled a waif in someone else's silken dishcloth, her skin bleached by the sheen of the material; a sort of sickly bimbo without style. Suits she could handle, dresses not, but she still craved a dress. She longed to flounce away from her own reception with a wobble of fluffy skirt.

'Hope Michael's in when I get home tonight,' Rose announced cheerfully. 'As of yesterday, he was leaving for Timbuctoo.'

Never mind the perfidy and wickedness she dealt with on a daily basis, if wonderful, solid, kindly Michael were to scoot, do a bunk, lose his bottle about Rose, then Helen really would lose her faith in human nature. It was frayed already, but not that much.

''S all right. He's twitchy, that's all. I mean, he's the one with all the family complications I ain't got. He's the one who's got to cope with his Aunty Mary, Uncle Stephen and 'orrible little cousin, Jim. To say nothing of all his mates at work, ribbing him, warning him marriage is the end of life as he knows it, and telling him he shouldn't be marrying someone like me. He's bound to listen sometimes. I can see the pressure, really. Thank God for his mother. Are all men such babes, Aunty H?'

She seemed unfazed, much to Helen's relief. Opposite her seat, a man lowered his newspaper to look at them. His eyes rested first on the tube map above their heads; then he appeared to examine the roof of the carriage; then stared briefly at Helen, longer at Rose, frankly curious. Rose noticed.

'Hello,' she said boldly. 'Nice weather, innit?'

He smiled, nodded acknowledgement and retreated behind the newspaper again. Helen noticed immaculate shoes, casual trousers of some synthetic fabric and a pair of brown hands, before the train rumbled into Oxford Circus. As she passed towards the door, she noticed the top of his head, the skull shiny brown, like polished wood. The indentations in that sculptured skin showed up in the station's artificial light, the dome oddly tactile, so that she almost wanted to reach out and touch it, like the knob on a banister. She compounded Rose's cheekiness with a grin of her own, surprised to feel a frisson of attraction for an impertinent stranger so completely bereft of hair.

'Are you always like that with men on the tube?' Helen asked as they crushed together on the escalator, where it seemed the whole world had suddenly joined in a headlong rush to escape the subterranean oppression. She always expected someone to begin howling with rage on the up escalator out of the underground, because of the sheer slowness of it and the pushiness of passengers, but resentment was more conservatively expressed. Behind her a shopping bag, carried like a weapon by a determined woman, brushed her legs. She turned, somehow expecting to see the bald head further down. It was a foolish expectation, even in an ideal place for strange hallucinations. Rose was answering her as they put their tickets into the gates and started up the stairs, avoiding the inevitable someone who could not manage the machinery and held up the queue.

'He wasn't a stranger,' Rose shouted back.

'Who was he then?'

'He's a doctor. Saw him yesterday. Stared up my fanny; must have recognized my voice. I talked too much.'

She did not elaborate; Helen did not ask. Shopping fever had descended on Rose's brow and her face wrinkled with concentration. There was the mild state of madness induced by Oxford Street in all its tawdry splendour; the one place where Helen failed to detest crowds.

There was method in the madness, too. Unlike Bailey, who shied away from shops like a frightened filly, crept into them and out again as if he was on a secret mission, Helen and Rose stood at the threshold, breathed in the scents of the perfume counters and knew they were home. The method was no method; there had to be a purpose to justify the expedition, but the purpose could be abandoned. It took Rose half an hour to fall out of love with the idea of a dress (Look at this, Aunty H . . . I wouldn't wear it to go to bed in . . .) and fall into adoration with the idea of a trouser suit she had seen (perfect shape, foul colour). They were on the trail; out of this place, on to somewhere else, looking without real expectation for a facsimile of a suit with the same buttons, but not that tasteful and over-bred shade of sludge. In the meantime, Helen had purchased three pairs of stockings and a hair-slide and Rose had bought a pan. If that was all they got, it really would not matter.

Heavy on the blood sugar, though, as Rose put it, necessitating frequent sit-downs and caffeine fixes. It was understood, after initial quarrels, that Helen would purchase these overpriced beverages and also the cake, which

373

was part of the proceedings, the paying arrangement being an acceptance of Helen's motherly role and their unequal financial status.

'*They* know how to shop,' Rose said enviously, counting the bags of two delicate tea-drinking Japanese ladies in Liberty's café. 'They've got fifteen carriers each.' She sipped and put down the cup with a clatter.

'All right, Aunty H, now tell me what Anna told you.'

Typical Rose, waiting for the right blood-sugar level, never really forgetting anything; but that was another thing about large shops. All the ladies, as well as the minority of men, sipping liquids and giving one another their whole-hearted attention, talked nicely in whispers, like a lot of low-voiced conspirators. Revolutions could be planned here; coffee-shops in the anterooms of spending halls were exactly the right kind of place for secrets and the baring of the soul. Indiscretions would be taken away, wrapped in tissue paper, back to the realms of suburbia where they would no longer exist.

'I don't think I can tell you. She didn't swear me to secrecy or anything, but she didn't want you to know.'

Rose nodded, curious but unperturbed.

'I s'pose I've got to respect that. Did you tell Bailey?'

'No, but I might. In fact I'm sure I shall, but then, he doesn't know her. There's a difference.'

Rose nodded again, mature about such things, well versed in the need for respecting confidence. She was a fabulous gossip, loved it; she also knew what not to repeat and what not to demand.

'Did you like her?'

'Yes. Yes, very much.'

Such value in the faint praise offered like that. Rose finished a mouthful, sat back and rubbed her stomach.

'I shouldn't have had that, Aunty. On account of the traditional pre-wedding diet,' she said without much conviction, using the pastry fork to subdue and then eat the last of the crumbs, only satisfied after the last was swallowed. 'Two more questions, Aunty, then I'll leave it alone, promise. First, was she raped, and second, could you help?' She mimicked the Redwood voice.

Helen was choosing words with the care which so often infuriated Rose. All she wanted was a quick response, the flush of shopping fever temporarily suspended.

'If she's telling the truth . . .' and Rose noted that the 'if' was not emphasized, merely used to introduce that lawyerly note of caution she so loathed, '. . . then she was assaulted in a way designed to make a complete and utter fool of her. Using means so silly that the telling of it would make a fool of her all over again, because it sounds like a joke. Her assailant was someone she admired, with a cruel sense of humour. She's adamant about not going to a professional. Perhaps it helped that I didn't laugh.'

Rose chose not to say that this all sounded like a load of cobblers.

'And she's equally adamant she won't say who it was.'

'Protecting him?' Rose asked incredulously, always dismissive despite herself when Helen got formal. Shop till you drop with this woman, she'd told Michael, but never say you know her.

'No. Protecting herself from further ridicule. She might be coming round for a drink and a meal next week. That might help more. And she loves her work. That will help too. Did what I could, Rose. Not much.'

'Sure you did.' That was enough. Some kind of result, Rose supposed; enough to mean it was time for her to abandon interest. It surprised her to hear that Anna loved her work, that wasn't what she had heard, but if Helen liked Anna and Anna liked Helen, something had been achieved. Helen always underestimated her own power. She doesn't even know how lucky I feel to know her, even when she gets things wrong, Rose thought, scraping back her chair, treading respectfully over the distinctive bags which fanned out from the next table, moving gingerly with the steps and smile of a cat. She had no time for people buying porcelain.

'Why are you so afraid of getting married, Aunty H?' she asked as they passed through handbags. Neither had much use for leather; shocking prices.

'Dunno. I suppose because I did it once, hated it and found out I'd married a thief. He didn't even know the meaning of truth. An utterly lovable thief.'

'Must've been his body.'

'We've got an hour,' Helen said in a voice grim with resolution.

'Monsoon? Principles?'

There it was, fifty-five minutes later in neither of these premises, but hanging in the window of an establishment neither had considered. Not a dress, not a trouser suit: a jacket made in heaven.

CHAPTER SIX

'If, at a trial where any person is for the time being charged with a rape offence to which he pleads not guilty, then, except with the leave of the judge, no evidence and no question in cross-examination shall be adduced or asked at the trial, by or on behalf of any defendant, about any sexual experience of a complainant with a person other than that defendant.'

Shelley Pelmore understood shops better than the back of her hand. She had haunted shops ever since she was allowed out on her own. West End shops were the stuff of dreams when she was a kid, especially the ones where music boomed and nobody cared who you were and you had to shout to ask the price of anything. Not that she had even whispered in those distant days, or dared to ask particulars of what she could never afford. On one single occasion, she had been stopped by the store detective, leaving with a vest tucked up the sleeve of her jacket. A vest, of all things! Nothing gorgeous, just an ugly piece of thermal underwear, chosen on a November afternoon, simply to find out if thieving was as easy as someone had said it was. Her informant had lied about the ease, but it had been a bitter wintry day, and Shelley's wise reaction on arrest by a woman who resembled her mother was to burst into tears, say she was sorry, but oh, she was so cold and it was colder still at home. A pretty child; thin, pinched, distressed, she had been forgiven with a brisk pat on the arm, accompanied by a kindly warning. Even now, she could still feel the shock of that hand on her sleeve.

She had felt genuine distress, a mixture of shame and horror over her own incompetence, but by the time she was halfway home, she could see she had been wise in learning her lesson with a vest. Anything more covetable would not have been forgiven as easily. Shelley never did it again. It diminished her love of big shops for a few days, but the light and warmth, the colours and the merchandise, were too strong a lure. It was preordained that she would work in a shop of large proportions and escalators, another childish passion, and only a question of time, she told herself, before she would own a shop of her own. Progress was slow, pay was lousy; she was not much further forward but it had ceased to matter.

The problem was that shops had lost their allure; she was waiting for it to come back. It was quite a while now since anything gave her a buzz, unless it was skin.

'Can I help you, madam? Just browsing?'

Suit yourself, you old cow.

Shelley had moved from hapless trainee in a department store to experienced sales assistant, almost to floor manager, until she'd had that fight with another girl which put her out of the running, although, mercifully, not out of a job. She had learnt from her mother, knowledge retained

like a talisman, that to be out of a job was the greatest disgrace on the planet, so she stayed for a while, although she
knew she was not going to progress any further. Instead
she took a sideways move into a far classier, up-market
South Molton Street designer boutique, which felt like a
kind of promotion. Escalators wearied her by then.

A friend of hers, who was leaving to have an unwanted
baby, had recommended Shelley on a temporary basis. By
the time she wanted the job back, Shelley was well dug in
amongst the expensive clothes, indispensable to the manageress and not to be ousted by a mere plea of loyalty. End
of friendship; so what? Shelley had other friends, other
distractions; she flitted among the silk chemises and linen
jackets, dressed in the shop's stock which suited her model
figure, shining with suppressed sexuality; a brooding presence which gave the display an added cachet. She despised
the fat customers all the more, because she knew their
secret ambition was to look as sultry and tempestuous as
she did inside these clothes.

She had told Ryan some of this. Something about the
frustration of selling to fat cows with no looks and much
more exciting lives. And about being best friends with the
manageress; the kind of friendship which led her into clubs
and pubs as a willing ally, trailing along with a couple more
girls, all exceedingly slender, with the unspoken misunderstood purpose of giving the older wiser woman some
kind of support as she cruised the bars, looking for something special with a bank balance to match. Shelley never
did know when she was being used. As friendships went,
the one with the manageress could be blown away in a puff
of smoke, but Shelley had never known that, either.

'What you been up to? Two days off and thinner than ever, well, I don't know. What's the matter, Petal?'

'Period pain,' Shelley drawled. 'Won't happen again.' Knowing she was being watched. Let down this brittle creature more than once and the coveted job and the fun which went alongside might be at risk, and worst of all, the man of her dreams and nightmares would not know where to find her.

Derek was right: Shelley was tired to her bones and might well have been better resting at home. She was too nervous and edgy to be at her best. When the phone rang at the back of the shop she jumped, and when she steamed the creases out of a blouse her fingers were nerveless and clumsy.

Perhaps, if she told the manageress what she had endured so recently, there might be sympathy; or disbelief. Besides, she was unsure of her ability to tell the story in the way she had told it when they took the statement; any repetition would confuse. She panicked when she thought of having to repeat it, live through it all again. The only person she wanted to talk to was him. She painted her face, teased her hair and waited.

Late afternoon; the two brown hands appeared in front of her on the display cabinet which housed the underwear: pure silk, made only for those with sufficient time or domestic help to keep them beautiful. The display was a fine froth of cream and lace: colour of the month, *café au lait*. His hands on the glass were enormous and alien by contrast.

'I'll have two of those, miss. Please.'

380

'The briefs, sir? Which size?' Her voice trembled; her fingers fluttered among the lace.

'Your size.'

'Any. You choose.'

'Your colour.'

She wrapped them with an attempt at the air of indifferent insolence she had perfected with the fat ladies, her heart beating like a gong and a sheen of sweat breaking out on her face, pausing in her fussing with the tissue paper to swipe her hair back from her forehead.

'How would sir like to pay?'

He handed over the card without a word; she put it briefly to her lips before passing it through the machine, stood watching the slip emerge for signature as if that piece of paper held the secret of the universe. 'I must see you,' she mouthed at him as he bent to sign. The bag rustled as she handed it to him, noticing with a kind of anguish how the varnish on her nails was chipped and untended. They had taken scrapings from under her nails, a sample of saliva from her tongue and swabs from her vagina; she wanted him to know all that. She wanted him to know how well she had done and how bravely she had endured. She ached to touch the burnished crown of his head, finger the smooth and repellent ridges of his skull, but she desisted.

'What a lovely day,' he said loudly. 'Far too good for working.'

'Yes,' she said. 'No choice about it.'

'Ah well. Perhaps you'll be able to take a walk in a nice shady park later on. If not today, tomorrow? Something to look forward to . . . so wonderful to have these places.'

'Perhaps,' she said.

Watching his retreating back, she felt the sweaty mix of revulsion and excitement which made her stammer. The breath of the manageress was on her neck. Long manicured fingers, without chipped nails, straightened the back of Shelley's collar, patted it back into shape, feeling beneath it the dampness of her skin, sidling round to check the price of the sale.

'Three times in a month that mean old baldy's been in here. The mistress must need some pleasing, or is he a conquest of yours, sweetie?'

Shelley suddenly had a vision of the rape suite in that faraway police station as a place of safety.

Maybe the life of a well-off Irish Catholic lady would be better if she had worked. A little job in a shop, perhaps. Brigid Connor watched the afternoon light turn dark and felt down her spine the threat of a storm. Late summer brought these alarms; she was less afraid of the thunder than the lightning. Oh dear Lord, if a storm were to burst over her head, she would run and hide in a cupboard, and if the devil himself had come to the door, she would fling her arms round his neck. Such nice eyes that doctor had, so kind. It was he who had stumbled upon the truth, only by letting her talk without saying anything. All she had wanted was for him to find something wrong with her, something which would make sex impossible, but there was nothing to be found. Maybe it was he who had sent the cutting from the newspaper. Maybe it was one of the girls. Brigid eyed the drinks trolley. It was Aemon's favourite affectation, as if they ever threw cocktail parties.

She knew she would succumb, despicable though it was to be sipping anything other than tea at four in the afternoon, with a storm coming on as well. If her husband found her laid out and comatose, she would blame the lightning which brought with it that everlasting fear of the wrath of God. Punishment; the apartment destroyed in a bolt from heaven which would consign them to hell and then do the worst thing of all, bounce them back, the same as they were before.

Taking a tincture was a new habit she had learnt from the parish sisters, who were not, she had come to realize, quite as obtuse and fatly comfortable as they seemed. Perhaps one of them had sent the newspaper cutting.

There was a ritual which had come to precede the tincture habit, like many of her rituals, which she vaguely recognized as a sign of something not quite right, although with the clarity of vision afforded by the first drink she could say there was nothing unusual about her own neuroses. It was beginning to occur to her that her careful rationing of drink might not be such a brilliant idea. Aemon had a thing about women and drink; hated it. Should he find her under the influence, it would either make her untouchable or, if it did not, she could sleep through the whole process. For the moment, she could not bring herself as far as putting that theory into action. Pride of a kind forbade it and, besides, she did not have a lifetime's experience of practice. Life might have been different if she had learnt, long before, to enjoy the taste of alcohol.

It did such dreadful things to the skin, so she'd heard. Made a female flushed and wrinkled before her time, her mother said. Made a man inherit the belly more suitable to a pregnant woman, so she had noticed of Aemon. Ah, drink is a terrible thing, sister. She thought all this as she ran the bath, thinking at the same time that only a woman with nothing to do bathes twice a day, but so the ritual demanded. It was a variation of the idea that a bath was therapeutic, relaxing, good for the soul and the body, cleansing enough to eradicate past and future sin. Sins such as taking the pill, denying Aemon his ambition for a son, offending God on both counts, and then telling the doctor all about it. Brigid simply liked this bathroom as a fantastic resort; it was big, beautiful, blousy and soft at the edges.

So was I, once, she thought, sadly, looking at her depleted figure in the comforting, obfuscating steam of the bathroom mirror. Tits, of course, famous for her tits, straining at a T-shirt and well able to pass the pencil test first tried at school. A girl had good tits if she could move around easily with a pencil held beneath each. She sank into bubbles, arose in front of the mirror, the top half of her festooned with foam, which she wiped off, using her hands, to save the towel.

'You're a highly attractive, healthy woman, yet, Mrs Connor; hardly a wrinkle. You could mother children if you wanted. You can do whatever you want, but from what you tell me about your lifestyle, maybe that could be improved . . . if you're worried about your own appeal, don't. That's not the problem, is it?'

So said that fine-eyed doctor, and she supposed that her appeal, as he put it, defined her existence. Being handsome, or not, was what dictated life and got one married out of a poor life into a rich one with a bathroom like this. She held the newspaper cutting over the steam and wondered again who had sent it. Whoever it was might have been kind, or, equally, malicious.

The print blurred in steam as Mrs Brigid Connor read, yet again, about the woman who claimed her husband had raped her, buggered her, generally messed her about. Asian names, therefore not applicable to herself, even if the result of the case had been hopeful, which it wasn't. All very well, they said, this business of marital rape, but it was difficult to prove. Almost impossible. Brigid had set a little store by this piece of paper, watched herself squash it in one fist and pull the lav chain with the other hand. She was a kind of hostage in here, dreaming of ways out. Using the law was unthinkable: she'd never dare and Aemon would always win. In the heat of the water, she cleaned her fingernails with a toothpick and removed some imaginary dirt from between her toes. There might have been a faint hope that Aemon preferred his wife less aggressively clean in the same way that he would like her to be dressed in something other than an apron – her standard uniform when she was cooking. She was a woman kept, in a certain style, maybe, but still kept, in a towelling robe which took the damp off her skin and smelt, vaguely, of rose petals, with the underlying musk of moisturizer. Perhaps all these ablutions made her smell of a tarts' parlour; she didn't care.

Brigid was hovering round the drinks in a flurry of delight, towelling robe knotted tight, perfumes in order, with at least an hour to spare and the first big gin down before there was any chance of himself being home.

Speaking for herself, she couldn't understand why anyone bothered with the tonic. Lemon and ice out of a silver bucket, that was fine. She was standing with the second tumbler cooling her palm when the doorbell rang. Modest in the towelling robe which clutched her throat and reached her ankles, she moved to answer it. There was a porter downstairs who was supposed to deter Jehovah's Witnesses and double glazing people. Brigid never hesitated about answering the door, in fact she often prayed for it to ring. As far as she was concerned, the only danger in her life already lived here, and he was not expected for a blessed interval yet.

There was the man with the nice eyes, the one who had understood all she had tried to avoid saying between the lines of expressing non-existent symptoms. It seemed like a long time ago, but it could only have been a matter of days. He smiled, of course, that is what any visitor does, and stood on the threshold, waiting for the invitation to come further. 'Oh,' was all she could say. 'Oh, it's you; do come in.' Flustered and a little unsure whether she was pleased, embarrassed, puzzled. Brigid's thoughts would have been clearer, except for an overriding guilt of the most obvious kind. She was still holding a tumbler of neat gin in one hand. Amply covered, but not properly dressed, at four-thirty in the afternoon did not give a good impression either; the most she could say for herself was that she did not look like a slut and she was, at least, thoroughly washed.

'All alone?' he said politely, not needing a response. The place somehow smelt of someone who was all alone in it far too often; there was not a dint in a cushion to show

386

where anyone had sat. 'I was passing,' he added. 'Thought you wouldn't mind if I called. It seemed to me, you see, that you were rather unhappy. It stuck in my mind that that was the case. Forgive me if I intrude.' He had moved to the picture windows. 'What a lovely view.'

The threatened storm had not emerged and the summer skies were clearing, leaving a sky of non-uniform grey and patchy cloud. Brigid knew every detail of the view; she had stared at it for hours. Knew that they stood at the tallest point of Clerkenwell and from here, the best apartment in the place, she could see the huge buildings which only looked poetic from a distance. From car level, driving round those streets, they seemed treeless and depressing; from here the amount of greenery was surprising. There was even a glint of canal water, and the sweet umbrella of St Pancras Gardens.

'You aren't intruding,' she said.

'I thought you needed . . . therapy, Mrs Connor,' he said softly, still facing the window.

'Therapy?' she echoed, watching his hands, held behind his back, the fingers on one hand tapping the knuckles on the other. All of a sudden she felt slightly woozy, the effect of a large shot of booze on an empty stomach and the first still doubtful sensation of fear. Such nice eyes.

He did not answer and his silence was unnerving.

'Would you like a drink?' she asked, noticing the quaver in her voice.

'No. Put it down and come and sit beside me.' He motioned to the shiny leather sofa; a long, deep, squashy piece of furniture which sighed noisily as they both sat, a further cause of embarrassment.

'Therapy, Mrs Connor. For a lovely mistreated lady.'

There was no expression of appetite on his face, only neutrality; the bland look of a scientist examining a specimen which has aroused interest rather than passion. He had seized the lapels of the rose-scented robe, pulled it down over her shoulders and pinioned her arms before she had an idea of what was happening. The knot of the tie belt was neatly unlooped; he pushed aside the volume of thick soft flannel. She stared down at herself, mesmerized, helpless, then closed her eyes in protest at her own exposure. Her mouth was dry. Carefully, he released one full breast and took the nipple into his mouth. There were the soft gurgling sounds of a baby at the breast; she had a dim memory of that, the most erotic experience of her life. First the right teat, then the left, like a child feeding, wet and warm until the mouth withdrew, leaving the nipples hard and pointed. She felt the brush of his slightly shiny shirt against her skin, his mouth trailing a moist line down her abdomen, his delicate fingers pushing apart her thighs without much resistance, although her fists clenched and she gritted her teeth. In a state of paralysis and profound shock, it was all she could do.

'Hush,' he murmured. 'Only therapy, Mrs Connor. You poor darling.'

The endearment, spoken so softly before he buried his mouth and she felt his tongue, was as shocking as his actions. Brigid had not heard a term of endearment, however vague and anonymous, in many months, only hoarse words of encouragement; hissed instructions, such as, move yourself, no, not that way; grunts of approval or discomfort. The uttering of the word 'darling', simply

388

increased the paralysis. I should be screaming, she told herself, and braced herself for the effort of the shriek which failed to emerge. All she could hear was the sound of her own breathing and all she could register were his hands beneath her buttocks, raising her with supreme gentleness to his mouth. She kept her now wide-open eyes fastened on the ceiling light above her head, an elaborate thing of glass and chrome, as new as the sofa. A wild confusion of thoughts made her dizzy again, among them the knowledge that the scream would not be heard, that in a moment she would wake from a nightmare and find herself still warm from the bath, that her nipples were not erect and that this man was not a virtual stranger, but her husband. Or that he was that other boy, from all those years ago; the one she first loved. The ceiling light moved back into focus; she was counting the bulbs, six of them, and their shininess reminded her that she was in the present and that what he was doing to her was monstrous and if she was still alive she must shout or move, summon some power to resist, spit out that bile which rose in her throat.

She struggled to free her arms; moved one leg, ready to kick; raised her head, the better to scream; arched her back and felt him pressing on the inside of her thigh, so that the leg she had bent was pinioned, the calf hanging loosely over the side of the sofa, his fingers pinching muscle. And then, to her own horror, she ceased even these pathetic attempts to stop him. Tingling warmth spread as far as her hips, sparkling sensation concentrated in her groin, making the mouth of the orifice feel enormous. She tried to close her legs, squeeze sensation into submission, suppress it, ignore it, wrench back control for her own treacherous body, but it was too late and the mind would not co-operate. Brigid Connor shuddered into sexual climax, moaning, biting her lip and drawing blood.

'Ice in your drink?' he asked. His face, with the nice eyes and the skull the colour of the polished walnut banisters which led up from the foyer downstairs, loomed above her and she closed her eyes, unable to look at him. The sofa exhaled as his weight left it. There was the sound of soft steps and a tinkle of glass, then he was back. 'Cool you down,' he muttered, or at least, there were words she only remembered later. She had been flushed hot, still fluttering. Then she felt the cubes of ice he rubbed between her legs, the ice melted from the bucket she had so carefully prepared, so that the ritual of the drink was less disgraceful and more like the ceremony of tea; it was then, and only then, that she screamed.

Later, the door closed behind him softly. There was fresh ice in the container. There were gifts on the table she had never noticed: flowers and chocolates. The crackly leather of the sofa was cleaned with detergent and Mrs Brigid Connor was back where the whole episode had begun: in the bath, weeping softly and numb with shock which the gin he had poured did not lessen. She tried to gather her far-flung, never-too-sharp wits to eradicate from her mind what he had looked like, what he had worn. A smart shirt of some shiny man-made fabric; trousers, beyond recall; nothing he had removed. No jewellery, no hair, no traces.

Brigid Connor had wept for imagined sins all her life, but she had never ever known such terrible, excoriating shame.

★

Rose Darvey had made intermittent efforts with the internal décor of the house she shared with Michael, and the various attempts at creating harmony showed the influence of Helen West. Helen's basement flat had been transformed into a sunny place full of yellows and blues; Rose liked it so much, the colours had become stuck behind her eyeballs. She was not a dedicated housekeeper any more than Helen, but she was still a compulsive nest-builder, wherever she had lived, and Rose had lived in many places since running away from home. She had made each of them clean and respectable; she was a devil with a paint brush which she used to put her mark on a place, but that done, enthusiasm waned. Frills, ornaments and dolls had disappeared from her life since Michael had arrived. She had adopted a minimalist attitude to furniture out of necessity; kitchen equipment was rudimentary because she refused to accept cast-offs. The walls were pale yellow, the blind blue-and-yellow striped and the mugs and plates echoed the theme. Rose thought that having a wedding present list for her friends and Michael's relatives was both absolutely gross and patently greedy. All she told everyone was buy something blue or yellow, and, if anyone could afford it, an electric drill for him.

They were lucky with this house. Rose had the low salary of an apprentice and a little nest egg from her granny; Michael's police wages were respectable; they weren't so badly off and it would get better, which meant that home improvements were not much of a priority. There was nothing which could not wait. The real priorities in Rose's life were loving him, working hard, getting on and having as much fun as possible. The paintwork would wait and the plants could die.

'Are we all right then?' she asked him as soon as she came in from work and saw his broad back at the kitchen sink, washing up the dishes from her breakfast. It was the nature of his shift work that they did not see one another every day, not when he worked nights. Sometimes three days passed. He did not reply. She put her arms round his waist; he flicked detergent foam onto her nose; she squealed and punched him lightly in the ribs. Then they were in one another's arms, hers scarcely reaching round his torso, the pair squeezing the breath out of one another, with enough oxygen left for a deep and endless kiss which seemed to involve every muscle and raise Rose's toes off the ground. When they withdrew, by an inch, she reached up and pulled his hair, looked at him with bold, questioning, playful eyes.

'Not leaving then?'

He held her head steady with two damp hands, kissed her again on the forehead, the nose, the lips.

'Thought I might postpone it. You know, think again, maybe in forty years, unless it upsets the grandkids.'

She looked at him seriously. 'How many do you think there'll be by then, Daddy?'

'Dozen or so. Give us a kiss.'

The reconciliations after disagreements were always thus. She had grown up in a house full of growling silence and threat; she could not bear bad feeling to persist. It got into the brickwork, she told him; then your house falls down. They fell to chattering. There was an accumulation of news on the days when he had come home after she left for work. A policeman's partner had to learn independence. Rose knew it already.

'Speaking of children,' he was saying, resuming the washing-up. 'Did you go to that clinic?'

'Yup.'

'How much did that cost?'

'Not much. I told you. I wouldn't have gone there unless Anna had persuaded me it was the best and she could get me a discount. It's very posh, but she was right. It's more comfortable than the doctor's – and there's no queue.'

They kidded on about children, wanted them madly, but not yet. So far, Rose had taken her pill, didn't like it any more than he. The idea of anyone spending much of their youthful life taking strong drugs of any sort struck him as fundamentally flawed; Rose teased him that it was his talent as a sportsman that made him think of all drugs as poisonous steroids. She giggled.

'Come upstairs, lover, I've got something to show you. You won't believe this.'

There was a bathroom and one and a half bedrooms at the top of steep stairs, their own room faced the road. Once the junk was cleared out of there they would move to the back, for the sake of greater privacy. There was a railway line shrouded by trees at the rear, a road with houses facing them in the front and no urgency about making the switch. The curtains in the front room were also blue and yellow. The offending dead plant, the ostensible cause of a row which had really been about something else, no longer dwelt on the window-ledge.

'This is what they gave me,' Rose said. 'A cap, like we

393

said I ought to get. Anna told me how to put it in and said I'd got to practise with it for a week . . . and then go back, but I don't think I'll bother. There's a doctor there, asks all these questions . . . And you do feel a prat, trying the thing. I was glad it was Anna.'

'You mean she shows you, or you show her? Funny thing, isn't it?' He was trying to hide his distaste at the sight of a round rubber sphere nestling in a blue plastic box. It was the most unsexy object he had ever seen, reminding him of his baby cousin's teething ring.

'How on earth do you get it in?'

'Well, I'm not about to do the whole demonstration,' said Rose indignantly. 'And it isn't easy, I'm telling you.' She picked up the tube of jelly which came out of the same bag as the box. 'You put this stuff down the middle and round the edge,' she did so as he watched with some fascination. 'Then you squeeze it in the middle and, well, you know, insert it up your what's-it. Oh, shit.'

Rose had begun to giggle again. The cap was slippery, difficult to handle; a comic object with a wired rim, skipping out of her hand as she stood by the window, flying through the warm air with sudden momentum, resuming the spherical shape she had been trying to contain, landing, bouncing and finally rolling to a halt on the pavement below. They looked at each other and dropped to their knees like a pair of combatants evading a sniper, hiding their heads below the level of the window, desperate not to be seen. Michael raised his chin up to the ledge and peered over; Rose followed his example.

The cap lay slightly to the left of their front door, glistening slightly and looking like an accusing eye. Both heads: hers dark, his fair, ducked down again. Rose turned to slump against the radiator, clutched him and howled. 'Shh,' he said. 'Shh.' Great gulps of laughter consumed them. 'You go and fetch it . . .'

'No, I can't, I can't . . .'

Entwined again, comfortable on the floor with the old blue carpet and the dead plants and the curtains fluttering in the breeze. It was a quiet street, rarely deserted; there would be eyes in the opposite windows. The kiss was resumed where they had left off in the kitchen, turned into something soft and sweet and urgent; the only sound was the rustling of clothes until there were no clothes, and Rose saying, I love you, I love you, I love you . . . Him, saying the same.

The evening sun was lower in the sky by the time Michael next looked out of the window. He stood, this time, with the coverlet from the bed round his waist, looking down into the street once, then again. He nudged her.

'Hey, Rose . . . it's gone . . . it has, someone's nicked it.'

The doorbell chimed. Rose scrambled to her knees.

'Do you think it's someone wanting to give it back?' he hissed.

'No,' she said, scrabbling for her clothes and looking at her watch. 'It's your mum and dad.'

'Down the drainpipe at the back?' he suggested lightly. Rose, dressed on top at least, had stuck the modest portion of herself out of the window and shouted down to the two greying heads below.

'Coming!' she yelled.

'Oh no,' he gasped. 'Oh no, I can't stand it.' And Rose had the grace to blush.

Chapter Seven

'**Sexual intercourse is a continuing act, which ends upon withdrawal. If, therefore, a man becomes aware that the woman is not consenting after intercourse has commenced and he does not desist, he will be guilty of rape from the moment that he realises that she is not consenting . . .**'

'*I did not consent to becoming what I am,*' *he wrote on his pad.* '*I am tormented and thus entitled to torment . . .*'

Wait a minute. He did not torment. He redeemed, gave pleasure, liberated; that was what he did. But there was this infection, coming through from the outside world, pushing him into this demeaning state of having to consider and reconsider the consequences all over again, becoming obsessive about the text, then reassuring himself. All he ever had to do, according to these texts, was to avoid penetration with any portion of his own body. (The tongue did not count; it was, in any event, almost entirely immune to infection; nor did a finger or an implement such as a syringe with a purely medical purpose. Such a penetration was not a rape.)

He sighed with relief. Books seemed so much more reliable than a computer screen in the sunlight of the day. Books were such solid items of furniture, demanding more effort to turn pages heavy with knowledge. Effort always equalled reward.

Next he read an article on baldness, advocating that the female of the species should note the bald man's legendary virility and, therefore, pursue him with the same lack of scruple she would use in the hunt after any other male. He shook his head, irritated again to find himself considering consequences. There was not a single hair left to fall from his body for collection by a forensic scientist, and that was not his fault either, nothing he had ever intended, simply another joke.

He rarely perspired; he was comfortable in clothing which was mostly synthetic, closely woven and highly unlikely to shed fibres fit for microscopic examination. So, as long as he kept his bodily fluids inside his body, he was safely beyond detection, unless, of course, someone not only protested, but complained. But women, in particular, were far too ashamed of pleasure to do that.

Love me, for what I am. For what I give you.

Stop that! Turn the pages.

'. . . Dilation of the cervix at virtually any stage of gestation will generally bring on uterine contractions which in turn, lead to expulsion of the contents of the uterus. In vitro decapitation, or foetal pulverization, were preferable to Caesarean section . . . Use a syringe with soapy water . . . Stir up the contents with a long sound . . . like pudding.'

They should be grateful for me, for all I know and all I have to give.

Teaching them about pleasure without pain or consequence.

Filling them with comfort; filling them with air. Ending it.

★

'There is many a cleft stick with rape cases,' Redwood intoned. Someone sniggered and he ignored it. 'Redwood on Rape' sounded like a type of vegetarian delicacy. The *double entendres* would be indigestible and all the worse for being as unintentional as his dreadful puns.

Standing in a lecture room, he resembled what he might have been in another life, possibly should have been, Helen thought with a rush of sympathy. An absent-minded professor, more at home with the written word and a legal text than he would ever be putting it into practice. Abysmal manager, worse public speaker, and, although he managed to suppress his knowledge of his own shortcomings most of the time, there was the occasional desperate realization of them which made him tearful. On the forum, doing his stint on an obligatory afternoon's training, Redwood tried to wield an illusory power. He still had some of the excitement of an academic to whom news, which has already travelled a continent, feels as if it has come to him first.

'What the law says,' he announced busily, brandishing the notes which were already circulated to everyone in the room, including those members of staff who had not been able to formulate an alibi or leave the building beforehand, 'is that men can be raped.'

'It says "rapped" in my copy,' someone muttered.

'Typing error,' he snapped. 'Use your common sense.' He cleared his throat. 'There was never, of course, a time when men could not be raped. I mean they could be buggered, but it wasn't called rape, it was called buggery, for those under a certain age, whether consenting or not; once sixteen, now eighteen, but not with someone over twenty-one if they didn't mind, and anyway, you could sometimes charge gross indecency as well, but only in a public place. And now it comes under the rape umbrella. Very important to phrase the charge right.' He beamed; they all sat, bemused. Old news did not improve with his retelling.

'It's *all* rape, you see. So if a woman's been buggered, she's been raped; likewise a man. Vaginal or anal, it's all rape, is that clear? One section of one Act only. But you can always have indecent assault and buggery, if you like. In some circumstances. All depends what you can prove.'

This time the muttering was definitely Rose, but by the time Redwood swivelled his head and stared at her, the crown of her spiky dark hair was all he could see, her face bent in assiduous concentration on the notes in front of her; the model pupil, with nothing to give her away, apart from one long and slender leg extended over the other with a shoeless foot twitching madly, even whilst everything else about her remained completely still. Out of the corner of his eye, Redwood saw the door of the room open to let inside a palpably reluctant latecomer, giving Helen West the opportunity to slip out in his wake.

'A man can be raped,' Redwood continued less certainly. 'In fact, he has to be raped for it all to come under the same blanket of the same charge . . . What's the matter with everyone?'

By now, Rose was the only one in the front row who was completely immobile. She looked the very soul of concentration, the foot still, with a shoe on it.

'The same rules apply about consent, too. Oh yes. And evidence, of course.'

At the end of the lecture half of them were grey with

399

sleep. Someone thanked Redwood for so enhancing their knowledge of the law, adding, beneath his breath, that it had done very little for the communal libido. They trooped out, smirking.

Once he was back in his room, Redwood wiped his brow and set about preparing tea. He had a secretary fit for this purpose, but he considered it bad for morale to have her make him hot drinks when she should be using her skills to type up memos and translate all those bureaucratic orders from above. Anyway, he positively enjoyed making tea to his own specification, drinking it out of the china cup he had brought from home. The interlude brought an illusion of civilization, all the better if he was not interrupted, so that when Helen entered after the briefest of knocks, she found him frowning. It crossed his mind to mention the fact that he had seen her leaving the lecture.

'Can I discuss something?'

It was a suspiciously humble request. He looked immediately for something with which to attack her in pre-emptive defence.

'In a minute, Helen. Look, is there anything you can do about the acquittal rate in your sexual assault cases? I've been looking at the figures; not good, not good at all . . .'

'You mean that losing every other one is hardly a fine track record? Well, I know what we could do about it. Send potential defendants on training courses, and tell them that what they have to do first is acquire a few previous convictions so that their fingerprints and DNA are on record. Then make sure that when they go in for an attack, full moon or whatever, they leave copious traces of bodily

400

fluids and fibres from brand-new flannel shirts made of pure cotton. And then we could train the victims never to associate with men under forty they haven't known since birth, and should they be so foolish as to suffer attack, at least ensure they acquire enough bruises to make it clear they didn't enjoy it. Would that do?'

'Be serious.'

'I am being serious. There's a high acquittal rate because any case which isn't entirely clear-cut – the woman raped at knife-point situation in a public carpark – is always a risk, even if there's some corroboration for what she says. Look, I want to talk to you about one in particular. Just to clear my mind, OK?'

'Rather than discuss it with Mr Bailey?' Redwood said cunningly. Helen's relationship with Bailey had always been a matter for speculation; Redwood did not approve.

'I don't discuss every case with Bailey, and oh, by the way, we're getting married, sometime, soon.' This was said in a rush. 'So I may need a day off, but if you could listen a minute . . .' She may as well let that news slip, she supposed, although it wasn't the purpose of the interview. For all his failings, Redwood could be a good sounding-board and that was all she needed. She was meeting Anna Stirland that evening and Helen wanted to be sure of her ground, although she was really sure already. Showing her insecurity, by asking about what she knew. Redwood nodded, stunned as usual by any tidings he had insufficient time to absorb.

'Supposing we have a woman, good character, sound of mind and limb, who invites a man she fancies round to her own house for a drink and a chat. He's perfectly well aware that she's very attracted to him, although in a shy kind of way. It's romance she wants, sex as well, but not yet. He pounces on her, causing her to injure herself, inserts an ice stick up her vagina and leaves. A joker, you see. She's so completely humiliated, she makes no immediate complaint to anyone until the nightmare of it makes her crack up, by which time she's comprehensively destroyed all physical evidence, such as stains, and her injuries can't be dated. If she named him, currently she won't, would we look at it?'

Redwood was unfazed, shaking his head before her recital ended, only amazed by the speed of her delivery.

'Look at it? Yes, provided it came through the police in the usual way. Then we'd turn it down. Even if we had a name. He'd walk out of a charge of indecent assault before the judge heard the end of the opening speech, you know he would. Defence? He wasn't ever there and she's a fantasist, or, he was there but nothing of the kind happened. The delay in reporting it makes it a complete non-starter. Why on earth are you asking?'

She hesitated.

'Confirmation, I suppose. Don't you ever do that? Seek a second opinion when you already know what it is? Call it frustration. What can the law offer a woman like that? Decent, responsible, maybe a touch obsessive. Oh, I don't know, I just hate the fact she hasn't got any form of legal redress . . .'

He lowered his face towards the fragrance of his tea.

'She doesn't deserve it if she won't ask for it. And I suppose what her recovering spirit needs is a spot of revenge? The best therapy? We all know about victims recovering far faster if their assailant's found guilty.' Redwood liked to

402

see himself as a closet psychiatrist. 'Supposed to limit the extent of the damage. Well, if counselling won't do for her, there's only one way I can think of for her to get her man. How can she expect redress if she won't even accuse? One way. A frivolous thought, of course.'

The tea interrupted, a sip of it restoring his good humour.

'Tell me your frivolous thought. You don't have many.'

He sat forward over his desk, the china teacup nursed in his hands, his face lit with a grim smile.

'She'd have to lure him back. Make him do it again. Only this time, collect.'

'Collect what?'

'Evidence. Injury, fluids, blood.'

Silence fell in the room, apart from the sound of a man sipping his tea, enjoying his little joke.

'Well, I can hardly tell her that,' Helen said flatly.

The noisy sipping of liquid was her signal to leave.

'Helen, if you're being asked for unofficial advice, rely on silence. The law's changed on the right of silence too. But not that much.'

Anna Stirland chose to walk to Helen's house that evening. It settled her mind – even a long walk, full of carbon monoxide fumes for the first half. She lived on the fringe of two districts, adjacent to where the summer dust lay in a ground-level cloud, disturbed by traffic, the identity of the place fractured by the massive dissections of road and rail. Even with the high proportion of inebriates and the rough trade in drugs and flesh prevalent in the environs of the stations, the area held her affection. It was a mixture of styles; a jigsaw puzzle with missing pieces; a dumping ground which solidly defied rejuvenation. There were terraces and squares, apartments carved from old institutional buildings, 1960's breeze-block monsters, flanked by traffic, opposite what she thought of as the church park, a green awning with a challenging if dirty statue near the gate. Anna walked down a fume-filled gulley, gazing with interest at the fly-by-night business enterprises which flourished in the brick-built caves of what had once been the arches of a railway viaduct. The furtive inhabitants suited caves; they dealt in cash and basic commodities. From here, a person could get a car rebuilt, a lorry disguised, a bathroom or new shop refitted overnight, a bus stolen to order; buy candles, bulk deliveries of halal meat, mirrors, take-away food, but never pay with credit card. Outside the station, there was a rank of panting taxis, eating up the travellers who emerged in clumps, anxious for the next destination. Avoiding the crowds, of whom the travellers were the minority and the drunks a sizeable proportion, Anna cheated and took the bus for the next mile uphill to the Angel.

Free of the immediacy of her own environment, she had time to relax and confess to herself that she had looked forward to this unsolicited invitation. Despite the circumstances of the second meeting with Helen, the bullying involved in the introduction at a time in her life when she doubted her judgement about anything and everything, she had already told herself that it was rare to like a person so spontaneously if it was not mutual. Therefore, if she liked Helen, Helen liked her. That kind of conclusion was not sound in a situation where lust was involved, Anna thought ruefully, but otherwise, yes, it was fair enough. She had usually known, although not always immediately, whom to trust. It was important to her to believe that Helen West was extending some form of friendship, as opposed to pity, or unfulfilled duty; even curiosity would have been better than condescension.

On the high pavement of the Angel, she began to walk again. The traffic was no less frenetic but less commercial, and here, the restaurant smells prevailed. There was one every twenty yards, not always with the same identity as its counterpart of the same time last year, wafting forth scents of spices, hot oil, curried chicken, tortillas, tomato sauce, bread, humanity, full bellies and good times. Anna thought of old friends and evenings out, wondered why it was that old friends could not help in her current condition, not that she had asked. Perhaps she wanted to keep her reputation with her old friends, not let them see her diminished; it was as if she owed the old friends a consistency she did not owe to the new. She paused to look at a menu in a window, cheered by the lights and the thought of food, horrified by the prices and slightly contemptuous of those who only came out because they could not cook.

It was then that she saw, up ahead among the straggling pedestrians, a shiny bald skull. It made her stop so abruptly that a girl running along behind cannoned into her with cross apologies. It was not him; nothing like him at all. It was simply a man, turning to smile at the girl he was ushering into a car; another younger man, dressed in garish clothes and possessed of a pricey motor, perhaps to compensate for the fact that his handsome head was as bald as an upturned bowl. He looked ten years the junior of her man. The car pulled out from the pavement with an arrogant burst of speed. Anna began to walk again.

How many lies had she told to Helen West? None of any significance; omissions rather than positive untruths, and she was not sure she wanted to remedy any of them. An irrelevant omission in failing to admit, out of a kind of shame which she resented herself, that while she had been a midwife for much of her life, and proud of it, she had succumbed to the lure of a better-paid job. It was a downright distracting lie to state that her bald-headed lover no longer worked in the same place, or had any command over her. How strange it was, the virtual impossibility of recounting the truth and nothing but the truth the way she could relive in her mind what that man had done to her, telling herself a slightly different version every time, each remembrance adding or subtracting sufficient details to distort the narrative. That was what trauma did to the mind, she supposed: made her doubt her sanity and threw integrity into turmoil. She doubted she could ever take an oath to tell the truth.

She passed a wine shop and a cinema queue, dawdling, and backtracked to look at the pictures advertising the film. Scenes of love, tension and violence made her shudder and she hurried on again. I want my old self back, she told herself, that is all I want. I want to walk around again with a perfectly normal set of reactions and a sense of humour. I want to be clean, decent and truthful. And what do I want from an evening with my new friend? I want her, someone, to know what it is like to have one's footsteps dogged by this all-pervading shame and anger. But I still can't tell the whole truth, which is that what he did to me

406

might well have been a brutal form of therapy to cure me of my silly passion. Nor can I say that, yes, I have seen him passing many times, even when I least expect it, although not nearly as often as I think I have, and that every time I have that real or imagined fleeting glimpse, like now I feel a panic-stricken sickness. A lump of gristle arrives in my throat and I think I am choking.

She had reached the crossroads where the restaurants gave way to trees. She stood for a moment, trying to remember the route she had memorized from the map she'd consulted before setting out. That was another symptom: lack of concentration. Dammit, she did not want to be suffering from a syndrome, or to be nothing but a mass of symptoms. She amended any expectation of what she might have wanted this evening to achieve. A shy foray into friendship, and if not that, a few hours' distraction would do.

'I can't cook, you know,' Helen said.

She lied, as well; that was all Anna needed.

The flat was a slightly untidy haven of multicoloured peace. Anna was aware of the moral superiority which came from the knowledge that she was a far better housekeeper than her hostess, and on far less money. She touched things, she admired, explored and settled like a wary animal. Most of all, she liked the garden: unplanned, overfull, big enough for a cat to get lost. She would have loved to get her hands on that garden.

Much, much later, after several glasses of wine and food in the form of an endless parade of snacks, Anna told Helen, lightly, speaking briefly, nothing heavy, that what

407

she really wanted was revenge, and Helen repeated, equally lightly, Redwood's cynical formula. Lure him back, make him do it again, collect evidence. She was only speaking in the context of the options available for redress rather than revenge; namely, none. They laughed about it; neither of them aware at the time of how the idea might take hold, like one of Anna's plants in parched ground.

When Bailey arrived, Anna left. He had made her feel welcome; her discomfort lay in the fact that she had never meant to stay so long and was not much at ease around men at the moment, even though it was nice to refuse his offer of a lift home and then be ushered into a cab. As if she was as normal as she seemed. A capable woman able to unlock her own door with that once-familiar pleasure in being home. Ashamed to feel so diminished by some incident which had not even threatened her health. And all the rest of her, still burdened with love and lies.

Bailey stood awkwardly in the kitchen, the way he sometimes did, as if he had never been inside the flat before, instead of a million times at the last count. There were moments when Helen wanted him to be in no doubt that this was her territory, others when she wanted him to meld in with the furniture, as comfortable as if he owned what was hers. His lack of resentment often amazed her; so did his humility and his complete acceptance of her ambiguous rules. She did not deserve him.

'Sorry,' he said. 'Didn't know you had company. Only I didn't want to be on my own.'

This was an admission, coming from him. There was far less of his almost obsessive reserve than there had been, but he was never going to be a man who admitted easily to need.

'Good. There's wine in the bottle and the night's young. Is it Ryan?

He nodded. Helen put her arms around him. His body felt like knotted wood, slightly softened by age, yet hardened by the tension which seemed to sigh through his voice.

'Never mind a drink,' Helen said, 'you need a massage. Hot bath, maybe. Tender loving care, all that.' She kept her voice free from anxiety but his pallor was alarming. Bailey was ever thus: resisting the river of emotion until the dam was ready to burst. She never remembered the ulcer.

'I need inspiration,' he said. 'And a different job. And,' he added, accepting a glass and something resembling a sausage roll, both swallowed with indifference. 'And . . . what was I saying?'

'Exactly that.'

He sat at the kitchen table, marginally relaxed. She was almost up to speed on the Ryan débâcle, she thought, but plenty could have happened in forty-eight hours. Such as some little snippet from the laboratory, some detail which made the whole thing worse.

'I've got to pass it over to that sanctimonious star, Todd,' Bailey said. 'I've got to. No choice about it. The girl's finalized statement is entirely convincing, needless to say. I've never bunked off a case before, and yes, I'm so angry with Ryan, I could spit.'

'Why did he do it?' Helen wondered out loud, feeling awkward about the fact that she had never felt at ease with Ryan, although confident she had hidden it. It was, in part, she suspected, a kind of jealousy. Ryan might know more about Bailey than she ever would; might even have a greater command over his affections.

Bailey rounded on her with red eyes.

'What do you mean, why did he do it? He might not have done it. Don't make assumptions.'

'Why not? You're sure, too, or you wouldn't be half as infuriated as you are now, or isn't it the thought of him being guilty which gets you down? You assume; you've got the evidence. Why can't I assume?'

He took a deep breath and attempted a smile. His stomach rumbled; the sausage-roll affair was a mere titillation, but the rumbling was his own fault for neglecting the simple business of eating. He had long since given up expecting, or even hoping, that Helen's fridge would automatically hold the makings of a man-sized meal. Sometimes yes, usually no; he was used to it.

'I'm sorry. I can't quite explain. I mean, I have to deal with my own assumptions and the evidence, which looks bad enough, but I find myself enraged if anyone else points the finger at him. Even when the stupid clot makes it worse, and even then I don't want anyone else suggesting that Ryan's guilty; I don't want to believe it, even though I do, actually, believe it. Am I making sense? No, I expect not. I loathe Todd.'

Helen stood behind his chair, kneading his shoulders. He reached for her hand and held it against the side of his face, resting his cheek against it. Bailey revelled in any sign of affection; he had been born and raised with a shortage which had turned him into a quietly demonstrative man.

'By an odd turn of coincidence,' Helen said, 'Anna, that

girl you just met, my new friend; she might have been interviewed by Ryan. About a month ago. If she'd made a complaint, that is. She lives on his patch. But she didn't and she won't. She thinks her complaint is too bizarre for anyone to take seriously.'

'Why?'

She would have liked to have told him, but she doubted it would have made him feel better.

'You've heard enough about sexual aberrations for one day,' she said. 'It'll keep.'

At about half-past eight in the evening, Aemon Connor delivered his wife into the hands of the police, more by accident than by design. It was not a measure he had ever considered appropriate for any member of his family, although when his daughters were small, he had found the prospect of having them imprisoned singularly tempting. Now, he could have wished them at home, rather than summering with the relatives he believed would have a more beneficial influence on making them hardy than Brigid ever would. To allow any stranger into his apartment, unless it was to admire the handiwork and commission a building on the same lines perhaps, was anathema, but there was little else a man could do when his wife would not get out of the bath.

Would not, could not; he was unsure of the difference, only that by the time he actually saw her in there, having put his foot to the flimsy lock which provided privacy rather than security, she was cold. Attempts to communicate through the door had resulted in her humming, softly at first, breaking out halfway through the first line of a hymn tune he thought he recognized, into a bubbly laugh which was devoid of any quality of joy. Well, as he told the doctor, he'd known since the beginning that Brigid, despite a sweet and gentle nature and a fine singing voice, too, lacked a certain something in the brain department, but this was another matter altogether. What he would never mention to the doctor was the fact that he considered his gentle wife such a conversational dead end that he fucked her out of despair. It was all a man could do in order to stay sane and as loyal as his faith demanded. Nor did he mention to the doctor that his wife had not left her cooling bath – cold, in truth, but on a day like this not chilly enough for any signs of hypothermia yet – by voluntary means. When she refused to respond to an order, he had seized her by the arms first, then the waist, and bumped and dragged her out of there, swearing mightily and calling on God for a witness. He had put that damn bathrobe on her, the one she hid inside so often to make herself look like a nun, shoved slippers on her feet by grabbing her ankles and forcing her tootsies inside. Aemon also failed to mention that her passivity during all these manoeuvres, which was not to be mistaken for co-operation, had given him an embarrassing stirring of desire; the one thing she could always do when no one else could, making her more infuriating than ever. Her skin was whiter than the morning milk, spongey to the touch. When he dumped her on the sofa, she had screamed, scrambled up to one end of it, curled her slippered feet beneath her and put her thumb in her mouth. Since this was the greatest sign of animation yet, he took it as a favourable sign.

He helped himself to a large drink to steady his nerves,

412

then another. She seemed happy enough, until she fixed her huge eyes on him and giggled. She took the thumb out of her mouth, formed a fist out of her hand with the index finger pointing at him like the barrel of gun, whispering, bang, bang, bang. Soon after that, he called the doctor.

The medic was a dark little man, half Aemon's size, pretending he had better things to do than interrupt his dinner. Aemon did not like Asians, for being so much better employees than his fellow countrymen. He liked this example even less when he turned into an interfering idiot with ideas of his own. He was beginning to mutter about his wife needing sedatives or whatever treatment was recommended for hysterical women, when she interrupted, opened her mouth and said, very clearly, 'Please take me away, I've been raped.'

Brigid rarely completed a sentence, so it was not surprising that Aemon's jaw dropped. When she went silent again and the doctor turned to him for explanation, he was the picture of surprised guilt. Brigid's fragile wrists emerged by accident from that cloying gown, as if she was trying to shake it off. 'I hate it,' she hummed, 'hate it, hate it,' again sounding both clear and absent-minded. She had slender arms, where the bruises were beginning to form from his efforts to get her out of the bath, livid patches beneath her skin; the only features the doctor seemed to notice. Apart from the flowers and the unopened chocolates which he took to be the guilty gifts of a guilty man.

He asked her politely if she was able to get dressed and come with him. She obeyed with a brilliant smile. Aemon stood by in silent confusion, for once, lost for words.

*

To Sally Smythe, summer was a silly season and she could only feel relief that it was drawing to an end. The gaiety of skimpy summer clothes was not enough to compensate for the fact that the warmth brought out of the brickwork vulnerable persons in all their disguises, and as they took to the streets and parks, so did the other type of vulnerable person who was likely to attack them. Oh, the lure of the great outdoors. The last person who had sat in the Rape House had been extremely dirty: a back-packing tourist girl sleeping rough until a stranger had decided to join her, not taking her refusal kindly. She had sat in here, with paper separating her torn clothes from the fabric of the chair, smelling, while they waited for the doctor. It went against Sally Smythe's instinct to prevent a person from washing. Mrs Connor was quite a contrast. She sat in the anonymous room like a shy cousin invited to tea, and she was as clean as a whistle.

Soft-spoken, too, apparently grateful for her surroundings which she stated she liked very much, speaking with the voice of a well-trained guest. Raped and/or abused by husband, Sally Smythe read the doctor's urgent guess. Mrs Connor seemed in no hurry. She might simply be there for the enjoyment of the hotel accommodation they would have to arrange soon. Would be nice to make some headway first, Sally thought; nasty bruises on the wrists.

'Who attacked you, Brigid? Please call me Sally. Did your husband get a bit . . .' There was not even the slightest scent of sex. Brigid smiled her brilliant vacant smile.

'Oh no,' she said, 'not this time.'

414

There were some victims who were much more responsive to a man.

Ryan worked in the garden until after dark, as he had done every evening since his suspension. Against all the odds, it was not the emptiness of the days which threatened him, when his wife was at work and his children, ever adaptable to new conditions, either pursued their independent social lives on a prearranged course as if nothing had happened, or wheedled him for entertainment. Trouble at work, was all they knew, whatever else they had guessed; Dad considering changing jobs after a few weeks' rest. His children were a source of solace, distraction and intense anxiety by day. It was in the evenings, with his wife at home, that he felt awkward, claustrophobic and guilty.

The problem with his garden was no more than the time of year. It was too soon to begin on preparations for winter, too late to plant or prune. He would normally have sat back and enjoyed the late summer season: the flowerbeds were weedless, although passing their best; his two fruit trees were free of blight and the lawn was healthy. There was nothing for it but to dig a pond.

Mary would have preferred him to concentrate on a number of things which required urgent attention indoors, but changed her mind. Anything which did not necessitate them remaining in the same room together for more than an hour at a time would do. If he was outside and she was in, they could behave normally. She would not be obliged to bite her own tongue in an effort to prevent herself from asking him, look, what exactly did happen on the night you went out with that girl? I know you haven't told me the truth. She would ask futile questions; each of them an accusation, a declaration of lack of faith which might be met with the mulish silence she dreaded, or the speaking of some truth she dreaded even more. There was a dull sense of *déjà vu* in all of this: there had been mutual infidelity in the past; enough evenings of silent recrimination, secrets and rows for neither of them to want a repetition.

She was brisk and calm. In bed, under cover of darkness, she had tried to make herself affectionate, but she could not pretend any real desire any more than he could respond. If he tossed and turned, it was better she did not know. The sleeping pills she had got from the doctor were remarkably efficacious, suppressing her boiling anger and letting her do what she needed to do: turn her back on him and sleep away the effort of being nice.

The pond had taken shape. Ryan, following instructions from an old *Reader's Digest* book, read first, dig your hole. The book did not mention what he was supposed to do with the resulting mountain of earth, except wheelbarrow it away to a site for a future rockery with the prospect of further time-consuming labour. Then, line your hole. Soon he could consider buying plants and fishes, then net to prevent marauders, then something to surround the pond. This task could go on for ever.

He was crouched on the edge of his hole, bone weary, rubbing soil from his hands. He stared at his nails, brown with the stuff and rubbed the fresh calluses raised by digging. Gardening without the impediment of gloves, as he usually did, gave a man hands like sandpaper. His wife had been known to complain. He wondered whether Shelley

Pelmore would remember encountering hands like that on her soft skin and, if she did not, would it be useful in his own defence? He could hear the question asked by a barrister with a voice to curdle blood: 'Surely, madam, you can remember if his hands were rough or smooth? Were they labourer's hands, madam, or those of a man at a computer terminal? Were they the hands of a man who digs a garden? You don't *know*?' In the last two years sitting in court to give moral support to the genuine rape victims who were his witnesses, Ryan had wanted to shoot the bewigged pompous farts who used questions like that to confuse.

Now, he would encourage it. He could take that girl and wring her little neck with his own calloused hands.

She was gorgeous, slim and lithe and gorgeous. Unquestionably affectionate, unlike his wife. So gorgeous, he could imagine burying her in a hole smaller than his pond.

The darkness of the August evening was not the real darkness of winter. His eyes had adjusted to it and he could imagine coming out here and seeing the glint of water, putting his feet in it on another night as warm as this, even though that was not what he was supposed to do with an ornamental pond. The strained voice of his wife floated over the lawn, shouting for him, trying not to sound impatient.

'Phone,' she said briefly, when he reached the harsh light of the back door, rubbing his eyes as he came inside. She watched, with resigned disapproval, as his dusty boots dragged dirt through the kitchen.

'Who?'

417

The phone had been so silent these last days, unless it was calls for the kids.

'Don't know. A woman, anyway. I asked her for her number for you to call back, but she wouldn't.'

Ryan rubbed his hands on his trousers and went into the hall.

'Help me,' said the voice. 'Help me, please.'

CHAPTER EIGHT

'Although juries must be told that "consent" in the context of the offence of rape is a word which must be given its ordinary meaning, it is sometimes necessary for a judge to go further . . . he should point out there is a difference between consent and submission . . . The jury should be reminded too of the wide spectrum of states of mind which consent could comprehend and that where a dividing line had to be drawn between real consent and mere submission . . .'

These were the words which excited him, would exonerate him if ever he needed it.

Both of the girls who had died had been afraid, although only initially. He would never have forced either of them, or any woman for that matter. The thought of doing anything so cruel shocked him. But even the most mature patient was timid, out of ignorance. There was nothing 'mere' about submission. One submitted to the dentist, the doctor, to life, even; submission was vital to survival. It was not a different state of mind to consent, but a close cousin. And in the end, one submitted to death; not consent, submission. What was the difference?

The law never mentioned redemption. The law did not believe in it.

The interior of the Rape House looked even more anonymous after cleaning. Plants, Sally Smythe thought; it needs plants.

'What did you do when he kissed you?' she asked the girl. There was silence.

'Nothing. I didn't do anything.'

'Well, he wasn't doing anything out of order at that point, was he? I mean, you didn't mind him kissing you?'

'No.' Her fingers continued to shred the paper handkerchief. 'I liked him, then.'

'They say you have to kiss a lot of frogs to meet a prince.'

'Pardon?' Sally smiled to hide a sigh, reminding herself not to get clever.

'I mean, we all have to experiment, don't we?' How condescending she sounded.

The girl's answering smile was wan in the extreme. They were not doing well and Sally felt as if she was wading through mud, not because of lies, but in pursuit of the words to frame the truth. Here was a plump girl, shivering slightly in the heat, preternaturally docile, although she had not been like that when the man she had liked took a deep-throat kiss as an open invitation to full-scale intercourse on the front seats of his van. She had fought like a cat, broken a window, all useful evidence, although it hadn't stopped him.

'Did he do anything else at first, apart from kiss you and you kiss him back?'

420

Another long hesitation.

'Put his hands . . . That's when I started to try and stop him.'

'Why? If you liked him?'

''Cos I wanted him to take me home. That's what he said. And it's all my fault, isn't it?'

She was crying steadily now, tears as plump as her hands. Sally moved the box of tissues nearer.

'Because I shouldn't have gone with him, should I? I shouldn't have fancied him at all.'

Sally gestured to her colleague to continue the good work and went into the kitchen. The slats of light which came through the Rape House blinds had begun to make her dizzy, but this girl had not wanted sunshine, she could only talk at all in the semi-dark.

The light in the kitchen was gloriously intense, reminding her of a tempting outside world and her own tired eyes. Brigid Connor had liked the kitchen, despite the view of a neglected backyard, or said she did, with her twittering politeness. She had even uttered thanks for a disgusting cup of soup; a charming lady, anxious to oblige, unlike the eighteen-year-old outside, who simply wanted to forget. Mrs Connor was so keen to please, so off-the-wall and, it had to be faced, so stupid, she would, and did, say anything as long as it received a smile, a nod of approval, or an invitation to continue in the same vapid vein. Didn't do so much talking at home, she volunteered; Aemon hated a chatterbox. She liked to take two baths a day, keep herself fragrant. She might have been in the bath when the man came to the door, but then again, she might not. He had no hair, that man. Your husband, Brigid? No, the man

421

with the gorgeous eyes. At which point, Brigid would put her palms over her own eyes, as if the sight of his had blinded her, and then remove the hands after a minute as if she was playing a game of peekaboo with a baby. They should all have been in a play-pen together. Nervous exhaustion, Sally concluded; premature senility or a reversion to infancy. But, throughout it all, there was something horribly candid in her guileless face. There were throwaway lines, addressed to the kitchen window or her own tea mug. He did, you know; he sucked me wet and dry, he did; never touched me. Something had happened.

Sally filled the kettle automatically. The medical examination which Brigid had not resented, although informing the doctor there was nothing to see, revealed old bruises on buttocks, fresh bruises on wrists and ankles. They had not gone as far as arresting the husband; policy dictated otherwise. Surprisingly, Ryan had always concurred with this caution; don't charge in without being sure; work out which of them has got a screw loose first. In this case, a husband yelling about issuing a summons against the Police Commissioner, with no trace of a stranger in the husband's house. Her dressing-gown fibres apparent all over his suit, as they might be, but nobody had raped her.

Nor had the husband brought the chocolates and flowers which lay on the table. She was his wife, for heaven's sake, and a good life she had too. She was perfectly capable of buying those things for herself. Chocolates and flowers, flowers and hearts. Something had happened, but Brigid Connor had gone back to her old man, and that was really that.

No hair, no name, but flowers and chocolates. And ice. Phone Ryan. No, she couldn't phone Ryan. Not now.

Nasty little ritual, this, although Todd rather relished it, everyone else around shuffled a bit, changing weight from foot to foot as if it was cold instead of so relentlessly hot.

Todd adopted the informal approach, only safe in front of witnesses, including the man's miserable little brief 'You know your rights, doncha? No need to say nothing, but silence ain't always golden.' Abandoning the strict wording also, handing him the sheet, which he received with a ghastly smile, like royalty receiving a perfectly repugnant gift and giving it to an aide. 'You attempted to rape Shelley Pelmore in the vicinity of King's Cross,' Todd intoned, leaving out the date for the sake of brevity. 'Got that? Anything to say?'

'Fuck off, you piece of crap,' Ryan said, before his solicitor could silence him. 'And where the hell's Bailey?'

''S all right,' said Todd, turning a benign countenance on the small man who was clutching Ryan's sleeve, judging from experience that unwise reactions often followed less-than-wise remarks. 'I shan't write that down. Hardly a response to the charge, is it?'

'Where's fucking Bailey, then?' Ryan demanded, louder. 'Where the fuck is he?' The cloth of his second-best shirt was bunched in the lawyer's fist.

'He's volunteered off the fucking case, is where, Mr Ryan. He wanted to go.'

Ryan reared back, pulling away. Controlled, sure, he had learnt control. He would not move; he knew he was powerless. He just wanted to look, for a minute, as if he was capable of butting his forehead down onto the bridge of Todd's nose. Todd did not wait. One swift jab to the solar plexus with the full force of vengeance behind it. Ryan doubled and moaned, thumped back against the wall.

Everyone was looking at the yellow paint above his head, pretending they were not listening to his breathing. It was in no one's interest to record either the aggression or the reaction. Sad, really. The defendant was not entirely reasonable; like everything else, it was all his own fault.

Police officers, so Bailey had often told Helen, commit the same crimes as other people since they are prone to the same temptations, although their rate of offending was considerably less. And people like me are appointed to investigate on a rota basis. You do not, cannot, train a young man into total self-control; no training course was going to rid him of testosterone or the desire for the things in shop windows he could not afford. He has to have power in order to be useful; it follows he will abuse it. There were plenty of occasions when you wanted the man to have the strength of a vicious young brute, so that he could survive other, less-inhibited vicious young brutes who did not care if he lived or died. You did not wish to see a piece of animated cardboard policing a riot, but what the public did want was the kind of paragon not generally born of woman, with a lion heart easily moved to aggression or compassion, but never to anger or dishonesty. The public wanted muscle power, intelligence and perfect self-control. Well, they could not have it.

Across the desk was today's interviewee. He was older

than most, ex-military, never learnt to control the cash requirements of the old wife and the new one, in deep trouble with money, making a false insurance claim. Not smart enough to get away with it. Following him would be the lad who bounced his torch back and forth across the head of a juvenile car thief. Bailey had more sympathy with him: that kind of crime had all the elements of rough justice. The sergeant with nowhere to go was claiming that he needed the money to pursue the course of true love, always an expensive commodity. I do not believe in the power of love, Bailey thought to himself. Dreadful things are done in the name of love, just as they are in the name of vengeance, and if anyone was ever again to say to him, I could not help it, when they talked about love, he was going to spit. Ryan haunted him. He went to take the phone call.

'Mr Bailey, sir?'

'Of course,' he snapped, regretting the recoil in Sally Smythe's voice.

'Sorry,' he went on, trusting her with a confidence to make up for the rudeness, 'but I'm interviewing a chap who is so riddled with self-pity I keep slipping through the holes and he's getting on my nerves. What can I do for you?'

All this was slightly overhearty, so she hesitated.

'You know what we were talking about when we met, about Ryan's little black book? The no-hopers?'

He did remember, all too clearly. That had been haunting him, too. So much so that he had mentioned it to Ryan's senior, and judging from the response of outraged laughter, wished he had not. She took silence as encouragement.

'Well, I think I've got another. Some of the same features. Ice.'

'I can't remember us discussing the presence or absence of that.'

'I can't remember us having much of a meaningful conversation at all,' she responded sharply, exasperation standing in good stead for confidence. 'But I should like to talk to someone and there isn't anyone else. No one who'll listen.'

He weighed it up in his judicious way. Perhaps there was something to be said for leaving Ryan to the tender mercies of Todd and the rule of law.

'I can't be party to any plan to get Ryan off the hook,' he said portentously.

'That isn't the point,' she said, more exasperated than ever. But it was, as far as Bailey was concerned. There was no other point.

You don't care any more about the things you cannot change, Rose had taunted. Rose could taunt until the cows came home, and still remain an ally. That was the nature of friendship, or at least one of its many facets. If Helen had ever had recourse to much by way of family life since she had made the decision to ignore them in the manner they had ignored her for several years, she suspected she might have known more about how friendship equates to other states of being, such as sisterhood, brotherhood, parenthood. Her own background forced her to treasure her friends; she was glad, in many ways, to have been cast adrift. She hated the idea that the ones you loved had to be related by blood to give you the reason as well as all the obligations attached. Perhaps she was cold in her narrow little bones. I wouldn't kill for anything except my handbag, she'd said to Rose.

There were not many friends: she was too picky, and even in the realm of friends, love had this random touch. In lieu of the family I secretly crave, Helen had once told Bailey, I would like my friends to have the following qualifications: I would like them to be courageous, but not necessarily brave; stubborn, doing the best they can with whatever they have been given; full of self-doubt but sure of self-worth; honourable, if not always, at least by inclination; the sort who neither screams nor whinges for help until they really need it and makes suffering the stuff of jokes.

To thine own self be true, he had said. And in the meantime Bailey had added, can they also be greedy, rapacious, dishonest, calculating? But of course. Nobody realizes, Helen had said, that you like people for what they are, which need not include conventional virtues, only the virtues you admire.

You said it, love. You like the people who are all the things you either are or want to be.

Am I cold?

No, just too analytical. I like you anyway.

She was sitting at her desk, crying with fury. There it was in the newspaper: the coroner's report, all on paper, no life to it at all. Girl found dead, two months before. Sweet twenty-seven. Pregnant, alone, a demise from heart attack. Nothing to show; not found for two days. How could it happen: death without cause in one so young? And how was it that she herself, so coy with friendship, so careful about the making of demands, considered not at all before she phoned Anna Stirland. Was it possible, she wanted to ask, to die of a broken heart?

No, no, Anna Stirland told herself, I rarely tell anyone what I do, especially now. Being a nurse covers so many questions, shuts them up nicely. Tell a man you're a midwife and he'll run for cover; tell a woman you work at a family planning clinic and she'll get you in a corner with anxious questions about her own thrombosis. Say you work in a hospital, they'll assume accident and emergency, like on the telly, maybe show you a blister or two. On balance it was best to keep quiet about being a nurse. They all want dramatic stories. They always avoid the question of pay and why you once thought you had some kind of vocation until the whole bureaucratic, form-filling idiocy of the NHS knocks it out of you.

All right; now I dispense pills, rubbers and other forms of birth control and assist in simple abortions. I wish I was still a midwife, really; but you could be a midwife for twenty years and still not be able to buy your own house. You can, if you work in a bank or sell cars. Abortion and the avoidance of pregnancy paid better and that was a fact, which was why a skilled and dedicated midwife worked for a private death clinic. She wondered if she might have been less vulnerable, less a potential victim, if she had been doing what she was good at; if she wasn't somehow defensive about what she did, since a person with such doubts about the nature of their work really did risk a kind of mental illness. Helen West had made her understand something, she said out loud as she walked round the park, namely that in her line of legal business there are no answers, no panaceas, no drugs which cure the problem. Anna had known that already, but she could not accept what he had done to her, even less what he might have done to others. Off his list, from the bowels of his computer and out of his notebooks, he would know exactly whom to choose for these little jokes. Because they, the patients, were like herself. They looked into his eyes and told him all their hopes and fears.

The park was the coolest place to be in the early evening. Not so much a park as a graveyard, sloping uphill away from the thunderous road into a canopy of old trees which left the grass, thin from constant shade, dappled with light. The gravestones were old, sticking up out of the ground round the church like gesturing fingers, the inscriptions long since worn away, making them little more than stumps of anonymous stone. There was no shame to sit up against them with a lunch-time sandwich. Few did; lying supine with a bottle of cider was more likely. It was not the kind of park which provided a landmark; not one of the perfect city parks which tourists in search of significant statuary would come to see. It was merely a green lung, always messy on the surface because of the leaves, slightly dusty because of the traffic; never entirely quiet. An old lags' park, with sinister overtones, a collection of bottles littering the grass each morning. Over the slope, beyond the sunken church, stood the coroner's court, prettily Victorian, and next to it, on more anonymous concrete lines, the mortuary. There were many reasons why the park was not to everyone's taste.

Anna Stirland liked it, from time to time, when it suited and therefore soothed a certain morbid turn of mind, or, in summer, provided such coolness when the streets shone with ill-tempered heat, but she could not see it as a trysting place. Unless you had come to frolic with the dead.

She hefted her shoulder bag, full of food she might or might not cook, but bought as a commitment to ordinary life, and made for the gates, surprised as she always was to notice how the sound of traffic grew so much louder away from the trees. She passed a girl, marching in the opposite direction, walking with an air of pretended purpose, the way a shy woman might walk into a pub to meet someone, not quite sure what to do with herself if he was not there, except stare ahead and around, as if preoccupied. Her face was vaguely familiar, so that Anna was tempted to nod at her. She saw so many youthful faces in the course of her job, she was never quite sure when she recognized a woman or girl, if work had been the context. Simply a girl, strikingly thin, patently anxious. There were times when Anna did not regret the passing of the first apologetic years of youth.

Shelley Pelmore came to a halt within sight of the coroner's court and paused. She felt less self-conscious now there was no one to see her looking around. She stood with her hands on her hips, bag across her chest, long legs ending in heavy shoes, a contrast to her short skirt and loose cropped top, as fashion dictated. She flicked hair out of her eyes and stared at the stained-glass windows of the court. It would always be dark in there, she reckoned, on account of the trees; lights glowed inside, as if it was winter. The building held no fears, nor the concrete block adjacent; Shelley had no idea of the purpose of either and no curiosity. She would never voluntarily have gone for a walk, least of all in a park, but this slightly seedy area held some attraction. Sex alfresco had a great appeal, like doing something forbidden. Shelley Pelmore had never had to resort to sheds or the backs of cars; sex had never been clandestine. It had always been Derek, blessed by her bloody mother and, apart from the initial naughtiness, profoundly disappointing. There had never been anything faintly wicked about it. None of this palpitating tension, this sense of being out on a limb, this dreadful enticing fear. This desperation.

He never smelt of anything and he had the quiet foot-steps of a cat. He could dance, too, this glamorous doctor. Shelley preferred to draw a veil over their first meeting, when she had talked her heart out, spitting out the partic-ulars of her life for his edification, receiving back his sympathetic warmth. And then his hands on her, feeling gently, asking questions with his smooth fingertips, making her laugh, even as she lay with her legs wide apart and the cool instruments probing. An intimate examination was something she had first dreaded, and then dreamt about.

Maybe it was the relief at not being pregnant after all which made her bold. You ever go clubbing, Doc? Come on down and meet me and the girls. He was a little old for her, of course; it would not do to place him anywhere near her friend, the predatory manageress. She must keep him away from her. Shiny brown head under artificial lights, beautiful exciting eyes. But, oh yes, in the end he was too good not to share.

'Hello.'

Behind her without a sound, arms on her shoulders. 'Where have you been?' she hissed.

'Missing you,' he said. 'All the time.' He was propelling her away from the court, towards the church where no one went. She stopped abruptly, thinking it was time to make a stand, to tell him she couldn't go on like this. The world and its expectations were tearing her apart. She dreaded the morning, the afternoon, the evening and this time she really had to do something about the pregnancy, or she would be in prison for the whole of her life. Would he help her, please? Oh God, he owed her that. She turned on him, ready to be shrill, to embarrass him by screaming at him. But he stopped her. He held her head steady with one hand meshed in her hair, his mouth clamped on hers, the other hand briefly inside the loose top, squeezing a nipple, hard, then down beyond the waistband of the skirt, over the still-flat belly inside her knickers, one long finger making her gasp. People would see; with eyes squeezed shut, she could imagine a crowd gathering, watching a man's hand snatch at her bush in broad daylight.

He pushed her gently into the deeper shadow of the church wall. She put both hands against it, feeling the cool stone scratch at her palms. He was behind her now, her buttocks supported against his thighs. Both hands fondled her breasts; then, bracing himself against her, he felt inside her thighs, parted the lips, slid his long fingers in and out, rhythmic and strong. Lovely, lovely cunt, he was murmuring, kissing her neck, feeling her legs slacken until she almost sat in his lap, the skirt round her waist, the G-string panties snapped, her breath ragged, her mouth forming, no, no, no, without making a sound, letting him do what he did. Legs straddled wide, coming round his fist in a writhing spasm and oh, God, no fucking with Derek was ever as safe or as dangerous as this.

She pressed her thighs together, trapping his hand for a moment, then relaxed with a shuddering sigh. It was at times like these, anger forgotten in a strange exhilaration, that she wanted to round on him, do something in return, fumble for the penis she had never felt and never seen, pleasure him somehow if only to even the score of need, or pleasure, or something. Other times, she would go home, practically howling for Derek and a straightforward unimaginative fuck to finish the business. Oh yes, he was safe. No risk of Aids or babies with this man. Safe enough to share with friends.

There was low laughter from him, as if from a man satisfied. She could not understand him, nor did she want to. One of her friends, Becky, hadn't liked whatever he had done, the silly cow. Now he was talking to her, his body shielding her from view while his hands stroked her buttocks, held them apart, kneaded them. In a minute, she would want it again.

'I think it must be gravity,' he murmured. 'Blood rushing to the right place. Something to do with the fact that we might still be meant to go round on all fours.'

She leant back against him.

'Would gravity, or whatever, pull this baby out?'

'No.'

'You said you'd help. I helped you. I don't want it . . . I don't want it and Derek would never let me . . . When will you get it out of me?'

433

'Next week, at the clinic. No hurry.'

He smoothed the skirt over her behind. Her panties were on the floor, she picked them up and stuffed them in her handbag. It always amazed her the way they could walk and talk, like a couple discussing what to have for tea.

'Last time I came to the clinic, you weren't there.'

'Sorry.'

'And you weren't here yesterday.'

'Sorry again.'

'I can't go on like this.'

'I know.'

Fear paralysed her. Fear of not going on like this, with this occasional, insane, sick-feeling excitement.

'I don't quite mean that. Oh, I don't know what I mean.'

She was shaking, hanging onto his arm.

'Next time,' he said, 'I'll make it all all right. Promise. Now you've got to go home.'

Her face hardened. She was not ready yet for a pat on the head and being dismissed.

'Monday?' she said. 'Monday? Talk to me. Talk to me, or I'll talk.'

He held her gently, a soft kiss, like a continental greeting, to each cheek.

'No, you won't. Promise. Anyway, what would you say?'

CHAPTER NINE

'My man', said Helen West, always confused as to whether she should refer to Bailey as her partner, boyfriend, or anything as simple as a lover, 'is in a state of grief and confusion. He mutters in his sleep about treachery and chocolates. And what haunts him, poor soul? Another man. Do I have a problem?'

The nurse laughed. 'Oh dear. And where is it you're getting married. In church?'

'Nope. Register office.'

'Oh. The one in Highgate's very nice.'

'Is it? I only know the one in Finsbury, on account of being married in it once before. I thought he said Finsbury.'

There was something disconcerting about the way she found herself chatting in the surgery, as if she were anxiously ill, instead of guarding against an impending change of status by the superstitious precaution of a medical check-up. Getting the body scanned: heart, cigarette-stained lungs, hearing and sight, just so she would know, within the usual inexact parameters, the state of her health. Ready to present for duty, sound in mind and limb, as if matrimony were a mountaineering expedition. Chronic illness and the wedding was off. The medical practice at the end of the road was small and valiant. Helen could feel herself becoming apologetic as soon as she crossed the portals and heard the sound of coughing. Even this cursory examination made her feel foolish and more than a little exposed; there was a certain, in her case, garrulous, vulnerability in being half dressed, even in such a clinical atmosphere. A feeling of putting the body up for judgement, as if either doctor or nurse was going to add some scathing aesthetic verdict to the general diagnosis. (Thin here, floppy here, and OK, what does this corpse think it's doing getting married at its age?) The most embarrassing thing in the end was how idiotically talkative she became.

Bailey did not only talk in his sleep, these days; he talked when he was awake. Expounding Ryan's idiocies; what little Sally Smythe could tell him about Ryan's theories. Ryan and other forms of gaol bait wandered through his dreams. Her bridegroom.

The marriage had not been discussed. Most of the time, she liked it that way.

Anna Stirland laughed, a great big uproarious laugh which Helen remembered from their first meeting and had not heard since.

'Talk a lot? Patients? Oh, yes, all the time. To be encouraged, if only they weren't apologetic about it. Why else would I do it if I weren't so curious about other people's lives?'

A drink after work, a chat about anything, a little people watching; turning out to be a good idea. 'Yeah,' Anna had said into her phone, not even cautiously enthusiastic. 'Yes, do me good. But one condition, mind.' A deep breath. 'Can we talk about anything other than my . . . attack? Honestly, it's weeks now, I'm much better, got my mind in gear.'

'What are you giving our Rose for a wedding present?'

'Wisdom?' said Helen.

'Not mine to give,' said Anna.

'Not mine, either. Impossible to wrap, anyway. A laundry basket, I thought, with a year's supply of all that boring cleaning crap: Jif, bleach, dusters. Then I thought I'd add in extravagant underwear. Not his and hers, only hers.'

'I thought I'd make them window-boxes. Evergreens, late-blooming things. It'll be autumn when they come back,' Anna mused.

'Rose doesn't look after plants,' Helen remarked, remembering the cause of the last Rose and Michael quarrel.

'No more does anyone, given some boiled root azalea or a drooping palm for the living room. She'll learn. You learnt with your garden.'

'Not really. I fiddle about, talk to it sometimes. Try and stop things throttling one another.'

'That's taking care. Michael will do it.'

'Was he a sweet child?' Helen asked.

'Oh yes, funny little squinty-eyed boy, went round with a bandage and specs, teased to death, then started to grow and grow. I met him out of school once; watched the other lads around him, baiting him, not even noticing how he'd grown. Michael picked one of them up, very gently, mind, lifted him into a rubbish skip and walked away. Never one to overdo revenge. I don't know Rose half as well. Didn't approve at first; love her to death now. I thought she was a gorgeous little slut; ever so glad I kept my mouth shut.'

'Gold dust,' Helen murmured. 'Hope the past doesn't come back to haunt her. Haunts me, and it isn't mine.'

'Should it?' Anna asked curiously. 'Colourful, I knew. but . . .'

'Sexual abuse from a dad who probably murdered her mother – I shouldn't have said that.'

Anna nodded, as if receiving information on the weather forecast. 'What privileged and lucky lives we lead,' she said crisply. 'Will she make a good lawyer?'

'I hope not,' Helen said vehemently. 'I do hope not.' She paused. 'Kills your fire in the end, see? If you believe in it, it makes you cold. All this objectivity. As bad as the form filling. Never being able to do anything well.'

'Like nursing,' Anna said neutrally.

'Even being a midwife? All that new life?'

'Even that,' Anna said, blushing furiously. Somehow, the evening died and they were no longer easy with one another. Anna looked at her watch.

'You've lost weight,' Helen observed.

Anna smiled, shrugged.

'Decided not to sell my house after all. I've worked hard enough for it. Besides, people want me to be better, so I thought I'd oblige them. Oh, it was all a silly episode,' said Anna, forgetting her own request not to mention it. 'Some throwback from his team sporting days, best forgotten.'

★

438

Ryan found the park again at about nine in the morning. No car, this time. The suburban train spat him out with the early commuters; he walked from that station to Euston. The air was as fresh as it could be in King's Cross; the park was sanitized by darkness and dew, the scrubby grass discernibly greener than in the afternoon. A man swept leaves, twigs and papers from the paths, moving with deliberate sloth, extending the task, enjoying it. The same old lag was sprawled on the same bench in a patch of sun. On a morning like this, the life of a drunken vagrant could seem almost romantic. Ryan trod by softly, noting, as before, the premature age of an old face with younger limbs.

The door to the coroner's court stood open. Ryan leant against the outside wall next to it and stared up at the gasometers. If you built these now, he thought, great circular edifices of metal, the size of large buildings, composed of naked girders, some fool would call it modern art. They looked like a skeletal casing for a bomb; they invited a daredevil to climb up there and feel the breeze. They were monstrous, crouching like guardians, dominating the view, and yet he liked them; because they had always been there. Ryan straightened his tie. Wearing a suit after nothing but gardening clothes for the last days felt like placing himself in a straitjacket, but if he had not worn this uniform, which he did with an element of pleasure, he would deny himself the credibility he needed in the absence of a warrant card. No one would demand to see it, or be aware just yet of its confiscation. He had never been a regular visitor to either the mortuary or the court or unexpected death, but the officers in the back room had seen his face once or twice before; so had the pathologist of the day. No one would question his status.

Inside the foyer, there was a desultory collection of relatives, assembled sombrely to hear witnesses repeat the facts leading to the death of Aunt Mary or brother John, then listen to the coroner's verdict. Death by misadventure; one kind of accident to which the deceased may well have contributed himself, common for a drug overdose. Suicide, which needed proof beyond reasonable doubt; accidental, which meant what it said, and, most rarely of all, rarer than anyone supposed, unlawful killing. The bereavement of these relatives was already old news: they were not in the first stage of grief, merely anxious, looking a trifle lost, waiting for someone to explain procedure, concerned to do the right thing. Ryan was not the only one wearing a suit, with the difference that at least one of theirs bore signs of moth.

The courtroom itself resembled a church with pews for seats plus the usual paraphernalia of judge's bench and witness stand. The sun glinted through the coloured windows, insufficient to illuminate an attractive restful gloom to the extent of making it possible to read small print. It was a place unconsciously designed to discourage hysteria; he found it difficult to imagine the staff even celebrating Christmas. Then he heard a shout of laughter from the office behind.

'DS Ryan. Dr Webb here yet? She promised me a word.' He introduced himself easily, nevertheless relieved to find his presence accepted. The pathologist occupied a desk, perched on it with the air of a regular visitor; she smiled sweetly.

'Oh, you again, Mr Ryan, with your awkward questions. What do you want this time?'

He felt as if he should be holding a hat in his hand, nervously turning the brim, like someone asking a favour from a duchess. Dr Webb was large, loud, extremely attractive and saw no reason why corpses, diseases and the inevitable fact of death should ever be discussed *sotto voce*, since she herself was congenitally incapable of whispering.

'A rehash of what we were discussing last time,' he said humbly. 'I seem to have lost my notes.'

She wagged her finger at him. 'Policemen should not be writing theses,' she said. 'And why should I mind repeating myself. Where were we?'

'I began', Ryan said, lowering his voice, 'by asking you if it was possible to kill a healthy young woman, leaving no traces, by the simple measure of inserting ice up her vagina. Could the shock of that cause a spontaneous heart attack?'

'And I,' she said impatiently, 'said no. Not unless she had a weak heart. I told you it would not otherwise be a question of the temperature of the instrument . . . not unless it was so cold it burnt the skin. It would be more a question of the length. A long icicle, maybe? Where would he get such a thing? No. He might cause an undetectable death, even without injury, if his instrument probed too far, against resistance – death by shock – women died this way in backstreet abortions. The cervix does not like interference. People have strange ways of having fun. Not an icicle; maybe a syringe.' In defiance of the prohibitory sign and any intimations of mortality, she lit a cigarette.

'What I wanted to know,' Ryan asked, 'is is there a technique a man could perfect?'

441

She considered and shook her handsome head.

'What technique? Technique for homicide, you mean? What a strange man he would be. Like an abortionist, he could perfect avoiding it, but not perfect the doing of it, I think. Your sexual murderer is more likely to be obvious. He does not have much control. He strangles, he bites, he stabs.' Hand and mouth, she gestured, biting, chopping.

There was a polite coughing from the far end of the room, where two of the coroner's officers sat with paper-work and phones, one looking at Ryan quizzically, trying to remember something, something he might have heard, perhaps. It reminded Ryan how much Dr Webb's voice carried; he remembered the waiting relatives, almost within earshot. Remembered also, his first protective chauvinistic impression, that a woman as beautiful as this should not speak so loud.

'Pleasant, outside,' he suggested. 'Shall we?'

She was, as always, obliging, and trailed her cigarette smoke into the warm outdoors. She sauntered into the park, stubbed out the fag end on a gravestone, sighed and looked at her watch.

'Pre-mortuary precaution,' she said, wiping her hands on her skirt. 'Takes away the smell. What next?'

'Another method of a man causing the death of a woman, in a sexual encounter, without leaving traces,' he began, pleased that he no longer needed to whisper. Her brow wrinkled.

'Ah yes. A similar thing. Death by blow-job. Shows there can be more things wrong with oral sex than just the view!' She roared with laughter. Ryan stood woodenly, looking at the grass, pressing down a ring-pull from a can into the earth. He noticed, with a sudden flush of horror, that he was wearing training shoes beneath his pressed suit trousers. He looked up again. No doubt the pathologist would cut off his feet for him if he asked her nicely.

'The vagina is full of delicate little blood-vessels. Vulnerable in pregnant ladies. The man doesn't do the normal: he actually blows into it. A bubble of air can enter one of the blood-vessels, travel round the system, get to the heart and poof! An embolism. You need ten cc. I told you. It's a bit like having an airlock in the central-heating system. She dies. No signs for me. Cardiac respiratory arrest.'

'I remember,' said Ryan, 'but could he be exact?'

'You ask for certainty, you can't have it; not in anything. More likely if you practise, but never certain. With a syringe full of air, more so. Oh, and only pregnant ladies, especially with vaginal verrucas.'

'How long would it take to die?'

'Oh, rapid. I must go. Is that enough?'

'Thank you. You've been very kind.'

'Good luck with your thesis. Don't come back soon.'

Another posse of relatives were huddled outside the entrance in order to smoke. They were a picture of controlled misery; Ryan guessed at the death of a child. He saw the officer who had coughed standing on the doorstep, looking over their heads, staring after him. No, he would not come back soon. Ryan turned and walked purposefully down the hill, wrenching off his tie, cursing his shoes. In this park he felt as if he was treading on skulls, one of them his own, and the shoes were simply a symptom of how far he had sunk and how much further he could go.

There was a man out there he had begun to hate long since. So nebulous a presence, the pursuit of him was similar to chasing a will-o'-the-wisp, a foggy London phantom, the discussion of whom would make him disappear into thin air. Unlike his own wife, who would stand by him until prison walls created the last barrier, and then, for the sake of the survivors, she would go.

The old young man slept, turned on his side to get the sun on his back. Ryan shoved his packet of cigarettes into a rancid armpit.

'Keep that bench warm for me,' he said.

'Look, Aunty Helen, when you and that old cadaver of yours get married, you will let me know, won't you? So I can come along and laugh? I don't know why the hell you're so neurotic about it.'

'I've told you as much as I can to explain it. And I'll tell you afterwards. But, frankly, can you see any point in asking you to grace the serious business of middle-aged nuptials with unseemly conduct? No, girl, get stuffed. This was always going to be a private arrangement, very short notice or I'd die of embarrassment, and don't ask why. Besides, Bailey can't ask Ryan—'

'I should think not!' Rose stormed. 'He's a fucking rapist!'

'—Overstatement and anyway, it seems to follow I can't ask my self-appointed, pain-in-the neck of a niece. There'll be a party, later, so you can offer felicitations and congratulations as appropriate, once the pair of us get used to the idea. If we ever do.'

'I don't understand you,' Rose stated.

Helen beamed at her.

'Good. If I were you, I'd avoid understanding. Tell me, is the man behaving well? Less of the nervous disorders?'

Rose considered.

'Most of the time, as good as can be expected, thank you, ma'am. Not always better, hardly exquisite in his manners, but not half bad, thanks. His lordship may still get the vapours when I let his botanical specimens die and when I spend joint money on going to an expensive clinic instead of allowing an ordinary doctor to get impertinent with me in the interests of birth control, but otherwise his health is excellent. How kind of you to enquire.'

'Is missy going to persist in this speech on account of watching a video of *Pride and Prejudice,* or can we get down to work?'

'Oh, did you see Anna?'

'Yes. Yesterday. She's going to make you window-boxes. You'd better look after them.'

'I'll use the bedroom one as a place to keep my cap. I'll plant it, instead of pinging it into the street, and grow little caplets . . .'

'Work, Rose.'

'OK, OK, but listen. You know I told you about the accident with the sodding cap? Well, it never came back, you know. I had to go to the clinic and get another one, didn't I? But the good thing was, it made Anna laugh. Laugh? I thought she'd split her sides . . .'

'Anna?' Helen queried.

'At the clinic. Where she works. Why else would I go to a place like that?'

'I thought she was a midwife.'

'Naa, not any more. More money in this.'

Only a little lie, Helen thought; only a small one. The sort of lie she always feared a witness would announce under oath; some little piece of secrecy or vanity which rendered everything else they said faintly suspicious, however true it was. She hefted the file off the floor and onto the desk.

'Work, Rose.'

'Fuck me. I forgot.'

'This one for trial. Read it, see if you agree. I've drafted the charge, you annotate the pages; six copies of each. Statements in order, so they tell the story in sequence. Code at the top for stuff which defence and prosecution might agree as purely scientific . . . away you go.'

Rose, astride the boxes in Helen's office, looked up, bullish and sulky.

'Look, I've read it. Cover to cover, honest. And I don't agree.'

Helen sat back. Examined her nails, thought of Bailey as Mr Darcy and thought, yes, there was quite a resemblance, not least in the fact that each had weaker friends.

'For God's sake, why?' she asked innocently.

Rose took a deep breath, as if about to sing solo and nervous with it. Helen's mind wandered; she reminded herself to ask some other time about this clinic Rose had mentioned.

'Because if you read her statement, it's perfect,' Rose blurted. 'Too perfect. The defendant's her ex-boyfriend, right? Can't stand the thought that she's left him for someone else, right? He gets lonely one night, comes round and

446

knocks. She says she's afraid of his violence, which is why she got rid of him in the first place, but she lets him in. All lovely. How are you? Just come round to ask, and how are you too? Have a beer, she says. Sit and watch this video with me, she says. Nice to see you after six months, she says. Where's that coffee?'

'On your left.'

Rose grasped the handle of a half-full mug, used it to weight the hand making gestures.

'Then he jumps on her. *He* says, she likes it; been giving him the come on for the last hour, *he* says. Wearing a short skirt and not exactly putting a blanket over herself, he says. While she says, look, the whole thing came out of the blue. Why would she ever want to screw this sod when the kid's asleep and her new man's expected home any time? Well, I reckon this old boyfriend used to beat her like she said; he comes on strong like she said; she struggled a bit and then decided to keep the peace. What's once more for old time's sake, eh? Look, I think she's telling the absolute truth; she weighed up rape against a broken nose and settled for rape. And I know there's bruises on her arms, which he says were there before, because the new chap isn't so gentle either; not a scratch on him, though. But put that in front of a jury?'

Coffee dribbled onto the floor; Rose ignored it.

'They're going to say, why didn't she slam the door as soon as she saw him if he was so bad? Why didn't she yell for help? By the time the defence has finished, no one'll remember how that's actually a difficult thing to do. They won't think like she would think: once more to stop him hitting me, and I won't shout because of the kid in the next

447

room. She'd do it, and he'd be able to say either she consented, or he'd every reason to suppose she did.'

'She could have slammed the door.'

'You don't; she didn't, but no witnesses. Balance of proof. Reasonable doubt. And you aren't going to get a six-year-old to testify about mummy's distress, are you? Not even you. As for the neighbours, they won't.'

Helen was out of her swivel chair, examining, through their own dirty windows, the administrative staff of the paint manufacturing company across the road. They had revamped their mottled grey walls to make them greyer still; the people merged with the décor in efficient silence. All busy about some executive decision. Life-threatening colour shades. She waved to no response.

'All right, Rose,' she said briskly. 'If that's what you think, we'll bin it.'

'What?'

'The rape.'

Rose looked horrified. 'It might work,' she stuttered. 'I didn't mean . . . It might . . . work.'

'A phrase not known in legal Latin. D'you want to argue this point past Redwood's budget? You said it. If you can see a reasonable doubt before you've even heard the arguments, what the hell will a jury see?' Rose was silent. Then she got up, opened the flap of a window, and made to heave the file out. Helen stopped her.

'No good either. You want this woman's life all over the street?'

'You made me say it,' Rose raged. 'You made me act God! You made me say we should turn it down, even when we think it's true. Sometimes you're a bitch, Aunty H.'

'Wish I was,' Helen mourned. 'I really wish I was. But we can't run cases we know we're going to lose. Truth is luxury. And I don't like playing God, either.'

The apartment block was a strange building; once a school or institution, Bailey guessed, converted into flats of an unusual size with large modern windows, so that the façade stuck out like a sore thumb in a terrace of smaller, less-gaunt dwellings which had all succumbed to historically conscientious planning regulations while this building had escaped. It sat on the corner of two roads, defiantly marking the boundary between one kind of territory and another. Before it lay the metropolis, behind it the leafier squares of Barnsbury's genteel streets. You lived here for the view, perhaps for a feeling of power.

There were benefits to the flexible routine of a rota, Bailey knew. He had always managed to evade any kind of job which imposed too much of a regime, except that dictated by emergency. His creative evasions were becoming more difficult to achieve in an age where the formulae of accountability took more time than the work itself, but still, he managed. Provided he did excessive hours and obfuscated, he could still function in accordance with his own clock, leaving time for eccentric assignments like these: checking up on Ryan's theories, following up Sally Smythe's kindred fantasies about the no-hopers. Beginning with the most recent.

He had phoned in advance and met with truculence, smoothed by Bailey's natural diplomacy until Aemon Connor's rudeness diminished into a grudging growl. Sure, the policeman could come round and waste his time;

waste his wife's time, too, for that matter, but not much of it. Ten minutes. There's little enough to say. She never did make a great deal of sense, he added.

There was a hotel-like carpet of more pretension than taste in the lobby and a tiny lift before Bailey reached the Connors' door. One myth, promulgated by the reports, was immediately exploded, namely that of a twenty-four-hour porter, sober or available at any given time.

Mr Connor was a man to whom anger was more than second nature; it was a state of being, only absorbed by frenetic activity, a constant position at the top of some heap, and the sense of achievement which came from physical exhaustion. Perhaps he was a cuddly bear when his children were around, but Bailey doubted it. Two teenage girls, he'd read, away for the summer, and, feeling the unnatural heat inside this high apartment, Bailey thought they were well out of it. There was no sign of the wife.

'In the bath,' Aemon said briefly. He looked at Bailey's outstretched hand, wondering whether to ignore it, but since the man was smiling, he took it. Bailey wondered if a palm so calloused could actually feel the difference between a firm handshake and a loose one, but refrained from asking. Something about the quality of his own hand seemed to mollify.

'It was you I came to see, sir,' Bailey said. 'A chat, before bothering the little woman.'

'She talks rubbish,' Aemon muttered. 'Always did.'

'They often do, women, don't they, sir?' Bailey sighed in sympathy. 'Oh, I am sorry. Not the right thing to say, is it? I don't mean any disrespect.'

450

'You've got it in one, boy.'

A slight warming of the atmosphere was established by mutual head-shaking sadness, like a couple of men contemplating the keeping of a pair of iguanas acquired by accident and without adequate instruction. Bailey did not feel in the least guilty.

'And I thought the whole thing was closed,' Connor muttered. He had half a mind to offer the visitor a drink. Not such a bad sort of man, for a copper, and besides, he wanted one himself. Late afternoon, work going downhill, hot as all hell, with scarcely an evening made in heaven stretching away in front of him; a drink seemed a good idea. Just a large one.

'So it is closed,' Bailey said. 'But you see, sir, there's an aspect of the sorry business which might, just might, impinge on another inquiry, quite separate. Now, it seemed like your wife was fantasizing about a caller in the afternoon when you came home to find her in the bath . . .'

'I often do. She lives in there.'

'Yes, sure, but not usually for so long? That afternoon, when you had to send for the doctor. Look, we know, of course, there's nothing in this rape allegation against yourself; monstrous, of course, but I'm working on the possibility she did have a caller. One who frightened her maybe. Shocked her, made her hysterical.'

Aemon was listening.

'I can't think who she'd let in. Parish women. The priest, she loves the priest, for all he's a stern fellow to everyone but the undeserving poor.'

'Salesman?' Bailey suggested. 'Electrician? Plumber? Delivery man? Doctor?' he added as an afterthought.

Aemon shook his head. He was suddenly furiously defensive.

'A doctor? Why the hell would she let in a doctor? There's nothing wrong with her, is there?'

'Well,' said Bailey, looking at the clenched fists and wondering why the mention of a doctor tending his wife should touch so raw a nerve, 'perhaps nothing obvious. Perhaps she was feeling ill?'

Aemon snorted. 'Often says so, never is. Like a horse, she is.'

And, like an award-winning actress, faded, but never beyond a cue, the subject of their discussion wafted into the room. White towelling robe, an overpowering odour of roses, hair wrapped in a turban. Gloria Swanson, Bailey thought; Marlene Dietrich with a softer washed-out face and a bigger bosom. Never a Jamie Lee Curtis.

'Did you call a doctor the other day, Brigid?' Aemon asked pleasantly, with only a hint of impatience. 'You know, the day when we all went on our pleasant little outing to the police station,' he added bitterly.

She flinched, shook her head and smiled brilliantly.

'We've our own doctor,' Aemon explained. 'Sound fellow, sixty-four last birthday. Couldn't scare a cat.'

'Have you ever been to see any other doctor, Mrs Connor?' Bailey asked her. She shook her head vehemently and spoke quickly in a childish voice.

'Oh, no, I wouldn't do that.' Her face flushed scarlet. Her husband had poured her a large gin.

'Ice?' he barked.

'Oh, yes. A lot.'

The ice bucket was divinely old-fashioned, Bailey

452

noticed; almost enough in itself to turn any ordinary drink into a cocktail. Aemon downed his drink in one without, in the end, offering anything to Bailey; it put him into a vastly improved frame of mind.

'Another doctor?' he chortled, stuck on the doctor theme. 'You'll be accusing her of going on the pill next. She'd never do that. Not when we still have time for a son. Another doctor! Perish the thought! She won't even take her clothes off for me!'

Bailey, to his own shame, joined in with Aemon's laughter; let it travel over his face, make his body move while he tried at the same time to catch Mrs Connor's eye.

'I only ask,' he explained, 'because we seem to have a man in this area masquerading as an innocent visitor. Possibly even a delivery man, sometimes, bringing in flowers and chocolates. He's bothered a couple of other women, that's all, got them upset.'

Aemon was thoughtful. 'You mean she needn't have been lying? She wasn't the only one being scared like that?'

'I wouldn't have thought lying was in her nature, Mr Connor.'

'Well, that's a relief. I hope you get the bastard.'

Aemon's eyes had strayed first to his watch and then to his wife.

Bailey saw her face, flushed and expressionless, as she passed an ornate mirror on her way to the window. A breeze moved the crystals of the chandelier making small clinking sounds. Mrs Connor leant against the window-frame looking downwards, intently, as if waiting for someone.

He saw scuffs on the glass, marks and streaks at odds with this daily-cleaned house.

She must have spent more time at the window today than she had in the bath.

God forbid he should be so happily married.

Ryan's blue folder. Two of them mentioning a doctor. Laughing it off.

Chapter Ten

'If, with intent to commit an offence . . . a person does an act which is more than merely preparatory to the commission of the offence, he is guilty of attempting to commit the offence.

'A person may be guilty of attempting to commit an offence (to which this section applies) even though the facts are such that the commission of the offence is impossible.'

Derek could remember their words, Mum and Dad and all the rest, but most of all he could remember the sharp intakes of breath he could hear when fellow men clapped eyes on Shelley.

She's a cow, Derek. Everyone's told you she's a cow. Pardon my French, said his sister. Let me tell *you* something, he would say, she's a lovely gel, just needs a decent bloke. She's done well, Shelley. Oh yeah, sure, she likes a good time, but she works hard.

He had recited this chapter and verse until it almost rhymed in his head, always singling out from the memory bank those times when Shell was really astoundingly pleased to see him. Times on which his devotion was more rewarded by her ten-minute enthusiasm than a starving pet with late-delivered food and everything forgiven. It was enough to nourish his dogged determination to keep by his side a bird as gorgeous and sometimes wanton as this. She could be a pain to live with, but they'd settled down, and oh, how his mates had envied him at first, whatever they said later. He could feel other men's envy like balm on the skin, massaging his fragile pride while they reappraised him.

'What you looking at, Shell?'

'Nothing,' she'd say, from her standpoint by the window, looking like a prisoner who would have knotted her bedsheets together in order to abseil out quicker than she could walk to the big front door. It was not such an imposing front door, either, simply double glazed and ugly, steel-framed, paintwork with condensation stains, and a notice politely requesting that it should be closed quietly. Most of the other residents favoured security. Senior citizens, Derek said politely, content to accede to their requests for errands and the mending of kettles. Past their sell-by date, said Shelley, with contempt.

And he was slowly, very slowly, discovering that his lady love, his dearest, his chosen partner in life, was a girl to whom kindness was not second nature, a bit of a bitch, in fact. Derek had resisted any such conclusion, squirrelled it away into the realm of non-being, just as he hid from her his ongoing terror of her infidelity. He dampened his exclusive passion for this elegant sulky creature into round-the-clock good-natured solicitude which he couldn't stop even when he knew it got on her nerves. Nothing was comparable to the fear that she might leave. Not only leave, but go elsewhere.

'You're always looking out of that window, you,' he teased. 'Anyone would think you liked the view.'

She yawned in reply. 'Think I'll go round and see Kath,' she said.

'I thought you weren't speaking to Kath.'

'Well, I'll try. There's nothing good on the telly.'

Of course she was going round to Kath's while he went out for the evening shift. Like hell she was. She had all the nervous excitement and the faked yawns of a girl who was revelling in the idea of a cosy chat with a female pal and the pal's mother over a kitchen table. She was positively twitching at the prospect of drinking cocoa.

'I think you ought to stay in,' he suggested. 'Get an early night.'

'Well, I might do that,' she said perkily.

His anger was always slow to build, easily hidden, only riled by lies. He knew what he was going to do and hated himself for doing it. He kissed her goodbye, went down-stairs noisily and ignored the prohibition against slamming the door. Then he sat in the covered bus stop on the other side of the road and waited. Derek did not bother to crouch, disguise his presence, or wonder if she might see him. He knew she would fly out of the block without look-ing left or right, all memory of him eradicated with the application of her lipstick. He could imagine the possible destinations, too: The Wheatsheaf, The Crown, the wine bar by the canal. They were less glamorous than the second-rate West End clubs she really favoured, but still places where a girl could perch and get a drink or five for nothing and look around. The way she did on the rare occasions they were out together; she'd rather look at the

457

wall than at him. But then in bed, later, it was another matter. Exquisite pains and pleasures from a sometime hoyden, sometime thumb-sucking youngster, sweetly demanding before the tyranny of sulks. Only a child.

There she went, like an arrow, long legs gorgeous in the late evening sun, and all at once the anger went in a sudden flush of longing for her, compounded by shame that he should sink so low as to follow her. No, he told himself; go for a walk, have a drink, calm down and then go home; have a showdown later. The conclusion that she was an incorrigible and convincing liar had been a long time coming. In fact, it might never have arrived with such finality in his slow but precise mind if he had not seen her, watched her with incredulous attention, when he had followed her the night before; seen her in the amusement arcade opposite the station, talking with gestures to that man, Ryan. The one who had been round their flat a long time ago. The one who was supposed to have raped her, reduced her to that humbled and whimpering state of need in which Derek had so delighted. He did not understand.

He had no head for drink, but he tried. He came from the same kind of stock as Shelley's mum and dad, less contemptuous of flesh, equally suspicious of drink, suspicious of a good time . . . Never take your eye off the ball, lad, or someone will have your job; ask about the pension plan when you apply at seventeen; life is for building a wall against the kind of poverty which killed your granny. Of course he had to sort this out with Shelley; you don't let go of anything you have. Not your bricks and mortar and not your woman. Especially if she was pregnant with your child, even if she thought that was her own secret. Ah, yes,

458

he knew. And she didn't know that he had guessed about what she had done the last time. For all her cunning, she was lazy about the details, as careless with the receipt from that clinic as she was with the receipts for the clothes she hid, as if he had not built every hiding-place. The echoes of this contempt, as well as the drink, made him maudlin for himself and the lost child; more for himself, he had to admit. Even in the pub, he wept a little over his second pint and almost enjoyed the sensation. An older man came and sat next to him, one of the regulars Derek usually crossed the street to avoid, although at this juncture in the evening, when he should have been at work, when he should have been a man, not a wimp, he found he did not much mind.

'You all right, old son?' It was said in a sedulous whisper, with all the solicitous secrecy of the confessional. Derek noted with rare observation that the face, younger on close inspection, was lit with concern. Derek rallied slightly, bought the drinks the occasion demanded, confirmed that, yes, he was fine thank you and they chatted about the weather in the time-honoured fashion of strangers keeping company, until Derek could no longer stand the smell of summer sweat which was days, if not weeks old, nor tolerate the sight of dirt-stained hands with brown claw-like nails, trembling round a glass. One and a half hours killed; he left with pleasant farewells to find the world darkening beyond the doors. The traffic was lighter, the air pleasant on his forehead, and the scent of diesel fumes almost a relief.

Then he waited indoors, half watching a long film, sipping the brandy kept for special occasions. Sipping, dozing until hunger woke him as the credits rolled and he could not remember what it had all been about. Only that it was one in the morning and Shelley was not home. He blundered around, found Kath's number and phoned. Grumpy response. No, why should she be here? Let me sleep. Who were her friends, then? Real friends? Few enough. Giggly girls who did not last: none that he could count; none who lasted long. The thought chilled him. He was, really, all she had.

That was it; she was stuck somewhere and, oh Jesus Christ, that man Ryan trying to buy her off or something; she would always listen to a man and she was always worried about money. We've got all we need, Derek could hear himself saying, and her saying, all we need for what? He was cold and stiff and shrugging into a jacket, banging that damned outside door behind him before he was quite fully awake, panic rising like sap, full of renewed love. Silly cow! Why didn't she tell me? There was the echoing voice of a mate, saying, she don't tell you fuck all, that's for sure, not a woman like that. Ho ho ho. Fancy a dull boy like you thinking a bird like that would ever confide in your shell-like . . .

He was walking by now, shuffling at first and then, as became a man with a purpose, striding like someone with a preordained sense of direction, although one he made up as he went along. First The Wheatsheaf, eight minutes' walk, faintly surprised to find it shut and barred. There was the feeling that they should open to his knock, purely on account of the fact that he was now wide awake, but he did not rap on the windows because he could see that even the manager had gone. He strode up Goods Way, silent in

460

a misty heat, down past the ever-so-twee Essex-type yuppies bar above the fetid canal; slowing down now, realizing that his stride had no purpose and all but the juggernauts were well asleep. There was a train rumbling by in his dreams. The whole of this vibrating area had settled into a kind of brightly lit somnolence; nothing here much, and such as there was, on the way to somewhere else. The work overalls he had worn all evening made him hot. She would not be out at a time like this; she would be home by now.

Home. The shortest way was through the park, from the top end to the bottom, from the road below the gasometers, downhill to the road home. Gates locked, didn't matter, over the top next to a building with lights on inside; he didn't know why it existed and did not care, because he only remained in this district on his way out of it, like the long-distance lorries, with Shelley. Difficult to explain to his parents, less difficult for hers to understand his longing for a clean modern cul-de-sac. Not like this, a place which could not change, where he was ten a penny and the noise never stopped. The park had seemed larger when he was a child; once upon a time, he could have reached it without risking death by automobile. The dangers posed by humanity in here after dark were surely no worse than those encountered *en route*.

Quiet though; too quiet for Derek's urban soul, untuned even to relative silence. Silent and deserted, until he saw him: the man from the pub, bent over a gravestone, looking as if he was taking swimming lessons on a float; arms and legs waving in unco-ordinated movements, thrashing at air rather than water. As Derek looked, he

461

slipped down the side of the stone and lay belly up, humming at the still branches above his head. As Derek listened, the humming changed to words in a musical singsong.

Derek went across to him, drawn by the antics and the sound. As he got closer, he could hear the words, Oh dear, oh dear, repeated rhythmically. Oh dear, oh dear, oh *dear*, oh dear, oh dear, oh dear . . . For some reason, it made Derek smile, so reminiscent was it of a puzzled child, and so stupidly innocent the man's spread-eagled pose, waiting for a kick or a command to get up. Derek remembered the empathy at the beginning of the evening. Never mind that the sentiment had been drunken, it had still helped, for a minute. The man looked up at Derek, smiled sweetly. Derek's curiosity was diminished by the smell, it was worse here against the comparative freshness of the grass.

'Swimming lessons,' the man said and laughed. 'Every night, my swimming lessons.' Then he stopped abruptly, struggled into a sitting position. 'Oh dear,' he repeated warily, as if remembering something. 'Have you come to find her, then?'

'Find who, old man?'

'Her, of course.'

He pointed in the direction of the church porch. A sudden light breeze shuffled the leaves in the canopy of branches. The glow from the street lights prevented total darkness. Derek felt his heart contract. The man had begun to shuffle away from him, crab-like, sensing a change of mood. Derek walked uphill again, slowly but certainly.

Shelley lay in a pose which aped that of the vagrant,

only more elegantly because she was incapable of adopting an ugly pose. Her legs were obscenely wide apart, one arm outflung, the other bent across her face, as if to shield it from the dim glow of the single light attached to the church wall. She could have been basking in the sun; she could, more like, have been lying in the way she lay at home in her own bed, after sex, guarding her discontented face from the prospect of the morning. Derek fancied he could smell sex as he squatted beside her peaceful form, catching the scent of perfume, betrayal, the rank odour of what she was: an alley cat. He moved the arm from across her face. Her eyes were open.

'Help me,' she seemed to whisper. 'Help me.'

He imagined these words, made them up later, the way he so often imagined Shelley pleading; but no help, not this time. Oh no, not this time. Never again was he going to believe in his little girl lost. There was nothing helpless about her; she was out in a filthy park, in the company of winos and that was what she had chosen. Her clothes were undisturbed; she was stretching, languorously, as though remembering the last man who had fucked her. Round her neck was a gauzy silk scarf; he felt it, recognizing none of the colours in this light, but knowing by the soft and buttery touch that it was expensive; not anything he would have given; not an item she was wearing when she had run from home as soon as his back was turned. The rage, held at bay by anxiety, returned in full force. He wanted to seize her head in both hands and bang it against the ground until it became indistinguishable from the grass; he wanted to fill her mouth with soil. Instead, he took the ends of the scarf which was twisted round her neck and pulled. Her head jerked; he pulled again. She made no attempt to resist, and, in that second, the rage died. A second or two, then he was loosening the scarf, slapping her gently on one cheek, then the other, saying, 'Come on, Shell, get a grip, come on girl.' Maybe she was drunk as well.

He got behind her, muttering encouragement, pushed her up so that she sat like a rag doll, supported by his weight.

'Put your head between your knees, Shell,' he urged.

There was no sound from her, not a single grunt of protest, not a breath. The trees had become silent again, accusing; making him realize she was dead.

He laid her back exactly as he had found her, even curving the arm back over her face. Although he had begun to tremble violently, there was precision in his movements and a certain fussiness in the way he wiped himself down. A trail of saliva ran from her mouth. Derek backed away, stumbled and finally tore his eyes from her face. The anger resurfaced, blinding. After all this time, you bitch, and you do this to me; well, I'm not going to prison for you, Shell, I'm not, I'm not, I'm not.

On the way out of the park, he looked for the tramp. The man was sound asleep, exhausted by swimming lessons, lying curled up by the same gravestone, snoring with his thumb in his mouth. Could she have been with him? No, the thought was clearly out of the equation; whoever it was had more power than that and she hated the smell of stale sweat. Somehow the thought of that filthy digit, stuck in the man's mouth with a tongue wrapped round it revolted Derek more than anything else.

★

464

When, in the sweet light of dawn, he reported his girl-friend missing, his complaint was met with indifference. Girls go missing all the time; what's a late night stop out between friends? Can't go into every case where a sweet-heart fails to phone home. When he explained that Ms Pelmore was a witness in a case against DS Ryan, who had been bothering her recently, the interest increased consid-erably, but he was still told to wait and see. Some hours later, well into the afternoon and after Shelley Pelmore had been found, conveniently placed for the mortuary, and the glad tidings had been announced on local radio, Todd was also informed that he had lost a major witness. But it was still late at night before anyone called at Ryan's door. Out of the ten-year-old mouth of his favourite babe came the lisping truth, before Mrs Ryan flung herself between the child and the enemy. No, Daddy was not in. He'd been out all last night, too. Silly Daddy, he was supposed to be dig-ging them a pond.

Sally Smythe went to the Rape House at eight in the morn-ing, scarcely refreshed by a day off in which she had resolutely refused to clean her own house. She resented the fact that, apart from anything else, the duties of dust-ing and checking supplies seemed to fall to her in the Rape House, these days, or maybe she had simply assumed them in the absence of Ryan, whose domesticity, fussiness, even, was surprising, especially since he confessed to being the opposite at home.

It was one of the things she liked about him, the fact that he did not wait for anyone else to wield the hoover, plump the cushions or make the bloody tea.

The key slipped into the lock with suspicious ease, the front door yielding without any of the customary shoving. Although two of the team were expected shortly with a woman found in the public lavs at St Pancras, claiming indecent assault, to her knowledge, no one had been here for two days. Which was why she was early to air the place; but the familiar smell of summer stuffiness was notable by its absence. Sally stood in the hall with the door closed behind her and listened to the silence. Her footsteps on the dun-coloured carpet of the stairs sounded unfamiliar.

There was a bed slightly disturbed and remade; the immersion-heated water was still warm from recent heating; the bathroom looked as if someone had been busy enough to wipe every surface, leaving a residue of cleanser. None of the cleaners they used on an intermittent basis was ever so thorough. The only sign of neglect was the used tea bags in the kitchen bin. Someone had been here. The place retained the residual warmth of a body. Sally thought of Goldilocks and the three bears. Whoever it was had rearranged the packets of cereal which, along with the packets of soup, was all the sustenance there was.

A couple of the lads from the nick taking refuge after a late night out? She knew there were several duplicates of an easily available, easily copied Yale key. The subject had been discussed when they first got the place and some bright young spark had dossed down here; a repeat performance was forbidden on pain of death. Victims deserved an environment free of stale male germs and beer breath; the Rape House was not a billet for someone who

466

found himself incapable of driving. And, in any event, Sally did not imagine that any hungover intruders would have been able to cover their tracks so precisely. This trespasser had gone in for overkill: the place was cleaner now than when he found it.

Ryan, she guessed; and even as she tried to shove that thought aside, it became so much a certainty, she almost expected to see a calling card propped by the fridge with apologies for depleting the supply of long-life milk. Why Ryan, she argued? Because the body concerned had oiled the lock and conducted a sort of loving maintenance as he went along; perhaps he had nothing better to do. He had always had a kind of affection for the place which Sally did not share; kept talking about wanting flowers in the backyard.

But even so, this behaviour was a kind of critical disrespect. How dare he? He was either taking her for a fool to assume she would not notice, or he was putting her at risk by assuming she would say nothing. It was an abuse of affectionate loyalty, whichever way she looked at it, as well as an abuse of the purpose of this house. Angrily, she threw up the blinds.

The phone rang. 'Coming round soon, Sal, OK? No one in a good mood, though. There's a hue and cry out for our Ryan, would you believe. Shelley Pelmore's dead, and he's jumped bail.' Sally stood with her back exposed to the window, gazing intently at the details of the bland river scene on the wall. She could have said something then; she could have put down the phone and got Bailey or Todd or whoever. Instead, she thought of Ryan, running, thought of him with profound sorrow and said, 'Well

467

there's a turn-up for the books. Oh, by the way, the front door's finally buggered, I had a devil of a job getting in, I'll get someone to change the lock this morning, OK?'

Bailey was changing his mind even before getting dressed. This jacket or this shirt? As if anything would make a difference to the weather. It was unlike him to be so indecisive, or rise sooner than he need, or to be so fussy about clothes. Helen never quite knew how it was that Bailey's suits and shirts marshalled themselves into neat ranks inside the hanging space he had built to include an ironing-board flicked up by hand so that a shirt could almost iron itself unaided. Her own wardrobe was a jungle; the choice of clothes made largely on the random basis of which were nearest and which were clean. Rose said clothes hung themselves free of creases automatically on a figure like Helen's and it was just as well. Helen was sitting up in his vast bed, watching him fuss around in the striped towelling robe she had bought him. She preferred its vibrant colours to his suits.

'Come here,' she said softly. 'Please.'

He did as he was told, half waiting to be asked, and sat heavily. A grey morning, she noticed. She put her arms round him, her chin on his shoulder.

'Begin at the beginning,' she said. 'I do like you an awful lot, you know. Even more when you talk to me.'

'What time is it?'

'You know very well what time it is. Early. Far too early for work.'

He was always like this, wanting to talk and wanting someone to force him to do it. Sometimes she had to take advantage of him in the early mornings.

468

'Ryan had a file,' Bailey said. 'If we'd searched his house, we might have found the duplicate, but we didn't, although Todd will sure as hell search his house now. The file's on the disk anyway. It was all no-hope fantasists who came in with weird stories about men they wouldn't, couldn't name, plus witnesses who couldn't help. I thought our Ryan might be keeping a book of screwball women who might not mind being screwed and could never give reliable information afterwards. There's a central register. You're only allowed so many spurious rape allegations before someone puts a question mark against your name. He was never fussy about type, Ryan; liked 'em all, in his way, but I didn't think he'd be so desperate. Although you never know. You never really know anyone.'

He slid in beside her and pulled the duvet up to his chest.

'But, if he was keeping the file for that, why keep the complaints of two women who died soon after he saw them? Unknown causes; heart attacks. Both pregnant. As indeed, it seems, was little Shelley Pelmore. Todd's flummoxed; and furious, which is why he phones me all day. Why I've got to help him nail the bastard.'

'Which bastard?'

'Ryan, the fool. For playing this so close to his chest. For fantasizing himself. Oh, I know he got his fingers burnt for even suggesting there might be a link between a few scared, confused, guilt-ridden women, where the method of attack described has no common denominator at all except for a total lack of forensic evidence on their persons. No semen, no fibres. He's either in their homes by some kind of invitation, in which case he brings flowers

469

and chocolates, or, in the case of the younger three, showing a penchant for the great outdoors, or his car, also by
invitation. No injury. A man they already know? Met in a
club, says one kid; came to my house, says another. And
the last recipient of chocolates and flowers says he has fine
eyes. Well, according to fiction and anyone old enough for
James Bond movies, creepy villains with great sexual
potency and black cats always have mesmeric eyes.
Personally, I think Sally Smythe has gone mad, too. And to
think this was a man I trained.'

'Trained, not only in the systematic forms of investigation, but also the empirical,' Helen said.

'Not that empirical. You can bounce things off a wall,
but only if you've got something to throw. Yes, I could kill
him and I know he could have killed her; Shelley, I mean.
He's capable of violence. More than one kind.'

He swung himself off the bed.

'Which is why I want to find him. I'm his best chance.
The preliminaries show that Shelley, too, died of
unknown causes. There was pressure on the neck, but it
didn't kill her. Oddly enough, old Ryan had been asking a
pathologist about how to cause death without trace, but
that's neither here nor there. There's nothing forensic to
connect him, nothing else either, if only he'll show his face
and say where the hell he was, they'll have to drop the
rape. The witness is dead; long live the witness! I hope he
was out on a bender.'

He sounded gleeful, Helen hated him. Hated that flash
of triumph in him which came from a death. A girl dead,
and him smiling about it, thinking of nothing but a grand
reunion.

'The witness dead. No evidence. Ryan being discharged. That's all you care about,' she said flatly.

'Not quite.' He dropped a kiss on her forehead. It felt like ice.

'Your mate, getting away with it. At the risk of a cliché, what about truth?'

'Oh, that?' he said, putting on a shirt without further indecision, scarcely pausing about the business of socks, underpants, trousers; always able to dress with speed. 'That can wait.'

'What about the fact that Ryan could be a rapist, a murderer?'

'That can wait, too,' he said, equally flat, his movements slowing down, less decisive. 'Truth often has to wait.'

'You detested that girl without knowing anything about her, and now you behave as if you'd dance on her grave.'

'That's an exaggeration.'

'What about compassion, then? Can you spell it these days?' she taunted, furious. This was her bridegroom, date fixed for the wedding, tomorrow, behaving like an alien with alien loyalties, underlining all her own doubts and fears. Bailey was all at once both defensive and apologetic.

'There's an order to things, that's all,' he began, then looked at her and decided not to continue, shrugged instead. They both knew she would not listen. Helen crept back inside herself and watched him go. The day was not only dull, but suddenly cold.

White was a cold colour. White flowers reminded Anna of snow and Christmas roses, and white daisies in a white living-room were just a shade clinical, even with the

471

curtains closed. Anna was about the work of creation; playing around in there with the curtains open, of course, because it seemed sinful to close them just yet, but trying at the same time to imagine the place after dark. She could wait until nine, she supposed, when the light slipped away, but that was too complicated. Greenery with the daisies and a light behind them would soften the effect, so would the colour of the curtains and the rich throws she had arranged over her old chairs, and the high polish of the table . . .

It had to be envisaged by night, because it was by night he would be there. She thought of how the evenings were becoming shorter and regretted the fact that she had painted the walls white at all. She could have made a cosy little snug of this room. Gone hunting for cheap second-hand curtains; velvet, perhaps, from that man in the market who had them sometimes. She could have had deep-green drapes. Suddenly she resented her own imagination and its shallow priorities. She had relinquished her vocation for the sake of this house and there were many days when she had thought she would sell her soul for the sake of going to a big department store and buying exactly what she wanted to beautify it, like Helen West had done, instead of the endless thrift required to achieve harmony. She chided herself for that ambition, too; having more money and choice would make no difference and would diminish the pride she had taken in her bargain hunting. Why would more money make any difference? The vast increase in her salary which had come from working in a private clinic had not made her happy either. As a substitute for a lover and a child, her obsession with this little house and large mortgage did not work. It was simply hiding a vacuum.

No, not daisies. Too cheerful and no scent. Something more fragrant was needed.

She had been smiling at him recently, exchanging the odd wry remark, and he had been reciprocating, convinced, of course, that all was forgiven and forgotten. If she sidled up to him and said, look, I'm cooking dinner tonight, why don't you come and share it? she was fairly sure he would say yes. He liked to be liked; he would want his reacceptance into the circle of her approval confirmed; he might not dare say no. Of course, a simpler form of revenge might be to poison his food, or indeed try to undermine his reputation, but she knew she was far too small fry to do that without her attempts being counterproductive. He would sail away and she would be sacked and branded as spiteful. No, this was the only way. It was not enough to injure him. He had to be humiliated and exposed and put on record. Anna's conscience was clear on that front; after all, the advice had come from a lawyer. The only way you'll get your own back, Helen West had said laughingly, is to make him do it again.

Roses then, in that corner; deep-red blooms if she could get them. And she would not promise seafood, although he had told her he liked it, because the cooking of fish made such a smell.

Anna shook herself. She had become used to lying.

She remembered the ice, the worst aspect of all; ice touching neck of cervix and being welcomed as if to douse the heat. That was the humiliation which cried out for

473

revenge, because that was what he did. He made the body lose control and take convulsive pleasure in itself, whatever the mind did.

And a nagging concern, which may have been jealousy, because the last name she had seen him extract from the records was gorgeous little Rose.

CHAPTER ELEVEN

'If the intercourse was with a woman of weak intellect, incapable of distinguishing right from wrong, and the jury found she was incapable of giving consent, or of exercising any judgement upon the matter, and that (though she made no resistance) the defendant had sexual intercourse with her by force and without her consent, that is a rape ... however, it was afterwards held that the mere fact of intercourse with an idiot girl, who was a fully developed woman, who was capable of recognizing and describing the defendant, and who, notwithstanding her imbecile condition, might have strong instincts, was not sufficient evidence of rape to be left to a jury ...'

'None of them have intellect! None of us has the kind of intellect which can prevail above need!'

He wrote on paper, the screen abandoned, knowing he should throw away this paper afterwards. His long slender fingers, unusual for an artist or surgeon, touched the vase by the desk and he did not know whether he was exhilarated or sad.

'Girls who are afraid of getting pregnant will nevertheless do a number of bizarre things in search of thrills,' he wrote.

'They are very willing to experiment, especially if they feel their experience leaves them behind their peers. So are those whose knowledge of sexual congress is nothing but a selfish coupling designed for the emission of seed and restoration of relative good humour of the male, usually an inarticulate young man who has never studied anatomy or physiology and considers that his greatest suffering to date is an unalleviated erection in tight trousers. Such a boy does not know the good fortune involved in this kind of discomfort. He does not know what real pain is.'

This was not part of the history he was writing, but he wrote it anyway.

'Despite disappointment,' he wrote, 'all young and youngish women are best approached in their secretory phase – immediately after ovulation – when they produce progesterone and, under the influence of this aggressive hormone, also a delicate watery mucus from the cervical glands. Progesterone production prevails for the first three months of pregnancy . . .'

He put down the pen, flushed with pity.

What chance has human nature against a cycle as relentless as this? Progesterone makes for imbeciles. The balance of the mind is disturbed; the body fair aching with desire, most easily pleasured. What price is free will to an empty womb which does not know it is empty for a purpose?

Sadness prevailed over exhilaration. It was the first time he had killed with such effortless proficiency, but there was no pride in it. Numbness and horror; more when he felt in his pockets and could not find the syringe, and then there was a moment of sheer panic.

There it was again: the wrong fear of the wrong kind of retribution, and then the old and crippling desire to be loved,

476

coming back with a force so strong he took the empty vase and threw it.

He was weary of this game. Sick of it.

Even if there was another candidate waiting in the wings. Sweet little Rose Darvey, marrying a clod of a policeman with whom she already quarrelled, soon, no doubt, to reach a stage of bitter discontent; as slender as Shelley; as sexual. With a background devoid of love.

And also, Anna. Who forgave him, although there was nothing to forgive. She accepted what he was.

Maybe, after all this, there was redemption.

I used to believe in the redeeming power of love, Helen West told herself, but now I'm not so sure. Maybe it's only suitable for those capable of redemption.

First undertones of autumn. A smattering of leaves on the window-ledge, desiccated by the dry heat, carried a long distance, looking burnt and almost tropical. An ominous strength in the warm breeze.

Perhaps it had been a mistake to encourage Bailey to speak his mind if she was going to so dislike the result. Honesty was often death to harmony. He had been so disgustingly jubilant, a boy let off the hook of anxiety because his little friend was not going to get smacked. Going out of the house wearing a loud tie which suggested premature celebration, perhaps limbering up to the prospect of an interview which could be fixed. She could imagine how it would go. Where were you, the night before last, DS Ryan? Out finding a new way of making a witness have a heart attack by a little playful strangulation? What every boy does from time to time? No, sir; nothing of the kind.

477

I was out and about in the business of my own defence against this heinous charge. Taking a break in order to get drunk with A, B and C, all of whom will stand alibi to squash any suggestion that I might rape or terrorize some poor little wench who once trusted me. Happens all the time, sir. Honestly, all I did was breach the conditions of my bail. Slap my wrist.

Helen could not concentrate. She looked at today's set of papers. A case with the usual qualified hope of whatever it was they called success, as if imprisonment was success. The best level of success in a rape case was the victim being believed; and then believed to the extent that there was no room for the jury to be distracted by sympathy for the accused. She was sick of this kind of Russian roulette. One sought a confirmation in the mind of the victim that she had not deserved this violation, without the whole process of law making the nightmare worse. *'Any penetration is sufficient . . .'* At the moment, Helen felt that a kiss from Bailey would feel like a bruise. Intimacy with a stranger she was supposed to marry tomorrow, who did not care about truth, only about his brutal little friend.

In the present case, as Redwood would say, the evidence was sound. With injuries like that, there was no question of consent and that was all which need concern her. Mary and John, whoever they were; their careers; their future life, were not hers to record. She judged the lives of others on the episodes she read; on evidence of misspent passion; love, turning first to disapproval, then to hate. She only evaluated them on a reasonable prospect of conviction.

Helen loved Bailey with reservations. Bailey loved Ryan

to the extinction of conscience. Yes, she preferred to know people only on paper. And she knew this angry litany of accusations against Bailey was unfair. He was not the only one tainted with hypocrisy. She was fuelling her own cowardice by blaming him for something. Anything would have done to excuse the fact that when she thought of marriage her feet were cold.

'I do not judge the living, I simply dissect the dead,' Dr Webb told them. 'But I liked your Mr Ryan. He said he was writing a thesis. Such a need for certainty.'

'The hell he was writing a thesis.'

Todd's ruddy complexion was pale with irritation. There was a sheen to his skin which might have been sweat or the rain, a half-hearted drizzle which dampened the hair and clung to clothes. They stood outside the mortuary, Bailey smoking, apparently nonchalant, impervious to the damp which the brown grass of the park drank greedily. If he looked at the grass long enough, he was sure he would see it change colour.

'Amazing,' said Todd. 'Absolutely bloody amazing that he should be asking you about how to kill women without trace and then one of them's found dead, on your doorstep, of a bloody heart attack.'

'Complete cardiac and respiratory failure. That was the cause. There is nothing to indicate that this death had anything to do with Mr Ryan's research. It's unusual, sure, for a healthy woman to die with such spontaneity, but not unknown. Strange things happen in pregnancy.'

'But he tried to throttle her,' Todd snapped.

'Someone tried, but not very hard. And, as far as I can

tell at this stage, she was already dead. Too late for the skin to bruise; she was already turning white and blue; she hadn't tried to defend herself. No, she just lay down in the park and went to sleep. No level on drink or drugs yet, maybe she took some pills. If there was a combination, well, who knows? Death by misadventure. I don't know about fibres and other stuff; nothing I could see.'

'He had to do it,' Todd fumed, talking to himself. Dr Webb stood back from him, Bailey noticed, looking at him as if he was a specimen on a slab, her posture revealing a mild dislike, but then Todd had this way of standing too close. An habitual invader of private space, as if he wanted everyone to share his flowery aftershave, worn as a precaution against mortuary smells.

'He knew all about it,' Todd said stubbornly.

'All about what? About an air embolism being fatal?' She was becoming irritated, felt that both men had her standing out here in order to make her accuse on evidence not yet gathered, purely to give them some sense of direction where there was none. They weren't even the officers investigating the death which she had not even called homicide.

'Look, an air embolism is fatal, but I do not know if one existed. And what do you think he would have to do to create it? Put a straw up her nose? A long blow-job?'

Todd sniggered. Nerves and embarrassment.

'Getting a quantity of air into a woman isn't easy. It has to get into her bloodstream. An injection would be best. Giving an injection isn't easy, either. How would your nice Mr Ryan know how to do that without leaving a needle mark?'

Bailey was silent; Todd sulky.

'But the fact he asked you . . .' he began, wagging his finger, hectoring, so that she stepped back even further.

'Means what? He first asked me about his thesis four months ago. Someone he knew, someone who'd complained of an attack, died mysteriously. Set him off thinking, he said, but he was slow to learn. Needed everything repeating.' Like you, she might have added, but refrained.

'Where is he?' Todd muttered darkly. 'Where the hell is he?'

Bailey thought of the Rape House and held his tongue. The rain fell harder as he looked downhill towards the traffic. He saw a man huddled by a gravestone, pulling his sweater up round his ears.

Ryan could live like that; Ryan could live in a phone booth. Ryan could be the perfect chameleon, changing colour with the landscape.

I never knew you, Bailey thought to himself. I never really knew you at all. He turned to Dr Webb, smiling his cadaverous smile.

'To kill a woman without trace, Doctor, would take some skill, wouldn't it?'

She looked at him with scarcely more approval than she had granted to Todd. They were both imbeciles, one slightly better than the other.

'Yes.'

'Medical skill?'

What did he think she meant? The skill of an engineer?

'Maybe a plumber,' she said. 'A medical plumber.'

*

481

That was what they all were, Anna Stirland thought as she tidied the third surgery, aligning the instruments in order, wiping the padded examination table with antiseptic and then putting a new sheet of paper over the top. Sensitive technicians in human tubing. The idea was to make them feel that internal examination was no more than having in the plumber to take a quick look at the drains, and all this was going to be as relaxing as half an hour on a sunbed, although rather more expensive. No prescriptions without examination, no surgery without express permission, sympathy unlimited, but absolutely nothing doing at all without money up front. The voice of the receptionist, asking how miss or madam would like to pay, writing down a credit card number like one transcribing a precious secret, was only as dulcet as her own asking, Are you sure this is what you want to do? It's only a little scrape, dear. Oh, hello, Miss Smith. Are you back again? How odd it was that even women in extremes of anxiety were prone to fall in love with the doctor and ignore the nurse. How odd it was that such a variety of people came here, even those whose general practitioners offered free access to advice and treatment they could otherwise ill afford. Ah, but there was something about payment which was supposed to guarantee quality and safety, discretion and soft, soft hands. Of course, one would have to pay for a clinic which offered such individual attention and such comprehensive appreciation of the whole female psyche. From the waist down.

Of course they did good, she argued with herself; they helped women avoid the ruination of their own lives. And they gave one doctor a playground.

Anna often fancied she could hear the echo of a baby crying in the murmuring quiet of this place.

She scrunched the used paper from the couch and put it into a sealed bin. A nice little girl, the one who had left, happy with her cap and happy with her life, and, like most of them, squeaky clean for her visit. If only they would not wear perfume, as if embarrassed by any possibility of their own smell. Clean underwear for the doctor, as if this was a brand-new date, and no thought about how he might be allergic to their artificial scent while being immune to what was natural. No, that little girl with her steady relationship and determined control over her own future would not be one the good doctor would choose.

It would be someone like Brigid Connor, Anna surmised. Someone who came in full of fear, who would have worn a paper bag over her head if she could, because the mere fact of begging a doctor to find something wrong with her, and then pleading for the means to avoid a late and dreaded pregnancy, was so obviously wicked that she had shaken with the fear of it. That was the type of person.

Anna told herself she only wanted to know what he was doing. Why it was he accessed certain personal details from the confidential records again and again, preferring the ones he had treated with conspicuous tenderness. Why he could continue to express such interest in the insecure, sometimes the downright ugly, and then treat her as he had.

Passing down a long corridor, footsteps silent on the carpeted floor, she paused to nip a bud from a plant. She took a deep breath, knocked and assembled a brilliant smile. 'Tonight OK, then?' was all she would ask. And he would say, 'Yes, fine.'

Her house would be bursting with flowers. The window-boxes she was creating for Rose were beginning to flourish in the backyard.

Rose stood by the office door, pulling faces at Helen's back. She had said hello twice to no response. Miss West gazed through the window and there was a suspicious smell of cigarette smoke. 'Tut, tut, tut,' Rose said loudly; Redwood would never forgive that. Major disaster, perhaps; general cock-ups in the administration of justice; poor timekeeping; innocent souls languishing in prison; cases lost by negligence; anything which would not easily be found out, but an infringement of the clear-desk and no-smoking policies was certainly a hanging offence.

'Wake up, Helen, there's a good girl. Oh, what are they doing now?' The occupants of the office over the road never failed to cause amusement. It was like watching a video without the sound; trying to decode the body language from a distance of twenty metres and through two panes of glass. Once they had all seen a fight and since then Rose and Helen watched all the time. Nothing quite as exciting had happened since, forcing Rose to invent a situation of seething rivalry between two men in suits lorded over by a lady of large size, indeterminate years and sultry authority.

'She's putting on weight again,' Rose said, pointing. 'Shame, after she was doing so well on that diet. All those apples. She'll have to stop pigging out at lunch-time. Hamburger and chips, I've seen. What's the matter? Speak to me. I've brought you a memo.'

'Great. Do you suppose someone has given her a memo

about her weight and that's why she hasn't spoken to anyone all afternoon? That one at the other end, for instance? The one who could be Redwood's cousin?'

Rose peered. 'Oh, yeah, for sure. He looks the type. They could do with a few plants over there. It always looks like an open-plan greenhouse recently visited by locusts. Oh, and I bought you some flowers to go with the memo, in case Redwood forgot; you know what he's like.'

A small and delicate bunch of freesias landed, without ceremony, on the crowded desk.

'Thanks,' said Helen, touched and, only as an afterthought, suspicious. 'What have I done to deserve this?'

'Nothing,' Rose said carelessly, running fingers through the spikes of her hair. 'Only I heard on the Michael grapevine about everyone being out looking for that bastard Ryan. They all had it in this morning's briefings. I didn't think it was the kind of news which would be making for a happy atmosphere at home, that's all.'

'No,' said Helen. 'It won't.'

She yawned and stretched. The scent of the flowers drifted upon her and she had a sudden and inexplicable urge to cry. Any act of kindness could have that effect, but she rallied since there was no point in public tearfulness if she could not explain it and she knew she did not want to make the attempt.

'So what does the memo say?'

Rose shrugged and offered a chewy peppermint, her panacea for all office ills.

'Reorganization. Again. Me to go to outer Mongolia and you to go to Special Casework. Extradition, forgery, counterfeiting, a lot of it about. No more rape.'

'That'll be the day,' Helen said. 'Which part of outer Mongolia?'

'Camberwell Green. He told me he thinks you're bad for me.'

This time, the urge to cry was becoming real.

'Maybe he just thinks rape isn't good for either of us.'

'C'mon, Helen. It isn't good for anyone.'

The afternoon was thunderously dark, the rain gentle and relentless.

Rain filled the pond which Ryan had dug in his garden and lined with polythene before leaving it incomplete. Mary Ryan, along with the youngest child, who was wearing bright-red wellington boots, both threw clods of earth into the hole which had been designed for exotic fish and now resembled nothing more than an overlarge puddle. The child whooped with delight; Daddy might as well have made him a scarecrow or a makeshift coconut shy, or simply have given him something to smash or throw things at. And where was Daddy now? And why had the house been turned upside down? All a game, darling; Daddy's lost his cheque book and these friends of his are trying to find it. And Mummy isn't saying anything about the note which Daddy left, which she destroyed not because it told her to do so but because it made her incoherent with anger. 'Got to go,' it said. 'Things to do, or we'll never get this sorted . . . can't explain more, yet.' As if he had ever explained anything at all. No, please believe me, I love you etc., not that sentimental words or promises loomed large in their relationship, but there were points like this when she might have clung to any endearment or plea for help.

So she had stood by, mutinous, unco-operative and mono-syllabic while the house was searched, only vaguely grateful for the fact that her status as a detective's wife, even one charged with rape and suspected of worse, meant that they were tidier and more considerate than they might have been. She remembered his tales, told with glee when he was a younger man, of how easy it was to trash a house when some guilty thief had flown. The only other saving grace was the absence of Bailey from the grim-faced number. She would have hit him with a hammer.

'Time to go indoors, love. We're soaked through.'

The child was too old to be playing such childish games. Retrograde behaviour, like her own in stuffing her face with chocolate and making herself feel sick. Maybe Ryan had dug the hole for the pond as a place to bury himself. She wished he had.

Then she looked at his flowers, the shrubs, the blooms, the riot of colour which had been his creation. In the damp air of the early evening, she tried to convince herself that he was incapable of savagery, but she could not. The only things Ryan loved were plants and children: growing things. Women were never in the same league.

Women could be stupid, but only as stupid as men. Stupidity was the place of last resort and Helen knew she had reached it when she realized she was calling herself a silly bitch and then correcting the description to say – on the top deck of the bus, watching as the rain ceased and a sky appeared, purple as a fresh bruise – that although she merited the description of silly, giddy, irrational from time to time, it wasn't a constant state of being and, try as she might, she was not what she herself would call a bitch. A female dog was never, as far as she knew, accredited with anything more malicious than a habit of fighting with a competitor when under the influence of hormones, and then fighting twice as hard to protect her young. It wasn't such a bad thing to be a bitch. Silly bitch was nothing more than a description for a kind of giddiness, a lack of steadiness in the head, an imbalance of vanity against reality, the optimism of prettiness against the ugliness of age and so on. It was Bailey who loved the Oxford English Dictionary, with its definitions of so many words which had become, essentially, so bloody meaningless. Like 'bloody', for instance. A word removed to the fringe of language, by misuse.

Helen got indoors, with the sky still purple, and set about the task of clearing up the kitchen debris, working to some mental calendar which told her rubbish was collected tomorrow. The desire to weep for no particular reason other than a universal sense of failure was still prevalent.

After a cursory rummage round, the sink was clear and the rubbish sack in the bin underneath was far too full. She rammed it down with force, trying to be deliberate. The second finger on her right hand shoved itself against the rim of the chicken soup can of the day before yesterday, standing proud with its nasty serrated rim. What a lot of blood, she thought bleakly; what an awful lot for such a pedestrian accident, and what a very distinctive, unmis-takable colour fresh blood has. She was running her finger under the tap at the time, wondering if traces of chicken soup could be infectious, condemning herself for choosing the kind of sustenance so bland to the taste and yet with a container so malicious. She was thinking, too, about whether the disablement of this little digit could stop her holding a cigarette for ever. The desire to cry was ever stronger.

She moved her finger from the kitchen sink, swathed it in layers of kitchen towel and still it bled. On the floor, in the sink, wherever she tried to keep it out of harm's way, it bled. She managed to avoid drops on the carpet, but any admonition to her finger did nothing more than make it spout blood even faster. She held it above her head, like a trophy, wrapped in kitchen towel and still it bled. The Elastoplast was somewhere, she forgot where, inaccessible. Finally, she went into the garden. Blood was surely good for the soil.

The rain had stopped, but the sky had turned from purple to a bleak grey.

Signs of neglect out here, Helen remarked to herself, crossing her hands across her chest. Anna Stirland said you had a care of your plants if you could stop them throttling one another. Which, revived by rain, they were about the business of doing; she imagined she could see them moving, the whole thing a jungle, praying for attention, made aggressive by nourishment.

Gloves, then; let the finger bleed inside the sleeve of her stiff gardening gloves, hanging by the door, awaiting a mood like this, when care and control of the garden seemed more important than anything, if only as a substitute for control over her own life. Nothing hurt when she worked in the garden; she would surprise herself later with the discovery of unconsciously acquired scratches on arms, legs and torso, regarding them proudly as symbols of the fact that, though she might not be an expert,

something in this small wilderness had received the benefit of her energy.

There was a school playground on the other side of the
high wall which bounded the back of Helen's garden and
made it so private. She liked the presence of the children
she never saw, although on days at home she heard the
raucous playground screams, always amazed at the sheer
exuberance of their noise and the deafening nature of the
quiet which followed. Remembering now, as it grew dark
and silent around her, how long it had taken to feel safe in
this garden. She pulled at the convolvulus which made the
ivy look shaggy, tore at it as if it was a real enemy and, as
the pile of weedy rubbish grew on the grass, she felt the
beginnings of satisfaction. The dark grew gently deeper,
summer dusk turning inky black, so that soon the only
light spilt from the kitchen window and it was silly to go
on. Helen paused, thirsty, and turned to go indoors.

It was then she saw a figure crossing the patch of light,
disappearing into the shadows. Her elderly cat had died in
the spring and its presence haunted her still, but she knew
it was not the cat, or any ghost. She was suddenly engulfed
with a fear which was at once strange and yet appallingly
familiar. There was more than one kind of ghost in this
garden. Bailey would not joke like this: he knew her fears
and respected them, but all the same she called his name,
her voice quavering uncertainly.

'Bailey? That you?'

Silence. The tree which shrouded the corner seemed to
sigh, shuffling a full head of leaves and loosening the very
last of the rain. The scrape of a shoe on stone.

It was a small garden by country standards, large in

urban terms, but now it felt enormous, the distance between herself and the back door the length of a long minefield. She stumbled in her headlong run to the rectangle of light which represented safety, her glove skidding against the rough surface of the wall, her hair flicking into her eyes, all of her sick with fear. Falling into his arms.

There were lights from the upstairs windows of the houses on either side, their promise a mockery. Her scream ascended unheeded as she had known it would; she was in the midst of a crowded street and it made no difference. The creature who twisted her body round so that he held her neck and clamped a dirty hand over her mouth might as well have been holding her over a cliff on a shoreline devoid of humanity for all the help she could summon.

'Shut up,' he snarled. 'Shut up.'

She nodded her head, let her body go limp. The hand moved from her mouth to her throat, his other arm pinioning her round the waist, pressing her against his groin.

'Lovely Miss West,' his voice murmured. 'And you never knew I cared.'

She could feel his penis stir against the soft flesh of her buttocks; his palm strayed to brush across her breast and a deep shudder passed through her. Then she began to tremble.

'Obviously mutual,' the voice continued. 'Always knew you fancied me rotten. Shall we go inside, love? Get ourselves comfy, eh?'

It was Todd who kept stating his wonderment about how Ryan could disappear, repeating himself stupidly without thinking about what he was saying. Bailey had no such confusion and he was bored of listening to the ramblings of frustration. Despite his years as an officer, Todd had never somehow taken to the streets; he had formed no affiliations there and still could not understand how a man like Ryan, who had so often failed to make his own way home in the evening, could remain at large now. Bailey thought the quickest way to flush him out would be to stop his credit cards; let him play cat and mouse if he would; he himself was tired of the game and angry with Ryan for prolonging it.

'I feel sorry for the boyfriend,' Todd said, nursing his pint like someone slightly afraid of it, sitting there in the uncomfortable company of Bailey, guilty for being in a pub at all, but knowing he would feel guiltier if he simply gave up. He was like a dog gnawing at a bone, turning it over with one paw and chewing the other end. If he had been Ryan, he would have given up on the subject long before now and gone on to his summer holidays.

'He seemed a decent bloke,' Todd went on.

'He probably is,' Bailey agreed, recalling a lad with a large ever-mobile Adam's apple and eyes full of tears, whose stress he had thought owed as much to fear as to grief. Eyes darting everywhere whenever they forgot to maintain a self-consciously sincere contact with those of his interlocutors. Lying about something, Bailey thought; the boy was suspiciously relieved to have it stressed that his dearly beloved had not died of strangulation, and even more suspiciously confused and angry to learn there had been no signs of sexual attack. Then he had cried. Bailey had disliked him even more than the manageress in the shop where Shelley Pelmore worked: a bitch from hell, who, even in the midst of genuine shock and tears, remembered to flirt. Bailey had failed to tell Todd that after this pint he was going back to see her.

'Did I hear tell you were getting married?' Todd was asking, trying too late in the day to be conversational. 'A triumph of hope over experience, is it?'

Only Ryan was allowed to tease and Bailey could feel himself about to snap, until he realized it had slipped his mind. Slipped? The thought of marriage had sunk like a stone. When was it? Next week? Tomorrow? Christ, tomorrow. Perhaps, after all, he was already married; to Ryan. Go home, Todd, he urged silently. Go home and let me get on.

'What? Oh. Yes.' Tomorrow. Jesus wept 'Excuse me a minute, will you? I've just got to go and phone her. She does like to know when I'm going to be late.' Todd nodded, with an understanding smirk which made Bailey cringe.

Bailey dialled, drumming his fingers on the shelf inside the booth. Perhaps there was something to be said for mobile phones; they would be mandatory soon for him, just like a radio for every beat copper, and then they could all stand around on street corners in common with half of the population, yelling at one another like lunatics. She answered after interminable ringing. Bailey imagined her out in the garden, or ironing a garment. Doing something frivolous and feminine, the way he secretly liked to imagine her, such as lying in a scented bath, with her tan-coloured skin turning pink.

'Look,' he said, before she could even say hello. 'You haven't forgotten, have you?'

There was a long pause, laboured breathing.

'Forgotten what?'

'Wedding,' he said tersely. 'I'm sorry, I was so . . . brisk this morning.'

'Have you found Ryan?' she asked.

'No.'

'What a pity. I expect he's closer to home than anyone imagines.'

Her voice was high; then she seemed to explode in a fit of coughing, ending as if she had been thumped on the back. There had been no coughing this morning, not that he recalled.

'I don't want to talk about Ryan. I've had it up to here with Ryan . . .'

'. . . But he's very close to you, I'm sure he is . . .'

Her voice was now so strained, it sounded almost as if she was trying to swallow. Choking on something, possibly laughter.

'Listen, love, are you ready for this? Ryan doesn't matter as much as us. Eleven-thirty in the morning. Don't be late, will you?'

Again, he allowed himself that fond imagination of Helen peacefully at home, sorting out her special-occasion wardrobe. He loved her clothes and the way she wore them. Then he heard the sound of clinking glass; a voice, which could only have been Helen's, turned sideways to the phone, saying shush. Then a male voice, very close, whispering, and the sound of smothered laughter. A cork being pulled from a bottle.

He could feel a sensation like a mild electric shock, then a feeling of despair. Shame on her, Helen drinking for

Dutch courage. Finding someone else for reassurance? That was it, then. Hadn't he always known there was a risk, a big risk that she would run away from commitment to him in the end, that marriage terrified her, and that his middle-class, professionally qualified, passionate but cool-as-ice Helen would decide she could do better than him and find someone her own class would approve?

'Bailey?' She seemed lost for words. It was only ever guilt which made her speechless.

'Look,' he said wearily. 'It's up to you, isn't it? I could call round later, only . . .'

'Not *later*,' she spat, then fell silent. Bailey could not think of a single thing to say. On the other end of the line, he could hear someone whistling in the background. Someone thoroughly relaxed in her house. Slowly, he replaced the receiver, unable to listen.

'You look so glamorous in those gloves,' Detective Sergeant Ryan remarked. 'So why doesn't a smart woman like you change into gardening clothes before she stoops to do the garden? I always do, myself.' Helen looked down at herself. The gloved hands were folded in her lap; they had made it awkward to hold the phone. She sat in the least comfortable of the kitchen chairs by the window, noticing, at his prompting, the dirt of her workday skirt and blouse, thinking, yes, perhaps she would be an all-round better person if she remembered to change her clothes before making an onslaught on the garden, and surely Bailey would know there was something wrong. Don't come *later*, come sooner. Feel concern for my cough. Wonder why I mention Ryan.

Ryan took the phone off the hook.

'Just in case he phones back, eh? Then he can think you're cosily engaged.'

'Why did you make him think someone was here?' she asked.

'I didn't make him think anything,' he said. 'I just told you to get rid of him before I hurt you and also because, if he comes round here, I'll kill him. Only he won't. If he thinks there's someone else here, he'll simply go into a state of shock. Not a jealous fellow, Bailey, just in a state of constant dread. He doesn't deserve you, you know,' he added, mimicking her voice. 'Oh no, never did.'

He took a swig from a tumbler of whisky: she looked at him with a mixture of amazement and contempt, shivering at the memory of his body pressed against hers. She noted the growth of beard, the training shoes, and felt strangely resigned now that she had spoken to Bailey, scarcely caring at that particular moment about the carving knife which glinted on top of the fridge, well out of her reach, but easily within Ryan's. She pulled at the gloves; the one on her right hand was firmly stuck; she tugged at it, grimacing, releasing it from her fingers, letting both gloves drop on the floor. Her hands felt light and cool; she pushed her hair away from her face, a small attempt to make herself tidier than she was, a minute effort in the difficult exercise of self-control. Ryan's eyes suddenly widened; she shrank from him in alarm. This was the moment, then; this was when the rapist would go berserk.

'Christ, Helen, I didn't do that, did I? Oh God, did I do that?'

She had put her hand to her face, the first gesture of

496

self-protection, noticed that it was covered in dried blood and fresh blood oozed from the injured finger.

'For God's sake,' he said, dragging her towards the sink by the wrist. 'Put it under the cold tap, you silly bitch.'

Always some act of kindness which did it.

Made her cry.

CHAPTER TWELVE

Perhaps I could love someone. Perhaps they could love me. Perhaps what has happened to me is all a figment of my imagination.

Perhaps I did love her. Little Shelley, who wanted the thrills, the decadence, the dirt. Or perhaps my current sombre mood is a reaction to murder.

But she consented, even to that. It was not submission, it was consent.

Women have such a capacity for forgiveness. Perhaps it is not too late for me. The love of a good woman.

I must not do this . . . now I have perfected it, my own power terrifies me, and it will corrupt. My hands itch to hold the implement, insert it between soft lips . . . nothing but the air we breathe . . .

Her life would have been wretched anyway. She would have made it wretched because she was far too afraid to change it.

Maybe it's not too late for me.

I could always try again. I could try and see if love redeems me. Redeems my flesh, and blood.

The blood ran away under the tap. She gazed at it, mesmerized, watching the pale pink of the water.

'Should probably have a stitch,' Ryan said. 'But a plaster would do. In the bathroom, are they?'

The bathroom was down the hall; the exit door next to the kitchen. She nodded, but he caught the enthusiasm of the nod and shook his head sadly.

'I'm not going to fall for that one, am I? You don't know where the hell they are. Women without children never do. Have kids, you get used to the sight of blood. Here, don't be a cry-baby.'

'I'm not a baby. I'm not.'

He grunted, doing a passable job with more paper towel and an elastic band from a dish which held assorted letters, paperclips, vouchers and bills. Then he seemed calmer. Shoved her back into her chair and sat opposite.

'Now you can get drunk if you like. Here.'

He had found a bottle of the heavy red wine she had been keeping for winter. In other circumstances she would have loved the sound of the cork. She thought of the damage a violent man could do with a corkscrew, such as gouging out an eye, making score-marks in skin. The wine was a warm claret; the first sip sat like a sour sponge on her dry tongue in the damp heat of the early night and yet tasted like nectar. There was more rain on the way; she could feel it gathering; the kitchen was stuffy. As if reading her thoughts, he stood and pulled down the window,

499

letting in the air. She imagined the front of her flat from the road, unlit and empty; a basement where no one was home. She had reached a state of subdued hysteria, preternaturally calm; the tears had dried to salt on her cheeks and she sipped the next mouthful as if she was someone standing on the edge of a party, trying to make her wine last and look busy at the same time.

'To what do I owe this pleasure?' she said. 'I mean a drink among friends is all very well, but I can't remember inviting you.'

'Must have slipped your mind,' Ryan said. 'Can't think how. Mind, I've been a touch difficult to find over the last thirty-six hours. Found a bed last night,' he leered. 'She chucked me out so I thought I'd better find another.'

Waiting in the back garden; getting into her house over the back wall from the playground, she thought; Ryan would know about that. She was hot and sweaty, conscious of her grubby clothes.

'We travelling rapists, see? We can't be picky, can we?'

She nodded and sipped a little more wine.

'Do you remember the first time I came in here? No you don't. It was when that mad youth attacked you. I happened to be passing.'

'I've never forgotten,' she said slowly. 'I let you in. I leant on that entry-phone buzzer until I passed out.'

'And never liked me since,' he said.

'True.'

'I often wonder if you knew that he was deep dark in love with you, even then. Bailey, I mean. Perhaps you didn't.'

'No, I didn't. I only knew about my own reaction to him.'

'And I was taking a long route towards finding out that

maybe my wife was the best woman in the world. Comparative studies, I think they call it.'

'You've a funny way of showing your feelings. She must be worried sick now.'

'What do you want me to do? Phone home? Hello, wife, it's good to talk . . . be back after a rape or three . . . See ya . . . Look at me, Miss fucking West. Look at me.'

He seized her shoulders in a grip which would bruise. Calmly, she looked. She had faced men accused of rape, possibly murder, always with a barrage of fences between them. The dock, the courtroom barriers, her own protected space. This was a hard-edged face on a muscular man, handsome in an obvious and sexy way she had never found appealing, like the good looks of a football star. Capable of kindness to children and animals. She made herself think that he had the brown eyes of a cow. In response to the scrutiny he had invited, Ryan blushed. He touched the paper-clad finger and started to speak.

'No, I don't like you much. Nothing personal; I don't like lawyers much. And I don't like what you do to him. But I thought I'd bust in here, rather than down at Bailey's gaff, because you might believe me. Also, it's the last place he'd look and I don't want him finding me, yet. I don't like you, but you listen. Bailey does, sometimes. Responds to signals, know what I mean? But he's always got something else on his mind. Jumps from one thing to another. Got a mind like a series of traps; comes of doing too many things at once. I know what he'd say. You're off the hook, laddie, if you play it right. What more do you want: justice? Got a cigarette?' For an answer, he rifled her handbag, lit one for both of them.

'But you,' he said. 'You listen. You'll take a leap for the fucking truth. Obsessive about it, you are. Or something like it.'

'I prefer evidence,' she said.

'So do I, doll, so do fucking I.' And then, to her horror, he began to weep, a controlled weeping which meant that he kept his hand near the knife on the top of the fridge while his eyes filled with fat tears, rolling down his chiselled cheeks and making him look like a clown. Weeping made him dangerous but also ridiculous; she did not like to see him weep, although she could not feel an ounce of pity.

'I don't want to look like this for my wife, see? I don't want her looking at me and saying I'm crazy. Mad or bad, what's the difference? Only that little Shelley Pelmore; she told me a thing or two. Wife wouldn't believe. Nor would I, except . . .'

'I need some more,' Helen said, extending her glass. He sloshed wine.

'Start from the beginning,' she invited. Let him ramble while she stalled for time.

He took a deep shuddering breath, spoke almost dreamily. 'It all begins with girls. Women, girls bored with sex or romance. Either with difficult histories, abuse per-haps, or simply unrealistic expectations of the whole thing. Girls who dread pregnancy; disappointed girls; girls afraid of it. Girls who want sensation, not through drugs. Screwed-up girls. Girls like Shelley Pelmore: bored with life, dying for a kick. Or another kind of girl, who can't wait to get rid of innocence . . . hungry for a man . . .'

'Which all girls are, of course, is that it?' Helen asked, attempting to jeer. He looked at her, half amused.

'In my experience, most of them. Don't interrupt. Girls, women with unfulfilled sexual needs or bad sexual histories, fantasize about it. I've heard a lot of fantasies about men doing amazing things with bottles, with implements, with ice, making them beg . . . Only then I heard a series of fantasies, like that, but all featuring a bald man with wonderful eyes . . .'

Helen stared at him.

'He seduced, he humiliated, he played jokes, he corrupted. He corrupts. That's what he does: he corrupts. And in two cases, two of these confused women died soon after they'd made their confused complaints about a man who visited them at home. We'd listened to them and turned them out. No forensic, they wouldn't give us a name, but they were humiliated. Two died of natural causes – pregnant kids. Then there was Shelley Pelmore's friend, picked out of the gutter; unhurt, apart from what she'd done to herself; half dead with shock. Something happened to her; some sexual trauma, I don't know what.'

He stared into the dark garden.

'Know what I think? I think the greatest humiliation for a woman is sex they've somehow invited, willingly. They let themselves in for it, innocently, and while they know it's wrong, the body responds. And when the body has responded, then the shame becomes excruciating.' He coughed. Even to his mind, this was extra fanciful and he couldn't explain what he meant.

'And then there was wee Shelley herself, who wouldn't say anything for the record, but somehow wanted to boast about something or someone. She says I met her twice; in fact I met her more than that. She told me about the

503

bald-headed man; she actually confirmed his existence; before that, I only had this odd unconvincing dossier on him. Shelley adored him, but she was afraid of him, teased me with bits of information about this demon lover who was, she said, "too good not to share". Shelley loved a kind of perversion; she'd persuaded a couple of her friends to try . . . she thought he'd made Becky come round the neck of a bottle. Wouldn't you like to know who he is? she'd say to me, and I'd say, yes I would, and what did he do to you last time? Once I'd got her a bit drunk, she'd tell me. He made me come against a park bench, she'd say. Used his dildo, used an icicle. They were con-spirators of a kind, Shelley and him: she was proud of it, but she was afraid of him, too. She set me up for the rape to stop me looking for him. They planned it. I fell into the trap, oh, so neatly.'

He smiled, ashamed of himself. 'It was easy, you see. All this drink and dirty talk. I fancied her; I let her tease me; I wanted the information; I prolonged the quest for it, even though it was him I was after; I half enjoyed it. And I really did leave her in the pub. I forgot the jacket; I think she hid it behind a chair. And she could see I had fingernails full of soil from the garden. As if I'd been grubbing round in the park.' Helen did not entirely follow, then remembered.

'You must have hated her for that. If that's what she did.'

'Hated her? Oh yes. Oh yes. "Hated her" would be the understatement of the year.'

She wanted to ask, Enough to kill her? And if so, how? But it was his mention of the icicle which somehow seemed more important. Ryan was in a world of his own, continuing without prompting. He seemed to have forgotten the knife.

'I hated her a bit less after she'd called me at home. She was frightened and wanted to see me. I met her once, but she shilly-shallied about, wouldn't really talk. Then a second time, much the same, in the amusement arcade. Then I lost my temper, wanted to strangle her. She went off in a huff. I followed. That park, by the mortuary . . .'

'Where she was found?'

'Yup.'

'And?'

'I left her,' he said bitterly. 'I was hungry and angry and I left her. I didn't think she'd be meeting him, but then I thought, shit, I bet she is. By the time I'd doubled back she was dead. And I thought, I'd better not go home.'

He paused.

'Such a pretty girl.'

He might think the place was home, decorated for Christmas, there were so many flowers. Anna thought perhaps she had overdone it. Once, twice or three times he had said how much he appreciated flowers; she had brought them to his desk. Snowdrops last winter, daffodils in March, never thinking then that there was something unconventional in a woman courting a man with flowers, as if she was being the male for both of them. She removed the lilies from the living-room: like the daisies they were too white and too much of a contrast to the roses. She wanted the room to have the atmosphere of a study rather than a boudoir; she was excited and he was late, and it was the excitement that bothered her most.

505

Keep a clear head, she told herself; just one glass of this stuff. The champagne, not quite real; an Australian look-alike, which is what she thought he would expect from her, rather than the far more expensive real thing, sent flutters of trepidation through her abdomen. She felt she was full of air.

Bruises, bodily fluids: evidence. She had a dim idea of how to create the bruises by replicating kitchen accidents she had suffered in the past. If she left the back-cupboard door open and belted it with her hip, that gave a hefty bruise, as she already knew. There was the cabinet in the bathroom; she had once hit her head against the open door when straightening up from brushing her teeth and now always kept it closed. The bruise, complete with a graze in the middle of her forehead, had looked quite dramatic and had given rise to teasing from colleagues. That one would have to be self-inflicted later; she couldn't meet him with a face like a balloon; she was trying to seduce the man, for God's sake. She caught sight of her face in the bathroom mirror. Well, she murmured to herself, that won't do it. A face to launch a million ships? This one wouldn't get a rowing boat out onto the Thames, and why was she so insanely cheerful? When the doorbell rang, she was composed, rehearsing words. Oh do come in, how nice to see you and how good of you to call ... the last words made her put her hand across her mouth and stifle a crazy laugh. She couldn't say such a thing, she really couldn't. She should go downstairs to her door and open it with decorum, hoping she didn't look overdressed or even faintly vampish with the extra make-up, but no perfume. The house was full of it, from the flowers.

He rang again, and when, with suitable stateliness, she let him in, she remembered to be casual.

'Sorry that took so long,' she said, smiling. 'I was out the back, come and see.' He bowed from the waist, giving her a glimpse of the top of his smooth head. There was nothing better to get a man indoors and unwary than a kind of distracted friendliness. Nothing sinister about his examination of Rose's evergreen window-boxes and a discussion of why, after a downpour, the flowering shrubs grew crooked. Good smells wafted from the kitchen. She chatted like a starling; she knew she was amusing. Hope these clothes are right, she thought. A pretty loose-weave top over an upholstered bosom, multi-coloured skirt almost to the ankles, neat leather pumps. Not particularly sexy in themselves; the pretty clothes of a plump, budget-conscious, working woman, better chosen than most and, only incidentally, easy to remove. He had brought flowers and chocolates. Such clichéd gifts annoyed her; wine would be better; they hardened her resolve, but there was one troubling feature. In some utterly bizarre way, she really was pleased to see him.

'What a lovely room this is,' he said when they took the second glass of the cold fizz into the living-room. 'How clever you are.'

It was as if he had never been here before. He moved from object to object, glass in hand, commenting on the watercolour seascape which had been such a delightful bargain, the bright-coloured porcelain of no known make which she had so artfully assembled on the shelves to make it appear striking and valuable, the pastel-patterned throws which made her chairs look inviting. 'I haven't the knack to do this,' he was saying; 'I can't create comfort, I wish I could. I have a living unit rather than a home, and oh, what's this?' holding, gently, the favourite of her few, carefully chosen ornaments. A small clay bird, nestling by the vase of abundant miniature roses.

He was turning back the clock; he was the soul of natural charm, behaving in exactly the right slightly shy, curious way; alert to her answers; concentrating his interest in everything which was hers; smiling appreciatively. It was exactly the way she would have wished him to act on his first visit. A courtier, humble but proud; the way a man should be if he was seriously interested in her. Oh praise, the wilful nature of it; she wilted and simpered beneath it. Her sofa was the perfect casting couch, the ironing-board was as absent as his memory of it, the burn marks on her arms as vague as they always would be, and her capacity for revenge was somehow dulled, and his mellowness was all too soon. And she was, because of the unusual amount of sipping which had gone on in the afternoon while she experimented with bruises, slightly drunk. More on hope and revenge and tension than wine, but still not entirely in control.

She laughed with him; she poured more wine; she shook her head roguishly, making the thick shoulder-length hair which was her finest feature move in tune with her own animation. Pressing the bruise on her thigh to remind herself of her purpose, she wondered, in spite of everything, whether clocks could be turned back. She ached with a sense of what might have been.

It was all going so much like clockwork, there was not even an audible tick. They ate by candlelight in the kitchen, the back door open and the smell of flowers com-

508

peting with aubergine, oil, spices. He had the right kind of admiration for the food, too: not exaggerated; asking how she did this or that, eating well, talking about work in between. Why he did this and not something else, mutual commiseration about the state of medicine. She found herself longing to tell him how much she wanted a child, the hideous and direct contrast between herself and most of the patients at the clinic, but that one would wait. She had thought, in the planning stage, that this might be a sexual ploy he could not resist. Now it seemed ridiculous. The food, eaten sparingly in her case, sobered her a little.

'Tell me,' she said, casually, as she moved dishes from the table and brought the perfect fruit and cheese, 'why is it you take so much more notice of some patients than others? So much longer with them? And then look them up on the computer after they've gone?'

His glance was suddenly intense, then he laughed.

'Do I?' he said. 'Do I? If I do, I take more notice of the unhappy ones who need me.'

She sat down again, her face flushed.

He leant across the table and took her hand, turning it over. Even in the candlelight, the V-shaped mark of the burn from the iron was visible on the underside of her wrist.

'How did you do that?' he asked gently. Anna let her hand rest where it was.

'You did it,' she said. Because it was too late for pretence. 'You did it.' Her voice had become shrill. He shook his head, in disbelief.

'Oh Anna, darling, I didn't realize.' Those fine brown eyes were full of sympathy.

*

509

Bailey detested the shop manageress with an intensity he had no difficulty disguising. Even conceding that his present mood would make him dislike any human specimen of the female sex, he wondered, as he sometimes did, how he was able to dissemble so easily. Natural talent, he told himself without any smugness; perhaps one shared by this glamorous harridan. Or perhaps she really did enjoy his company; she showed every sign of it. A bar-stool percher of the old school, difficult to age unless one looked very closely to see the crow's-feet round the ever-smiling eyes with their long lashes, or observed the lines on her forehead which were artfully concealed by the blond fringe. It was hair which resembled spun gold, looked careless and youthful in style, although he suspected it would feel like steel wool, solid with fixative. Bailey thought of the scar on Helen's forehead and her understated, sometimes untidy, elegance. Of course, she had always been too good for him.

The manageress had already established he was a bachelor. He had parted with several bogus particulars of his own life in order to advance the conversation and he suspected that what she had told him in return (a dreadful divorce, life so hard for a woman on her own) might have been equally contrived. They approached the subject of Shelley Pelmore obliquely, by the route of mutual flattery and three drinks each, Bailey pretending throughout that his interest in Shelley was strictly professional, while his interest in the manageress was anything but. There were times when he despised himself more than others.

'Such a divine-looking girl,' she gushed. 'I mean, really lovely. A credit to us, but wasted in a shop, really. Should have spread her wings a bit. But I suppose, in the end, it's best to knuckle down if life's given you a nice man, isn't it? So rare to find. That's what I told her, anyway.'

'But you went out together?'

'Oh yes, lovely fun. Just a bit of clubbing, you know.'

'He was tolerant then, her boyfriend?'

'And why not? She never *did* anything. Far as I know. Mind, there were a couple of blokes came in the shop, liked her. A lot. Oh yes.'

'Anyone in particular?'

Music came from the far end of the bar where the place merged into a club. She looked towards Bailey, who hated dancing and was grateful Helen had no time for it either, and had an unbidden thought that dancing with this woman would be like dancing with an easel: all sharp angles and a picture of a face in a frame.

'An Arab who was rather persistent. She made him buy so much, clever girl! Actually, a couple of those – both fat. Shelley would never go for a fat man. Oh, and then there was this beautiful chap; bald as a coot, but ever so attractive. I've got a feeling she used to see him outside, but I never was sure.'

'What did he do? I mean, for a living?'

'Oh, it's not my business to ask what anyone *does* ... not the men, anyway. They aren't usually buying lingerie for their wives, you know. But come to think of it, it said Doctor something on his credit-card slip.' She gave the distinct impression that the title of doctor gave a man a touch more kudos than that of police officer. Bailey could not blame her for that; most people thought the same. Most people were unwilling to talk to police officers; they would talk their heads off to a doctor. Suddenly he felt extremely uneasy and, for the first time, smiling into the woman's eyes, he also felt the first stirring of pity for Shelley Pelmore.

The mixture of one pint and three indescribable cocktails, as well as the frozen glance of the manageress after she had conceded that, yes, it was possible to reclaim a credit-card slip and of course she would do it tomorrow, only to find that whatever she promised, he was leaving her to her lonely perch, all combined to make him feel queasy.

The darkness was not complete; the rain began again and he was hungry and lonely. He drove, illegally he suspected, from the West End to Helen's street and parked outside. What price pride, boy? What does it matter if she has a drink or two on the eve of her wedding and decides, in the company of some old friend, that the best thing to do is regard it as a joke? Maybe it was his fault for taking Ryan more seriously than anything else this last week or three, behaving like a bear with a sore head. No wonder she needed a little last-minute frivolity. She wasn't the only one, he thought with a flash of irritation; what made her think he was so confident about it?

Bailey knew as he approached the door that there was someone inside. Empty flats echo with their own vacancy; this one did not. The front windows, visible from the street, were severely curtained, showing not a chink of light; that in itself was unnatural. The phone, when he had tried *en route*, was permanently engaged, for which he read, off the hook, and now repeated ringing at the door-bell brought no response.

All right, so he had his own key, but they had their own

set of rules and, godammit, he wasn't going to beat the door down to see her if she so clearly did not want to see him. If she wanted to hide, let her. He was hurt to the quick. Silly bitch; a phrase without meaning, but echoing in his head all the same as he got back in his car to drive home. Halfway there, he stopped, bowed his head against the wheel, weary beyond belief, and this time more than slightly nauseous. He felt overwhelmed by the kind of grief which had first afflicted him when he had been woken with the news about Ryan; a sense of panic about how empty life was going to be. Then, aware of the prospect of a passing patrol car, although he was confident by now, on completely unscientific grounds, that his own emotion had digested the booze at double speed, he continued. Speeding up dangerously on the final stretch as a last coherent thought occurred to him.

Maybe Ryan was waiting at home.

'Let me go,' she was roaring, beating at his face with her fists, scratching, pulling away, tugging towards the door, going on and on long after the car engine died away and she knew he had gone. Ryan held her back with almost contemptuous ease, even though she stamped and yelled like a fractious child. Restraint of hysterical human beings, children included, was second nature to him; he knew how to subdue, exactly how to spread his fingers across her face so that she could not bite, then let her punch and kick and tug until she was exhausted. A brief slap brought all resistance to an end; the sound of it in her kitchen, unnaturally loud above the humming of the old fridge, like the announcement of the finale.

'Silly,' he said, half apologetic, half impatient as he pushed her back into the same chair. 'Shh, be good, now. It didn't really hurt, you know it didn't.'

No more than the cut on her finger had hurt. There was only the humiliation. The sting on her face was less painful than the utter futility of resisting at all; the reminder of the ultimately debilitating truth that in a straight fight with a man, a woman is no match and that is the cause of a primeval fear and anger. Helen did not want to kill Ryan; she would dream at other times of watching him being slowly and relentlessly overpowered until he begged for mercy for this simple illustration of his own power and what he had made her do: lie to Bailey, deny him access, make him believe her a treacherous fool. A silly bitch. At the back of her mind was the real terror of what he would think of her and the awful realization that she cared for Bailey's good opinion more than that of anyone in the world. And then another realization filtered through her shameful agitation. It was that although she wished Ryan every kind of pain as she looked at him, speechless with fury, she was no longer afraid of him, and it followed, somewhere along the line, that she believed what he had told her.

He poured the last of the wine as if he was a solicitous host, continuing an interesting conversation merely interrupted by a telephone call.

'Bailey would dismiss all this as a load of nonsense,' he said conversationally. 'Turn me in for my own good. He doesn't mind speculation, as long as it's his own speculation. No point telling Bailey anything without evidence.'

She spread her hands on the table, willing them to stop shaking. Blood seeped through the paper towel, and she wondered vaguely what Ryan would do when he needed to go to the lavatory.

'The only thing I don't see,' he continued, 'is where my fantasizing ladies meet their bald-headed man. Except for Shelley and her friend, there's no common denominator, not the same backgrounds, clubs, dentists . . .'

'A clinic,' said Helen. 'A women's clinic.'

'A clinic?' he repeated stupidly.

'A place where women go,' she said, 'and tell a doctor all about their lives. The way we do.'

Tell me about your life, Doctor. Tell me what has made you such a gentle persuasive monster, so sure I would never complain, and would, after a time, want you back; want you until I ached in my bones. Something in the way you joked and made life deathly serious, but less than serious. Something about the hands, the eyes, who knows? Tell me I am drunk and my mind is not engaged in this, although this is what I wanted, isn't it? Revenge? I wanted to tempt this man into my body and then cry rape, because, even if I were not ultimately believed, I should have made him feel as powerless as he made me. Humiliated by my body's desire.

I must let him do this the way he wants.

He called me darling. He said, my darling, I am sorrier than I can say to have treated you so despicably, you of all people, the one I liked best, respected most, but I had to push you away as brutally as I could. You do see that, don't you? No, I don't, I don't . . . Listen to me, my love, he said; you are the only one who forgives. Let me make love to you. Please. Beautiful.

515

I am not beautiful, but I am here, obedient and waiting, nerves stretched like wire. Lying, at his invitation, on my own bed; he has resisted the casting couch. I must, repeat must, let him do this in his own way. I must pretend. I must be his slave in order to find out *why*, or how. Not criticize him for his failure to remove all his clothes; he has a broad chest, hairless, which is odd for a man of such dark skin, or is it, how would I know? How many men have I ever known? Only a few. Pretend enjoyment; he has promised that this, and his explanations afterwards, will make amends. Why does he wear those awful synthetic-fibre trousers? And he a man of such taste. Unbuttoned at the waist, though: when I reached to touch his nipples, he shivered. Pretend? I am not pretending.

Kiss, kiss, kiss. Tongue going down my throat, neither too wet nor too dry, tasting of the wine. Stay still, he commands; let me do this, let me admire you, please. Whichever way he wants, let him; I could not stop him if I wished and I do not wish. Breasts fondled like rosebuds, one held while he feels how wet I am, his knuckle kneading . . . I feel as embarrassed as if I were producing sap . . . I want him, want him; he must smell desire by now. Sweet words, too: darling, darling, gorgeous darling, a word which can be such a mockery and is not, here and now. I touch his head and close my eyes against my own naked-ness. Let him do it his way, that was always the plan, but I want him inside me, I do, I do, I do. Licking me like a cat with a rough tongue; I once heard a tale of a woman who made her dog do that, with a bigger, rougher tongue; it got to like the taste. Mutual release is what I want, but he told me to close my eyes and keep them closed and I do what he says. There is no light in here. The room is at the front with the curtains drawn and a bit of the street light coming through. I've always been ashamed of those curtains: cheap and nasty, and Christ – why call upon him at a time like this – Christ, I can't stop . . . go on, go on, go on. He's as cold as ice. Cold, cold, cold. Enormous.

I can't keep my eyes closed and open them to find myself in the arms of a man who kisses and caresses while I convulse around the neck of an empty cheap champagne bottle.

I wonder if he rinsed it first.

When he removes it, there is the loud and hollow sound of a cork being drawn. Wroop. Louder than the normal sound; a vintage cork, pulled with an echo and a sensation in me like a plaster pulled from a raw and weeping wound.

Breathe deep, you silly bitch. You asked for this; he knew all along and you, you . . . consented. Now he takes off his trousers like a man settling down for sleep, having done his duty, ready to confide, and I have never felt such hatred in my life.

I reach out to grab what is exposed. A firm fist with the greatest possible intention to cause maximum injury.

In my imagination, it could all come away in my hand. I handle an ugly, flaccid, unarousable piece of rubbery flesh which never ever responded to me. A brief fight for repossession, with one of my eyes drawn to the green bottle he has carefully placed on the window-ledge; him trying to speak, me trying to scream. Unable, but I frightened him. I could see the fear as I lie paralysed and he tries to slink away.

But you did consent, he says. I did what you wanted and I am what I am made, and I do, love, you.

Silly bitch. The phone was sounding in his ear. Bailey drew himself up onto his elbow, bile hot in his throat. He heard her voice and knew what time it was, the way he did; late for a man whose only recourse was sleep or food, and there was no food. On the edges of London, major capital of the wor!d, and he a sophisticated man in it, there was no food and his stomach heaved. The height of his eyrie, the multicolours of the duvet, all mixed on a palette with this dreadful sadness. A book lay unread on his pillow and he could scarcely hear.

Be there, she said, and I'll be there. Will you?

But the phone was silent. All he had received and all he could remember was the answerphone message from earlier in the day. Silly bitch, too late to say sorry and far too late to care. Then his skinny legs on the floor on the way to the bathroom. So who the hell was that? Colours blurred; voices, too, and his last surviving image was that bitch in the club, her with the spun-gold hair and a face with a scar on the forehead.

And a dim memory, too, of the phallic-looking syringe in his pocket, which the park vagrant had given him out of his own.

CHAPTER THIRTEEN

'As to the admissibility, in cases of rape and kindred offences, of the fact that a complaint was made by the victim shortly after the alleged offence and the details thereof, not as being evidence of the acts complained of, but as evidence of the consistency of the victim's account and as tending to negative consent . . . such complaint cannot be regarded as corroboration and it is a misdirection to refer to it as such.'

Wait for the morning, Helen said. The morning will shed the light of reason on all this. Neither my Rose nor Anna will answer their phones; why should they at this hour? Ryan could not quite leave it alone. Got to find him, he kept saying, long after two a.m.; got to find him.

What exactly has he done, Ryan?

He corrupts. Like I said, he corrupts. Makes women mad. Kills them; kills their spirit.

What evidence, Ryan? What offence?

Don't know. Got to get inside that clinic. If they've got records of all those women . . .

You can start a war. But you can't bust in there, can you? Even when we find out where it is?

I can't. You can.

Which was why at seven in the morning, showered, dressed and half crazy with fatigue, Helen was walking to Anna Stirland's house on the day she had arranged to be away from the office in order to get married at eleven-thirty. Perhaps that could be retrieved, but this was a priority. She was too tired to think in advance of what she was going to say, feeling an irrational anger against a nurse who lied, and, despite Helen's single effort to phone, failed to answer at antisocial hours, although, on reflection, an answered call might have achieved nothing. It was better to face her, feeling aggressive with anxiety, and say, look, Anna, I don't want all of the truth, only a little scrap of it. Such as, where do you work and what is his name? She would have been happier involving Rose; Rose would be good at this, but involving Rose meant more complication and, besides, Rose did not deserve it.

Crossing the road, even so early, was dicing with death. In the middle of an intersection where lorries stormed from left and right and she was the only pedestrian in sight, Helen felt anonymous and irrelevant, marooned amongst hurtling metal. A train rumbled over the bridge beneath which she stood; there was too much unsyncopated vibrating noise to allow for thought as she ran for the other side. The road surface was damp with drying rain; the freshness of the day swallowed in alien smells, and she wanted, at every third step, to turn back, go to Bailey, who, Ryan had said, would not listen either. So she also believed, reluctantly, because it was, after all, Ryan who knew him best. I may miss my own wedding, she thought, but Bailey would want me to do this.

Anna's door was as freshly painted as she remembered, the street quiet, with the traffic a distant backdrop, like the bass sound behind a tune. She knocked and rang and waited, repeated the process and waited again. Come now, she chided Anna in her mind; life is not so unsafe that you cannot open the door at this time of day to what might be a postman with a gift.

There was the rattling of a bolt and the door opened a crack. Enough to show something less than a vision of loveliness. A poached face, pale, puffy, otherwise expressionless and slow to function. Then it trembled into a half smile with lips moving uncertainly, halfway between a grimace and a frown.

'Oh no,' was what she mumbled. 'Go away.' And then, beginning to push the door closed, repeating it more urgently. 'Go away; this is all your fault.' Helen shoved herself forward and found that, despite Anna's bulk, the resistance was weak.

'I need to know where you work and what the baldheaded doctor's name is,' she shouted, standing in the hall and watching Anna pull her dressing-gown round herself. Anna began to laugh, an ugly sound which she seemed unable to control until the words forced their way through the chortles of someone sniggering at a dirty joke.

'What?' she asked. 'What! You, too? Well, well. I would never have guessed.'

'What do you mean?'

'Another one. Fallen into the trap of Dr Littleton's charms . . .'

'I don't know what you're talking about.'

Hangover, Helen was thinking. Big-time hangover here. She had that disorientated look. This was not a woman who was fit for work today, but Helen could not be concerned with Anna at the moment. She could not even feel vaguely sorry for depriving Anna of an hour or two's sleep which might have made a difference between feeling like death and a state where life was possible.

The kitchen was surprisingly clean for someone who had so clearly been on a binge. Bright, tidy, odour free, not a sign of a bottle or a glass. It took an obsessive character to manage to eradicate any sign of conspicuous consumption. Perhaps Anna was a little that way inclined.

'What time is it?'

'Not long before eight.'

'Oh, shit.'

She sat at the kitchen table and let her head fall onto her crossed arms. Helen prodded her impatiently.

'Who's Dr Littleton and which clinic?'

Silence.

'C'mon, Anna. The bald doctor. I need to know.'

'Wha' for?'

Helen thought wildly of something which would inspire an answer; something which would make the woman talk. The words were out of her own mouth before she had digested them, a natural cunning driven by a rush of adrenalin.

'Because Rose has been to see him and I don't like it. I need to know who he is, where he is.'

Anna stirred, raised her head and gave a long sigh.

'Joseph Littleton. The Wilson and Welcome Clinic,

Camden Street. Near the park.' The words seemed to exhaust and amuse her. Then she yawned. 'Do me a favour, will you? Tell them I'm not coming in to work today. Maybe never,' she murmured to herself. 'I'm sick of it.' She turned a half smile to Helen. 'That's why I drink, see?'

Helen had paused, conscious of some kind of lie, but unable to define it. She was aware of the sweetish taste of red wine still sour in her own throat as she left the house and walked away. She turned left at the end of the road, following her instinct while wondering all the time what to do. Should she go straight into the lion's den, with none of the legal power of a police officer to demand information which they would not give? Pretend to be a patient, asking for the only doctor she could name, and be told to come back next week? Or sit down somewhere and work on her slim talents for subterfuge, and all for what? What, after all, had the man done? Where was the offence, and where would be the proof?

The world was, by now, thoroughly awake, the traffic heavier, the noise greater and the adrenalin less. She wanted direction and she wanted Bailey. Instead, she walked to the unpretentious front door of the Wilson and Welcome Clinic, to read a sign which said it opened at ten-thirty. On the other side of the road was a café of supreme grubbiness, where Helen sat and waited, after she had struggled with the question of whether to phone Bailey. Ryan had pleaded with her not to do so; would she be able to phone Bailey, make the peace, make some explanation which would convince him without mentioning Ryan? She

523

doubted it, but knew she had to try. Summon up more subterfuge. So she stood in a phone box which stank of last night's booze and listened, three times, to the polite message which said he was not there.

I am going to miss my own wedding. But I am doing what Bailey would want me to do, aren't I? And my feet are cold.

When Bailey phoned Todd in the early morning to say that he was too ill to come to work, it was scarcely an exaggeration, but he still felt a frisson of guilt. He did not mention he had booked the day as leave; it would have meant nothing. But then if neither Todd nor any of the others had been wise enough to question the vagrant in the park, they hardly deserved him either. Especially since they were operating at cross purposes. His only hope as he knocked on the door of the South Molton Street shop, admiring the window display of silk, and thinking how a certain colour of chocolate brown would suit Helen, was that the manageress would be less brittle in the morning than the evening, or at least she would look her age. He received the credit-card slip from heavily ringed fingers; the thing presented like a lottery prize, with a brilliant celebrity smile. Maybe it was the effect of himself, looking so much less attractive and so much more sinister in daylight.

It was no trouble, with the use of a little official muscle, to worm out of the credit-card company the address of a suspected felon, who, it transpired, rarely used the facility and always paid his bills. Bailey found himself going back to King's Cross; floating out of the station, carried by the crowds who celebrated rush hour with absent faces and copious luggage. It would be nice to take the train. Up to Scotland or some deserted part of the Yorkshire moors; anywhere cooler and greener than here. He passed the red brick of the monolithic British Library, saw the cars grid-locked as he detached himself down a side-street and found the place.

It was a dusty old mansion block, with a scroll above the door, spelling out in stone that it had been built in 1914; time not favouring the pláce, but unable to diminish a certain dignity to the solid door, despite the lack of paint and the grime of the first-floor windows. Still, a block for renters rather than owners. A placard on the left wall announced that for 'Passports Inc', press the entry buzzer and follow directions to the third floor, while for 'Graficko', he should act similarly and go to the second. Small businesses, hoping to grow big; scarcely a sign of a resident, despite the plethora of other bells, and nothing showing the name of Littleton. Nevertheless, when he buzzed the business bells and the door opened without any challenge, the foyer smelt of old cooking, overlaid, some-where, with a fresher scent of bacon. Bailey knew he should have eaten *en route*. Helen never understood his hypoglycaemia.

Eleven-thirty, the register office. Ah well, she was not at home or at work; he had tried in call boxes, checked his own messages; best not to think about it. Easy come, easy go, you can't deal with neurosis. But down in the heart of him, a terrible misery made him hate the man he had come to find for his oblique part in all of this, or more aptly, for his part in Ryan's imagination and the need for Ryan's exoneration. Foolish of him ever to think that

Ryan's rehabilitation would be achieved by the death of that girl, Shelley. Her death had only put everything else into a melting pot. Bailey had accustomed himself to believing that the sometimes volatile Ryan could be capable of rape, but he knew he could not murder in cold blood. Hot blood, yes, he thought, as he climbed the stairs and looked through the gloom of dark corridors, wishing his spectacles helped to read in dim light the small printed cards in brass fittings on the mahogany-coloured doors. Not a calculated killing, planned over days; Ryan would never carry it through. Which left the bald man, this creature of a dozen fantasies, suddenly more substantial. There he was on the label at the fifth out of six floors; Bailey resented him, even for that.

The door was opened by a Filipino girl, whose pear shape, adorned with pink overalls and the hose of a vacuum cleaner gripped in her hand as she led it behind her, startled him. Likewise her disingenuous response, which was so unworldly wise as she smiled and explained about cleaning the place on this day of the week, and no, he was out, at work, she supposed, like he usually was, and of course his cousin could come in.

She had a face like a nice round cheese, eyes like raisins. He was expecting me, Bailey said; he told me midday at the latest, but I'm early. All that announced with the answering smile which could terrify a guilty conscience, but not this innocent. And if you don't mind, he added, I shall wait.

Of course. He's a good man, your cousin; good to me. But only, it seemed to Bailey, marginally good to himself.

An adequate flat, because of the generous proportions of the living-room, but still a chunk, carved from grander accommodation, with an air about it of the temporary and something suggesting the perpetual student, or the genuine academic to whom surroundings are transitory and a taste for comfort a distraction not yet acquired. The mean furnishings granted by a landlord, with little added; indulgence discovered in the kitchen cupboards when the Filipino girl obligingly left him alone and went on to her next job, closing the door behind her so softly she could have been in a convent.

The man liked food; he had all the taste of a delicate gourmet who lived alone. Packets of smoked salmon and trout, speciality soups, olives, lemons and a variety of flavoured oils and green leaves in the fridge along with free-range eggs and a vacuum-packed loaf labelled as containing sun-dried tomatoes. Nothing here a really hungry man in need of a high-cholesterol bacon sandwich in white sliced toast could really crave, but Bailey noted the bread for future reference and did a mental inventory of the herbs for interest only. With a cup of coffee made in the man's cafetière and flavoured with the man's skimmed milk, he strolled into the bedroom which doubled as study. He was Dr Littleton's cousin, after all.

It smelt of flowers in here. The whole of the small high-ceilinged room was dominated by the desk rather than the small single bed which was simply cramped against the far wall; the bed a white-coloured couch with a much-washed cover; bare walls. There were no posters or pictures to indicate interests; the room of a celibate, with a random selection of unmatched clothes on a rail. Bailey touched a

527

dozen polyester shirts, trousers of a synthetic linen-look mix and wondered. The only thing he liked about this man was the quality of his coffee and the fact he was good to his cleaning girl.

Perhaps there would be a clue to everything in the sheaf of notes spread all over the desk, the only untidy feature of the whole place and a complement to the piles of books on the floor. A confession, neatly word processed and double spaced. In a long life, Bailey had never come across such a thing, but this area, for sure, was where the good doctor kept a life.

The window was double glazed, making this room alone semi-quiet if not entirely so. Bailey could see why the place was unsaleable for development, what with that sub-dued roar in the near distance, the slight vibration of the underground which would rattle nerves on the ground floor and still echoed slightly at the sixth. He waited, listened to nothing, waited. He found a medical card for the doctor; fluttered his hands over piles of paper, and then began to read. He was sitting on a good chair, built to hold male weight; supportive without being cosy and, even so, the subdued traffic hum was oddly seductive; the room felt warm, but protected from another hot day. His own eyelids heavy as lead.

Time passed. When he opened his eyes, there was the doctor's life, told in code. And his own rumbling belly.

Two rings, then dial off, then ring again, that was her code for Ryan from the phone box outside the clinic, and when Helen reached him all he could say was, get in there, girl, like someone encouraging a greyhound. Well, at least she didn't have to phone work. The day off today had been organized well in advance, although she had not expected to spend it this way. Pretend you need an abortion or something, Ryan said. Helen stroked her own stomach, a trifle swollen from half a loaf of bread and three milky coffees from a thick white mug in a café where no one took much notice, provided she did not stay there long enough to interfere with the small breakfast crowd and the serious trade at noon.

There was no one of the doctor's description going out or coming in, but she could well have missed him. Her predominant feeling was one of intense foolishness. Trying to appear unconcerned, wishing she knew as much about pretence as she did about keeping secrets. All I want is sight of the man, she told herself.

Proof he exists.

The reception was small, comfortable without luxury, a sensible-looking place with a counter reached through swing doors and flanked by four armchairs. The glass-panelled swing doors muffled the noise of shouting. Leaning across the counter was a woman with a large bosom and red hair, clutching the blouse of the receptionist in one fist and shaking the other, yelling, 'I want that doctor; I want Dr Littleton ... where is he?' with the receptionist, trying to repeat, 'He isn't here, he isn't here,' her face flushed with panic as she tried to avert her head from the woman. It was difficult to detect what was being said, although the import was clear, the voice rising in insistence, the fist ready to connect, the receptionist looking round wildly for help, but it was not the kind of establishment which ran to a security guard and the door both in and out minimized sound. In an instinctive copying of Ryan's methods, Helen ran forward, grabbed the raised fist and twisted the woman's arm behind her back, her other arm round the neck, pulling her back, holding her still. The hold on the blouse was relinquished, the woman suddenly still.

'There, there,' Helen said in her ear. 'Now what was all that about?' What she did not know was how long she should hold her captive, so she let her go, slowly, patting her shoulder, making calming noises, the way she used to talk to her cat. 'Dr Littleton is not here,' she said calmly. 'That's a pity, isn't it? I was hoping to see him, too, but we can't, can we? Why don't you go home and phone him tomorrow?'

The aggression seeped away. The woman seemed accustomed to obedience; she produced a brilliant tremulous smile, straightened her hair and her cotton jacket and made unsteadily for the door. She wore a dress with a sweetheart neckline, appropriate for a little girl rather than a woman; she smelled of baby lotion, her arms shiny with it. Helen opened the door for her with a flourish. The receptionist sank into her own seat, gratefully.

'Get many like that, do you?'

'No . . . I didn't know what she was going to do . . .'

'Don't worry about it; hope she doesn't come back. Look, could you help? I'm Dr Littleton's cousin; I've been away for a while and wanted to make contact. Could you give me his home address? Oh, and I've got to give you a message from Anna Stirland. She won't be in today, touch of flu, but you know what she's like, probably fine tomorrow.'

It was easy. Stepping out into the road, Helen looked right and left for the redheaded woman, grateful for her intervention which had made the difference between co-operation and the lack of it. She found that she was shaking, caught between a desire to laugh and another to run, with an underlying shame at how easy it was for a person who so prized truth, to be a liar.

She looked at her watch. Was there any point calling Bailey again? To say what? A lovely mess, this was. A gut-churning mess which was set to damage life beyond repair and there was nothing she could do to redeem it, except be braver and more reckless than she felt. A silly bitch.

Bailey made toast out of the bread with the sun-dried tomatoes, detested it and chewed it solidly, without bene-fit of butter, since there was none of that. At least the bread had been vacuum-packed, otherwise he might not have chosen it, reluctant as he was to touch what the doctor had touched with his own fair hands. The doctor's bathroom was as clean as his kitchen; it was not a lack of hygiene that made his skin crawl.

'Juniper extract, overdose fatal,' he read. 'Hellebore and aloes . . . iron dust, ivy . . .' all used to effect an abortion. 'Internal douching, strong brandy, water as hot as possible, brine vinegar . . .' Abortifacients, first swallowed and then inserted via syringe as time passed and more was known. Abortionists using a Higginson's syringe, or an enema with soapy water, stirring up the contents of the uterus with a long sound . . . Syringing was the commonest form of death because it was the commonest practice . . . it risked the inclusion of air . . . death by air embolism could

531

produce a fatal airlock in the lungs and brain within minutes of the procedure. Fat embolisms may be produced by soapy particles used in solution. But most, death from air, entering the bloodstream via vulnerable dilated blood-vessels . . .'

And in the doctor's bathroom cabinet, two packeted syringes. Sixty millilitres, bladder wash, womb irrigation, for the use of, like the one he had left in the park. Nice souvenirs the man kept.

He was an historian of his trade, that was all; nothing more sinister than that. There were library cards and certificates and, in the drawers of the desk, the history of a long and failed legal case. The doctor seemed to divide his interest between obstetrics and law. Not a humorous person, Bailey surmised; there was nothing in his book collection which suggested the least desire for entertainment. Bailey started in on the legal documents, wearily but intensely interested, sitting on the edge of the chair, his body tense, so that when the doorbell went, he sprang to his feet clumsily, cramp in his calves, scattering paper far and wide, then moved in ungainly fashion towards the door. He had a right to be here, he told himself: he was the doctor's cousin, and beside the doctor, a picture of health.

Rose was feeling in a mood of more than usual insolence. Even though she thought it was nonsense, there was something about the impending state of being a married woman which had a stimulating effect, as if it meant joining the real world, giving up the conversation of a girl and entering a club of those who could justifiably moan about men from a position of established authority. The wife. As in a nagging wife, scolding wife, she-who-must-be-obeyed wife; mustn't let it go to her head, it was only the party which mattered, but all the same, another life began here and she had no regrets about the one she was ending. What day of the week was it, now? Days of the week did not matter in this office or a courtroom; there was no routine which made the same thing happen on successive Mondays, not even a canteen with the same weekly menu. The only reason she was thinking about the days of the week was counting down. One afternoon and two working days to go, and then she and Michael would be off to Majorca, via the wedding, of course. Such a lot to do. Sneaking out of the room she shared with five others, down the corridor where she joked with the workmen who were replacing the lights, into Helen's office where she could use the phone in peace in order to check the progress of the damned cake. Being a busy bride-to-be and making them laugh in the shared room was all very well, but there was a limit to how much they could take. Rose knew colleagues did not always like you for being so volubly happy; there were times in her own working past when she had teased a wedding candidate, mercilessly, with the crudest jokes she could find and she wasn't sorry for it.

Standing in Helen's room, wanting to tell Helen about the dress, watching the staff across the road in the early afternoon, she leafed through Helen's diary. Now why had Aunty H wanted a day off? The page-a-day diary had a line through today's date with the initials B-RO. Didn't mean much, possibly an interesting assignation with a washing-machine man. Rose saw the supervisor of the paint people opposite sitting near the window, chewing in what Rose imagined was a furtive manner; she felt sorry for those who could not eat as they pleased and stay thin, as she could, and, in the same breath, thought of Anna. Give her a call, too. Leave her a message in case she forgot to organize the flowers.

She was surprised to get an answer. Wasn't anyone but herself and those in the immediate vicinity at work today? Was the rest of London at home in this muggy warmth? Anna's voice was cool but apologetic, saying wasn't it unutterably silly and downright embarrassing to have got measles at her age? Confining her to home quarters, forbidding her the joys of weddings or flowers; sorry, sorry, sorry.

The woman over the road continued to chew and Rose tapped her fingers on the desk impatiently, mouthing commiserations, chatting a bit, being as nice as she knew how and all the time thinking, well, never mind the flowers, then, who needed them? Knowing that Anna's measles were more important than her floral decorations in a few days' time, but nevertheless annoyed, because it meant something else to do. She didn't much care about bloody flowers, but other people did.

Get well soon, then. See you after Majorca. Byeee.

What did RO stand for?

Register Office? The old cow.

The two cousins of Dr Littleton met on his doorstep without much more than an initial shock of recognition. The progress of Helen's day was making her immune to surprise and her heart had been beating so fast with fear at what she might encounter, this kind of surprise was a relief.

'Hello.'

'Do come in,' he said politely. 'Who referred you? Was it treatment you wanted, or merely a consultation?'

His smile was false; she felt suddenly and profoundly ashamed.

'I'm glad you're here, though I don't know how or why,' he continued, waving her in blithely as if he owned the place. 'I've been needing some help. Doctor Titillation here has an interesting desk. Needs some deciphering.'

He sat on one side of it, she on the other, like a pupil at an interview with the headmaster.

'I can only presume that you know something about the resident of this not-very-nice apartment,' Bailey went on in headmasterly tones. 'The theory being that he used his job at a clinic to pick out disturbed or unhappy women, either pregnant or not; gained their trust; offered or foisted upon them some kind of alternative treatment and then raped them.'

'A kind of rape.'

'A kindred offence, then. Which all were either too ashamed or too confused to report accurately. There is another category who actively enjoyed his powerful attention, but, in the case of Shelley Pelmore and two before, there was a real risk of them blowing the whistle. So, using a method he had perfected from study . . . or practice of old abortion techniques, he persuaded them into co-operation with the use of a syringe created an air embolism, which killed them. It may not have been deliberate. It may have been accidental. They may have asked him to do it. Are you with me, so far?'

'It couldn't be accidental.'

'Yes, it could. It could be in the course of an abortion. And, anyway, there's no one alive to say otherwise. If you consent to sexual experiment, or to cheap makeshift abortion, are you consenting to death? And although the good doctor is prolific in his notes, including love-letters so ambiguous they may as well be in Greek, his jottings do not include confessions. Although he gloats a little about his lack of hair and his choice of fibre-free clothes, there's nothing else to indicate either a criminal mind, or a conscience.'

'Where does this leave Ryan?'

He looked at her quizzically, saving questions for later. A hard stare which left her uncomfortable.

'Ah, the good doctor could be very useful there. He's very kindly kept the particulars of several victims, if you can call them that, including Shelley. By which I mean he's copied personal details from the records of the place where he works and brought them home. Incriminating, in a benign kind of way, since names on his list coincide with a series of women who went to the police with vague complaints which, at best specified his appearance, at worst nothing. The doctor's list is longer, of course. Includes Lady Hormsby something, lives near you. Ever met her?'

'I may know ladies. None with titles.'

'He stocks good coffee, this man,' Bailey said. 'Which is kind of him, since he had no idea he would be offering hospitality to strangers.'

'I'm no stranger. I'm his cousin; to get this far.'

536

'So am I.'

'But I'm the only cousin on the distaff side whom he longs to see,' Helen said, desperate to make Bailey smile in this oppressive room. 'He and I have corresponded for years. We were childhood friends. We played doctors and nurses. Very clever boy he was. Only the slightest tendency to rape. Had an ambition to be a plumber. He knows me well.'

'How lucky for him. I don't,' Bailey said.

He left the doctor's desk and paced the room.

'How odd, how little one knows. I was contracted to marry a woman who looks vaguely similar to you, an hour ago. I hithered there on the dot and thithered hence, in case she arrived, but it was all in my imagination that she had ever meant what she said. So I came back to act the doctor. Do you think I look the part?'

Helen felt that if she touched him, her fingertips would freeze from cold. Bailey's skin was pale; he looked old.

'You look like Doctor Death.'

'It's only the names he collects', Bailey said, 'that make him deeply suspect of naughty play. A new phrase I've invented. Like your legal phrase, it won't work. Although it will work, to prove Ryan had a bona fide investigation, an honourable intention in his silence, and there is another candidate for the attack on Shelley and her untimely death. We can blame everything on this doctor. Except . . .'

Then he laughed, but she could not laugh with him. He paced the room again, still laughing.

'This man,' he said, 'needs beating up on a street corner. Like we were allowed to, once. A kick in the balls. If his balls, or his prick, would suffer.'

He seemed to find all this funny, extremely funny. He removed a large handkerchief from his pocket to absorb the tears of laughter. Fountains of water appeared on his gaunt cheek-bones, showing up the contours of his face. He looked cunning: a fox with a shiny nose; she found it repellent.

'Where was I? Oh, yes. Only Ryan could pursue a rapist who can't rape. Can't rape anyone, this customer. Impotent. Ugly. Chemotherapy burns. He sued them over his cancer treatment gone wrong, but it got him nowhere. Poor bastard.'

Helen sat stunned.

'No wonder he likes his food,' Bailey added irrelevantly. 'And another thing. If the good doctor comes home, I have no right to be here. No search warrant, no nothing, since there is not a scintilla of evidence that the man committed any crime, only evidence that a series of women fantasized about him, unpleasantly. That might be enough to restore official faith in Ryan, provided the doc does not get a lawyer and, quite rightly, stop us referring to illegally accessed private papers. In fact, it would be highly convenient all round if the poor blighter left the country and never came home. Where is Ryan, do you know?'

She felt as if she was giving him a blow beneath the ribs.

'At my house. Doing the garden.'

He faced the window, unable to look at her. Picked up the strange-looking vase which was the only ornament, studied it and put it down carefully.

'The poor emasculated doctor has no one to trust,' he said. 'I think I know the feeling.'

538

Chapter Fourteen

'The charges of rape and attempted rape are
punishable with imprisonment . . . other than in the
most exceptional circumstances, an immediate
custodial sentence should be imposed following a
conviction for rape in order to mark the gravity of
the offence, to emphasise the public disapproval, to
serve as a warning to others and to protect women.
The length of the sentence should depend on all the
circumstances.'

●

There were no newspaper headlines about rape or even
the sexual peccadillos of cabinet ministers. Parliament was
not in session; the late-summer news was dominated by a
new royal scandal and the abduction of two British children by their Spanish father. The last week in August had
brought more rain and the trickling home of the holiday
crowds. West End shops swelled with mothers and
teenagers, quarrelling about the most appropriate clothes
to wear for the new term at school. Members of Aslef, the
union for railway workers, went on strike, and for
two blessed days, the larger stations were as hushed as
museums.

A doctor who had gone missing failed to return home. It was thought by his employers that he might have made a sudden and inconsiderate decision to holiday abroad with a cousin.

A man in North London referred his wife to a psychiatrist for her habit of wandering the streets on the rare occasions she consented to get out of the bath; a hitherto unknown form of agoraphobia was diagnosed.

Miss Rose Darvey prepared, with glee, to change her name. 'I never liked it in the first place,' she said.

Detective Sergeant Ryan was admonished by his superiors. His reinstatement was close to a foregone conclusion, pending the convening of the right kind of committee. Someone was obstructing it.

A famous English cricketer announced he was gay.

Ryan and Bailey sat in the latter's large clean flat, watching the sunset. It had been a long lunch.

'I suppose I'm meant to feel sorry for the bloke,' Ryan was saying. 'And I suppose, in some ways, I do. Fancy, overdose of chemotherapy, you said? Ouch. It's more difficult to be terrified of a chap with such an affliction and a prick as useful as a chipolata. Why the hell didn't he win his negligence case?'

'Because he'd interfered in his own treatment. Thought he knew best. Misdirected a technician. Arrogant.'

'So some of this was his own fault? Naa, you can't say that. Getting cancer wasn't his fault. I mean, it isn't as if you ask, is it? Make a prayer, like, go on, God, disfigure me, why don't you?'

'He was brave, apparently. Stoic, philosophical,

courageous in the face of pain, all that. And is admired as a doctor for his holistic, sympathetic approach.'

'Oh yeah? Loves his patients, you mean?'

'And still, poor sod,' said Bailey softly, 'wanted to be a lover. Don't we all?'

'Steady on, guv,' said Ryan, not wanting to get maudlin, or not yet, anyway, and then getting angry. 'I mean, steady on. What do you want me to do? Be sorry for this fucking ghost with no balls? What did he do, then? What did he do? He had trust, sacred trust, the sort you and I get in a month of fucking Sundays, handed to him on a plate. And he used it. For what? Some kind of fucking revenge. A power trip. Made girls hate themselves, made them mad for him, made them trust him and then killed them; or made mad fools of them while he fucking experimented.' He was speechless with rage. 'I mean, what kind of fucking wanker does that? Gets a job like that?'

'Your use of the word fucking in this context is hardly apposite,' Bailey interrupted primly. 'And he might not have had much choice about his job.'

'The fucking hell he would! He's a doctor,' Ryan shouted. 'He ain't judged by his balls! And a fucking doctor, like any other man, should know that disease and disappointment is what you get from being alive. You've got no licence to spread it. And just because you've taken some fucking Hippocratic oath that's going to keep you all right with the pension plan, you don't have the right to abuse. Jesus, Bailey, you've gone soft in the head. Stop finding fucking excuses. There was pleasure in what he did; love wasn't involved. He was experimenting with lives; he was full of self-pity, the worst. Can't you see evil any

541

more? Even when it puts its tongue into your mouth? Sod the excuses. He's still a monster, because he knew what he was doing. There aren't any excuses. I just wish one of his women had found a way to retaliate.'

His anger faded into a dull ache. He settled himself back into the depths of the enormous sofa, squinted round this minimalist but colourful room and thought, benignly, how he had always considered it a bit cold, although it wasn't really, and quite comfortable, even with all that space. At least he didn't have to walk across the carpark-sized floor for the next sustenance, which stood at his elbow. Personally, he preferred the clutter and noise of his own home, like everyone did, despite the superior quality of the whisky and, really, if he had to choose between the two, he liked Helen's place better than this. Now there, even with his many reservations, was one hell of a woman. She had spent hours on the phone with his wife, squaring it all up, so that he could go home and explain it again, knowing he was halfway there. He felt suddenly ashamed at his own good fortune and his own role as the one who persisted in getting away with it. And Bailey's reluctance to condemn enraged him. He would never dare ask if Bailey had ever actually believed the rape charge against himself. If he had actually done it, Bailey should have shot him. That would have been justice, instead of all this analysis and trying to understand. Ryan still wanted something.

'It wasn't all in my mind, was it? He does exist, doesn't he? Can I tell a liar from a lover? I dunno.'

There was this fact about Glenmorangie: it kept on tasting good. Not as good as the first sip, but still good.

'No, he wasn't entirely a creature of fiction. Maybe fifty

542

per cent the fevered imagination of those reporting on him, but more than a grain of truth.'

'The man's a bastard gone to ground, wherever he is. Where the hell has he gone?' Ryan grunted, resolving privately, as he had publicly, that he personally was never going to search. They would turn over what they knew to the medical establishment, let them hound him out. If Littleton could not practise, he had no base for manipulation. It irked him that that was all they could do.

'Where's he gone? People asked the same questions about you a couple of days ago,' Bailey said. 'What makes you think you're the only one with licence to disappear? The doc's got plenty of money. Goes where he likes, and when. Earned money, own money, a mixture of both; mystery man. You're a shit, Ryan. Why didn't you trust me?'

Ryan remembered to pause and think about his answer. Bailey had spent years teaching him that.

'Didn't. Couldn't. You had a job to do and you know me too well. You knew I could have gone off the rails; you know how close I've been . . . Besides, I wanted to hit you for not being able to spring me out of there. I wanted to hit you. Kick you. In the balls. But you were always out of reach; like Helen always seems.'

'Helen isn't out of reach,' Bailey said. 'Merely absent.'

'Are you accusing me of fucking it up; the wedding, I mean? Well, stone me; if you have to get married in secret, you ain't got a lot going for you, have you? I didn't believe you'd ever do it; nor did she. Funny what she said in the middle of the night.'

Then he found Bailey standing over him. Pulling him

up by the sleeves, shaking him like a rat, the sound of cloth tearing. Controlled violence of some intensity, designed to intimidate. It had been a good shirt, once.

'Oh, for God's sake, leave it alone, will you? Would I ever touch your woman, you stupid idiot? Even less, would she touch me? Hates my guts; don't fancy me either. Nor me the other way round, if I'm being frank. Leave off, Bailey. There, that's better.'

Bailey returned to the opposite chair, calm as a sleepy spider. Jealousy had not really featured in his action; merely a vague suspicion that Ryan's sabotage of his own marriage plans had been, in some sense, deliberate.

'She talks in her sleep, that's all, and she talks loud. Carries through to that sofa in the living room where she parked me for the night. All sorts of stuff. Like she thinks she don't live up to a man like you. Well, thinking the way you think – namby-pamby, forgiving everybody – she may be right.'

Ryan became restless, the way he did with emotion in anything other than a professional context. He could handle weeping women, provided they were strangers. Emotional men were another matter, and besides he was not being entirely truthful. He'd always thought Helen was a very tasty piece, likeable or not.

'So what's the state of play now?' he demanded. Bailey misunderstood, deliberately.

'Oh, stalemate. There's not enough of anything to justify getting out a warrant for the doctor's arrest. The verdict on Shelley Pelmore will come back as death by misadventure. The pathologist suspects embolism, but can't put a hand on her own cardiac machinery and say for sure;

could have been a freak result of the couple of drinks and couple of paracetamol she had on board . . . If the doctor came back, we could question him, that's all. And if he said nothing, that would be that. And we could go back to the women in your little black book, but since they gave unreliable accounts first time round, they'd never be credible. And then there's this Anna Stirland, who's off sick and told me on the phone she's not saying anything. Amen. Can't force her. All we know is that he couldn't be a rapist. Not with his equipment.'

It was repetition of old ground. Ryan was sick of it.

'Do you have to pay a cancellation fee if you don't turn up at the register office?' he asked politely.

'Only what you've paid already. They're used to it, apparently. Some don't turn up. Others turn up every few years.' Bailey was not going to be drawn further.

'I hope they don't reinstate me before I finish the pond,' Ryan said.

Helen was not to be drawn either.

'All right. If you didn't get married, now that Ryan's off the hook, you'll do it, won't you?' Rose was asking.

'Stand still. The label's sticking out at the back. There.'

'. . . Only don't do it without me. Promise?'

'Promise. Cross my heart and hope to die. You look . . . well, wonderful.'

''S all right, innit?'

Rose stood before the full-length mirror, stuck out one hip and crossed her eyes. Her hair was soft and full, a compromise between spikes and curls. Small nuggets of silver sparkled in her ears. The dress was a short-sleeved shift of soft crimson. Designer label, courtesy of Oxfam. Who would know, Rose had asked, and if they did, who would care that it cost five quid? Must have been a person who got too fat for it and gave it away in a fit of pique. My good fortune; meant for me. I'll do the same. Watch me, lover, watch me.

Standing back, Helen compared the effect to a young Audrey Hepburn *en route* to breakfast at Tiffany's. This was no sacrificial lamb; this was breathtaking.

'I sort of wish this was in church,' Helen said. 'So the vicar would faint.'

'Stuff 'em all. S'long as Michael likes it. Here we go.'

Michael at his mother's, chewing his knuckles; Helen and Rose in the upstairs bedroom, watching for the car, making the last unnecessary adjustments to perfection. It wasn't so much the dress, Helen thought later, as Rose's total appearance that brought gasps of admiration on the town-hall steps; it was the poise, the complete assurance, which brought tears to her eyes and a pang of non-malicious envy to her heart. Oh, to be like that, to have such belief that you would make everything work and that what was broken you would fix.

If she had ever had that kind of confidence, she no longer had it now, but she rejoiced to see such utter certainty in another. There was such a thing as true uncomplicated love. There was, but it simply needed belief in itself to flourish. A childhood deprived of it, perhaps, so that it was easy to recognize and vital to preserve in a tight fist. That was what Rose had: a rigid grasp on reality. Her kind of true love was not so fanciful after all.

★

There was a brief exchange of vows; the hall was full to bursting, extra chairs provided. On Rose's express instructions, issued on pain of death, each woman was dressed to excess. I want you costumed over the top, she had ordered. There were hats with feathers a foot long, puffy taffeta skirts, ear-rings the size of tin lids, plenty of sheer thigh, and a total inability on the part of the crowd to keep quiet. Chatter only fell to nothing during the making of promises, when a snuffling into handkerchiefs replaced it. Standing next to her, one of the few men who looked at ease in a suit; Bailey dug into his pocket and handed Helen his hanky. The extra-wide brim of her overlarge deep-blue sombrero, worn low over her forehead, hid the act of blowing her nose.

'I don't want anyone sitting down,' Rose had said of her own reception. 'It creases the frocks. I want 'em all moving around, eating and drinking and showing off and talking to one another.'

Which they did in the hotel room with buffet and garden attached, where food was less important than drink and the sixty of them, chattering, made a fine volume of noise amid too much of a squash for anyone to notice the dearth of floral decoration. Bailey unbent from his great height, enjoying himself, Helen hoped, since she was herself, out of relief as much as anything else, because it was turning into exactly the kind of thrash Rose had planned. They would probably leave before the lights came on in the garden and the music, Rose's secret weapon to subvert the tendency to speeches, began to invite dancing.

'What kind of dancing?' Bailey asked suspiciously.

'Any old kind of shuffle. We've got three generations here.'

'So I can waltz, can I?'

'We can watch, first.'

He took her hand. They sat in a corner of the garden; he observing, with evident pleasure, the ranks of Michael's aunts and uncles towing each other about with concentrated movements, some serious, some laughing throughout.

'I don't know if it's possible to have a wedding without relatives,' Bailey shouted above the din.

'No fun at all,' Helen agreed.

'I think I've only got two left,' he added. 'I don't know what I've done with them all.'

'Me neither.'

'Look, Helen,' he was bellowing. 'We can't go on like this, we really can't. It's no good, it's become a neurosis.'

She could feel herself freeze. She did not want a conversation about the issues between them; not here, not now.

'Why am I so bloody frightened of dancing?' he asked plaintively. 'Do you reckon it goes back to school? When I trod on Gloria Smith's toes and she screamed as if I'd raped her?'

Music swelled in Anna Stirland's house. She was busy with the flowers. The backyard was a profusion of late-flowering stock, mostly leaves. The wedding-present window-boxes had been dismantled and added to the borders, making up for the gaps where she had picked the blooms she would otherwise have left to fade into

548

blowsiness on their own stems. Whenever life was more complicated than usual, it was always a comfort to have extra flowers in the house, and the irony was that her aunt, the kindest relative a motherless woman could have, had added to the quantity by sending more, in commiseration for sickness, accompanied by a note saying she would miss Anna at the wedding and would love to see her when she was better.

To look at happy snaps, Anna thought, standing rose stems in boiled water; or, God help her, a video.

The hot-house blooms provided by the doctor as his hospitality gift had been binned, long since. Their falling petals and rancid leaves made a mess.

She went upstairs slowly and added a touch of fern to the arrangement beside the bed. Even with the window open and a gentle breeze, the scent of the room was heavily floral, as if a housewife had gone mad with artificial air freshener and a ton of pot-pourri, all of it underlaid with a bite of antiseptic.

'All right?' she asked him sweetly, stroking his brow. The skin was the texture of candle wax. Beeswax, more precisely; yellowish rather than white.

One of the skills she had inadvertently acquired as a midwife, taught by an older mentor, was how to lay out the body of a dead baby without crying throughout the process. And although the laying out of the body of a grown man was, of course, substantially more difficult, she thought she'd made a reasonable fist of it. Even if poorly done, it was adequate to preserve him with the help of preservative, which was easy to obtain for those who knew how. There was that artist who used it to exhibit a dead sheep. Not that Anna had any intention of putting the doctor on show, aware as she was of her own lack of equipment and her serious shortcomings in the funereal arts, and even more aware that this was a temporary measure. Nor did she like the fact that he lay with his head on one side, revealing a handsome profile, in a pose which made him look, somehow, shy. The left side of his face, unfortunately badly damaged as a result of repeated blows from the champagne bottle, lay snug against the pillow. Anna was fairly sure that it was not the facial injuries which had proved fatal . . . they rarely were . . . the blow to the back of the neck had done it, but even so, he had taken his time while she fussed around, doing what she was good at, namely, nursing; her skills entirely confused by the ambivalence of her own wishes about whether he should live or die. In the end, he decided it for her.

'What good were you ever going to be to me?' she had asked him. 'Whatever did I see in you?'

She knew she would have to get rid of him soon before she put the house back on the market and made all those other decisions about her life, but she was fairly sure, between moments of acute anxiety, that she would find a way. As for the vexed question of whether this remaindered hunk of manhood deserved the fate she had merely encouraged him to receive, it was not a discussion she could afford to have with him, or with herself, at the moment. Conscience was a luxury and his skin was so cold, even in the cooling heat of the season, he no longer seemed entirely real. A figment of the imagination. A shadow of substance.

Anna sighed at the enormity of the tasks which lay

550

before her. And, at the end of them all, she supposed she would have to paint the house, again.

Someone would buy, if only for the sake of the yard.

Dusk turned to darkness. She went downstairs, slightly reluctantly. In his own particular way, he was company. Never had such a handsome man remained in her house so long. In the kitchen, she fiddled with the radio until she found Classic FM. They were playing Strauss.

'He does a passable waltz, old Bailey,' Rose remarked to Michael. 'But a waltz! When was he born?'

'Same year as my mother,' Michael said. 'Don't worry about it.'

The music ceased in preparation for a major change; all part of Rose's plan. In the interlude of silence between prerecorded orchestral palm-court schmaltz and the heavy pulse of disco sound there was the audible sound of a bleep from Bailey's belt. Half of the spectators understood, half not; there was laughter and a smattering of sympathetic applause. Rose grabbed Helen by the arm. 'Look,' she said, 'even if he goes, you don't have to, do you? We ain't hardly started yet.'

Helen followed Bailey out to the foyer. She was accustomed to interrupted evenings, but, on this occasion felt it was either preordained or prearranged and she liked to see him leaving in good spirits.

'Grand wedding,' he said, pausing by the door of his car. 'Does it matter, do you think, that we missed the boat? Or is it more important that, at some stage, we actually had the will to catch it?'

'That is what matters,' Helen said, 'isn't it?'

551

'Sure you don't mind going home on your own?'

'Course not.'

'Of course you don't,' he murmured. 'Comes naturally, doesn't it? You'll always want to go home alone and I shall never be sure of you, shall I?'

'I don't deserve you,' Helen said.

Back later; see you soon; take care; be in touch; adieu; so long; call me. There were a dozen different phrases which meant goodbye. Including a gap, where neither could say anything at all.

So he thought she'd been crying in the service out of sentiment, did he? Instead of crying about an ending rather than a beginning. At least he had left her his handkerchief.

Perhaps the desire for her own company first was unnatural. Perhaps she should see a doctor.

Perhaps tomorrow, in the wilderness of a blank Sunday, she would try and find Anna Stirland. Tell her about the party. Discuss the benefits of the single state, the reality of true love, the importance of hope, the dignity of living alone, and the comfort of growing things.

THE NATURE OF
THE BEAST

Frances Fyfield

'The best female crime writer in this country'
Sunday Express

Amy Petty is dead. But Amy Petty is alive . . .

When an inter-city service travelling from Kent to London joins Paddington, Hatfield and Selby in a deadly list of notoriety, it isn't only fate who decides who is killed; one passenger uses the opportunity for argument to spill over into murder; whilst another – blonde, beautiful Amy Petty – sees the train crash as an opportunity to leave her life behind.

But why would Amy want the world to presume her dead? Is it because of her husband – the rich, charismatic and evil-tempered Douglas Petty – currently embroiled in a libel action against a national newspaper? Or maybe it isn't the present that Amy is running from. Maybe it is the past from which she cannot escape . . .

'A compelling story . . . as always, her portrayal of the human psyche is to the point, often witty, but rarely comfortable'
Minette Walters, *Daily Mail*

'Frances Fyfield has the same ability as Ruth Rendell to show the dark side of ordinary people . . . a book that grips from the beginning' *Sunday Telegraph*

'As ever, the writing is graceful, witty and elegant, and Fyfield's cool eye misses nothing and spares nobody' Donna Leon, *Sunday Times*

ISBN 0 7515 32312

A HELEN WEST OMNIBUS:

DEEP SLEEP
SHADOW PLAY
A CLEAR CONSCIENCE

Frances Fyfield

'Her knowledge of the workings of the human mind – or more
correctly the soul – is second to none' Ian Rankin

DEEP SLEEP

The death of a respected pharmacist's wife is accepted by all except
Helen West, a prosecuting solicitor. Her suspicions are only shared by a
confused child and a drug addict, and are dismissed by her awkward and
pragmatic partner, Detective Superintendent Geoffrey Bailey. Then an
unexploded wartime bomb causes an evacuation and in the dark streets
one lone man prepares to murder again.

SHADOW PLAY

Mr Logo is a familiar figure in the courts, frequently accused of indecent
assault, but invariably acquitted due to lack of evidence. He is
frustratingly familiar to the Crown Prosecutor Helen West, who again
has just failed to prosecute him. This isn't the only set-back in her life:
her long-term relationship with Geoffrey Bailey is even more brittle, and
she has to deal with the insubordination of her office clerk, which
unwittingly sets in motion events which push Mr Logo's rage and dark
passion to lethal extremes.

A CLEAR CONSCIENCE

Helen West's personal life is in need of repair, and she decides the first
move is to tidy up her home, helped by her cleaning lady, Cath, who
is trapped in a miserable marriage. Working by day with domestic
violence cases, Helen finds it too easy to turn a blind eye to Cath's
unhappiness, but then her personal and professional lives collide as
she witnesses the destructive forces of love and guilt, and finds herself
applying her own version of justice.

ISBN 0 7515 3283 5